PROVENANCE

Frank McDonald

—————◆—————

PROVENANCE

An Atlantic Monthly Press Book
Little, Brown and Company–Boston–Toronto

ATLANTIC-LITTLE, BROWN BOOKS
ARE PUBLISHED BY
LITTLE, BROWN AND COMPANY
IN ASSOCIATION WITH
THE ATLANTIC MONTHLY PRESS

Published simultaneously in Canada
by Little, Brown & Company (Canada) Limited

PRINTED IN THE UNITED STATES OF AMERICA

ACKNOWLEDGMENTS

For their comments, ideas and time generously given at various stages of this book, I would like to thank William Coleman, security consultant; John Taylor of the National Archives; Marco Grassi, conservator; Raymond Perman of Christie's; David Nash of Sotheby Parke Bernet; Barbara Guggenheim; Jane Livingston of the Corcoran Gallery; Father Joannes Quasten, for his guidance through the catacombs; and art dealers Stephen Hahn, Barry Sainsbury, Sam Salz, David Carrit, John Richardson, Eugene Thaw, Alexandre Rosenberg and Clyde Newhouse. I am particularly grateful to Matila Simon, art historian, writer and critic; and finally to my editor, Peter Davison.

For
The House of Cloghroe
and all that it once was

"PROVENANCE (prŏv-ə-näns') n. The place of origin; derivation. (French, from *provenant,* present participle of *provenir,* to come forth, originate, from Latin *provenire: pro-,* forth + *venire,* to come.)"

The American Heritage Dictionary of the English Language

"Lay not up for yourselves treasures upon earth, where moth and rust doth corrupt, and where thieves break through and steal:

"But lay up for yourselves treasures in heaven, where neither moth nor rust doth corrupt, and where thieves do not break through nor steal:

"For where your treasure is, there will your heart be also."

Matthew 6:19–21

PART ONE

———◆———

1979

I

In a cavernous seventeenth-century Roman palazzo on a narrow cobblestone street near the Vatican, Monsignor Hans Weiller sat motionless and inscrutable as a Buddha. Monsignor Weiller, a stout, unwrinkled man of sixty-five, rested his elbows on the ornately carved arms of a Venetian pearwood chair, while supporting his rounded double chin on the back of thick clasped hands. The weight of his head on the backs of his hands squashed his pursed thin lips upward into a petulant look of contempt. Beneath drooping, half-closed eyelids, his washed-out blue eyes looked down with supreme confidence at a Siberian jade chessboard.

Behind the calm facade, however, the nodules of his brain pulsed with impatience and anxiety, waiting for the reports from London, Paris and New York. He glanced at an ormolu and marble clock on the side table. It was five o'clock. Still time. Surprisingly, in spite of the distraction, he had played a remarkable game of chess. He had approached the contest as he would have attacked a finely baked fish. He had peeled away the skin, separated the flesh from the bone, and now he was ready to savor the meat.

Across the table from him, his opponent, the esteemed head of the Vatican's "Commissione Di Archeologia Sacra" and member of the Curia, Austrian Bishop Alois Schneider, no doubt knew the end was near. The portly old man looked as though there were already a hand at his throat.

In the early stages of the game, the bishop appeared to have provided adequate defensive cover for his king. Midway, however, Weiller introduced a brilliant twist to the Wathier Variation of the Rook's Gambit Declined and broke his defenses. Schneider had stayed in the contest until the twenty-fourth move. Then he had made another mistake, placing his queen in jeopardy. The rest, Weiller knew, was foretold.

While his opponent sweated away another ounce of weight, pondering his devastated board, Weiller sat back. He placed his plump hands over the rounded front edges of the armrests. The clock now read five-fifteen. Not long. London and Paris would be reporting within the hour. The word from New York would be much later: about three o'clock the following morning.

Coldly, he looked across at the bishop's glistening face and watched him raise his left hand. The light from the fire reflected in his ruby episcopal ring as he moved his queen's pawn to knight-five. The bishop glanced up at Weiller and smiled apprehensively.

That was it. The queen was exposed like a virginal child, defenseless and innocent. Weiller slowly lifted his right hand from the armrest and stretched it across the board. Like the pincers of a huge lobster, his thumb and index finger opened, then gently closed on his rook. The fingers, holding the piece, moved straight across the board, capturing the queen. Then the hand slowly retreated to its place on the armrest.

The bishop sat back in his chair, smiled weakly and bent his head in a brief, formal bow of surrender. "Magnificently played, Monsignor."

"A worthy opponent, Excellency, is worth a thousand victories." He reached to his right for a crystal decanter. "Another apéritif?"

"Delighted."

Weiller leaned across the table and carefully filled the bishop's glass with *carpano,* a dark, cornelian-colored vermouth. "Don't you think there's a wonderful clarity about chess? A purity of morality from which a player cannot deviate?"

"Exactly, Monsignor. There is no right or wrong in chess. There's only deception, tactic and strategy, and knowing what your opponent is going to do before he does it."

"Like war, Excellency."

"I agree," the bishop acknowledged. "Like chess, there is a purity of morality in war."

"Even Hitler's war?"

"Why, of course! I spent many years in Berlin before the war, representing the Vatican. I've always thought the Teutonic ideal made political and economic sense. Of course, as an Austrian, I have very ambiguous feelings about the Germans."

Monsignor Weiller smiled benignly. "I understand," he said, swirling his vermouth around the edge of his glass. "Speaking objectively, of course, not as a German, I must admit over the years I've slowly come to that conclusion myself. One could almost agree with some of Hitler's ideas. He was flawed, but far from mad. As the West declines, and the Christian peoples are surrounded by their inferiors, one can credit Hitler with understanding a great many truths, particularly about the Jews and their allies the Communists."

The bishop nodded. "Take Italy today. Look what's happening. Scum has permeated nearly every aspect of our society. The germ carriers are poisoning our civilization and culture."

"It worries me, too," Weiller sighed, rubbing his finger around the rim of his glass. "But what can one do? Thank God for the Church."

They sat in silence for a moment. Weiller poured the bishop another glass of vermouth and added a drop to his own. "On to more pleasant subjects," he said. "The excavations in Monte Verde are moving along satisfactorily."

"I'm delighted," the bishop enthused. "We've been anxiously waiting for the results."

"It's an archeological job, basically," Weiller said. "The care we've taken . . ."

"I understand, Monsignor."

"It's not merely a matter of clearing away the rubble."

"Of course not."

"Still," Weiller said, a hint of rebuke in his voice, "it has been three years. The permits took so long!"

"As you know, the Church moves slowly, Monsignor. It's built upon a metaphorical rock. . . . But it moves, almost literally . . ."

"Like a rock."

"Yes. You're very understanding, Monsignor."

"The world needs more understanding, Excellency."

Weiller sipped his vermouth and stared into the fire. "You must come on a tour some day. The Catacombs have a medieval feel about them."

"They're much older than that, Monsignor Weiller."

"Of course."

"We considered electrifying the galleries . . . briefly. But to tell you the truth, the tourists wouldn't have stood for it. They prefer the torches."

Weiller muttered: "I don't blame them. Well, as you can see, we're very near to breaking through. In a few days, I suspect, the inner chamber of Monte Verde will be open again."

"After how many years? Thirty? When was the cave-in? I've forgotten."

Weiller looked toward the wood-beamed ceiling as if consulting

Heaven. "The cave-in? I believe, Excellency, it happened in June nineteen forty-four. . . ."

II

The evening sky darkened over Paris as the Air France 747 hummed toward Charles de Gaulle International Airport. From a seat in first class, a trim, rugged-looking man in his middle thirties, wearing a tan suede jacket, stared down at the flickering lights below.

Under the harsh glare of the overhead reading light, the hard lines of his face—a broad forehead, straight nose and strong jawline—were softened somewhat by the animation in his blue-gray eyes. He was happy to be back home and it showed in those eyes, which, under normal circumstances, seemed to scrutinize rather than observe, were expressive and yet surprisingly unrevealing.

The man's name was Alex Drach, and as the city took shape below, he sat back, ran his hands through his black curly hair and recalled, as he always did when he returned, his earliest memory of Paris, of his foster father, Jocko Corvo, and of his life with the Corsicans.

Alex was only four years old then, playing on the balcony of the Corvos' tiny apartment in Pigalle and screaming with delight every time Jocko magically made a one-franc piece appear and disappear in thin air. There was something wonderfully special about that stifling-hot August day. He didn't know why it was so special, only that it was. Jocko's wife, Mama Louisa, wearing the new pink dress she had stitched together from scraps of black-market fabric, was also sitting on the balcony, fussing with a bouquet of flowers, watching for the first sign of the Americans.

Jocko, in his best dark suit, broke into song, his voice so loud that the atonal couplets of the Corsican national anthem resounded off the walls of the buildings across the narrow street.

"There was a time when God was man.
Napoleon! Napoleon! . . ."

The clatter of grinding treads smothered the song. From around the corner, a convoy of tanks and trucks lumbered toward the Place Pigalle. They were German.

Suddenly the street exploded. From rooftops and windows a fusillade of fire poured down on the column. A flaming bottle spiraled through the air and plopped into the open turret of a Panzer tank, and within seconds the tank was a mass of yellow flames.

Further down the street, another tank pivoted and fired at a nearby building. An 88mm. shell tore into the facade, sending a spray of chipped cement and broken glass in all directions.

In the same instant, directly below the balcony, one of the open trucks lurched wildly, mounted the curb and slammed against the building. Someone screamed, *"Heraus! Schnell! Aus!* Get out!" The soldiers, scrambling from the truck, were caught by rifle fire in midflight. They tumbled to the sidewalk like tin soldiers. One German vaulted over the tail of the truck, crouched alongside it and then, in a desperate search for cover, leaped into the building through its smashed front door.

For Alex, the rest was like a dream. Jocko dragging him off the balcony. Heavy boots running. Fists pounding on the door. Louisa clutching him tightly, cowering in the corner and muttering a prayer. Then there was a knife in Jocko's hand and he was springing across the room. A terrifying explosion. The door burst open and a gigantic German in shiny black boots filled the room. But Jocko was behind him, even bigger. His powerful arm snaked around the German's shoulder. The knife flashed and suddenly a thin red smile appeared around the soldier's throat.

The German slumped to the floor. Standing over him, Jocko said only one word, *"Giustizia!"*

Alex never forgot that moment. The black boots, the face of the German, the eyes rolling upward, the red smile. Nor the word that Jocko uttered over the dead body. It was a word he would hear often, a word intimately bound up with the honor-bound, codified Corsican world that had been his for the first fifteen years of his life. Justice! It was a word that echoed in him now, just as it did the first time Jocko, his voice hard and bitter, intoned it.

Alex eased back in his comfortable seat. He tightened his safety belt, and as the aircraft circled for its landing, he reflected on how good it would be to be back in Paris. His base of operations might be New York, but his home, though he had not lived there in years, was Paris. Not the Paris of luxurious hotels, the George V, the Meurice or the Plaza-Athénée, although he had stayed in them all. Nor the picture-postcard Paris with its expensive restaurants and luxurious shops. His Paris was none of these.

The Paris he loved, because he knew it as a child, was that of the steep narrow streets of Montmartre, where, among the pimps, prostitutes and thieves of Pigalle he had grown up as part of the closely knit Corvo family. He wondered what his life would have been, had he remained with them, for he had spent the past twenty years in a very different kind of world.

Since the age of fifteen, Alex Drach had lived, studied and worked in New York, where he had become part of the supposedly civilized and sophisticated world of art. He had, in fact, become something of an art scholar, but one with an unusual bent. He specialized in tracking down and recovering stolen art. Swag hunting, he called it irreverently.

He had tried teaching after taking his degree in art history, but standing in front of a group of self-centered, adolescent students held little appeal for him. Even though he was extremely popular with his students, he suspected they had attended his lectures for all the wrong reasons. Since he was the youngest full professor on the faculty, students tended to identify with him. The young men admired him because they had heard about his unusual moonlighting activities. That a professor would spend time hunting lost or stolen Rembrandts stirred their imagination. Women students found him attractive. His remoteness, he presumed, had inspired their sexual fantasies rather than an appreciation of art. Alex was flattered by the enthusiasm of his students but found the teaching experience banal. More and more he began to devote his time and energy to his security business.

As an art security specialist, he had seen the art world from the underside, and knew that in many ways it was more violent and corrupt than the world of Pigalle. To the sophisticates of the art world, however, the ritualized, closed society in which he had been raised was savage and brutal. But that didn't matter. A part of him, the best part of him, would remain Corsican forever.

Not that he didn't enjoy his work. He did. He had chosen his profession deliberately, not only because of its financial rewards, but also because of the risks involved. He was highly paid because he was the best, a man in command of his craft. Still, while the money pleased him, more important was the satisfaction he derived from coping with the technical problems of recovering stolen art. As for the risks, he had a need to live on the edge. That too was Corsican.

The plane touched down smoothly and then slowed as the engines fired in reverse. Alex took a deep breath, unfastened his seat belt and reached for the leather valise he always carried. It was small enough to tuck underneath the seat in front of him. He liked it because it saved time. He hated waiting for his baggage.

Deplaning into De Gaulle International, Alex felt as though he were in a futuristic maze. The airport was like a gigantic spider-like spaceship whose hollow oval core was fed by Plexiglas tunnels that drew passengers in and out on conveyor belts like parcels in pneumatic tubes. He cleared customs in the outer ring without incident. The rippling rubber conveyor belt then led him down to a "satellite," where he boarded an escalator to the street level below.

Through sliding glass doors, he stepped into the bitter January cold outside the terminal. As he slipped on his Burberry, he noticed three clerics engaged in quiet conversation. One of them, the one with steel-gray close-cropped hair, had been on his flight from New York. He remembered him because he had thought it unusual for a priest to be wearing a tiny silver stud in his left ear.

Alex waited on the curb only a few minutes before a low-slung, bright-red Citroën screeched to a stop in front of him. The passenger door flicked open, and the driver, a tawny-haired woman with large brown eyes, smiled up at him mischievously. "Welcome to Paris," she said.

The girl was Jocko's niece, Araminta. He couldn't believe it. She was all ovals, the curve of her eyebrows, the shape of her face, the fullness of her breasts. She possessed a maturity unexpected in a girl of nineteen. He smiled. "There've been some changes."

"You just haven't been around enough."

"That's my misfortune," he said, laughing. He pitched his case into the back, lowered himself into the front seat and kissed her on both cheeks.

"Perhaps you'll stay awhile this time," she said. Then she deftly shifted into first gear and sped away.

"How's Jocko?"

"Like any father of the bride," Minta replied. "He's nervous."

Alex grinned. "I can imagine." The Citroën moved into the right lane of the *autoroute* to Paris. "Will we make the reception?"

"Don't worry; we've just entered the Roissy-Paris time trial. I can do it in twenty minutes."

"I only hope we're alive when we get there," Alex said, eyeing Minta nervously.

She glanced at him and winked, then downshifted around a curve and accelerated.

Moments later a silver-gray BMW moved rapidly around the same curve, keeping pace with the red Citroën in front of it. In it three clerics rode in silence. One of them in the left back seat expertly assembled an Ingram M-11 submachine gun. With its stock telescoped it was exactly 9.75 inches long and weighed 3.5 pounds. To the M-11 the cleric fitted a Sionics silencer. On full automatic the Ingram could quietly spit out fifteen rounds a second. The only sound heard would be a mechanical click followed by the zing of the subsonic cartridges. The weapon was perfect for the job: easily concealed, effective and quiet.

III

Although the rain had stopped, a heavy, asphyxiating fog hung like a gray shroud over London. Hurrying through the rush-hour crowds, dodging umbrellas and the pools of water that dotted the uneven sidewalks of the West End, an aging and breathless Hugh Jenner cursed the damp chill that cut through him like a blade. He longed to be out of all this, he thought, out of the damp. The cadaverous existence of his daily routine, the sluggish days at the Ministry, that dilapidated and bureaucratic anachronism, had taken thirty-three years of his life. It had both cradled and cramped him, afforded him protection from the real world, but at the same time prevented him from really ever living fully in it.

There was only one consolation, the knowledge that in a few more months, five to be exact, he would be free and able to fulfill his lifelong dream of retirement. He would move to his sun-drenched villa in southern Spain. Wondrous days lay ahead. He would have time, finally, to lounge on the front terrace, sip sherry, and gaze out at the endless blue sea beyond.

Comforted by such reveries, Hugh Jenner pulled the collar of his trenchcoat tighter around his neck, plunged his hands deep into his pockets and plowed on, hunched over, as if moving against a stiff gale of wind.

Apart from his dreams of spending the rest of his days lying in the sun, Jenner had another obsession, his lack of hair. When, as a young man, he started going bald, he visited London's most eminent trichologist. The series of treatments proved to be very costly but of little practical use. Jenner continued to lose his hair. After that, he tried to ignore his balding, and for a time accepted the consolation of a friend who told him that it was a sign of uncommon virility. He liked that, but in the end resorted to a black wig, one that had suited him when he bought it fifteen years ago, but now that he had aged, contrasted sharply with his heavily lined face and poorly fitting false teeth.

A low-level administrator, extremely low in the grand scale of things at Whitehall, Jenner had spent thirty-three years conducting briefings and writing reports about the criminal justice system in Britain. The reports were certainly not brilliant, but they were detailed and precise enough to be useful to junior grade Ministry officials who never read them but pushed them upward through the bureaucratic maze.

Now, as he ritualistically did every evening at half past five, Hugh Jenner had left his carefully arranged desk at the Home Office and walked to The Ark, one of London's more nondescript pubs. At The Ark, it was his custom to have a few drinks before heading home to his bachelor flat in Albany, just off Piccadilly. In that respect, Jenner's routine never varied. He believed that habit instilled virtue, that people without regular patterns had no traditions and, therefore, no substance.

When he reached the pub, Jenner entered the downstairs bar, where he exchanged greetings with several of the older regulars gathered around the fireplace. Jenner nodded stiffly and then mounted the well-worn stairs to the upper lounge, crowded with a group standing shoulder to shoulder in front of the massive mahogany bar. He edged through the crowd, waved to a few acquaintances, one of them the pub's champion darts player, whom he admired, and took his customary place at the far end of the room. Ordering a pink gin, he dug into a bowl of oily peanuts and mused about the bright sunshine and easy life-style of the Costa del Sol. The image of the beautiful young boys who flocked to southern Spain in the spring and summer warmed him as much as the taste of the gin.

Having quickly downed one drink, Jenner was inspired to order another, unusual for him, a sober, retiring personality whose temperament was considered somber by those who did not know him. Certainly few, if any, of the regulars at The Ark knew him well. That he was different from the others at the bar, Jenner always regarded as his secret.

As he watched the faces of the men standing around him in the smoky glass mirror behind the bar, he observed that they were the typical habitués, brokers, bankers, more than a few solicitors and barristers, mostly middle-aged, all enjoying the institutional reassurance of their own solemn, self-righteous company. He listened to the inconsequential banter without being a part of it. Indeed, despite a sense of well-being in harmony with the evening's mood of camaraderie, he felt lonely. These really weren't his kind of people.

As Jenner's attention wandered down the bar, he noticed a man he had never seen before. Slim and elegant, he wore a continental tailored suit with tight-fitting trousers, a jacket contoured in the Italian style and a magenta silk foulard artfully tucked into the neck of his pale blue shirt. Too stylish for a businessman, Jenner guessed, possibly an actor, a designer or even a dancer. Jenner liked to think he could read people's occupations by the way they dressed. He had trained himself to do so, or felt he had.

The young man ran his hand through his straight blond hair, looked into the mirror and caught Jenner's gaze with his globular blue eyes. As their eyes met, the man gave Jenner a friendly nod. The two exchanged cautious but embarrassed smiles. Jenner knew at once what this intimate communication meant.

Although exhilarated by the exchange, Jenner was a careful man, especially around the pub. He had never dared to make a contact there. No thank you, he had told his intimates, he was perfectly happy in the closet. He had to be. His position at the Ministry, his pension, everything would be ruined if "Home" knew. Pretending indifference, Jenner directed his attention back to the bowl of peanuts and casually ordered a third pink gin. But he was unable to restrain himself. Again and again, his eyes returned to the man's reflection in the mirror.

Finally the unthinkable happened. The man moved down the bar and took a place next to him.

"I wonder if I might join you," the man said, with just a trace of an accent that Jenner decided was Scandinavian.

Although he could not hide his curiosity, Jenner did not know how to react. His instinct told him that something was not quite right, but in the euphoria of being approached by such a fine-looking specimen half his age, he ignored his fears and extended his right hand. "Please. Would you like a drink?"

"Delighted. A glass of wine, if I may. My name's Baruch."

"Last name?"

"My only name."

"Hugh Jenner. A pleasure."

Baruch explained that he was a journalist from Sweden. He also quietly admitted that he was in London for the night and had not yet booked a hotel room. His overnight bag, in fact, was in the cloak-room.

Jenner, whose generosity at that moment amazed even himself, offered Baruch a place to stay. At first the blond man demurred, but at Jenner's insistence that his chambers were only a few blocks away, finally agreed. Casually Baruch rested his fingertips on the back of Jenner's hand in a gesture of affection.

Jenner was warmed by the display but quickly withdrew his hand. He stood as erect as a colonial officer about to review his troops, placed his hands on his hips, arched his back and looked up and down the bar to see if anyone was watching. Unable to mask his feelings, he whispered to Baruch that it would not do to be so open in the pub.

"Discretion," he said, self-consciously. "You know . . . we're not so relaxed as you are in Sweden."

They then left the bar, picked up Baruch's overnight bag and walked together into the misty night.

At Albany, where Jenner lived, he and Baruch climbed the stairs to the older man's third-floor chambers. Entering, Jenner paused for a breath. He pressed his hand to his chest, reached in his pocket for a tortoise-shell pillbox, took out a white tablet and chewed on it hastily. A tiny white bubble from the tablet appeared in the corner of Jenner's lip.

"Are you all right?" Baruch asked, a concerned look on his face.

"A touch of angina . . . ," Jenner said, flushed with embar-rassment and passion. He unlocked the ornate door and they walked in.

The drawing room was swathed in dark brown and lit by a large chandelier, a spiderweb of crystal that twinkled flirtatiously overhead. A clutter of antique furniture made the modest front room seem even smaller than it was. Jenner offered Baruch a seat on a green velvet couch, which was flanked by two high-backed velvet chairs. On the mantelpiece a cluster of figurines and statues competed for attention with two gigantic ivory tusks that projected upward from either side of the fireplace.

"Do you like it?" Jenner asked.

Baruch hesitated a moment, sniffing the red carnation he wore in his lapel. "I'm just a bit surprised," he answered, glancing at a Lichtenstein print of a hand pinioned by the heel of a boot. "The contrast . . . the decor is so different from the way you dress."

"Oh that. We all dress this way at the Ministry. We have to blend in. . . . This is the real me," Jenner said, gesticulating about the room.

"But that painting isn't really in keeping with the rest," Baruch said, pointing to a painting of an eighteenth-century nobleman playing a lute for a group of fashionably dressed ladies.

"Oh, that!" Jenner said. "The Watteau. Rather special, don't you think?"

"How did you come by it?"

"I found it in a little gallery on Duke Street. Do you like it?"

"Decorative, but rather sentimental."

"Yes, but it has an interesting provenance. It was looted by the Nazis during the war."

"How exciting!"

Jenner's face brightened. He began to light candles about the room, and in their golden glow his lined face softened. He felt young again. "I'm so happy we met," he said.

"I, too, am grateful for this chance meeting. I'd always heard the English were stuffy."

"I knew you were for me the moment I saw you in the mirror."

"It's such a delight to make new friends. You seem so different, Hugh."

"Would you like some wine?"

"Of course," Baruch said. "You're so kind."

Agitated now, Jenner went to the bar and began to open a bottle of white wine. He could hardly take his eyes off Baruch, lounging gracefully on the green velvet couch. As he pulled the cork free, it crumbled and some flecks fell back into the bottle. Annoyed at his clumsiness, Jenner put the bottle aside, took another, and opened it more carefully. This time the cork came clean. Only the best, Jenner told himself, only perfection for Baruch tonight. Pouring two glasses of wine, Jenner offered his guest one of them. "These are Montefiore, the finest crystal," Jenner said.

Baruch smiled in appreciation as he raised his glass. "They're beautiful, so thin and fine that the glass would be invisible but for the wine."

A mellow glow rose in Jenner. He reached across and touched Baruch's upper arm. The biceps felt like iron. The power in the muscle stirred him. He admired the breadth of the shoulders, the short muscular neck, the bulge of the chest under the form-fitting shirt, and the face of chiseled granite. "How charming." They watched each other and sipped in unison.

"I see you have a fireplace," Baruch said. "Would it be a bother . . ."

"A fire? Of course not, my friend. How thoughtless of me."

"May I help?"

"No, not at all. Just a moment. I'll get it going in no time. The grate is always prepared. Just takes a match."

As Jenner stooped to light the fire, the blond man took a clear, plastic vial from his pocket, uncapped it quickly and emptied a few drops of liquid into Jenner's wineglass.

Returning to his guest, the fire now ablaze, Jenner removed his shoes and curled into the opposite end of the couch. It was the culmination of a perfect evening, Jenner thought. How handsome this one was, how strong, how Germanic. It was so good to look forward to a beautiful night of loving. "May I offer a toast?" Jenner said. "To a chance meeting that I'm sure will change our lives forever."

Baruch smiled demurely and watched Jenner put the wineglass to his lips. The toxicant took effect almost immediately. Moments later an overwhelming drowsiness swept over Jenner. He nodded. Too many gins before the wine, he thought. Then just before he passed out, he realized it was not the gin or the wine. He had been drugged. He couldn't believe it. All these years and now this. Betrayal was so unfair.

Baruch did not move immediately. He had plenty of time. He pulled a pair of thin surgical gloves from his jacket pocket, slipped them on and as he did so walked to the Watteau hanging on the far wall. He took it, opened his case and carefully placed the painting inside. Every now and again his eyes shifted to the sleeping figure at the end of the couch. He then went into the bathroom and filled the tub with hot water. Thoughtfully, he placed some bath oil in the water, then tested it with his finger. He returned to the couch, quickly undressed Jenner and then, gathering him into his arms, carried the sleeping figure into the bathroom and lowered him gently into the tub.

With Jenner nicely settled in the warm water, Baruch reached into Jenner's mouth and removed his false teeth, placing them in a glass of water on the sink. Then he opened the medicine cabinet and extracted a razor blade. He took each of Jenner's hands and slashed the arteries running from the base of the thumb around to the delicate underside of the wrists.

Then he dropped the razor blade into the water and watched as Jenner's head slowly sank. As the water turned pink, then red, he was amused to see the dead man's toupee slide from his head and float along the top of the water, where it stayed, modestly covering Jenner's exposed genitals.

Returning to the front room, the assassin walked around the apartment, picked up both glasses and took them to the kitchen, where he carefully washed his own and replaced it in the cupboard. He lightly rinsed out Jenner's glass, took it back to the drawing room and splashed a little wine into it before placing it on the table. Then he gathered Jenner's clothes from the couch, went to the bedroom, and laid them neatly across the bed. Then from his overnight bag he withdrew a black suit and cleric's collar. He changed quickly, making sure to transfer the red carnation from the blue to the black jacket. He put the discarded clothing in the bottom of the case, covering the painting, took a last look around the room and left, closing the door quietly behind him. As he descended the stairs, he removed the surgical gloves and stuffed them into the pocket of his trousers. He glanced at his watch. It had gone even more smoothly than he thought it would. He had time for dinner at the Chelsea Rendezvous before catching the plane for Rome.

IV

Ray Fuller glanced at his watch. 7:55. It was almost time. In a few minutes the auction would begin and André Rostand had not yet arrived. From his seat in the third row of the main salesroom of Sotheby Parke Bernet, Fuller checked the entrance. He was worried. Perhaps at the last minute Rostand had decided to bid by telephone to insure his anonymity. That way the opposition wouldn't know what they were up against.

No, Fuller told himself, the Vermeer being sold was too important. Too much was at stake. Just before the auctioneer took his place on the rostrum, the old man would appear. Rostand's timing was uncanny that way.

As Rostand International's chief accountant, Fuller had known André Rostand for over thirty years. The man was shrewd. His entrance, just as the first lot was called, would be calculated to produce the maximum psychological effect. It was as if the auction could not begin without him.

Fuller wondered. Perhaps there was an agreement between Rostand and the chief clerk. A request was all that would be necessary. Small courtesies like that always came easily for Rostand. Someday, Fuller would have to ask him about it, though not tonight. Tonight, Rostand would be in no mood to joke about such things.

During the past few weeks, there had been a change in the old man. He had become sullen, impatient with idle chatter and preoccupied about something. Fuller had never seen him like this before. Perhaps Rostand was getting too old to handle the pressure. Maybe it would be better if he handed over the gallery to the next in line, his son Philip. The thought horrified Fuller, but perhaps the time had finally come. Whatever the problem was, Fuller was certain it had to do with that night's sale. The historic importance, and particularly the immense value, attached to the jewel of the auction, the Vermeer, had attracted collectors and dealers from all over the world.

Over the years, Fuller had attended many auctions, but never such a glittering one as this. Except for the seat reserved next to him for Rostand, not one of the seven hundred red velvet chairs in the main salesroom was empty. Even in the adjoining galleries, where a thousand more spectators were seated in front of closed-circuit television screens as large as double doors, there was standing room only. Although most of these people were mere observers, there to see and to be seen, there were serious collectors among them. Fuller noted a German steel magnate attended by two beautiful women who looked like starlets; a celebrated English fashion designer with his longtime male companion; and a Swiss investment banker with his wife. They were all Rostand's clients. Fuller knew the biographies of most of the important ones. That, after all, was his business.

Almost without exception, these people controlled vast financial and cultural empires. He called them the Illuminati. They all knew each other, of course, vacationed in the same resorts, attended the same parties and slept with each others' wives—mixed doubles or singles, it didn't matter. They were all friends. Fuller smiled. How they marveled at their own self-importance. They had arrived in gray Bentleys and sleek, chauffeur-driven Rolls-Royces, the women wearing Halston, Dior and St. Laurent, the men more somber in ruffled shirts and black ties.

Still, these people were not the real competition. Illuminati never openly bid themselves. Sprinkled throughout the crowd were agents or dealers acting for them. Discretion was all important. The less the IRS knew about who owned what, the better. Art might be sacred, but it was also big business. More than an investment, it was the world's last free currency, a socially convenient way to hedge against inflation and avoid bothersome exchange control regulations, the perfect way to move assets across borders without declaring them.

So it was the dealers and museum people they would have to watch. They would be the ones bidding for the Vermeer. From a list Rostand had obtained from his informant working inside Sotheby's, Fuller mentally checked them off.

Christopher Ashton, the blond, aristocratic director of the Metropolitan Museum, was in his usual spot, seated directly in front of the auctioneer's stand. He could be counted upon to pounce from the start. Never the reserved type, Ashton loved the action. And why not, Fuller reasoned. He always bid with other people's money.

Charles Duranceau, the wily Paris dealer, had positioned himself as he always did, in the most inconspicuous place he could find, along the wall on the far side of the room. The chameleon-like

Frenchman wore a cream-colored dinner jacket as if to blend in with the beige walls behind him.

Close to the front, in the second row, sat Julian Johns of London, a young, urbane man with a photographic memory for pictures, an insatiable ambition and all the right social connections—especially among very rich, older women. By the age of thirty, Johns had already established himself as an eminently successful dealer. There were rumors that the heiress to Brazil's largest industrial conglomerate was his lover and might be backing him. If that were true, Johns could offer some resistance. On his own, however, he wouldn't be able to match Rostand's personal resources.

On the other hand, Dr. Leopold Marto, seated across the middle aisle, directly opposite, was a much more formidable opponent. Spindly, balding and darkly tanned even in January, Marto was in his early seventies, though he looked much younger. Known to pride himself on being able to run four miles every day, Marto also liked to surround himself with beautiful women, as evidenced by the young blond Swedish model who was seated next to him. Fuller shook his head. He understood power and the attractions it held for some women. But this he couldn't accept. To him, Marto looked like a wizened old athlete, almost repulsively muscled for someone his age.

Comparing the list to the audience, Fuller noticed that Nando Pirelli had not arrived. Something was wrong. For him attendance at an auction like this was mandatory. The dapper Italian loved excitement and spectacle. Assuming a mistake of some sort had been made, Fuller carefully scanned the crowd and spotted Pirelli as he entered the salesroom. In his late forties, the Italian was a suave, sophisticated man whose tanned unlined face and glossy black hair belied his age.

Fuller watched Pirelli walk down the far side of the room and greet Bertram Bez, a stoic Iranian art dealer interested only in high-priced art. Instead of sitting together, however, they conversed for a moment, then parted and remained standing on opposite sides of the room. Fuller thought it odd that they had purposely decided to stand, particularly the bulky Bez, a man loath to exert himself physically in any way. Yet they were in a perfect position, he noted, to observe the bids as they came from the floor.

Fuller shrugged and anxiously began to thumb the red, cloth-bound catalogue Sotheby's had prepared for the sale. Again he checked his watch. By tradition, important paintings were auctioned in the evening and Fuller calculated the sale would be over by ten. It would be the consummate social event of the season.

Opening his catalogue, Fuller examined the large color photograph of the Vermeer and its provenance.

Jan Vermeer van Delft
Lot 10. PORTRAIT OF A TAVERN MAID
c. 1660. Face slightly profiled. Full length, the maid turned partially to the right, in a blue dress, with a white mantle. A green cloth drapes an entrance way leading to the room beyond.
Oil on canvas   19 × 18 in.

Provenance: Rostand & Cie., Paris 1895
Armand Baumont & Cie., 1895
Auguste Donnet, Paris 1899
Charles Donnet, Cleveland, Ohio 1947

Literature: B. Bechtol, *Dutch Pictures of the Baroque,* Amsterdam 1932, p. 278.
Max S. Bottarri, *Vermeer, A Catalogue Raisonné,* London, 1953.

How exquisite it was, he thought. *The Portrait of a Tavern Maid,* a small, radiant canvas, was treasured not only for its precise beauty, but also because it was so rare. It was one of the world's most coveted paintings, one of only thirty-five masterpieces by Jan Vermeer, the Dutch master who painted three hundred years ago. Almost all of his works now hung in museums and would never come on the market again. The few Vermeers still remaining in private hands were owned by families whose wealth was as great as that of some small nations. Perhaps once or twice in a lifetime a Vermeer might come up for sale. Indeed, to own a Vermeer was to belong to such a select company that to sell one could mean only one thing, the imminent decline or end of a family dynasty.

The Tavern Maid was of particular importance to André Rostand. It, after all, had been the beginning of the Rostand art dynasty.

Fuller knew the story well. Rostand's father, Aaron, then a young dealer in Paris, had purchased a heavily varnished old painting in July of 1895 for only two hundred francs. When he had seen it the first time, hanging among hundreds of other paintings, it had taken his breath away. He knew at once that he had discovered a lost Vermeer. Aaron was then only twenty-five, but it was his greatest coup.

The purchase made him famous and eventually its sale to another Paris dealer for twenty thousand francs provided the money he needed to open an art gallery on the Faubourg St. Honoré, the neighborhood that was then the center of the French art world. From that time, Rostand International grew to become the world's preeminent art gallery.

In the years between and by a circuitous history, *The Tavern Maid* found its way into the possession of a distant relative of the Paris dealer—one Charles Donnet, of Cleveland, Ohio. Now ill and in need of money, Charles Donnet had placed the painting with Sotheby for auction.

Fuller snapped the catalogue closed as the spotlight over the auctioneer's stand flicked on, highlighting the stage. Suddenly the room quieted. Then the spotters and assistant auctioneers took their positions like outfielders around the room, while a gray-uniformed attendant marched nervously down the aisle, carrying an empty easel. He set it down carefully on the brightly lit stage, checked that its feet were properly secured, then walked away. It was time.

Unnoticed by Fuller, seated in the rear of the main salesroom, was a man with dark glasses, dressed in the simple garb of a cleric. He was a curious exception to the high fashion and elegance on display around him, more so because he was chewing gum, his heavy jowls moving in a gentle motion, rather like a cow chewing its cud. Little else about the man attracted anyone's attention. His seat had been reserved by the Vatican's special envoy to the United Nations.

V

Outside, New York was strangely still and quiet. A light snow had blanketed the city earlier that afternoon, muffling the sounds of the streets. Large snowflakes continued to fall past the streetlights. Crunching his way toward the auction house from his offices at Rostand International, André Rostand could feel the cold. The light cashmere overcoat he wore was more suited to the temperatures of the firm's limousine than to the freezing streets, and he had forgotten his gloves. A cherrywood cane with a silver knob was tucked securely under his right arm. Rostand, in his late sixties, was short and solidly built, with a barrel chest and large shoulders. Dark-complexioned, he had a broad nose, thick gray hair and brown agate eyes that glowed with intensity. Dubbed the "Art Baron" by the world's press, André Rostand had for decades been the ruler of an art empire with galleries in every major capital of the world.

Tonight not even the cold could distract him from thoughts of the Vermeer. He calculated that the bidding would go as high as four million dollars. For his part, he was prepared to go even higher, to four-million-five, if necessary, though he hoped he would not have to. It depended on the opposition. Marto would bid, of course. Bez and Julian Johns would challenge as well. And, according to rumor, some outsiders—Japanese buyers—might bid seriously, although Rostand did not think that likely. No, Marto would be his problem, the rival with the most staying power.

Nevertheless, he was determined, the Vermeer would be his in an hour or two. The only thing that worried him was the conversation he had had at lunch some weeks before with Marto at the Metropolitan Club.

Marto, his chief rival, had proposed that they form a "ring," a secret organization of dealers working together to control the international art market. Marto had recently formed Art Intrum, a mutual fund investing in art, for that purpose.

Marto was right, of course. The market in art had changed. Now, a gallery had to buy Cézanne, Degas and Renoir paintings as though they were commodities like grain—or, more appropriately, gold. Few investments provided a safer or better return on capital. Only a limited number of masterpieces existed, and only a small number of works by contemporary artists could be expected to add to the basic supply. Art, especially rare art, would only increase in value, perhaps as much as ten to fifteen percent a year.

Yet André had not liked the proposal. A Rostand never went into partnership. The way Marto had pressed the offer had also put him off. There had been an air of menace in the way Marto suggested it was in Rostand International's best interests to join forces. André wasn't sure what that had meant, but he didn't like being threatened, even subtly. Besides, it was Marto who needed him, not the other way around.

As André approached the heavy glass doors of Sotheby's, he passed a line of double-parked limousines, the drivers clustered in groups, smoking and gesticulating in the cold winter air. A few, recognizing him, wished him a good evening. He thanked them and went through the front door into the lobby, removed his coat and handed it to a waiting attendant. The cane, which he carried at every auction for luck, he kept. A second attendant rushed up to lead him to the main salesroom, where a young woman dressed in a full-length green evening gown greeted him.

"You're just in time, Mr. Rostand," she said, smiling.

Rostand returned her smile, viewed the crowd and nodded. "You've got quite a turnout this evening, Marlaina. Should be a good sale."

"Yes, it should be exciting," she said, as she handed him a copy of the catalogue. "The code tonight is Oscar Wilde. Good luck."

Rostand accepted the catalogue, smiled again, and walked down the side aisle to take his customary place beside Fuller.

"It's about to start," Fuller said unnecessarily.

"It's freezing out there," Rostand said, laying the cane across his lap and rubbing his hands together. He opened the catalogue and observed that beside each lot number Marlaina had provided him the confidential bids left by prospective buyers not attending the auction. In addition, she'd also given him the reserve, or lowest price, the seller would accept on each painting. The figures had been coded using the acronym, OSCAR WILDE. Each letter beginning with "O" represented a numeral from zero to nine. This was one of the most closely guarded secrets of the auction house. Rostand wondered how long it would be before they caught up with her. He made several calculations, then looked up. "Where's Marto?" he asked.

"Directly on our left, across the aisle," Fuller whispered.

"And Bez?"

"Up front, near the first row. Pirelli's on the other side. Duranceau . . ."

Rostand shifted in his seat to catch a glimpse of Pirelli just as the auctioneer, slim and impeccable in a dinner jacket, made his way with a broad smile up the aisle to the steps at the right of the stage and then up to the old mahogany rostrum. On cue, two salesroom clerks and the alternate auctioneer took their places like a phalanx in front of the stand. Sydney Morrow, the white-haired record keeper who knew every major collector by sight, bent over his ledger.

The auctioneer swept the room with a professional eye, making certain that his spotters were in place. Most of them were eager, attractive young women who not only added glamour to the sale but were also responsible for making certain that even the most furtively signaled bid was promptly relayed to the rostrum. In the closed-circuit television rooms, the auxiliary auctioneers tested their micro-phones and assured their audiences that all bids would be clearly transmitted.

Satisfied now, the auctioneer in the main salesroom rapped his gavel three times. The room hushed.

"Good evening, ladies and gentlemen. There will be fifteen lots of fine old master paintings offered this evening. We invite you to begin with Lot Number One, a magnificent Tiepolo."

Immediately, two uniformed porters carried a large canvas onto the stage, placing it reverently on the easel.

"I have fifty thousand to start," called the auctioneer.

As the bids flowed from the floor, the spotters picked up the subtle and intimate communications from the crowd: a touch of the lapel, an adjustment of glasses, a hand raised.

"Seventy-five thousand . . . one hundred thousand . . . do I have one hundred twenty-five thousand?" Every gesture, every pencil tipped, head motion, raised eyebrow or catalogue closed represented a small fortune.

"Two hundred thousand on my right! Two hundred fifty thousand! Do I? Yes. In the back, I have three hundred thousand."

Rostand, arms folded in his traditional no-bid position, watched as Marto entered the bidding. For Rostand, the way a man bid was often an index to his personality. Ostentation could suggest bravado or a lack of determination. Hesitation, sometimes a ploy which he himself had used, might mean confusion. Overeagerness could be at-tributed to inexperience, as might a show of temper. Humor was al-ways out of place.

"Three hundred fifty. I have three hundred fifty. Do I have four hundred thousand?"

Marto was completely relaxed. Rostand could detect neither hesi-tation nor eagerness. The old man worked like a machine, flicking his pencil in a tiny arc, responding immediately to each increment as it was bid.

Turning his attention to Pirelli, Rostand detected a certain play-fulness in the Italian that was wholly unconvincing. Pirelli had en-tered the bidding just after Marto, challenging at two hundred thou-sand. Then, at three-fifty, he had shaken his head, withdrawing from the competition. That was curious. Pirelli was too experienced, too astute to think that the Tiepolo would go for less. Perhaps he was "split bidding," starting strong, then visibly backing off. Others, inexperienced in the auction room, would be put off balance, and the momentum of the sale would falter. At the same time, Pirelli would have someone else take up the bidding for him, someone secretly connected to him.

"I have four hundred thousand. Four hundred fifty! To you, sir!"

That was strange. The Tiepolo was Bez's kind of picture, yet he was not bidding. Why was he staying out? Was he waiting for the Vermeer?

At the five-hundred-thousand mark the bidders were reduced to two: Duranceau, the Frenchman from Paris, and Leopold Marto.

"Against you, sir," the auctioneer intoned, looking at Duranceau. There was a moment of hesitation as the Frenchman pondered what he'd do, and then his eyes gave him away. Rostand didn't know precisely what it was, but he'd seen the man's eyes leave the rostrum for a moment, and it was clear that he was ready to withdraw. He bid, as Rostand thought he would, but it was his last. Marto flicked his pencil, topping the bid by another twenty-five thousand and the Frenchman folded, ignoring the auctioneer's appeal. The Tiepolo was knocked down to Dr. Leopold Marto for five hundred thousand dollars.

The sale had begun auspiciously and the audience burst into applause. Even Rostand clapped. The gesture was not so much appreciation of what had gone before as it was a release of tension. He realized that he hadn't moved a muscle while the Tiepolo was on the block. In an effort to relax, he began to rub the silver knob of the cane, while glancing from side to side, reading the room. He was an expert at it. Even as a child, attending auctions with his father at the Hôtel Drouot in Paris, he'd had an extra sense that enabled him to gauge the mood of the players in a salesroom, the degree to which they would take risks on a given night. Tonight the air was drunk with art and money. It reminded him, in some ways, of the Paris he knew in the 1930s. The decorum and glitter were the same.

A long sigh of appreciation swept through the crowd as the porters delivered Lot Number 2, a splendid Caravaggio. Its play of light and shadow was remarkable.

Fuller leaned toward Rostand, keeping his eyes on the painting. "Marto must have plenty of backup to bid so heavily so soon."

Rostand shrugged, folding his arms again. "Perhaps."

"I don't like it," Fuller whispered.

"I suspect he's got a buyer for the Tiepolo. It doesn't matter. He's here for the *Tavern Maid*. As we are."

VI

In Rome Cubitt Keeble was usually wakened by her maid at two or three in the afternoon. She exercised, bathed, went out for lunch or to shop and then came home and began to prepare for Madame Gérard's.

Cubitt loved the night, drawn to it as if by a powerful lover, especially the early morning hours after midnight when for her the world came alive. An ethereal beauty of pure English descent, she was as breezy as the wind, a born wanderer and a hustler.

Ever since Cubitt had dressed up in her mother's clothes at the age of seven, she had always wanted to be either a model or an actress. She started out in London at seventeen taking her clothes off for a photographer. Five years later she had climbed to the top, her face appearing on the cover of *Harper's Bazaar* and *Vogue* in the same month. But even a highly paid mannequin's life was not so easy. She worked hard, got home late after a long day's shooting and collapsed.

Then at twenty-five, it was all over.

Young one day, old the next, she was past it. New faces overtook her in fresh waves that flowed regularly from the agencies. But she was lucky. She had survived longer than most.

It was then that Madame Gérard discovered her. They met in London one afternoon at a photographer's studio and the next day Cubitt packed her bags, closed up her little flat in Chelsea and moved to Rome. That was two years ago.

Now she lived in a richly furnished apartment overlooking Rome's Borghese gardens and as was her custom every day, she lay immersed in a steamy bath, fed by thirty water jets strategically placed to massage her spine, waist, hips and thighs. She loved to float in the pneumatic tub, adjusting the dials that controlled the temperature and pressure of the water. She spent hours there, reading, drinking Campari and soda, and studying her face in the mirrored ceiling. In the mirror, she thought she was better in profile than straight on. In profile she had the face of a finely cut diamond. Straight on, she was soft and inviting. The duality, a hard yet inviting look, was part of her style. She cultivated it. Men found the combination irresistible.

She stood and took a huge terry cloth towel from the heated rack and dried her long, taut body. She thought of how she wanted to look that night.

Madame Gérard had briefed her. She would be expected about ten. The men would be the conventional types, socially acceptable but looking for something unusual. Cubitt decided on an innocent, wide-eyed look. It would be more effective.

Conjuring an image, she spent a half-hour combing out her long blond hair, trying first the newest asymmetrical style. She embellished her hair with first a flower, then a ribbon and finally a few jewels. It was not quite right.

She tried again, this time a modified chignon. Too severe. She undid the chignon, bent over from the waist, and flipped her hair over the top of her head. Holding it there with one hand, she fixed it in place with pins and worked it into a delicate braid. She gazed into the mirror. Perfect. The style gave her an old-fashioned look that enhanced her long graceful neck.

The makeup took longer. She lightly applied mascara, and then thickened the curve of her brows with a fine-line eyebrow pencil. She wore a pale tone of lipstick, rather than the lush red she usually used and outlined her lips with brown liner. Finally, she added a touch of rouge to her cheeks, stepped back from the mirror, and turned her head from side to side. She approved.

Still naked, she went to the wardrobe and selected several evening gowns with accessories for each. The relationship between clothes and a woman's body was symbiotic, she thought. A dress was a signature. Of course, she knew that gestures were equally important—the way a woman moved, used her eyes to look at others or crossed her legs when she sat down.

After trying on the dresses, she chose a silk wrap of pale almond by Chloe. The dress would complement the golden highlights in her hair. A single strand of baroque pearls might have been elegant, but in the end she decided against them. A pair of emerald earrings and a drop of Yves St. Laurent's Opium was enough.

It was nearly ten o'clock and at last, she was ready. She did not know who Madame Gérard had chosen for her that evening, but she was not often disappointed.

The man would be more than rich, he would be wealthy and, of course, influential. All of Madame Gérard's clients were. Cubitt only hoped that he would also be attractive, though it didn't really matter. Most of the men were close to her father's age, overweight and graying. But there was one difference between these men and her father: money. Her father had never had the wealth to smell so expensively or dress as finely as they did. It made a difference. For Cubitt it was simple. Wealth and power were the sinew of love.

She left the dressing table, drank the last of her Campari and soda, set the glass down on a silver tray and left her bedroom. On the way out of the flat she hooked over her arm the Fendi fur coat the maid handed her and descended by elevator to the courtyard below. There she slipped into the driver's seat of her black Alfa Romeo and sped off to the Piazza Navona and Madame Gérard's.

VII

Nestled in the front seat of Minta's Citroën, Alex Drach gave himself in trust to the motion of the car. Lulled by the sway and purr of its engine, he leaned back and watched the lights of the oncoming cars. An early evening mist had settled over the French countryside and on low-lying sections of the road they plunged through wispy patches of fog. In the clear, a full moon was rising. It seemed to be racing with the Citroën, skimming along through the trees that flanked the highway. As the car plunged back into the mist, Minta's face was lit by the reflection of the headlights.

Alex looked at her. Remarkable, the changes that had taken place in four years. He remembered the gangly, awkward, undeveloped girl. She had always been precocious and friendly. Every time he had visited the Corvos, she had attached herself to him, not in any pestering way, but in an easy, comfortable manner. So often had he met her there that on the rare occasions she wasn't around he had noticed her absence. She could be habit-forming, he thought, especially now that she was a woman. With her long thick hair cascading over her perfect shoulders, a slim waist, the firm bust, a mischievously arched mouth and those long legs, she was a remarkably beautiful young woman. It was as simple as that. Yet not so simple. Suddenly, he felt older.

Minta broke the silence. "They're looking forward so much to seeing you, Alex. Especially Madelaine. She made such a lovely bride. The wedding was beautiful."

"I'm sorry I didn't get there on time. I couldn't get away sooner. What's her husband like?"

Minta smiled. "His name is Pascal, but we call him Manetta—'Little Hand.' Jocko says he's a gift from the Saracens. You know: dark, supple, a real Moor."

"Sounds dangerous," Alex said, watching the mist dance in the headlights.

"He is," she remarked. "I wouldn't want him for an enemy." She pressed a button and the wipers started sweeping across the windshield with authority. For a while then she drove in silence.

"How come you never married?"

Alex's voice took on a playful tone. "Who'd have me?"

Minta glanced at him. "I would," she said nonchalantly.

Alex laughed, while a series of reactions flitted through his mind. At first he was flattered. Maybe he wasn't so old, after all. But then Minta was Jocko's niece and part of the clan. He'd have to be careful with her. "I bet you say that to all the boys."

"I certainly do not," she said. "That's more your style." She arched her eyebrows mockingly. "I've heard all about you and your women."

"What women?" Alex asked.

"You know very well, Alex, you're always with some beautiful creature."

Amazement showed on his face. "Who's been telling you all those stories?"

"You know how the Corvos are. News travels fast, particularly when it's about you. So tell me, what are they like?"

"Nothing to tell," he said.

"All those broken hearts, and nothing to tell?"

Drach enjoyed the needling. He liked Minta's irreverence and more, her directness. "Honestly," he said. "I'm not serious about anyone." He paused. "How about you? Any boyfriends?"

"Many. But no one special."

"I know what you mean."

They were halfway to Paris now and the fog was heavier, with visibility cut to a few hundred yards. Fewer cars were on the road. Suddenly, in the sideview mirror, Alex caught sight of a pair of powerful headlights approaching at high speed. They surprised him, not because of the speed at which they came, but because it was the first car that night that had been able to overtake them.

Minta was in the left lane as the vehicle closed on them and began to pass on the right. Instead of overtaking them, however, the car slowed and kept pace beside them. Alex glanced to his right. In the glare from the headlights he saw the car was a BMW. In the same instant, registering a gray metal snout that protruded from its rear window, he ducked.

A string of explosions shattered the windows around him into crystal webbing. Alex heard Minta scream and felt the car lurch as she wrenched the wheel to the left and jammed her foot on the brake. "Keep going! Don't stop," he shouted. Another swath of fire sliced into the side of the Citroën, two rounds slapping into the back of the vacated leather seat where he had been sitting only a second before.

The Citroën bounced off the iron barrier in the middle of the *autoroute,* careened to the right, then catapulted forward ahead of the BMW. Minta slammed the gearshift into second and brought the Citroën under control in the right lane, her right foot pressed to the floorboard. In less than five seconds she was into third gear, up to fifty miles an hour, hurtling toward Paris.

Alex turned in his seat and looked back. The lights of the BMW loomed larger through the fog as the gap between them closed. He glanced at Minta. "Are you all right?"

"I think so," she replied, her voice quivering. She shifted into fourth gear and continued to accelerate.

"Keep going; you're doing fine. Remember, this is a time trial."

She smiled grimly. "Who are they? What do they want?"

"Don't think about it. Just keep your boot down."

Ahead of them on the *autoroute,* two sets of taillights became visible. In the right lane, the lights were amber, green and red. In the left lane, they were two tiny red dots. As the Citroën bore down on the two vehicles, Alex could see a *deux-chevaux* lumbering past a large refrigerator truck. Both lanes were blocked.

Minta decelerated and then, without hesitating, slammed her foot to the floor. The Citroën veered to the right onto the graveled shoulder, where, for a split second, her tires held, throwing the car forward, past the truck and out onto the *autoroute* once more.

Alex drew a deep breath, exhaled and looked back. The BMW, blocked for a moment, lay at least a hundred yards behind. Minta's maneuver had given them precious seconds. But not enough. The BMW would close fast. Alex looked at the speedometer. It read 130 kph—something over eighty miles per hour. "On a track, you could earn a living doing this."

Minta braked, shifted down and while all four wheels went into a screaming slide, she rounded a sharp curve on an incline to the right. "I prefer bumper cars," she said. "And cotton candy . . ."

"I promise you a carnival if we get out of this," Drach said, looking back. The BMW, now only a car length behind, slid desperately around the same bend and bore down on them. They passed a beat-up Renault. Its driver, Drach thought, looked at them as though they were maniacs. Then they flashed past a phosphorescent sign: "Exit 15—1 km."

Drach took another deep breath and looked at Minta. Her face was drawn, her lips pressed tightly in concentration. "We're going to try something up ahead," he said. "Do exactly what I tell you."

Minta nodded. Drach checked the odometer. A three was becoming a four. He calculated the distance. Three quarters of a kilometer. The timing would have to be perfect.

"What do you want me to do?" Minta asked, nervously glancing into the rear-view mirror.

"Get into the right-hand lane, and when I tell you, turn the steering wheel sharply to the right. Do it as fast and as hard as you can. At the same time, take your foot off the accelerator and downshift into second. Got that?"

"Hard to the right. Into second gear . . . Right?"

"Right!" Drach checked the odometer again. A half-kilometer to go. The question was, would they make it? As Minta crossed into the right lane, the BMW swung out and moved up to overtake them on the left. In the glare of the lights Alex could see the silhouette of the driver and two passengers. He was playing it very close, and he was playing with Minta's life. His hands slipped between the front seats and grasped the handbrake, his fingers opening and closing around the grip. The flexing eased the tension he felt in the pit of his stomach.

As the Citroën dipped and cut through a patch of thick fog, a yellow number nine rolled past the window of the odometer. They broke through the fog, and on their left the headlights of the BMW edged almost parallel with their own. To the right, Alex could make out the entrance to the exit ramp thirty yards ahead. "Are you ready?"

Minta leaned forward. "Ready."

Drach looked through the left rear window of the Citroën. He could see a metal nozzle raised and aimed in their direction. At the same moment, the Citroën flew past the exit ramp. Drach yelled, "Now," and pulled hard on the handbrake, locking the rear wheels. Minta whipped her steering wheel sharply to the right and slammed her foot onto the clutch. The Citroën spun into a right-angle turn, while a burst of machine gun fire ripped through its front left fender, shattering a headlight.

The Citroën slid viciously to the right and continued to spin, its tortured tires screaming in accompaniment to the bellow of the engine downclutching into second gear. Finally, it came to a dead stop facing in the opposite direction from the one it had been traveling seconds before. The radius of the turn had not been much more than the length of the car and less than the width of the highway.

Drach looked back up the *autoroute*. The BMW had already disappeared in the mist and fog. "Take the ramp," he commanded as he released the handbrake. "Hurry. We don't want to die in a crash now."

Minta shuddered, shifted into first gear and circled back up the ramp. At the top of Exit 15, she stopped.

"It's all right now, they won't be back. They missed and they know it. But they're not going to chance driving the wrong way on the *autoroute,* not the distance they have to go." Minta buried her face in Drach's shoulder. He put his arm around her and gazed back down at the fog-shrouded lights on the *autoroute* below. He held her for a moment and then he was out of the car, walking quickly around to the driver's side and opening her door. She slid into the passenger seat and Drach lowered himself behind the wheel. He eased the Citroën onto Route Number 7, and half an hour later, battered and with one headlamp, the Citroën sliced through the late evening Paris traffic, wove around the Porte Maillot and headed up the Avenue de la Grande Armée. The lights of the Arc de Triomphe, like beacons, loomed directly ahead.

VIII

Philip Rostand slumped in the comfortable leather back seat of his hand-tooled Bristol. Caught in Rome's heavy traffic, he impatiently drummed his fingers as he watched the procession of chic women and dapper men parading toward the Via Veneto. A handsome man in his late thirties, Rostand was fashionably dressed in a dark-blue pin-striped suit. He never wore an overcoat. Instead, this evening for warmth he kept his jacket collar turned up, with a cashmere scarf dangling casually over one shoulder.

He looked at his watch and calculated the time of his arrival at Madame Gérard's. He was going to be late. As a man of precision, he was upset. His dark muscular body began to sweat. He was a man who needed to have his way.

He reached into his breast pocket and withdrew a tiny silver pill-box. His hand trembled as he opened it and reached for a small white tablet. He swallowed, leaned back, and waited for the blessed effect.

Ten minutes later, no longer sweating, Philip glanced out the window at the warren of streets running off the Corso, and as the driver stopped near the Piazza Navona, he gazed at the Church of St. Agnes, the martyr. Whenever he saw the ancient building, he remembered the story of the thirteen-year-old saint who was stripped and stoned to death on the site in the fourth century. The story titillated him. Sometimes he dreamed about Agnes, how the jeering crowd gazed at her nakedness, and then watched as her hair grew miraculously long enough to cover her body. He would have to ask his astrologist what the dream meant.

As the Bristol rolled to a stop near the Palazzo Pambisti, Rostand's chauffeur nervously leaped from the front seat and opened the rear door. "Be here in an hour," Rostand commanded as he emerged. The chauffeur, a young Frenchman, nodded stiffly as Philip walked through the massive mahogany doors that led into the Palazzo's interior courtyard.

As the elevator doors opened, a middle-aged man in tight leather trousers passed through the lobby trailing behind two large black poodles. Rostand smirked. Probably double-gated, he thought. The elevator man held the door with a white-gloved hand and Philip stepped forward. "Madame Gérard's, please."

The operator nodded and was about to close the door when a voice echoed through the lobby. " *'Spetta! Per piacere.'*"

A moment later, a young woman with a mink coat flung over her shoulder stepped into the elevator. The operator smiled. "Madame Gérard's, *sì?*"

"*Sì!*" She flicked a glance at Rostand and smiled. The elevator doors closed and the operator and two passengers stood in silence.

Rostand stared at her, liking the cheekbones, reddened by the cold wind, the long blond hair and, as she unbuttoned her coat, the fashionable silk dress that revealed the outline of her breasts. He hadn't seen her before. Another wonderful discovery by Madame Gérard.

"You alone tonight?" Rostand asked, ignoring the elevator man.

"No. I'm meeting a friend," she replied.

"*Un fils de* Madame Gérard, eh?"

She looked into his eyes, but made no reply.

Rostand jammed his clenched hands into his pockets and they rode the rest of the way in silence.

At the top floor of the Palazzo, the elevator doors opened. The tinkle of glasses underscored by a low murmur of voices floated from the main reception rooms. A heavy, maternal-looking housekeeper dressed in black greeted the pair as they stepped into a large marble entrance hall. Without a word, the woman took her coat off, flipped it to the housekeeper and disappeared down the corridor.

Rostand waited for a few moments in the hall wondering whether to follow her. He decided not to. He gave the housekeeper his scarf and asked in fluent Italian for the blond's name.

"*Sì, sì.* She is beautiful," agreed the housekeeper, nodding vigorously.

"No, no. *Signora, como si chiama la* . . ." Rostand, very frustrated now, pointed down the corridor in the direction Cubitt had gone.

The old woman's eyes glimmered. "Ah. Signorina Keeble, *una ragazza gentile, molto gentile* . . ."

Rostand smiled and shook his head. "*Sì, sì. Grazie, Signora.*" "Keeble," he thought, "probably English." He stepped into the reception room. Its fifteen-foot-high ceiling was indirectly lit, like an atrium open to the sky. The lighting, the gold-papered walls and the marble floors created a mood of luminous luxury.

Philip threaded his way through a crowd of formally dressed, suntanned men and women, sipping champagne in clusters of twos and threes.

Every man, he knew, was distinguished for either his pedigree, his power or his purse. They ranged in age from twenty-five to sixty, and were of various nationalities. Philip felt akin to them. They were, like himself, men who had inherited their wealth. They were not nouveau riche.

They all had one other thing in common. They were "fils de Madame Gérard": her boys, who by virtue of being there, were introduced to the most talented, intelligent, desirable and expensive women to be found anywhere in Europe. Of course, each paid Madame Gérard handsomely for the privilege.

For the women present, a night at Madame Gérard's could lead anywhere or nowhere. They were under no obligation to sleep with the men they met. Often they didn't. At first.

Madame Gérard, adapting a variant of the Japanese tradition of the geisha, insisted that each of her "girls" was a free agent. Those who did establish a sexual relationship usually maintained the liaison for years. Few ended up marrying, but a woman could lead a very comfortable and luxurious existence if she were sufficiently discreet. In all, an evening at the Palazzo Pambisti was a very nice arrangement for everyone concerned, especially for Madame Gérard.

Philip accepted a glass of champagne from a waiter in a black shirt and white vest, and spotted Madame Gérard standing in the middle of the room. An inch or two taller than most of her guests, she was a striking woman. Large, but not heavy, she was perfectly proportioned. In her fifties, she wore a full-length dress of midnight blue. Her eyes glowed knowingly above a strong straight nose and a mouth that showed strength and determination. As she crisscrossed the floor introducing her guests to each other, she projected an aura of someone unafraid to stand out in a crowd. That confident, almost queenly carriage attracted people to her like a magnet.

No one knew very much about Madame Gérard. The story was that she had come to Rome during the war from eastern Europe, escaping, it was said, from the Nazis. She had opened up a small brothel, catering only to Italians. She seemed to specialize in political figures, and for that reason, many suspected she had special entrée to the highest circles of government and the police. Her girls were never bothered as a result. Some thought she might have worked for an intelligence organization for a time. Where better to have secrets unfold than in a brothel? But that was only speculation, like everything else about her.

Philip Rostand had known her for twenty years, ever since his father, André Rostand, had brought him to the Palazzo for his initiation to sex, another instance in which his father had tried to run his life.

André had taken more interest in the affair than had Philip, to the point of selecting the young girl Philip was paired with. Philip had always remembered that night with resentment. It was a fiasco, but before he left the girl he made her promise to keep his personal failure a secret. If Madame Gérard knew, she had never indicated it. She could be counted on to be discreet.

Philip walked across the room and edged his way into the circle that surrounded her.

She saw him coming. "Philip. At last, you've arrived. It's been a long time!"

"Too long." Then, taking her firmly by the arm, Rostand led her aside. "Is he here?" he asked.

"Who?"

"Maurice!"

"Of course, come with me. He's so Californian!"

She started to move toward the hallway, but Philip stopped her. "One other thing, Madame, a slight favor." Philip's upper lip lifted in a thin smile. "A very small favor. I want to meet one of your girls. A Miss Keeble."

"Cubitt! How do you know her?"

"I don't. That's the point."

Madame Gérard's eyes lifted in mock horror. "But I've already arranged that, and not with you. She's with Miles Cattell tonight."

"That baby!"

She smiled. "He's attractive, and charming. They suit each other."

"But, Madame . . ."

"I'm terribly sorry."

Philip took Madame Gérard's hands in his own. His face took on a conspiratorial look. "Do you remember the Degas you liked so much, the one that hung in our gallery last year?"

Madame Gérard smiled. "The two dancers?"

"Exactly. The same one. It's been sold, but undelivered. A slight mistake could be made and you could have it. At a minimal price, of course. What do you say?"

"It's unethical. For you, and for me."

"But think about it. Wouldn't it be lovely in your bedroom? Just . . ."

"Philip, enough!" she said. "I make no guarantees. You understand that, don't you? But I'll have a little talk with Cubitt. Just a word, understand. No commitments!"

"No commitments, of course," Philip repeated.

The two walked from the reception room into a glass and chrome paneled study where heavy lacquered furniture and brown satin couches contrasted with the sweep of a white Berber wool carpet. Stretched out on one of the overstuffed sofas was a slender, casually dressed young man. With his open, form-fitted shirt and gold neck chain, Maurice Tucker, a curator for the San Francisco County Museum, was the archetypal sun-tanned Californian.

The young man looked up and waved at Rostand. "Hey, Phil, I've been waiting for you." Tucker glanced down at a woman in a low-backed green dress. All Philip could see was a bony, sloping spinal column, white skin and a shock of medusa-like red hair. The woman was sitting on the floor, at the foot of the couch, sniffing a line of cocaine from the surface of a table. Tucker continued, "I've been playing with Olivia."

Olivia looked up at the sound of her name, her head three inches above the rest of her body. She smiled absently through lips darkened with grape-red lipstick, but took no further notice of the three figures standing above her. She returned to the line of white powder.

"Olivia," Tucker called to her, "my friend has arrived; why don't you go take a pee!"

Olivia looked up again. This time a frown creased her forehead. "Maurice, must I?" she whined. "I'm having such a good time."

Madame Gérard took Olivia's arm. "Come with me, darling, you and I should have a talk." Obviously displeased with the woman, Madame Gérard pulled Olivia to her feet and led her to the door.

The men waited until both women were out of the room, then Philip walked over to the built-in cabinet that housed a bar, a television set and sound equipment, including a reel-to-reel tape recorder. He set a glass on the sideboard, mixed a Pernod and water and turned up the amplifier. "Do you mind the music?" he asked.

"Not at all," Tucker said, lighting a cigarette. "By the way, what kind of place is this?"

"I'm surprised, Maurice! Don't you know Madame Gérard? You might call her work old-fashioned matchmaking. Much more like a salon than a brothel. And a good place to do business."

"Speaking of business, my friend . . ."

Tucker's hand went into his jacket. "I've got some interesting news. We had a trustees' meeting last week. They've agreed on six retrospectives over the next three years. I've made a list of the artists to be exhibited." He withdrew a piece of paper from his jacket and handed it to Rostand. "They're all relatively unknown. We should make a killing."

Philip smiled for the first time. In his hands he held one of the museum's most carefully guarded secrets, information that would enable him to make a small fortune. Once a museum had a showing of an artist's work, a dealer could be assured of a good market. Rostand would immediately instruct his buyers to acquire each of these artists' work at minimal prices, perhaps as little as a few thousand dollars apiece. Then, he would wait until the museum canonized them, and sell off the works at a spectacular profit. "What about purchases?" he asked.

"We've budgeted up to three million this year. It's almost certain we can acquire the Mexa, one or two Rauches and a set of drawings by Ernst Kapalow."

"Why so conservative? I thought California was the home of the avant garde?"

"These artists are safe. The board doesn't really like the contemporary scene, makes them uncomfortable. They don't understand it."

"I don't either!" Rostand said with a smirk. "But I know how to make money if we control the market." Rostand walked over to the couch, licked his finger and dabbed it in the residue of white powder on the table. He rubbed a little on his gums and took a sip of Pernod. "Nice combination, Maurice."

"I'm doing the buying," Tucker said.

"For the museum, you mean," Rostand corrected.

"Of course. You'll be doing your own, but there is the matter of money."

"You'll receive your regular payments in cash, as we agreed," Philip said. "I'll be in touch with you within a few weeks. Where do you want to take delivery?"

"Zurich. I'd never take that kind of money in the States."

"Fine. Is there anything else?" Philip asked.

"One thing. What about your father? Are we going ahead with this without his knowing about it?"

Philip's lips tightened. "Don't worry. That's not your concern."

Tucker sniggered. "When's he going to retire? He must be nearly seventy by now?"

Philip shook his head. "That, Maurice, is the big question. Never, if he were to have anything to say about it."

Suddenly the door of the study burst open. Olivia, swaying in the doorway, pouted, "Maurice, I've been waiting long enough. Are you coming or not?"

"Darling, of course I'm coming." He walked over to her and as they embraced he winked at Philip. "We're finished now."

Philip reached for Tucker's hand, shook it and moved to the door. "As I said, we'll be in touch." He looked at Olivia and pitied Maurice. "She's breaking his balls," he thought, "probably never gets enough." "Pleasure meeting you, Olivia. Perhaps we'll all get together sometime." The two men exchanged a friendly nod and Philip left the room.

IX

André Rostand's judgment was confirmed as the sale continued. Marto's pencil remained in his pocket as the Caravaggio was knocked down to a Swiss dealer for $375,000. Nor did he bid on Fragonard's *La Malheureuse,* which the National Gallery in Washington bought for $875,000. Nando Pirelli and Bertram Bez bid actively for a small Frans Hals, but each demurred at the $120,000 mark. Eventually, it went to the Carnegie Institute for $25,000 more. As for Rembrandt, it was an unhappy evening. His *Portrait of an Old Man* was "bought in" by Sotheby's, having failed to meet a reserve price of $2.5 million because its provenance was questionable. That disturbed Rostand very much. The Bez Gallery had an enormous stake in the Rembrandts it already owned or had access to. It was unthinkable that the Iranian would fail to bid and permit the tawny canvas to be carried offstage in ignominy. André shifted in his seat and coughed. There was no mistaking the signs. A ring, not individual dealers, was doing the bidding here.

In the box, the auctioneer gazed out at the audience with the empty glance of a squid, calling each bid in the chill impersonal tones of a BBC weather forecaster. For him, the evening so far had been more than a success. In the space of an hour, nine lots had been disposed of, with two world records being set. Except for the Rembrandt, all of the paintings had been sold at prices that exceeded the catalogue's estimates.

It was then that the Vermeer appeared, brought from Sotheby's vaults by a single nervous porter flanked by two gray-uniformed guards. In a simple gilt frame, the portrait floated toward the stage on a tide of applause. Rostand shifted in his chair and held his breath. He had seen the Vermeer only once before and remembered the way his father had described it, lingering over the details, his nasal voice tinged with admiration. *The Tavern Maid* was typically Vermeer, a perfectly balanced painting portraying a world so calm as to be frozen in time. A pale, silvery light bathed the young woman, who stood alone in an isolated hush.

Before the night was over, *The Tavern Maid* would be home again, Rostand thought. After all these years, she would belong to a Rostand again. Auguste Donnet never appreciated it, not really. Nor had Charles. Now the painting would be cared for as it should have been. The gallery would honor it with a special exhibition and afterward keep it safely in the vaults at Iron Mountain.

"Lot Number Ten: Jan Vermeer's *Portrait of a Tavern Maid*. I have an opening bid of one million dollars."

Immediately, several bids were directed at the rostrum. The microphones whined as offers filtered in from the side galleries too. Within a minute of the opening bid, the price had reached the three-million mark.

Fuller looked at Marto. The old man had his pencil ready, but had not yet bid. Nor had Rostand. Some in the salesroom would offer early bids so that, at cocktail parties, they might boast of having bid for a Vermeer. Marto and Rostand would wait for their moment.

That moment came at four million five hundred thousand. The bidding had slowed considerably. Only the Met's Christopher Ashton and Julian Johns remained when Leopold Marto flicked his pencil through a forty-five degree arc. Rostand remained immobile. The longer he waited, the more determined he would seem. When he did bid, Marto would know that he had come *to buy*. Such a tactic tended to intimidate.

"I have four million eight hundred thousand," the auctioneer declared. "Four million eight hundred thousand!"

Marto's pencil snapped through its tiny arc.

"Four million nine hundred thousand! On my right! Four million nine hundred thousand." As Ashton and Johns both folded their arms, André Rostand unfolded his and lightly touched the white pearl stickpin on his lapel.

"Five million," the auctioneer instantly cried out in response to Rostand's signal. "I have a bid of five million dollars! Five million on my left!"

The audience craned to see who had made the bid. Rostand's gesture had been too delicate for most of the excited crowd to notice, though the cognoscenti never doubted the bidder was Rostand. They knew Aaron's story, too. The tale was legend. Of course Rostand was bidding.

Marto's pencil snapped through the air.

"Five million one!"

Rostand touched his stickpin.

"Five million two hundred thousand! Five million two hundred thousand. Do I have . . . ?"

Rostand was worried. Something was beginning to gnaw at his stomach, something he hadn't felt since the war. Bez, Duranceau and Pirelli had not bid, and it was clear from their expressions that they would not. They were all there simply to enjoy the show. The excitement showed on Pirelli's face. Excitement, but not tension. The knot in Rostand's stomach grew larger. He began to twist the cane in his hands.

Marto's pencil flicked. "Five million three hundred thousand!" It was as if the bid were a stone dropped in a still pond. The audience shifted, tension rippling outward to the edges of the room.

"Do I have five million four? The bid is five million three." The auctioneer was looking at Rostand. "Five million three," the auctioneer repeated. Calmly, the baron touched his stickpin.

"Five million four hundred thousand!" A world record had already been set, and still the bidding continued. The auctioneer quickly turned in the direction of Leopold Marto.

Marto remained immobile for several seconds. Fuller leaned forward. The audience held its breath. The pencil cut the air.

"Five million five hundred thousand dollars!"

Fuller glanced toward Rostand, still twisting the cherrywood cane. The habit disturbed Fuller. It was out of character. It suggested a case of nerves. Then he understood. They were being *ringed*. Bez, Pirelli, Marto and God-knows-how-many-others were in it together. They were squeezing Rostand out. Fuller now understood what had happened with the other lots. Bez and Pirelli bowed to Marto's bid for the Tiepolo, Marto allowing Bez to take Lots 6 and 7. Pirelli stayed out of that, but then bid alone against Johns on Lot 8. Rostand slowly touched his stickpin.

"Five million six hundred thousand!" The audience gasped. Like an automaton, Marto once again flicked his pencil.

"Five million seven! Five million seven hundred thousand is bid!"

The moment had arrived. Waiting patiently for the auctioneer to repeat Marto's last bid, Rostand felt the silence of the crowd. Then, with only the microphones' quiet hum filling the room, he jump-bid. In a voice that barely exceeded a whisper, he cut the silence: "Six million dollars!" The crowd gasped.

The auctioneer, stunned, looked straight at Rostand. " 'Six million'?"

Rostand nodded. He had never wanted anything so much in his life.

"Six million dollars!" the auctioneer declared, sending the audience into an explosive ovation. Overhead, the chandeliers rocked and tinkled.

Rostand glowed, sensing victory. He wouldn't keep *The Tavern Maid* in Iron Mountain. It would hang in his office at the gallery. He would never sell it.

"Six million," the auctioneer repeated evenly. "Six million dollars." Engulfed by the applause and almost inaudible, he turned to his right.

André, who saw no further reason to stay, rose, glanced at Marto and started to leave, accepting the applause around him as he made his way toward the exit. Marto would be a fool to go higher, he thought.

Only the auctioneer saw Leopold Marto's pencil snap through the air.

"Six million one hundred thousand is bid!" intoned the auctioneer. "I have six million one!"

The call sent a spasm up André's spine. He froze in midstride. As the crowd's applause faded in disbelief and then welled anew, this time for Marto, André slowly turned toward the rostrum.

"Do I have six million two?" the auctioneer asked, in a dignified tone.

André, standing near the exit, looked at the auctioneer. His shoulders slumped in resignation. He waited a moment, calculated again, then shook his head, turned, and walked out of the salesroom.

From the lobby, André heard the final verdict: "Six million one . . . I have six million one hundred thousand. . . . Once . . . twice . . . sold . . ." As the gavel banged three times, André Rostand hunched into his overcoat and stepped out into the cold.

X

The mural Cubitt Keeble was looking at depicted a group of flesh-colored nymphs frolicking in a dark green forest. Together with five men and two women, she sat around a large oval table in the corner of the reception room. They were drinking chilled champagne and taking turns telling stories in Italian, French and English. She was enjoying herself, but found all but one of the men surrounding her dull.

The man on Cubitt's right was an Englishman, a descendant of a British duke, who was so boring she feared he would vegetate with the woodwork.

On her left, the corpulent German publisher in a black coat with red lining was even worse. He kept telling her about his latest publishing coup. He had, he said, just discovered a major writer with the sacred fire of talent. Cubitt abhorred his pomposity. She had met him once the year before at San Moritz, wearing a blood-red and black ski suit.

The man across from her, Miles Cattell, held promise. Young—and Cubitt told herself—unexpectedly goodlooking, the blue-eyed Cattell was the ex-equerry of the Prince of Liechtenstein. More importantly, he was the son of Dominic Cattell, head of one of Europe's oldest banking houses.

After several glasses of champagne, Miles was in a giddy mood and Cubitt was teasing him along. He was a regular at Madame

Gérard's, receiving an invitation from her whenever he was in Rome. Cubitt eyed him carefully, attentive to every detail of his personality. She considered him sexy and his stature in her eyes was enhanced by the five million dollars attached to his name.

Cubitt saw Philip Rostand walking toward the table, but pretended not to notice. After her conversation with Madame Gérard, she knew he was interested in her. She knew very little about him, except for the fact that he was an art dealer. She would wait and see.

Philip greeted the others. Then, with a possessive smile, he introduced himself to Cubitt.

"Rostand . . . ," she said, "as in art dealer?"

"More like arch-dealer," the corpulent German quipped, laughing aloud and greatly enjoying his own joke.

Rostand took no notice of the German's jibe. Instead, he looked at Cubitt and replied: "And you're Cubitt Keeble, as in . . ."

"That depends, Mr. Rostand."

"Please, call me Philip."

"Philip . . ."

Rostand took a chair and edged it into place between Cubitt and the German. As he sat, he searched the room for the waiter and ordered more champagne. The bottle arrived almost at once, and for several minutes Rostand made polite conversation with those around him. Finally, he turned to Cubitt. "I suppose everyone asks, but wherever did you get a name like Cubitt?"

"Everyone does. And the answer is I chose it myself. I was christened Elizabeth, which was nice enough. But I prefer to be more enigmatic."

"I thought so."

"What makes you say that?"

Rostand looked at her for a moment. "I like to think I read people well. It's my business to appreciate quality." He paused. ". . . And to acquire it."

Cubitt laughed uneasily. He was obviously a man who knew what he wanted, and she felt slightly out of control.

Philip leaned closer to her. "Could I see you home tonight?"

For a moment, Cubitt was silent. She needed time to make that decision. "Perhaps," she replied, sitting back to sip her drink.

Rostand persisted. "I think it would be worth your while."

Cubitt wondered if that were really true. Cattell was obviously interested, and she was attracted to him. However, she reminded herself that she had to be pragmatic. Madame Gérard's comment had swayed her. Rostand, she had said, could take her a long way.

By midnight, most of the guests had paired off and left. When Miles Cattell rose to leave, only Cubitt and Rostand remained at their table. "Are you ready?" Miles asked, extending his hand across the table.

"Perhaps another time," she said. "I'm a bit tired tonight."

Cattell looked stunned. He stepped backward, nodded curtly, mumbled something about the next time and left.

Cubitt saw that Rostand was bursting with delight. She took out her compact, applied a bit of color to her cheeks and added a line of red to her lips. No need to look so innocent now. "Are you happy now?" she asked Rostand, closing the case.

"Delighted."

"Shall we go, then?"

Madame Gérard ushered them to the elevator, with an arm around each of them. "Don't be too hard on him," she said. "He means no harm, even though he's a bit pushy."

Philip laughed and said, "You know me too well, Madame."

As the elevator slowly descended, Cubitt thought about Rostand. In the past few months she had developed an acute sensitivity for the men she'd met at Madame Gérard's. Some of them had been art dealers; and she'd found that, like everyone else, they came in different sizes, shapes and temperaments. There were a few scholarly types, but very few. Others were frustrated artists or compulsive collectors who chose to deal in works of art because it gave them an opportunity to live and work with beautiful objects. That type was rare as well. Most, she'd found, were in it for the money. Philip, she guessed, was one of those. And yet there was something about him that disturbed her. Perhaps it was the hint of angry narcissism she sensed in him.

Outside, Philip took her by the arm and led her toward the chauffeur-driven Bristol. "Your place or mine?" he asked.

Cubitt stopped in front of the Palazzo. "Neither," she replied, wrapping the Fendi fur more tightly around her. "At least, not tonight. Let's have a drink at the Hassler."

Rostand patted Cubitt's shoulder and nodded twice. He took her by the arm and led her to the Bristol. The chauffeur, standing discreetly in front of the car, moved to the rear door and opened it. Cubitt and Philip settled into the plush leather of the back seat.

Philip took her hand as the car drove off. They were silent for a few moments, then the voice of the chauffeur came through the rear speaker, "Where to, sir?"

Rostand pushed a button on the armrest. "The Hassler," he ordered.

The hotel bar, overlooking the Spanish Steps, was small but ornate. Its single narrow room was festooned with mirrors set in gold baroque frames that reminded Cubitt more of a ballroom than a bar. They had entered the bar shortly after midnight. The maître d' ushered them past several couples clustered at the counter and led them with a great deal of ceremony to a corner table with a view of the Spanish Steps.

Cubitt looked down the length of the bar to see if she recognized anyone. There were only strangers. Romans didn't frequent the Hassler.

Across the table from her, Philip was talking about Madame Gérard. "She's a remarkable woman. What do you know about her?"

"She's a very private person, and she's been very good to me."

"Where did you meet?"

Cubitt recounted the story of how they were brought together through a photographer in London. As she told the story she sensed that Philip was checking her background, probing rather than making conversation. She also noticed that with every question, he became increasingly agitated.

Philip raised his glass and found it empty. A waiter appeared instantly. "Another, sir?" Philip nodded, quirked an eye in Cubitt's direction, and ordered for both of them.

They sat without speaking for a moment, gazing out at the lights of Rome.

Philip leaned back against the green leather upholstery of the carved banquette. "You interest me, you know. Most of the women I meet are bitches who don't know their place."

Cubitt looked down into her drink to hide her reaction. There it was again, that intense almost irrational anger. She looked at him closely, trying to size him up. He couldn't intimidate her. She decided that he was an angry man and surprisingly insecure, with a whole series of facades to disguise it. His face changed from moment to moment, fluctuating between a pout and a glare. She wondered what troubled him. For the moment, however, she was reluctant to probe. Finally, she replied, "I don't see any point in competing with a man."

Approval appeared on Philip's face. "Do you know anything about art?" he asked.

"Very little."

"But you know a lot about people."

Cubitt had a feeling of being slowly cornered. "Something . . . ," she said.

Philip made a theatrical gesture, beckoning the waiter with a snap of the fingers. "Another Martell." He seemed to take pleasure watching the waiter scurry away. He turned back to Cubitt. "I was thinking," he said, "you might consider working for me."

Cubitt sat back and took a long look at Rostand. "You're joking."

Philip grinned broadly. "Cubitt," he paused, letting her name float in the air between them for a moment. "I'm serious. I could use someone like you."

"Doing what?" she said, eyeing him suspiciously.

Philip leaned across the table. "It's simple," he said. "You get around. You know the right people. You have access to their homes. You know when someone's marriage is in trouble. . . ."

"What's any of that got to do with art?"

The waiter returned to the table and from the silver tray set a brandy snifter filled with amber liquid in front of Philip.

"Everything," Rostand replied. "When a marriage breaks up a collection often goes on the market. I'd like to know before it happens. Or when an estate is being sold, or someone is financially in trouble, an art collection is often the first thing to go."

"Sounds like a spy to me."

"In a way . . . But in the art business, we call them *runners*. All dealers have them, any dealer worth a damn, that is. We have them all over the world."

Cubitt smiled, and for the first time she thought she was beginning to see the real Philip. "You're being serious."

Philip raised an open hand and laid it over his heart. Cubitt noticed the fingernails had been immaculately manicured, the cuticles buffed back, the tips of the nails filed into perfect arcs. Their luster could only have come from a bottle. He was one of the few Americans she'd met over the years with hands like those. "Of course, I am!" he said. "You'd work on a commission basis getting a percentage of anything you find."

Cubitt wondered how many runners Philip recruited like this. She smiled.

"I know exactly what you're thinking, but I want you to work for me, not the gallery. I want you to give me a list of everyone you know interested in art. Anyone who's ever bought or sold a painting, collects them or talked about collecting. Then I want background information on all of them. Where they live. What they do. The status of their bank accounts. Married. Divorced. Happy. Unhappy."

Cubitt lifted her glass and took a long swallow. She held the glass between her fingers and stared at Philip for a moment. "I can see the ethical level of the art world is just a notch above the prostitution racket."

Philip laughed, but once again his dark muscular body began to sweat. "It's a business just like any other."

"I see," she said. For a long moment she gazed out the window, feeling a surge of excitement grow within her. She looked back at Rostand. "When do I start?"

"Tomorrow. You're going with me to New York in the morning."

"You're out of your mind."

"If you're going to work for me, you've got to see how I operate. After that, you'll meet my father. Protocol, you know."

"You've got everything figured out."

Philip nodded twice. "Everything but the next step." He sat back in the banquette and withdrew his tiny silver pillbox.

"What's that?" Cubitt asked, watching Philip slip a small white tablet into his mouth.

"Which?" The pillbox snapped closed. "The pill or the next step?" he asked.

"The pill . . ."

Philip shrugged casually. "Just a few grams of phenobarbital for the nerves."

Pheno and cognac, Cubitt thought: a hell of a case of nerves. Then, aloud: "And the next step?"

"A minor matter really," Philip said, the muscles of his face visibly going slack. "We must decide where we go from here. Your place, or mine."

Cubitt saw her triumph reflected in Philip's eyes. They were beginning to glaze from the effect of the pheno, but he was watching her with rapt attention. Cubitt nodded and smiled, more to herself than Philip. "Yours would suit me fine."

XI

André Rostand, deeply shaken by the loss of the Vermeer, returned home by cab to his Fifth Avenue apartment directly opposite the Metropolitan Museum of Art. He went to the library, set the cane on his desk and poured himself a glass of his favorite cognac, a 1939 Château Fontipot.

Picking up his drink, he crossed the room and opened the drapes. Ignoring the shimmering lights of the city below, he stared out of the window and tried to review the events of the past hour. He realized, however, that he was in no condition to think clearly. The sound of the auctioneer's gavel echoed in his brain like a sledgehammer striking an anvil. He would never forget the personal humiliation of that final moment. Nor would he ever forgive himself for underestimating Marto. Sheer stupidity. It had cost him dearly. Only once before, in France during the occupation, had he ever felt so vulnerable. But he had been younger then, and more resilient.

Even five years ago the formation of a ring would never have been such a threat. He would have had a dossier compiled on each of its members, estimated their worth and outbid them. Marto's ring, on the other hand, was much more powerful than anything he had encountered before.

It was also clear to him that Marto had planted an informant inside Rostand International. There could be no other explanation. During the past six months, he had tried, and failed, to acquire a number of important paintings. Just when he had been on the verge of securing these masterpieces, inexplicably the sales had fallen through. In every instance, the paintings had gone to rival dealers connected to Marto's ring.

Coincidence was out of the question. The ring, using Art Intrum as a front, operated inside as well as outside the auction room. They had organized an international network of dealers that knew in advance the people Rostand was negotiating with and what he was offering them. With this kind of information, Marto's group had simply moved in and outbid him.

Rostand nervously began to pace the walnut paneled room. He

needed time to think. He was certain there was a leak, and that someone very close to him had to be responsible. He shook his head. He had always been cautious, so careful about security, compartmentalizing his staff so that no one, not even Philip, had a total overview of the gallery's inner workings. To find the one betraying him, he would have to go outside the gallery. He needed someone shrewd enough to handle Marto and yet honest enough to be made privy to the gallery's inner workings. He needed someone he could trust.

The situation was critical. If Marto succeeded in pushing him out of the auction room, Rostand International would become secondrate. His runners, men and women he had recruited over the years to move among the wealthy and powerful, seeking out that vital tip that led to the purchase of a rare art treasure, would begin to freelance, or worse, start working for the opposition. His sources would dry up. He would no longer be selling important works of art, but would be reduced to dealing second-rate junk. There was no money to be made that way. A fifty-thousand-dollar painting could easily sit around the gallery for years. A million-dollar masterpiece could be sold anytime. No, the problem was never selling quality. The problem was finding it in the first place.

André walked to his desk in the corner of the room, unlocked the top drawer and took out a black notebook in which he kept a coded list of the names of his most trusted runners. He underlined three names.

Next, he picked up that morning's *New York Times* and turned to the Business and Finance section. He noted the over-the-counter price at which Art Intrum was trading and using the closing quotation of thirty-one dollars and fifty cents, made several calculations. That done, he felt better.

Rostand sipped the cognac and glanced at the small gold clock on the mantelpiece. It was just past eleven o'clock. He would have to hurry. Philip would be in bed, though one could never be sure.

Dialing the operator, André placed a long-distance call to the Excelsior Hotel in Rome. The call went through immediately, but there was no answer in Philip's suite. André told the operator at the hotel that he would try again later and hung up. He was about to dial again when the door to the library opened. Looking up, he saw his wife, Jane, meticulously groomed and dressed, standing in the doorway.

In her late fifties, Jane Rostand had frosted gray hair, which was cut short and combed straight back, giving her face a rather boyish look, a look accentuated by her high cheekbones and a slightly up-turned delicate nose. She was tall and slender, beautiful and well preserved. Not by accident, but by design. She believed in ointment and oils, moisturizing masks and skin treatments, sunlamps and, most recently, cosmetic surgery. She also ate sparingly, exercised daily and maintained an unvaried regimen of early nights and late mornings. Just returned from La Costa, a fashionable health spa in Southern California, she had the tanned face and body of a woman half her age.

"Come in," Rostand said. He returned the phone to its cradle, stood and walked around the desk to greet her. "I'm surprised you're still up."

"I thought I heard you come in. How did it go?"

A thin, almost bitter smile was the baron's only response.

Jane frowned. "Four million wasn't enough?"

"Nothing would have been enough. I was ringed. . . ."

"By whom?"

"I'm not certain, but I'm sure Marto's behind it."

"How high did they go?"

"Six million one."

"My God! Six million! That's incredible." For a moment she stood before him in silence, then added, "I'm sorry. I know how much that painting meant to you. . . ."

He shrugged.

Jane turned away and crossed the room to the large bay window overlooking Central Park, where she busied herself with the drapes, first closing them, then making certain each fold was perfectly in line. "Do you like them, André? I just had them hung. I had the same style made for my bedroom. The rose color is perfect for this room."

"Perfect," he said, absently.

As Rostand watched his wife fiddle with the drapes, he noticed a subtle difference in the way she looked, something about her face. He wondered what it was. There was a change in the shape of her eyes. Finally, he realized that because she had recently had both her upper eyelids lifted, the space between her eye and brow was firmer, wider and more contoured. When she had told him about the clinic and op-eration, he had objected. He thought her preoccupation with the way she looked was grotesque. She had gone ahead anyway, insisting that it was the way one looked, not the way one got that way, that counted. Maybe she was right, he thought, if it made her happy.

"What are you going to do?" Jane murmured.

"I'm not sure."

"Can you beat them?"

"I'll know in a couple of weeks when the Jannis collection comes up for sale in London."

"You're going yourself?"

"Yes."

"What about Philip? Can't he handle it?"

"Not this time," André said gruffly. "I can't trust him." The moment he said it, André knew it was a mistake and regretted it.

Jane's retort was instantaneous. "It must run in the family," she snapped, wrapping her red velvet dressing gown more tightly around her as if girding for battle.

Rostand retreated to the edge of his desk. "Look, Jane, the Vermeer is gone and I've got other problems at the gallery. I'd rather not talk about Philip right now."

"Why not? He's your son."

"Genetics has nothing to do with this."

"You've never given him enough credit or encouragement. You . . ."

Rostand cut her off with a wave of a hand. "And you have?" he snapped.

"Always," she countered.

Rostand walked over to her. "I don't want to discuss it, Jane. I have some calls to make, so if . . ." He took her gently by the hand and led her to the door.

"Just one thing," she said.

"What is it?"

"What time do you want breakfast brought to your room?"

Rostand smiled. She could be so subtly brutal. "Don't bother," he said smoothly. "I'll have breakfast at the gallery." André opened the door, kissed her on the cheek and then, as she went down the hallway to her bedroom, closed the door.

Returning to his desk, André picked up the phone and dialed. After several rings, a husky voice answered.

"Hello, Ray?"

"Yes, Mr. Rostand. I'm sorry about tonight. We were . . ."

"I know, Ray. Listen. Where is young Drach?"

"In Paris, the last I heard."

"I want you to find him. Get in touch with his office the first thing in the morning. I have something for him."

"Yes, sir. But . . . you know Alex; the last time he refused."

"I know that, but this time he may be more interested. Just tell him I want to see him, that's all."

André hung up and then, as he always did, made a short notation of the call, its time and purpose, in a notebook he carried with him. He was precise about such matters. He was also careful about making certain nothing was left on the top of his desk, not even the Fontipot, which he replaced in the liquor cabinet. He paid a staff handsomely to do such things for him, but he thought it unnecessary and unwise to have others clean up after him. More than a quirk, it was his conviction that small things revealed a great deal about a person, and that the less his subordinates knew about him, the better.

André sat back in his chair and sipped the last of his cognac. Jane was right, he thought. He felt little affection and even less respect for his son. Not that Philip wasn't astute or competent enough to run the gallery. He was a shrewd dealer, ambitious, cunning, and tough enough to stand up to the competition. But competence wasn't the issue. Underneath, Philip was sour, even depraved. He wished it weren't so, but that was the truth. His son would never understand the usefulness of benevolence.

After turning out the lights in the library, he left the room and from the front-hall closet selected a heavy fur-lined coat. He quietly opened the front door and slipped out of the apartment.

Outside, the snow had stopped falling, but he could still feel the cold. He walked the six blocks to East Seventy-fifth Street, where he turned the corner and continued east until he came to an imposing three-story brownstone set back off the street. He found the key in his suit pocket, walked up the steps and opened the front door.

The warmth of the house and the sweet smell of incense that permeated it cheered him immediately. He removed his coat, laid it over the arm of a yellow brocade chair and then adjusted his tie before the hall mirror.

As he stood there, the man's face he saw reflected in the mirror was much older than the one he saw inside himself. The years had taken their toll. His flesh had slackened and his once-dark hair had thinned and turned gray. But he felt younger than he looked. He seemed to need less sleep now than he once did, and he had plenty of vitality left. More than that, his eyes were still good. That was the most important thing. His eyes. Everything depended on them, everything from buying a painting to appreciating a woman's beauty.

"André!"

Rostand looked up the winding stairway leading to the second floor. From the landing above, with a tumble of blond hair surrounding it, a small, almost childlike face peered over the bannister. It was Marlaina. "Hello, what are you doing up there?" he asked.

"I'm just out of the bath," she replied, her high-pitched voice warm and friendly. "Make yourself a drink in the front room. I'll be right down. . . ."

XII

Entering its final turn, an Alitalia jet yielded altitude as it swept through the rain over Rome. As the plane rumbled toward Leonardo da Vinci Airport, in the first class cabin, Baruch gazed idly through the window. His blue eyes flickered across the lights of the urban landscape below: the Vatican, Coliseum, Piazza Venezia and the Tiber running through the city like a black ribbon.

The view bored him. He had seen it so often in the past five years. Too often, he thought.

On the seat beside him was a leather case, lightly held in place by his right hand. A red carnation in the lapel of his tailored clerical suit matched the color of the ruby cufflink that gleamed atop the leather bag. His fingers drummed to a beat no one else could hear.

At the Arrivals Hall, Baruch ambled through the green zone of the customs area unchallenged. He did not go to the baggage area where luggage from London Flight 217 was being off-loaded, but walked straight through the electric doors leading out of the terminal. He spotted the black Alfa at once. It was in the same place it always was. He greeted the chauffeur and then disappeared into the back seat behind the car's smoky glass windows.

An hour later, he was being driven along a narrow Roman street near Vatican City. Before a massive door, its wood dried and cracked with age, the Alfa smoothly glided to a stop. Baruch left the

Alfa, grasped the door's iron ring and rapped once. A loud boom echoed within. Underneath the ring, a small brass plate the size of an envelope read: "Society for the Preservation of Religious Monuments and Shrines." Baruch smiled thinly, appreciating the irony of the inscription.

As the door swung open, a blond, heavy-set man garbed in a priest's cassock greeted him politely. "Ah! Baruch . . . Monsignor Weiller has been waiting for you."

The young priest reached for Baruch's case, only to be silently rebuffed. Baruch's hand failed to release the handle. The two men smiled at each other, then walked on through the atrium, passing a stone fountain where water dripped quietly over a crust of green slime.

They moved into the Palazzo's interior, to a large foyer, where the curate asked Baruch to wait. Seating himself in a heavy leather chair dating to the time of Pope Julius II, Baruch felt the fatigue of the day's efforts draining him. He picked up two pamphlets that had been placed on the table in front of the chair. Both were by Monsignor Hans Weiller. Both were esoteric studies of some aspect of the Roman Catacombs. Baruch leafed through the one entitled *Die Römischen Katakomben,* realized he couldn't read German, and flipped it back onto the table.

As he was about to glance at the second, Hans Weiller strode briskly into the foyer, his footsteps echoing on the marble floor. Rising, Baruch extended his hand. "I didn't know you were an author too."

Pleased, but self-depreciating, Weiller murmured, "Pamphlets . . . a few things I've learned . . . hardly literature, Baruch." When he saw the flight-bag, Weiller's smile disappeared. "Well," he said, "to business."

Taking the bag firmly in hand, Weiller led Baruch up two flights of stairs and through a series of empty rooms, coming at last to a studio.

Placing the case on a long wooden table, Weiller turned to Baruch inquiringly. "No problems, Monsignor," Baruch said, walking toward the table to open the case. "It's here."

Weiller nodded, turning his attention to the leather case. The lock sprang and Baruch opened the bag. From the case he withdrew the fourteen-by-ten-inch painting of the *Lute Player* by Watteau.

"You've done well, Baruch." Weiller took the painting and held it to the light, examining it carefully. "Still in perfect condition." He walked to an easel, set the painting upon it, and rapidly began emptying tubes of various colored paints onto a palette. He turned to Baruch. "Betrayal is the worst sin."

"I know."

"I had an unfortunate call from Paris this evening. Rolf failed. Drach escaped his punishment."

Baruch removed the carnation from his lapel and, twirling it by its stem, sniffed it. "Is there anything I can do?" he said evenly.

"Thank you, my son. I've given Rolf another chance to redeem himself. But if he returns without accomplishing his task, then, like the unprofitable servant, we shall cast him forth into the darkness outside, where there will be wailing and the gnashing of teeth."

Baruch smiled. "Like Brother Sebastian," he said.

"You found him?"

Baruch nodded. "His mortal remains went out with the ebb tide in the Thames."

"And the dealer, Thaw?"

"He, too, has been punished."

"As he should be. . . ." Weiller rolled up the sleeves of his cassock. "Now, if you'll excuse me, Brother Baruch . . ."

Baruch withdrew as Weiller returned to the Watteau. The Monsignor spent a few minutes mixing paints, then cocked his head and gazed at the painting resting on the easel. For the next few minutes, he did not move, oblivious to the existence of everything but the Watteau. It wasn't the finest example of Watteau's work, but it was still worth a small fortune. More than that, it had great sentimental value. The painting had been presented to him by the Reichsmarschall, a token of the great man's esteem for the work he had done during the war. It was the only painting he'd kept with him since those days, and it had been with him ever since, except for the few weeks the traitor, Brother Sebastian, had it.

The Monsignor lifted his hand to his right cheek and began to stroke the side of his face. He felt the anger rise in him at the thought of Sebastian's betrayal. He had been one of his first recruits, his most trusted aide. Then he had left and taken the Watteau with him. Sebastian had been a fool to think he could get away with it. He should know he could never elude Baruch.

Weiller's attention returned to the Watteau. He had already settled on an appropriate theme, a scene of a church nestled in trees. He remembered the church just as it was, one he had visited often when stationed in Paris. He took a brush and mixed a tiny amount of black, white and blue pigment. It produced the precise shade of gray he wanted. He stood back, took one more nostalgic look at the Watteau, then began systematically daubing tiny brush-strokes of oil paint over the masterpiece.

XIII

It was a momentous occasion. Jocko Corvo and his wife, Louisa, stood at the front entrance of the Fantasio, one of Pigalle's most popular nightclubs, greeting their guests on this great night, the night of their daughter's wedding reception. In his exuberance, few relatives and friends escaped Jocko's bearlike embrace. Louisa, a short bulky woman with anthracite eyes and a pear-shaped face, chattered in a voice high with excitement, and directed the guests toward the reception room where the tables were laden with chestnut-fattened roast pig; *figatelli,* a spicy pork sausage; *broccia,* an aromatic goat cheese; and straw-covered jugs of Corsican red wine.

Jocko was a stocky muscular man with a low flat forehead, a boxer's broken nose, spadelike chin and thick black hair heavily flecked with gray. He knew and loved everyone that night, even the cooks, waiters and bartenders, who, like everyone else in attendance, were members of his clan. Jocko measured his strength that way—not by his brawn, nor the size of his muscles, but by the number of cousins he could count.

The Corvo clan was one of fifteen tightly knit Corsican families that had emigrated to France during the last two hundred years, ever since the time of Napoleon. Jocko, as head of the clan, slighted no one. He was a humble man but no one in Pigalle doubted his power. The white envelopes stuffed with money and the wedding gifts in honor of the bride and groom attested to that fact. More than that, no one failed to notice the fob watch medallion which hung across his vest. It was a gold medallion bearing the moor's head crest of Corsica, and though no one mentioned it, there was an unspoken recognition of its meaning. The medallion symbolized Jocko's membership in the Union Corse, an organization whose very existence in

France had always been denied, but whose power stretched from the parched hills of Corsica to every corner of France. The "Union," far more powerful and deadly than its counterpart, the Mafia, controlled organized crime throughout the country, from protection rackets and smuggling to gambling and prostitution.

There were now hundreds of guests crowding the tables in the nightclub's dancehall. Some danced on the raised platform festooned with flowers and colored lights, others sat at the round tables drinking the rich red wine. The bride, Madelaine Corvo, passed festively from table to table, accompanied by her groom, the quiet, dignified Manetta. Her maid of honor, a few bridesmaids, and her brothers, Marco, Franco and Domenico, formed an entourage around her. At each table the guests pinned money around the skirt of her wedding gown. It was an old Corsican custom, one she consented to only because of her father.

Outside the Fantasio the music and laughter of the reception flowed through the streets of Pigalle. Alex and Minta, parking the red Citroën, heard the party from two blocks away. As they drew nearer the Fantasio the carefree sounds eased the tension of the harrowing escape from the BMW.

Alex felt as though he were home again, secure in the familiar surroundings he knew as a boy. Pigalle, he remembered, was small. He could walk it from end to end in twenty minutes. Though its forty square blocks were packed with more dancehalls, discothèques, sex shops, bars and brothels per square foot than any other place in the world, to him the area bounded by the Rue des Abbesses to the Boulevard de Clichy was the safest he had ever known. There was, he had learned, a more honorable code of morality in Pigalle than anywhere on the upper East Side of New York.

The first person to see Alex and Minta enter the reception was Madelaine Corvo. From across the room she shouted happily, "Alex!" Her face radiant with excitement, she flew across the room and threw her arms around his neck. Alex held her tightly and kissed her three times on each cheek as other members of the family gathered around them. Madelaine embraced Minta and then turned to Manetta and introduced him to Alex.

Manetta's dark eyes looked at him directly. Alex was impressed that they did not waver or look away. Manetta did not smile, but Alex sensed that he was a man he could respect. Marco, Jocko's eldest son, handed Alex a glass of wine, which Alex raised to toast the bride and groom.

Alex then walked across the room toward Jocko and Louisa, who were standing by the bandstand. A ripple of attention swept over the room as Drach made his way through the dancers toward the two people he accepted as his parents. Alex remembered some of the older guests and acknowledged them with a glance and a nod of his head. He was pleasantly aware of the affectionate welcome these people showed him. Nowhere else would it be the same.

At the bandstand Alex leaned over and hugged Mama Louisa. She had gotten broader but that was all that had changed. Her eyes still glistened, wet with happiness and affection. At his side he heard Jocko's familiar voice. "Welcome home." Alex turned and threw his arms around him. Seeing his cheerful, buoyant grin raised his spirits. Still, he had to tell him. Alex put his hand on Jocko's shoulder and whispered in his ear. Only Manetta, standing a few feet away, noticed something amiss in Jocko's face.

Still smiling and with gruff good humor, careful to appear natural, Jocko glanced around the room and explained, "Alex has traveled four thousand miles to be with us. Before he has too many *pastis* I want to have a talk with him. Araminta, you too." His arms around Alex and Minta, Jocko led them away.

On the second floor of the Fantasio Jocko had constructed a room without windows, but with eight doors in the Corsican tradition. Eight was the ritual number that insured escape in the event of trouble. It was called the vendetta room, and there all matters of importance were discussed. Jocko filled three glasses from a bottle of *pastis*. "So tell me, what is this? Who has dared to harm my family?" He walked to Minta, handed her a glass and put his arm around her, his eyes burning with anger.

Alex took a sip of the yellow fiery liquid, savored the familiar licorice taste, and then briefly recounted what had happened. After Alex had finished, Jocko began pacing the room, his index fingers hooked into the two pockets of his vest. "You said a BMW. Did you get the license number?"

Drach shook his head. "No chance."

"It doesn't matter; they'd have stolen plates anyway." Jocko continued to pace, then stopped and turned to Alex. "I'm sure it's not vendetta. We have no blood feud with any other clan. If we did, I'd know." He paused, then asked, "Is there anyone in New York? Have you made enemies?"

Alex shrugged. "None that I know of."

Jocko frowned. "Don't hide anything from me. If there are problems, I can help."

Alex smiled. "If I had problems, Jocko, I'd tell you. There's no one else I trust as I do you. I know of no reason why anyone would want to kill me."

"But there is a reason," Jocko said. "We must find it. Men kill for many different reasons. Passion, the love of a woman, money, revenge, power. Think. Which applies to you?"

Alex glanced at Minta. "This has nothing to do with a woman, at least not that I know of. But something unusual did happen. I received a strange phone call a week ago. The caller gave his name as Jenner. He said he worked for the Home Office in London, and that he'd come into possession of a painting that once belonged to my family, a Watteau, he said. One that was lost during the war."

"Part of the Drach Collection?"

"Yes. *The Lute Player.* I'm supposed to examine it on my way back to New York."

Jocko took Alex's empty glass, refilled it, and poured himself another drink. He looked at Minta. "I'm fine," she said. Jocko gulped down his drink and began pacing again. "Where did Jenner find this painting?" he asked.

"In an art gallery in Duke Street. He thought I should know about it in case there were others around."

Jocko walked over to Minta. "Would you leave us alone for a few minutes," he whispered. "I want to talk to Alex about something."

Minta nodded amicably and kissed him on the cheek. At the door, she turned and looked at Alex. "Promise me a dance when you're finished."

Alex smiled. "It should be the other way around," he said.

After Minta left, Jocko motioned Alex to take a seat at the large round table that dominated the room. "There are things about your parents I've never told you," he said, "things that perhaps you should know. Especially now if your father's paintings still exist. What happened tonight may have some connection with them." Jocko reached inside his coat pocket and withdrew a long black case. He opened it and took out two cigars. Alex shook his head, declining

Jocko's offer of one. A match flared, and Jocko puffed repeatedly until the cigar tip glowed red.

Alex waited patiently for the old Corsican to begin. He should have been exhausted. He was into his second day without sleep, but the events of the past few hours had wound him up beyond thought of fatigue.

Through the smoke Jocko peered at Alex. "The man who phoned you; what was his name again?"

"Jenner."

"Not Hugh Jenner?"

"Yes. Do you know him?"

Jocko nodded slowly. "After the war, he came here. He worked for Allied Intelligence and he asked many questions." Jocko puffed on his cigar, and mumbled to himself, "After all these years . . ."

"Why did he come here?" Alex asked.

"He was investigating your father's death." Jocko paused for a moment, then added, "There's something I've never told you before, Alex, but I think you should know before you talk to Jenner. Your father was a *collabo,* a collaborator!"

Drach's eyes flickered, but, apart from that, the expression on his face did not change. He remained calm. Paul Drach was no more than a name to him. Who he was, or what he did, had no bearing on Alex. Somehow, though, his father's death was apparently connected to the attempt on his own life. "Why didn't you tell me this before?"

"I saw no need. Such things are better left in the past." The Corsican stood and started pacing the room. "But now we must talk. It's a painful story, one I myself try to forget. It's to do with your father's collection. It may sound strange to you, but I've always believed it was cursed. Both your parents died because of those paintings, and you'd be dead, if I hadn't intervened."

He walked to the bar, poured another glass of *pastis* and then returned with the bottle to sit across from Alex. He sipped his drink, puffed on his cigar, and told the story.

PART TWO

—————◆—————

1940

Jocko sat in the kitchen of the thick-walled townhouse of his employer, Paul Drach. He was listening to the German-controlled radio announce the new laws that were to govern the lives of all Jews living in occupied France.

Four days earlier, on the morning of June 14, 1940, the first troops of the German Wehrmacht had passed through the Porte de la Villette, the principal northern artery to the heart of Paris. First the lone point men came, steel-helmeted, their bayonets pointed skyward reflecting the bright June sunlight. Then Panzer tanks, followed by speeding staff cars. Then column after column of soldiers, pushing their way through the narrow streets, into buildings, stores, offices, seeking, hoping for resistance. There had been none. The French were helpless, now subject to the *Übermenschen,* the all-powerful Aryan race destined to conquer and rule the world.

Jocko spat on the floor. "Children of the Reich!" he muttered. *"Merde!"* He thanked God that Naomi Drach was safe in Monte Carlo. There, because of the principality's neutrality, she was safe from the Germans. And just in time, he thought. She had left only three days before the Nazis had occupied the city, sent away by Paul because she was Jewish.

Before she had married Paul Drach, Naomi de Montrose had been one of the most sought-after women in Europe. Her beauty, spontaneity and intelligence had attracted scores of suitors. That she was the daughter of Baron Edmond de Montrose, head of one of France's leading banking houses, had made her even more desirable. Many men had pursued her, but none had conquered her, or even held her captive. None, that is, until Paul Drach had come along.

Jocko shook his head and then began mopping the floor of the kitchen, thinking how difficult it must have been for Paul to let his wife go. Why Monsieur Paul had stayed behind now he wasn't sure, but he suspected it had something to do with the art collections he was guarding for some of his Jewish friends.

After Naomi left for Monte Carlo, Paul had shut down part of the house and let the rest of the staff go, retaining only him as its caretaker. It was a great responsibility for a twenty-year-old, one that he took very seriously.

Jocko had known Paul Drach ever since he was a child. The Drachs were an immensely wealthy family, French Huguenots, who had built a combine of seven iron and steel mills stretching the length of France. Jocko never liked Théodore Drach, Paul's father, a man driven by some inner need to dominate others. But Paul was different. He was kind and considerate, a *bon patron,* who had treated him with trust and respect.

The telephone rang and Jocko went into the study to answer it. He picked up the receiver. At the other end a muffled voice—Jocko was certain it was a man's—warned him that Paul Drach's name was on a list of suspected subversives drawn up by the Gestapo. There was very little time. Jocko asked for more details, but his answer was a click at the other end of the line, and the phone went dead.

He put down the receiver and went directly to Paul Drach.

Paul listened quietly—then went to his bedroom, where he changed clothes and packed a suitcase. He had made plans for just such an eventuality. Together, he and Jocko left the house and drove to a warehouse on the Boulevard St.-Germain. There, Drach had hidden a 1935 Citroën truck and fitted it with a false front in the loading space. Painted gray, with no other identifiable markings, the false front concealed enough room to accommodate his family's most precious possessions, a collection of fine Impressionist paintings, together with a few Old Masters, a fine Watteau, called the *Lute Player,* among them.

With Jocko's help, Paul hurriedly encased each painting in its own wooden bed, cushioned the cases with straw and filled the front end of the truck. A wooden partition was shoved into place and drums of used clothing and dry goods loaded in the back end. In the glove compartment, a set of false papers documented Paul Drach as a chauffeur whose destination was given as Tours, though his real destination was Tulle, roughly 460 miles farther south. There, in Vichy, France, he would be safe.

Dressed in "bleu de travail"—blue overalls and gumboots—Paul, tall and slender, climbed up into the truck. He gave a thumbs-up salute to Jocko, pulled a cap down over his head to cover his straight blond hair, and started the engine.

Jocko slid the warehouse door back on its creaking rollers, and steamy sunlight filled the cool darkness inside. The engine sputtered, then revved. A smoky blue haze rose in the dim light.

Jocko walked to the front of the warehouse, checked the street and gave a signal that all was clear. Paul shifted into first gear and eased the truck into the midmorning traffic. Jocko closed the warehouse door and then climbed up into the cab of the truck beside Drach. They drove slowly east on the Boulevard St.-Germain until they reached the Place Denfert-Rochereau, where they veered south toward the Porte d'Orléans.

It was one of those sultry summer days that Parisians love. The streets were alive with men, women and children enjoying the hot June sun. Still, an ominous tension gripped the city. Everywhere the black, white and red swastika flag of Germany fluttered from public buildings, apartment houses and hotels requisitioned by the Wehrmacht. Every few blocks there was also a black, red and white sentry box which controlled the movement of Parisians in their own city. Like locusts, the Nazis were swarming everywhere. Roadblocks and concrete pillboxes pimpled the surface of the city.

Paul and Jocko calculated that if everything went according to plan, they would make the first checkpoint in fifteen minutes. They had worked out the routing carefully. It would have been foolish to move at night—too few trucks on the road. The best time was between ten in the morning and two in the afternoon, when the flow of traffic was at its peak. The more cars and trucks on the road, the better their chance of getting through.

Six routes led in and out of Paris. They had canvassed them all. In cafés or bus shelters across from each checkpoint they gauged which set of guards was lax, which more thorough in scrutinizing identification papers and cargo. In the end, they had selected the Porte d'Orléans as their departure point. There, the paunchy blond sergeant spoke no French and seemed good-natured. A quizzical look from a driver, a shrug or two, and the exasperated German would invariably wave the vehicle on. A truck was more prone to inspection, but only on an irregular basis: they had estimated one of every eight.

Even if they were inspected, a cursory look would reveal a few drums of old rags. Only if the tarpaulin were completely removed and the false front of the van uncovered would the paintings be found.

At the Porte d'Orléans, Paul maneuvered the truck in line behind the other vehicles waiting to pass through the checkpoint. In front of them, a *gazogène,* a car powered by wood burned in a wash-boiler bolted to the trunk, sputtered feebly. Behind them, there were several *vélo-taxis,* cabs that had been cut in half, leaving the back end suspended by two wheels and hitched up front to a bicycle.

As the line diminished ahead, Jocko noticed that there were two soldiers manning the checkpoint. One held a rifle at port arms while the other questioned each driver. Jocko reached into the glove compartment for Paul's *Ausweis,* a pass to travel freely in and out of Paris, and handed it to him. Then he stiffened. The paunchy army sergeant usually in command of the checkpoint was not on duty. He had been replaced by a lieutenant in the S.S.

They discussed whether to pull out of line and return to the warehouse, but decided against it. They were too close to the barrier. To leave now would attract attention. They would certainly be stopped and questioned.

Paul drove into the checkpoint, the truck backfiring as it decelerated, and stopped. The S.S. lieutenant approached Paul's window and politely asked for his papers.

Too politely, thought Jocko.

Paul presented his *Ausweis.* "I'm carrying old clothing and textiles to Tours," he said casually.

The German took the paper and scrutinized it, his eyes squinting in the sunlight as they moved down the page. He stepped back, then walked over to another German officer, a major in the S.S., and handed him the papers.

Paul looked across at Jocko, his eyes filled with anxiety. Jocko wiped a sweaty palm on the side of his pants and watched the two German officers intently. As he examined the papers, the major absently rubbed a wine-red birthmark on his cheek.

When the S.S. lieutenant returned to the cab of the truck, he extended an open gloved hand through the window and curtly demanded, "Your identification, *bitte.*"

As Paul reached for his identification, Jocko saw a half dozen black-uniformed soldiers, rifles lowered, surrounding the truck. Simultaneously, both doors of the truck swung open. He felt a Luger jammed into the base of his skull. "Come out slowly," a German soldier commanded.

By the time he had recovered from the shock, he was out of the truck and being shoved toward a black Horch sedan, its rear door already opened. He was pushed down into the back seat of the car, where a burly S.S. sergeant yanked both his hands back, locking his arms and wrists inward. Frenchmen in their cars and *vélos* averted their eyes and moved around the cars.

Jocko looked into the back seat of another car and saw Paul looking at him. For a moment there was an intimate communication of solidarity, and then a foul-smelling, coarse hood was shoved over his head. A pair of rough hands moved over him everywhere, carefully searching for nonexistent weapons. For some reason, the phrase *No heroics* kept running through his mind.

He was barely able to breathe. Jocko's mind reeled. How did they know? Was it the *Ausweis?* Or the truck? The doors of the car slammed shut. Who had betrayed them? The car accelerated, turned in a tight circle and headed back into Paris. No one spoke.

He tried to get his bearings, but the twists and turns soon muddled him. It was only when he heard a brass band playing that he realized where he was. Each day, at the stroke of twelve, a company of German soldiers marched down the Champs Elysées to the Place de la Concorde. They marched to the tune of "Prussian Glory."

Suddenly, the driver downshifted, swerved right at a sharp corner and abruptly came to a stop. Jocko was dragged from the back seat and led up a flight of steps into a reception hall. There the hood was removed. Paul was already there.

All around them there were black-uniformed guards. On their tunic collars, they wore the twin silver flashes of the S.S. Behind a long, chest-high desk, a thin-faced guard told them to empty their pockets. "That too," he said pointing to Paul's watch.

"What are we here for?" Paul said angrily.

Jocko saw the black rubber truncheon coming. Paul twisted to his right but not enough. The blow glanced off the base of his spine. "No questions," the guard who had struck Paul shouted.

Two other guards, much younger, pointed in the direction of a door to the left. Paul walked ahead of him, through another room and into a long, brightly lit corridor. Two hundred feet farther on, at the end of the passage, they reached an iron grate. One of the guards rattled the padlock.

From the other side, a guard descended some stairs and unlocked the grate. They were led down another flight of stairs into a dark, gloomy cell block. The air was cool. It smelled sweet and pungent. It reminded Jocko of rotten fruit. Or formaldehyde.

Jocko counted the cell doors as he passed them. Less than halfway down the cell block they reached cell number thirty-three. The guards stopped them, pushed them up against the wall and waited while another guard from the other end of the cell block came toward them. Each time the guard's left boot hit the floor, a cluster of keys attached to his belt jangled. When he reached cell thirty-three, he pulled a ring of keys from his belt and selected one. The sound of the key in the large padlock and the slipping of the bolt echoed throughout the cell block. The iron door swung back and they were shoved into the dark cell. The bolt slammed home, the padlock snapped shut and the jangle of keys faded down the cell block.

In that dark prison cell, Paul and Jocko spent the time encouraging each other, fortifying each other's strength. They were equals now in every way. For two days, they were left alone, and then Sergeant Horst Schlenker called.

Schlenker, an interrogator, was known at Gestapo headquarters for his "rigorous examinations." His job was simple. He took prisoners reluctant to tell the S.S. interrogators what they wanted to know and subjected them to a certain number of tortures until they agreed to talk or died. It made very little difference to Schlenker either way, although he had one curious quirk. He didn't like to torture a man on a full stomach. It got to be messy that way.

Paul and Jocko learned to lie on the straw-covered floor and listen for the food cart. If the cart stopped at their cell, they knew they would be spared another day. If it didn't, they could count on seeing Schlenker that day.

In the blackness, they could hear the doors of the cell block bang open and close. The sound of the cartwheels came down the corridor. They estimated it was two cells away. Then the cart started rolling again. It passed the cell next to them and continued on.

"No, God, not now," Jocko muttered to Paul.

A painful spasm rippled through Jocko's stomach. His face and neck beaded with sweat. He stood and felt his way to the corner nearest the door, where a hole in the concrete flooring served as a toilet. He retched. Nothing came. His eyes watered and tears ran down his face. He gagged once more and crawled back to the corner and waited.

"Courage, *mon ami,* don't be afraid. They want the locations of the paintings—and that they cannot get from you."

They did not have to wait long; minutes later the guards came.

The iron green door swung open and bright light burst into the cell. "On your feet," a guard snarled.

They both stood, but the guards took only Paul. They seized each of his arms and began to drag-step him out of the cell. Paul looked back and over his shoulder and shouted, "Take care of Naomi, my friend."

"Go with God, Monsieur Paul," Jocko cried. "Go with God."

Jocko never learned what Paul Drach went through that night. All he remembered were the screams that floated down from the "examination rooms" above. He tried to blot those screams out, but even worse was the sudden way they ended.

Two weeks went by and then they came for Jocko. Dazed by the bright lights of the cell block, he was led through a series of corridors to an interrogation room, where the major he remembered at the checkpoint was seated behind a large desk. The German smiled politely, offered Jocko a chair in front of the desk and, to his amazement, offered him an apology for his confinement.

The German introduced himself as Major Hans Montag of the S.S., and explained that because Paul Drach had cooperated fully, there was no need to detain Jocko any longer.

Bewildered, Jocko accompanied Montag to the front of the prison. There, Jocko's personal belongings were returned to him and a release paper typed up and handed to him to sign. Jocko left the Gestapo headquarters. He felt uneasy, but greedily gulped the air, the first fresh air he'd breathed in two weeks. Curiously, he felt almost grateful to the Nazi.

He boarded a bus that would take him back to the Drach townhouse. Seated on the upper deck, he recorded everything with his senses. The sensation of speed merged with the street scenes to form a collage of human energy: the laughter of the children running home from school; the pumping legs of young girls, skirts flying, bicycling along the avenues; the jabbering of the matrons in the market waiting for change. Everything was so glorious, so beautiful.

He skipped off the bus and ran down the Rue des Bordes Valmore to the front steps of the gray stone house overlooking the Seine. He opened the front door and walked inside. There was only silence, that, and the strong odor of death. Jocko went into the front parlor and found Paul, hanging by a rope from a chandelier in the middle of the room, dead.

Later, Jocko learned that while he was in prison, the Nazis had found the hidden repositories, the "Jewish Collections." One after another they had been seized. At each location it was the same. Paul Drach, bruised but treated with deference, accompanied the Germans and made it obvious to all that he collaborated. Released by the Gestapo, Paul had returned home and the same afternoon committed suicide.

Burying Paul was one of the hardest things he had ever had to do. No member of the Drach family was present. There was no funeral, just a simple burial in the Passy cemetery. Afterward, Jocko telephoned Naomi in Monte Carlo and told her the sad news. Despite his protestations, she insisted on returning to Paris. Later that month, she came back to Paris and took up residence in the family house.

The following spring, she gave birth to a son. She did not go to a clinic. It would have been too dangerous. To have registered the child's name would have documented his existence in the files of the S.S. For a Jew, that could be fatal.

Louisa, Jocko's young wife, acted as midwife. After the birth, the Corvos offered to take Naomi and the baby to live with them in Pigalle, but Naomi refused, preferring to remain in the large empty house. Her life was not easy. She was the curator of a residence in which two-thirds of the rooms were shut off and blanketed in dustcovers. It was dreadfully lonely, but a kind of peace settled over her, though nothing soothed the pain of Paul's death.

In the spring of 1942 she planted the garden behind the house with beans and cabbages. She lived in the house, cleaning, knitting and taking care of her son. Apart from what the garden produced, their diet consisted of rutabagas and a few eggs from the hen in the backyard. The meat ration was minuscule, so small she joked with Jocko that it could be wrapped in a Métro ticket. To make matters worse, the Germans had forbidden Jews to shop at any time other than between the hours of three and four in the afternoon. She was, therefore, unable to buy anything that was in short supply. By the time she got to the store, everything was gone.

The Corvos tried to help Naomi out as best they could and Jocko remained on as an unpaid housekeeper. Every morning he faithfully pedaled across Paris on his bicycle to give her a hand. His first job when he arrived was to make a fire. He used a poker to rake the cold ashes from the night before, saving the biggest lumps of coal. He picked up a few scraps of newspaper, crumpled them into tiny balls under the coal, and sprinkled them with water. They burned more slowly that way. A six-page newspaper, even without coal, could bring a liter of water to boil in fifteen minutes.

He lit the fire and then, to create an updraft, placed a sheet of paper over the front of the fireplace. When he removed it the wet balls of paper were burning and the coals glowing red. The rest of the paper he folded and shoved under the coal bin for use the next day.

While the fire warmed the front room, he would go into the kitchen and light the "stove." The gas and electricity in Naomi's house had been cut off, but Jocko had ingeniously made a new cooker for her, four ten-gallon cans welded together. For fuel, he taught her to use the same paper method he had used to light the fire in the front room.

Then, on a frigid day in December 1942, when the child was nineteen months old, it happened. Jocko got up that morning at his café just after seven. The first soft grays were beginning to lighten the winter sky outside. He leaned over the edge of the bed, moving carefully so as not to disturb Louisa, and picked up a pair of shoes.

He got out of bed. The room was freezing. Shivering, he quickly put on his clothes, topped by a heavy woolen sweater. He left Louisa asleep and quietly went downstairs. He pushed back the sleeves of his sweater, made coffee in an open pot and poured himself a cup. He sipped it slowly, and grimaced. The taste was loathsome. But what could one expect from coffee made from acorns and chick-peas? Then, he went outside into the cold, took his bicycle and started off to work.

When he neared Naomi's townhouse, just as he did each morning, Jocko leaned forward and, as fast as he could, cycled the last few blocks along the Rue Bellechasse. His short legs pumped tirelessly, like the pistons of a locomotive engine. He picked up speed and sailed past the Maison de la Légion d'Honneur, imagining himself leading the field in the Grand Prix of French cycling. His breath vaporized in the cold air and he began to perspire as he took the last curve.

Halfway up the block, he glanced up. It was as if a wall had suddenly risen in front of him. There were Germans in front of Naomi's house and a convoy of buses lining the street. People from several houses were being led to the buses. He braked and got off his bike, wheeling it up the street, past the bus in front of the Drach house. Under the disapproving frown of the German guards, Jocko looked into the buses and saw men and women inside, a yellow star sewn onto each of their outer garments.

Instead of taking the garden path leading to the shed behind the house, Jocko continued to walk to the end of the block and loitered at the corner. A moment later he saw her. *"Mon Dieu,"* he gasped. "Madame Drach." He stood gaping at Naomi, her head bowed, her slender shoulders slack as she was led, clutching her child, to the rear of a bus.

Naomi handed the child to a young woman standing at the back of the bus and was about to step up herself when the guard in charge of the detail stopped her. "Wear this," he said, pinning a piece of paper to her coat. Naomi climbed aboard the bus, took the child and then glanced at the paper on her coat. On it her name was written out in capital letters, and below that, the one word, *Auschwitz*.

Down the street, Jocko's hands tightened over the grips of the handlebars and desperately he tried to think of something he could do.

The bus engine revved and the rolling prison started up the block toward him. As it passed, he saw Naomi raise her hand in a gesture of recognition and farewell. Without knowing why, Jocko turned his cycle around and, without hesitating, raced after the bus.

For the millions of Parisians still in bed, the dawning of that December day brought them a holiday, the Feast of the Immaculate Conception. It was a day to attend Mass, relax and stay at home with the family. But to Naomi and the seven hundred other prisoners herded together on a train of cattle cars lined up in the Gare de l'Est, the Feast of the Immaculate Conception was a very different day. For them, in the gray, frosty mist of the station, their long agony was only beginning.

The processing took very little time. At the station, the men and women were separated, their names taken down, and then they were led to the train. Naomi was loaded onto a car jammed with seventy-five other women. There was only one window, crossed with iron bars, and though it was freezing, within a few seconds, the air inside the car was stifling.

Jocko saw all this as he stood outside the *gare* beside a telephone kiosk. He looked up at an old Gothic watchtower and checked the time. It was almost noon. He had been there four and a half hours.

He didn't know why he waited. There was nothing he could possibly do. But he couldn't leave. Next to him an old Frenchman mumbled, "Auschwitz." Jocko had never head the name before. He nudged the man next to him and asked, "Auschwitz, what's that?"

The old man smiled sadly. "A concentration camp, young man. They're being resettled in the eastern territories conquered by the Nazis."

"Resettled! But they're French!"

"Not to the Germans. Nor to Vichy. They're Jews."

Suddenly the couplings between the cars banged together like links in a chain, and slowly the grating wooden carriages began to roll down the sidings of the station. Jocko waited a few seconds and then, with tears in his eyes, remounted his bicycle and started pedaling home. He had gone only a block or two when he shook his head and, as if drawn by some unknown force, turned around and frantically began pedaling after the train. Without reason or a plan of any kind, he was determined to follow Naomi's train, no matter where it went, as long and as far as he could.

Three hours and forty-four kilometers later, he was still pedaling furiously in pursuit of the prison train. He knew that the train would have to pass through Saint-Dizier and refuel before carrying on to Nancy and the German border. That was two hundred kilometers ahead. He knew he could go the distance, but as he pressed his legs to the limit, he began to despair of ever catching the train. At each rail junction, he stopped for a moment to ask how far behind he was. Panting for breath, he always received the same answer, an hour and a half behind. And no matter how hard he tried, the interval remained the same. Still, he refused to stop, not even for a brief rest. He was a man obsessed, if necessary, committed to pursue the phantom train across the breadth of France.

At that moment, unbeknownst to Jocko, the Resistance had blown up a main transformer in a power station outside the market town of Fontenay-Trésigny. The switching station at the rail junction a few miles away had shut down and the train had been forced to stop.

While waiting for the lines to be repaired, the Germans had backed the train transporting their prisoners into a tunnel so as to avoid the risk of an air attack. Inside the cattle cars, ignorant of what was happening farther down the line, the prisoners thought the Germans were trying to asphyxiate them. Black, acrid smoke spewed from the locomotive and poured back into the tunnel, almost suffocating the prisoners.

Ten minutes later, Jocko came pedaling down the twisting road toward the Fontenay junction. What he saw brought a hoarse roar from his throat. Four hundred yards away, the nose of the locomotive protruded from a tunnel. He picked up speed and within a few minutes rolled to a stop in front of the junction's station house. He wheeled his bike to the side of the building and looked around.

Ahead, up the track, he made out a group of railwaymen talking to several guards from the convoy. One of the men pointed up the track and the guards trooped on up the line in the direction he had indicated. From a safe distance, Jocko followed them until they reached a siding well beyond the junction. There, the Germans found another train, this one filled with sheep. They drove the sheep from the train and had one of the railwaymen back it from the siding. Minutes later, the other train edged its nose out of the tunnel and moved up the track as far as the junction.

When the prisoners were led from the tunnel, among the coughing, blackened women walking up the tracks, Jocko recognized Naomi. Still holding her baby boy, she stumbled along behind the hundreds of other women transported with her. Without thinking, Jocko ran forward and with his handkerchief began wiping Naomi's drawn face. The guards stared but did not interfere.

At first she didn't realize who he was, but after a moment of hesitation, she started to cry. Rivulets of tears ran through the soot on her face. By some stroke of luck or feeling of kindness—he would never understand—Jocko was permitted to walk along beside Naomi as she was led to the cars waiting on the other side of the junction. The guard shrugged indifferently and allowed the two to stumble along together. Her hair askew, her eyes watering, she clasped Jocko's hand and mumbled an indistinct phrase to him.

"Yes, Madame. I'm here. What is it?"

"Take my baby. Take him. Take care of him," she said, pushing the child into his arms.

Jocko looked around at the guard, who looked the other way.

Jocko took the child. "I'll see that he's safe, Madame. Don't worry. When you come home, he'll be safe and healthy."

Naomi clutched his arm and said, "If ever the time comes, and you need help, ask it of Paul's friend, André Rostand. Just tell him that I told you so. Whatever you need." She was pushed on then, leaving him behind. He had reached the limit he could go with her.

After a time, he could not remember how long, he watched the guards from the convoy scurry along the train slamming the cattle doors shut. The train of human misery was ready to roll.

There was a resonant bang as the wagons smashed together. The first lurch was followed by a slow movement of the train from the junction. As it gathered speed, Jocko stared at the car Naomi had been shoved into and, as the train disappeared down the white folds of the countryside toward Nancy, he wept. Only when he could no longer see its receding form rounding the last bend at the head of the valley, or hear the screech of the locomotive in the stillness of the empty junction, did he move. He wheeled his cycle around, and once again started pedaling, while against his body, secured by his belt, Jocko carried a little boy back to Paris. Alex Drach.

PART THREE

1979

I

When Alex woke the next morning, it was late, about eleven by the angle of the sunlight streaming through the lattice bedroom window. He lay with his eyes open, looking about the room at the familiar objects he had grown up with in his Paris home: the little bookshelf in the corner, the long mirror hanging on the secret door that led into the attic, the old pinewood chest of drawers.

By the time he and Jocko had finished talking the night before, it was nearly midnight. The wedding cake was about to be served, so they agreed to talk again in the morning.

They returned to the reception, the cake was cut, and several toasts were drunk. Madelaine and Manetta had one final dance and then whisked themselves away on their *lune de miel*.

Jocko, not so exuberant as before but still polite, sped his guests' departure. The doors were shut, the chairs stacked and the lights dimmed. The only ones left in the Fantasio were Minta, Louisa, Alex and Jocko, and two broad-shouldered figures seated in semidarkness in the corner of the room. The two bodyguards were friends of the Union Corse, their presence a precaution on Jocko's part to assure the protection of Minta and Alex.

They had all said goodnight and Alex went upstairs to the room he had slept in as a boy, collapsing exhausted into bed and falling into a deep rejuvenating sleep.

Now, refreshed, the next day, his thoughts returned to the events Jocko had described the night before: to the tall slender man whose name he bore. It had been an incredible story, forcing him to confront events that had taken place nearly forty years before. As a child, he had wondered what his unknown father had been like, what kind of man he was. He had seen photographs of Paul Drach, especially a faded black and white photograph that had rested on the Corvos' mantelpiece. It showed his father, together with his mother, standing arm in arm, in front of an old Parisian café. They looked so happy there, smiling into the camera, optimistic about their future. He'd always imagined his father as gregarious, open and honest, while his mother seemed possessed of a vitality and charm that could captivate anyone.

Now, after what Jocko had told him, it was hard to absorb the shock of learning his father had been a *collabo*. But was he the sort of man that would collaborate? Whatever had happened to him that week he was held by the Gestapo, it must have been a terrible ordeal. And who was Major Hans Montag? Where was he now? Alex pictured the German living in retirement, perhaps in Bavaria, on a farm, in peaceful undulating countryside.

The main question came back to him. Who was trying to kill him and why? Was it linked with the past? Whatever the truth was, he must know it. One thing was certain, the truth was connected with the painting that had reappeared in London. Whatever, Alex thought, flipping the blankets aside, today the hunt would begin.

He swung out of bed, bathed quickly and dressed in fresh clothes. Then, packing his suitcase, he descended to the kitchen where he found Jocko, Louisa and Minta having breakfast. Jocko, dressed in a red flannel shirt and baggy corduroy trousers, gave Alex a chair and asked, "Feeling rested?"

"After what happened," Alex assured him, "I slept surprisingly well."

Louisa took a large bowl and filled it with hot milk and coffee. She set the bowl down in front of Alex and offered him a freshly-baked croissant. Alex buttered it and slapped on an extra dollop of black currant jam. As he ate, he noticed Minta staring at him. He smiled and winked at her. "What are you thinking about?"

"You," she replied. "What are you going to do?"

"For starters, I'm going to finish my breakfast. . . ."

"Be serious," Minta said. "Where are you going next?"

"To London, as planned."

"Isn't that dangerous?"

Alex shrugged. "I'll be all right."

"No you won't," she pouted. "You'll be killed and I'll never see you again. Besides, you promised to take me to a carnival."

"Be quiet, girl!" Jocko shouted. "This is a serious business!"

Minta said nothing. She only frowned, folded her arms and hunched back in her chair, furious.

Jocko turned to Alex. "There's an old Corsican saying. At the birth of a son, Corsican fathers flip a franc over the cradle of a child. If the coin comes up heads, the boy becomes a criminal. If it's tails, he'll be a policeman. If it lands on its side, he may work for a living.

The point is, no matter where you are, I can protect you, officially or unofficially."

Alex grinned. "I know that, Jocko, I'm grateful. But don't worry. There'll be no *lamentù* chanted for me by this clan."

"*D'accord*. But don't hesitate to call on me."

"Thanks, I won't."

They finished and then Alex gathered his things. Accompanied by the family, he walked to the front entrance of the Fantasio.

Jocko, his eyes moist with emotion, put his arm around Alex's shoulder and said, "Your last name is not Corvo, but you know I've always regarded you as a son." Then, from his pocket, he brought out a heavy gold medallion. "Wear this," he said. "It might come in handy some day."

Alex took the medallion and opened it. As the facing slid away, the point of a razor-sharp stiletto an inch long emerged. Alex grinned. "I see what you mean," he said.

"It was my grandfather's," Jocko said. "He made it for a similar kind of situation. I'm told it worked very well then."

Alex turned and embraced Louisa. "Take care of yourself," she said, kissing him on both cheeks.

Minta rushed up and threw her arms around him. They held each other for a moment and then she whispered, "Come back soon."

He nodded. "I won't forget the carnival. Or the cotton candy." After that, he left.

II

The headquarters of Rostand International was located in a magnificent nineteenth-century building in New York's fashionable East Seventies between Madison and Fifth. Formerly the residence of the French consul in New York, its creamy-white cut-stone facade and imposing Georgian windows bespoke solidarity, tradition and wealth. That was what André Rostand had in mind when he purchased it shortly after World War Two.

As André's black limousine rolled to a stop before the gallery, two gray-suited men emerged from the front entrance. One man hurried to open the rear door of the limousine while the other held the large mahogany-paneled gallery door open.

From the back seat André Rostand stepped onto the pavement, looked approvingly at the way the sidewalk in front of the gallery had been cleared of the snow that had fallen the night before, and then walked briskly through the open door. He handed his blue cashmere coat and gray Gelot homburg to a third man, also wearing a gray suit, who, like the others, doubled as guard and receptionist, the former function being the most important.

Each guard had been carefully selected by Rostand on the basis of his previous record. All were former policemen and all were totally reliable.

On his way to the elevator, Rostand stepped into the main exhibition room to see that preparations were under way for the benefit to be held later that week on behalf of the Hebrew University in Jerusalem, one of Rostand's many philanthropic interests. Thirty important Impressionist paintings, Renoirs, Degases and Matisses chief among them, had been brought into New York from his Iron Mountain repository and were meticulously hung around the room. Other exhibition rooms in the gallery were filled with works lent for the occasion by some of his principal clients. He made a mental note to cable his thanks to each of them.

He went to the elevator, where a guard nodded deferentially and pressed a button. The elevator doors opened. Rostand entered the elevator. First the gilded gates and then the paneled mahogany doors closed politely. The elevator was unattended. With a short thick finger, Rostand pressed the button numbered three on a brass control panel.

At the third floor the doors slid open at a slightly faster rate than they had closed. Rostand turned left and walked down a wide carpeted hallway with light sluicing down from squares of translucent glass. He passed by several doors spaced at discrete intervals until he reached one marked "Library" at the end of the corridor. This door was different. It was a mahogany-encased steel door, through which entry was restricted to a select few: the library staff, Ray Fuller, one or two trusted aides, Rostand's son and himself.

Rostand pressed a white ivory button. The heavy doors slid open and he walked into a large windowless room. Along two walls heavy wooden filing cabinets stood twelve feet in height. The other two walls were covered by bookshelves on which rested every important art periodical published around the world. The collection of books about art and related subjects was stored in a series of adjacent rooms—a collection rivaled only by the Frick Art Reference Library and the Fogg Art Museum.

The books, magazines and sales catalogues were not the reason for the importance of this room, however. What was important was contained in the long row of filing cabinets. There, cross-indexed by artist, title and collector, was a complete photo-catalogue, giving Rostand the disposition and condition of every major work and most minor works of art throughout the world. Every major painter, from Giotto to Pollock, was represented. Their works had been photographed, indexed, then computerized. With a push of a button Rostand knew in an instant where every one of these paintings was located, who owned it, its condition, provenance and value. With this information, he was able to remain one step ahead of rival dealers who had to rely on word of mouth or memory to locate a work of art they wanted. The library also maintained a detailed system of dossiers on the world's important collectors, museum directors, art critics, auctioneers and other dealers. These dossiers not only revealed the current status of their professional situation, but a great deal about their personal lives as well.

It had cost millions to establish this intelligence and millions more to maintain it. But it was worth the price ten times over. It was the key to Rostand's success, the heart of his power.

A scraggy little man whose tiny eyes were hardly visible behind thick bifocals scurried from behind an enormous desk cluttered with photo-slides and index cards. "At your service, Monsieur Rostand," Pirrone, the librarian, said.

Rostand handed Pirrone a slip of paper. "Give me a printout of these three names, please. Send them up as soon as you can."

Rostand returned to the elevator and took it to the sixth floor. There, he walked to the end of a carpeted hallway lined with English landscapes, nodded to Harper, his aide, and went through a white paneled door to his office.

Rostand believed that a man's office, like a painting, was the culmination of a thousand nuances. The office was small and modestly furnished with dark wood furniture, a beige carpet and waxed paneled walls. Warmed by a blazing fire in the white marble fireplace, the room was simple, unpretentious and essentially utilitarian. Personal paraphernalia were not conspicuous, though there were a few antiques placed around the room. One was the old green leather-topped desk his father had used in Paris. Three other mementos rested on the mantelpiece above the fireplace: a red and white porcelain peacock; a cherrywood cane; and a Daniel Quare bell-top clock of silver-mounted ebony.

There was also a colorful touch in the room, a vase of freshly cut flowers that rested on a pedestal table in the corner of the room. Every day a florist delivered fresh flowers. Today they were gardenias. Next to the flowers there were a few books, recent issues of several art magazines and a silver cigarette box.

Few of his clients ever saw Rostand in this room. Most he met in the viewing rooms on the floors below. Those that were permitted into his office were usually surprised that there were no paintings in the room. Rostand's reply to this was most often couched in humor. He had too many to choose from. Had he told the truth, he knew, his clients would be shocked. The fact was that Rostand did not particularly care for the pleasures of art. He had an eye for quality, which he had inherited from his father, but it was basically the cut and thrust of the marketplace that appealed to him. He was first and foremost a dealer, relishing the risks involved in acquiring an art treasure, but not the object itself.

He thought again about the Vermeer. It was the only painting he had invested in emotionally. He looked above the mantelpiece at the empty space where the Vermeer would have hung. Strangely, the gap did not depress him. If anything, the loss of the Vermeer had somehow energized him. He felt refreshed and in command of himself, fully prepared to take on the challenge of Marto's ring.

At his uncluttered desk, he flicked the switch of the intercom downward and asked Harper to summon Ray Fuller. Then he reached for the sheaf of papers resting on the corner of his desk. They were letters—on the average no fewer than twenty—culled from the nearly four hundred that came into the gallery each day offering paintings for sale. Those his staff considered the most promising came to his desk for final approval. The few he initialed would be sent downstairs to the library for further research. Later a complete file on each would be returned to his desk. He would examine the files, and if everything were satisfactory, a viewing would be arranged. Only one in thousands ever turned out to be of great value.

Ray Fuller entered with a quiet knock on the open door. Silver-haired, brown-suited and soft-spoken, he was carrying a leather-bound notebook and three parchment-colored folders. He and André Rostand were about the same age, though Fuller looked much older. Emaciated from years of chain-smoking, gaunt and self-effacing, Fuller looked like walking death. Still, André thought, he seemed to go on forever. A stickler for detail, Fuller was meticulous, efficient, effective.

"These are the dossiers on the runners you wanted," Fuller said, handing Rostand the folders. Then, without being asked, he added, "I haven't been able to locate Alex Drach. I've left a message at his office. They say he's still in London."

Rostand nodded and directed his accountant to one of the two exceptionally fine Georgian wing armchairs in front of the desk. He trusted Fuller with the firm's accounts and with the gallery's most intimate secrets, primarily because Fuller knew everything about him. Even so, Fuller could not help him in what he had to do now. The risk was too great. If Fuller ever betrayed him . . .

André rejected the thought and began. "There are several things I want you to do," he said crisply. "I want a dossier on every member of the ring. Research can provide you with most of the details."

"Just Marto, Bez and Duranceau?"

"No. You'd better include John Richards, Ira Kellerman, Nando Pirelli, and Jules Feigan. They've all got links to Marto. I particularly want to know each one's individual assets, especially liquid assets."

The gaunt man nodded. "It'll be on your desk in the morning."

"Also, get me an accurate"—Rostand stressed the word *accurate*—"valuation of each item that's going to be sold at the Jannis auction. I don't want conservative estimates, either. I don't want to be cut short this time." Fuller made notes as Rostand continued. "Especially the Rembrandt, I can't afford to lose it."

Fuller looked up from his notebook, nervously clearing his throat. "The Rembrandt?" he asked in astonishment. "It's been burned, bought and sold so often that no one believes it's authentic."

"I know that," Rostand snapped. "I don't need you to tell me what I already know. Jannis bought a lot of junk. The drawings, even the ones by Leonardo, are nothing but autograph album examples. It's a checkbook collection that adds up to nothing but salesroom swag."

"Yes, sir, I understand. . . ."

"I don't think you do. I'm going after that collection, not because of its quality but because I can't afford to let the ring freeze us out of the auction room. The gallery, as we know it, wouldn't survive."

"Who's going to do the bidding?" Fuller asked.

Rostand stood up and walked over to the fireplace, picking up the cherrywood cane and rubbing its silver knob. "I am," he said.

"You're going to London, then?"

Rostand nodded, and continued to issue instructions to Fuller. The salesmen were to be informed that the gallery intended to sell as many paintings as possible over the next few weeks. Existing offers were to be studied and, provided only that they were reasonable, the transactions were to be concluded. Rostand emphasized the need to acquire large amounts of cash over the next months. Fuller was to arrange for mortgages on Rostand's French vineyard and château. Additionally, work on the twelve-meter yacht design that Philip was financing would have to be suspended. He would just have to put off his mania about being accepted for full membership in the New York Yacht Club another year.

The moratorium on the development of Philip's toy would be matched by Rostand's own sacrifice: the syndication of his stable of racehorses. The only condition was that he be given an option to buy the horses back within a year. He would, of course, be willing to pay a ten percent penalty on the repurchase. Finally, he instructed Fuller to ready his Lear jet for the trip to Europe. It was to be available the night of the exhibition. He expected to be gone three days and was to be kept informed by Telex as to the progress being made on his instructions.

As Rostand finished, he returned the cherrywood cane to the mantelpiece and walked back to his desk.

Fuller, standing now, asked, "Is that all?"

"Just one more thing. See to it that the Chagall lithograph I selected is delivered to our critic at the *Times*. On second thought, you'd better deliver it personally to his home. It's more discreet that way. Also be sure and make out a receipt in the amount of fifteen thousand dollars." Fuller nodded. "Don't forget to back date it," Rostand added. "That should keep him happy for a while."

As soon as Fuller left, André withdrew a tiny notebook from his inside jacket pocket, picked up the telephone and asked his secretary to connect him with George Asher in Zurich, Edouard Villot in Paris, and Michael Koenig in London. While he waited he examined the three dossiers Fuller had prepared for him.

The first one concerned George Asher. Asher, Swiss-born, lived at 2, Bahnhofstrasse, Zurich. He was forty-three years of age, a lawyer with a Licence-ès-Lois from the University of Geneva. Fluent in German, English and French, he was married and the father of two children. Socially, he was well connected. A descendant of Alfred Asher, the merchant banker, he had an impeccable reputation and, more important, was discreet. This last trait was indispensable to Rostand.

On the negative side, Asher was a difficult man to deal with, a little insensitive, even aggressive at times. This, André knew was a result of financial worries. Asher was a frustrated art dealer. A victim of the recession of 1974, he had been unable to attract sufficient clientele and had been forced to close his gallery. Rostand had heard about Asher's difficulties and offered to buy up his inventory at top value. Asher had agreed and soon thereafter started working for Rostand International. He had been an absolutely loyal "runner" ever since.

Edouard Villot was the subject of the second dossier. Villot was French, a forty-seven-year-old accountant, educated at the École Normale d'Administration. Divorced with three children, he was the eldest son of an admiral in the French navy. He was well liked socially and had developed strong associations with conservative elements in the French government. Villot was also anti-Semitic, but that did not bother André. Villot liked to play the edge, his latest exploit involving a political payoff to a French revenue inspector. In return for reducing his taxes, Villot had arranged, through Rostand International, to sell Picasso's *Guitar Player* to the inspector. The painting was valued at $250,000. The revenue official paid only $50,000 for it. Villot absorbed the rest of the cost, but his taxes were reduced twice that amount.

Despite the anti-Semitism, André liked the gregarious Villot, not only for his healthy streak of larceny, but also because the Frenchman always maintained a good table.

The third man André had selected was Michael Koenig. Born in Holland, Koenig lived in London, and at thirty-six, was a theater producer. Educated at the Royal Academy of Dramatic Art, Koenig was fluent in Dutch, English and German. He had never married.

Koenig had emigrated to London at the age of twenty-three, had good contacts in the London theater scene and was part-owner of a popular West End discothèque. Artistic and flamboyant, the theater producer was tolerant of what passed for sin. He also tended to break the rules. André had first heard of Koenig when the producer had tried to peddle a number of forged Légers. The phony provenances for the fakes were so amateurish that Rostand's buyer in London had spotted them immediately. When Rostand threatened to expose him, Koenig offered his services in return for silence. It had been a mutually rewarding relationship ever since.

The first call came through at 11:40 A.M. It was Michael Koenig from London, sounding jovial at the other end. "Mr. Rostand! How delightful it is to speak to you again. What can I do for you?"

André spoke concisely for two minutes. When he had finished, Koenig was only too happy to help.

"I understand completely," Koenig said, "but I'll need further instructions."

"You'll get them from me personally," André replied. "Be in the lobby of Claridge's at nine-thirty Tuesday morning."

"I'll be there."

André hung up, and three minutes later George Asher was on the line from Zurich. After a brief exchange of polite conversation, Rostand told the gnomelike lawyer what he wanted. Asher grunted his approval.

A meeting was arranged for two o'clock Wednesday afternoon, at the Hotel Baur-au-Lac. Without further pleasantries, Asher confirmed the appointment and rang off.

It was an hour later when Edouard Villot came through from Paris. In French, André inquired about his friend's family. Villot gave him an account of his son's latest escapade and then asked how he could be of service. The French accountant was given similar instructions to those of the two previous callers and told to be in the lobby of the Hôtel Crillon at precisely eight o'clock on Tuesday evening.

Villot expressed his satisfaction at being able to see his old friend again, wished him a safe journey, and the line went dead.

André made one final note in his appointment book—to have lunch with Blandford Donahue, the auctioneer who would conduct the crucial Jannis sale in London the following week. He thought a moment, and then decided on Claridge's for the engagement. It would be appropriate. The hotel was one of Donahue's favorites.

The morning's business completed, André realized he was hungry. He phoned upstairs to the gallery's private dining room, where meals were prepared by a French chef, formerly on the staff of Charles de

Gaulle. He ordered a cheese omelet, salad and a half-bottle of Chablis. Then he left his desk and, feeling pleased with himself, walked up one flight of stairs to the dining room and ate alone.

III

Today Nando Pirelli was eating alone, unusual for him because he was a man who enjoyed the company of others, especially that of beautiful women. There were, however, more important matters to occupy him this afternoon. One was Marto, a man who didn't like to be kept waiting. Pirelli glanced at the thin gold watch attached to his wrist with a black crocodile strap, finished his espresso and motioned to the maître d'.

While he waited for the bill, he observed the noontime crowd gathered at Les Pléiades, the lunchtime favorite of New York's art crowd. It was pretty much the same group he saw there every day: dealers, auctioneers, museum directors and critics, the powers of the art world exchanging privileged information and back-fence gossip in discreet corners around the room. Pirelli's smooth tanned features brightened as he acknowledged a friendly greeting from the director of the Whitney Museum who, in his usual spot at a table flanking the second column from the door, was consuming the same lunch he did every day: steak tartare, endive salad and rum raisin ice cream. Pirelli's stomach growled defensively. Not that he didn't like steak tartare. But every day? The monotony of it sickened him.

Across the room, Christopher Ashton, the Metropolitan Museum's *éminence grise,* was holding court at a table of six, delivering an impressive monologue on the cultural and social history of sixteenth-century Europe.

At the next table, the *Times* art critic, Neil Johnston, was obviously eavesdropping on the conversation his archrival—the editor of an art magazine—was having with a well-known painter currently exhibiting at the Museum of Modern Art. Pirelli thought the artist's work was overrated.

Pirelli took out his gold cigarette case, pressed a discreet turquoise button on it. The case flipped open and he withdrew a cigarette, lighting it with a well-worn gold Dunhill lighter. How far he had come. How different the world he now inhabited was from the one he grew up in as a child. What were the words to that song? "If my friends could see me now . . ."

Nando Pirelli was raised in a tough, gang-infested neighborhood in a poor working-class district outside Naples. From an early age he had been taught that muscle determined the difference between right and wrong. Then one day, at the age of fourteen, he watched three thugs beat and mutilate his father, a man Nando had idolized. His father had been the strongest man in the neighborhood, the final word in any dispute that occurred. That day, however, Nando Pirelli learned that physical force could only take a man so far. What else was needed, he didn't know. But he was certain he wouldn't find it on the docks of Naples.

Pirelli left home and went to Rome. There, he lied about his age and obtained a chauffeur's license, which he used to find a job driving a truck at night. Days, he wandered the chic avenues and streets of Rome, especially the Via Veneto, hungrily absorbing the incredible sights and sounds around him. The women, like movie stars, always seemed to be with rich and debonair men. That, Pirelli decided, was the kind of man he was going to be.

At the age of fifteen, he found a job as a delivery boy for an exclusive boutique. Most of his deliveries went to wealthy old ladies living in fashionable palazzos. With them, he discovered he was a great success. An impressively handsome young man, tall for a southern Italian, Nando had clear round eyes and a perfectly geometric face. He started to pattern himself on the men he saw on the Via Veneto, not the dock boy from Naples he once was. Soon he perfected the style and looks of a model picture in a fashion magazine, well talored and barbered, the kind of young man seen playing deck tennis on a luxury liner.

One day, at an elegant and spacious apartment on the banks of the Tiber, he delivered a dress to Signorina Marina Ferrara. She invited him to have a glass of lemonade while she went into her bedroom to try on the dress. Nando walked through the house. He had never seen such opulence. Then, he noticed the bedroom door had been left open. He edged closer to it and heard the rustle of clothing. He felt an overwhelming desire to know what a woman like Marina Ferrara was like. He retreated across the room as she appeared in the doorway wearing the gown he had delivered. She looked at him and smiled. "What a waste," she said. "A shame you're so young. Then again, maybe you're not." She motioned him toward her. "Would you like to feel my skin?" she asked, extending her hand to him. Overwhelmed, Nando took a step backward, never averting his eyes from the sleek lines underneath the red satin gown. "You *are* young," she said smiling. "But don't be frightened. I'll tell you what to do." Then slowly and deliberately, Marina Ferrara reached around her to her back and unzipped the gown, letting it fall to the floor.

Marina Ferrara was more than a sexual encounter for Nando Pirelli. She was an education. From that day on, he understood that a woman could do much more for him than ease an ache between his legs. Treated properly, a woman could teach him how to speak, how to present himself, and most of all how to acquire a new identity. In the years ahead, those women who shared Nando's bed and benefited from his formidable skills as a lover taught him a great deal. They also introduced him to the sophisticated world of opera, theater, fine restaurants and, more importantly as it turned out, to art.

During the next few years, with the money he saved working as a maître d', model and hotel clerk, Nando invested in the right suits, shirts and accessories that, together with his natural good looks and charm, allowed him to move from fashion shows and gallery openings to dinner parties without question as to his social background, upbringing and education.

Still, Pirelli thought there was something lacking. The image of what he wanted to be had not fused with what he was. Just as muscle wasn't enough, good looks and charm could only carry him so far. He needed money.

At the age of twenty-five, Pirelli was offered a position in a small, inconsequential art gallery, off the Via Nazionale. The owner of the shop, recognizing Nando's appeal to women, realized that it could be a powerful asset in the gallery's business. Pirelli understood this, of course, and exploited his talents. At the same time he was learning a great deal about art, though he viewed art as a means to an end, not an end in itself.

One day, after Nando had sold the most expensive painting in the shop, the owner congratulated him and told him that if Nando stayed on, within a few years he would no longer be working for a salary but would be given a share of the business. "There's a future for you here, Pirelli."

Nando smiled to himself. The man was an imbecile. Nando Pirelli had no time to waste, nor was it his intention to be part owner of anything. He wanted his own gallery, and not in Rome where art was something you decorated your walls with, but in New York, where art was big business.

Pirelli worked at the shop off the Via Nazionale for three more years and quietly acquired a small collection of paintings. Then he left for New York. There, he opened up a gallery in an office building on the corner of Fifty-fifth Street and Madison Avenue. Unlike the walk-in, open-window type of gallery up the avenue, Pirelli's sixth-floor space was a setting in which to do "business." With subdued gray slate floors, removable white plastic partitions, and simple appointments, he created an austere atmosphere similar to a modern museum.

He then began to deal in Contemporary art, buying paintings cheaply and discreetly, just as the art boom of the 1960s began. He could not have established himself in New York at a more opportune time. The sluice gates of fortune opened wide for anyone dealing in modern American art—action painting, abstract expressionism, color field and pop art. The American wave swept the world and Pirelli rode the crest of it.

As prices skyrocketed, Pirelli hired a corps of young salesmen, each of whom handled a group of artists and carefully selected customers. The salesmen were instructed not to discover new artists but to make money. They were to concentrate on those artists who were well known and popular, to understand the meaning of downside risks, advances, staggered payouts from Swiss banks, promotional tie-ins, international exhibits and handsome full-colored catalogues. Pirelli became a master at manipulating the marketplace, notorious for the methods he applied. He exploited the notion that if a high price were paid for one work by a given artist, everything that artist did could be sold at approximately the same figure. Pirelli, therefore, supported the exorbitant prices "his" artists commanded by artificially bidding up prices at auctions and by working out discreet deals with collectors. He went to any length to protect his investments. If necessary he even bought the paintings himself at auctions to maintain the price level he had established.

Now there was one more step to be taken. He had invested wisely. His inventory was worth millions. He was rich. But he had learned something else over the years. Like muscle and charm, money wasn't enough. He wanted something more. He wanted influence. He wanted his name to be recognized. He wanted power. That, Pirelli knew, was where Marto came in.

Nando extinguished his cigarette, took three crisp ten-dollar bills from a silver money clip and paid the check.

Leaving Les Pléiades, he made a point of stopping at a table near the entrance, where he chatted amiably for a few minutes with an assistant curator of the Guggenheim Museum. She was known to the regulars at Les Pléiades as the Feminist Dragon Lady. Nevertheless, when Pirelli asked her to dinner, after looking about the room and hesitating momentarily, she accepted. When he took her hand and kissed it, she flushed. And when he left the restaurant, she watched him go. It had always been that way for Nando Pirelli.

IV

After passing through Customs and Immigration at Heathrow Airport, Alex changed a thousand dollars cash into pounds sterling, then went to a phone booth near the front entrance of the terminal. He dialed Hugh Jenner's number at the Home Office.

While the phone at the other end of the line double-buzzed he scanned the airport lounge, examining the faces of the other passengers rushing to queue for buses and taxis. A heavy-set man with a plaid sportscoat and a camera dangling from his neck entered the kiosk next to him. Drach watched him as he heard an answering click and hum on his line. He inserted tenpence in the slot beneath the receiver. The operator at the Home Office responded, and Alex asked to speak to Mr. Hugh Jenner. A moment later, Jenner's extension rang. Alex waited while it rang half a dozen times. There was no response.

The operator came back to him. She asked in a polite voice if he would like to speak to Mr. Jenner's assistant, Mr. Deakin. Alex replied that he would. The phone rang again. A man's deep baritone voice, his diction clear and vowels perfectly rounded, responded by asking if he could be of any assistance.

Alex introduced himself, and explained that he had an appointment with Hugh Jenner that afternoon. Could he confirm? Deakin told Alex to hold the line while he consulted Mr. Jenner's appointment book. A moment later Deakin verified the appointment and invited Alex to come directly to the Home Office.

Drach rang off, noticed that the man in the plaid jacket had disappeared, and walked to the entrance of the terminal. He remembered the last time he had gone out through the sliding doors of an airport. Any one of the thousands of people surrounding him now could be a potential threat. It's too damned easy to kill someone in a crowd, he thought. Whoever they were, there was no doubt they were professionals. He didn't relish the thought. Once he had been lucky. The next time it wouldn't be that easy.

He queued for a taxi and shrugged. Forget it, he told himself; don't let it get to you. But it was only when he sat deep in the back of the taxi en route to London that he relaxed, listening to the hiss of the wheels rolling over the wet streets and focusing on the rain-mottled pavement reflecting the light from the shop windows. Although it was only three o'clock, it was already growing dark.

The taxi driver cursed under his breath and slammed his foot on the brake. They were caught in a snarl of traffic around Trafalgar Square. Alex decided to go the rest of the way on foot. He paid the fare from the back seat, not wanting to expose himself by paying in the usual way from outside, through the driver's window. He left the taxi, darted through the traffic and into the back entrance of Whitehall.

At the Home Office, he was expected. He climbed three flights of stairs and was shown into the office of a pasty-faced, gray-haired man in his late forties who introduced himself as George Deakin. To Alex, Deakin looked like the sort of man much in demand by Hollywood film studios to play the part of the archetypal English gentleman.

Over gold-rimmed spectacles Deakin peered at Drach and took his seat behind a large mahogany desk littered with papers. "You made bloody good time from the airport," he said jovially.

"I took a taxi," Alex replied, and sat down.

"Ah! Yes! Public transportation being what it is . . ." Deakin leaned his head around the partition and shouted to a young blond woman reading a historical paperback, "Any sign of the old boy yet, Gladys?"

"Half-a-mo, sir, I'll try again." She picked up the phone and dialed.

While they waited, Drach looked around the room. The office

walls were painted a dull green, the wooden floor was bare, and the room furnished with plain hard furniture. A desk, filing cabinet and a few chairs completed the austere decor. There were no pictures, no personal touches of any kind except for a set of dirty teacups on top of the filing cabinet.

"Not a sign of him anywhere," Gladys shouted.

Deakin grunted. "Have you tried him at home?"

"Several times," she replied.

"Not at all like him," Deakin said, shaking his head. He looked at Drach with an embarrassed smile. "I know the old boy wanted to see you. He told me a bit about it. A painting, wasn't it?"

"Yes, a Watteau," Drach replied. "It once belonged to my father."

"Yes, I saw it after Hugh found it. He bought it for next to nothing."

"Do you know the dealer's name?"

"No, but I can probably find it. When you see Hugh he'll tell you."

Drach nodded. "Do you think Jenner would mind very much if I called on him at his home this evening?"

Deakin twirled a gold ballpoint pen in his hand, then began to doodle on a little scrap of paper. "A bit unusual, isn't it?"

"It's an unusual situation, Mr. Deakin."

Deakin stopped doodling. "How unusual, Mr. Drach?"

"I'm not sure, myself, but I think it might be a good idea to talk to Mr. Jenner this evening."

A tea-lady, pushing a trolley, came into the room. She poured them two cups of tea and offered each a packet of Merities biscuits. "Tell you what," Deakin said. "If Jenner doesn't show up by the end of the day, I'll send you 'round to his pub. He never fails to call in there."

"Fine, I'll do that. . . ." He sipped his tea, then asked, "Has he been with the Home Office long?"

"Since nineteen-forty-six. He came to us from the War Office. Mixed up with Allied Intelligence. Very hush-hush, you know."

Alex smiled sardonically. "Of course."

They finished their tea, but by half-past five there was still no sign of Jenner. As Deakin gave Alex the address of Jenner's pub he quipped, "Probably on a 'batter' last night."

V

The Rostand limousine glided across the Queensboro Bridge, then began to bump through the potholes of the snow-banked East Sixties. From the back seat, next to Philip, Cubitt watched the midafternoon crowds hurrying along the slushy sidewalks of Third Avenue looking for bargains at the post-Christmas sales. The limousine drew away from the light, turned west on Sixty-seventh Street, then north again, passing the smaller but more exclusive shops along Madison Avenue. Cubitt had shopped up and down Madison Avenue on previous junkets to New York. As they passed her favorite, a little dress shop called Kamali, she promised herself to get there in the next few days.

A few blocks farther north, they were in front of Rostand International.

Philip was out of the back door onto the sidewalk before the doorman had a chance to respond. Philip helped Cubitt from the back seat and then pushed past the guards into the handsome sandstone building.

There was a quiet omniscience about the way the attendants gathered around Philip. He handed his scarf to a receptionist, while the luggage was carried past them by one of the guards. Thirty seconds later a secretary descended a sweeping set of carpeted stairs and handed Philip a sheaf of papers.

"Mr. Rostand. Your messages."

Philip thanked her. While he looked through them, Cubitt, her stiletto heels clicking on the white marble floor, walked into the exhibition room. Carpeted in deep gray pile, as solemn and quiet as a chapel, the room was a place to absorb the contemplative genius of great art. The paintings were exquisite, she thought. She also knew enough about art to calculate that at least ten million dollars' worth of pigment and canvas surrounded her. Lost in thought, she did not hear Philip approach from behind. "They're Impressionists and Post-Impressionists," Philip whispered. "My father isn't interested in anything painted after World War Two."

"I know they're Impressionist paintings. I'm not a visual illiterate. I also know that paintings made between World War One and World

War Two are referred to as Modern, and anything after that is Contemporary," she said sardonically.

Philip grinned. "Sorry to be so condescending. You'd be surprised how many people don't know an Impressionist painter from an Old Master."

Cubitt looked at the ceiling. "I am curious about one thing, though. What are those rectangular objects hanging from the ceiling? They look like thermostats."

Philip looked up. "They're part of our security system," he said proudly. "I'm responsible for that side of things. Those are very sophisticated gadgets. They're sound detectors that can pick up anything within a range of eight thousand square feet."

"Anything . . ."

"Anything from water dripping to heavy breathing, depending on how sensitively we want it to register. The sounds are picked up and relayed to our alarm system. They're only one part of the security system I've installed," he added, taking her by the arm. "Come here, I'll show you."

He led her into an adjoining room where two guards sat before a series of television screens and a console flashing with multicolored lights. As they entered the room the guards jumped to their feet.

"At ease, gentlemen," Philip said, the tone of his voice dropping an octave.

Cubitt smiled to herself. At times, Philip could be a little boy. She half-listened as he described the extremely costly and complex "hardware" he had installed. "We have all the standard kinds of physical intrusion detection devices: vibration strips on the windows, microswitches on the doors, in addition to a layered system of interlocking alarms controlled by this computerized console." He pointed to the flashing lights. "I've also installed infrared and sonar devices that pick up motion. They protect the paintings in the exhibition rooms." Then, pointing to the closed-circuit television screens: "These monitor the entire gallery as well."

"It's like a fortress."

"Impregnable."

"I'm impressed," Cubitt said, taking his arm as they left the room. They walked back across the main floor, its white marble glowing with a kind of golden aura created by hidden spotlights recessed in the ceiling twenty feet above.

Cubitt squinted up at the molded ceiling and thought that the antique crystal chandeliers, with their candlestick bulbs, twinkled like stars. She looked down as they approached the closed elevator doors attended by a clean-cut, rather severe-looking man who might have been the dean of discipline at an all-boys school, except for the obvious bulge on his right hip beneath his gray suit coat.

They stepped into the elevator and slowly descended two flights to the subbasement level. "The air, light and humidity are carefully controlled down here; you'll see why in a minute," Philip explained.

They walked toward a heavy iron door with a multicombination lock. While she waited for Philip to run through the combinations, Cubitt thought the whole procedure rather melodramatic. She felt as though she could read the minds of the men who had constructed such a tomblike structure. It had to be the post-Crash mentality of the early thirties.

Then, as she walked through the door into a brightly lit steel-vaulted chamber, she understood. Repository racks full of various sized paintings lined the repository walls. The air reeked of that unique musty smell that only oil paint, aging varnish, gesso, jute canvas and timber, blended together, can produce. There was the constant hum of a generator in the background.

"This is our midtown repository," Philip said solemnly. "We have other repositories in a bomb shelter at Iron Mountain, in upstate New York. Several others are in Europe."

"Just how many paintings do you own?"

"That, my dear, is a state secret. But I can tell you there are over two thousand in this room alone."

Cubitt calculated. Conservatively, that was over three hundred million dollars. "It's incredible," she said. "This isn't an art repository; it's a bank vault."

Philip led her back toward the elevator, shoving the heavy iron door back into place and spinning the tumblers.

They took the elevator to the fourth floor and passed through the gallery's heavily carpeted viewing rooms. Draped in pale-gray velvet, and devoid of furniture except for a pair of comfortable easy chairs set before two or three velvet-covered easels, the rooms were almost confessional in atmosphere, places where a client could sit and contemplate a painting for hours, if necessary. Some of Rostand's clients were known to have spent entire days in these rooms, simply staring at one of the treasures that was presented.

"We keep everything compartmentalized here," Philip explained, as they ambled through the viewing rooms. "For example, the buyers, those who actually do the purchasing, never do the selling. That way no one but my father and I has an overview of the entire operation."

"Very cautious indeed."

"We have to be. As a gallery we deal in two things. Art and discretion. Which reminds me. You'll have to sign a contract which pledges you to secrecy regarding anything you do or see on behalf of the gallery."

Cubitt's eyes narrowed. "I suppose I must."

"Don't feel picked on," Philip said, putting a heavy arm around her. "It's a little something everyone is obliged to sign, both on entering and leaving our organization. It's just a way of reminding the people who work here to be a little more discreet than they might otherwise be."

At the end of the hallway they entered a viewing room empty except for an awesome oil portrait of the Duke Cosimo de' Medici.

"We're offering this to a German industrialist," Philip said, walking toward the easel on which the painting rested. "It's a Raphael easily worth more than six million."

Cubitt's eyes widened. She took a seat in a cushioned easy chair, speechless.

From the table between the chairs, Philip handed her a gray parchment folder, fastened with a blue ribbon.

"This gives you the painting's provenance. Every client is presented with it, along with the art work they're viewing."

Cubitt opened the folder and quickly scanned its contents. In elegant black script, a short biography of Rafaello Sanzio was followed by a meticulous description of the painting. Below that came the names of the various collectors and dealers through whose hands the picture had passed. The page ended with a bibliography citing the references made to the painting by art historians back to 1854.

"You're selling more than art; you're selling immortality."

Philip laughed. "You're right. That's part of the sales pitch. A prospective buyer sits here, looks at the painting, reads the provenance and realizes he's not only buying a painting, he's buying social status as well. My father likes to say that when one owns a Raphael or a Rembrandt one becomes a direct descendant of the aristocracy of Europe."

"You're serious!"

"Of course. That's what sells art. Pedigree. That, a little psychology and lots of cash. Take the German industrialist, for example. He's become obsessed with the Raphael. He can't sleep, eat or work until he possesses it. Women can't compete for his attentions. He's even ordered ten thousand sheep from his estate slaughtered to help pay for the painting."

Cubitt looked at the Raphael resting in all its majesty on the easel. "Why is he taking so long to make up his mind?"

Philip smiled. "Oh, he's made up his mind all right. We're the ones who are delaying. My father told the German that he didn't think he was quite ready for a Raphael. He wasn't hungry enough. When he does buy it he'll appreciate it all the more." He paused. "So will we. It'll cost him an additional half-million."

Philip took her by the hand and drew her from the chair. "Come on, I'll show you the laboratory."

They took the elevator to the fifth floor and stepped directly into a room with a vast array of scientific equipment. Several employees wearing white smocks were bent over microscopes, surrounded by racks of chemicals, flasks, and looping rubber tubes. Others were carefully picking at a series of canvases stretched on easels or lying flat on table tops.

As they entered the room everyone looked up at them, then, as if recovering from a surprise, went right back to work.

Cubitt noticed that none of the technicians was a woman. For that matter, she had yet to see a woman in the gallery. She leaned toward Philip. "Am I the only woman employed here?"

"My father doesn't believe in mixing art and the weaker sex," Philip whispered. "He has a prejudice about hiring females. So do I, for that matter." He winked at Cubitt.

They moved to a nearby table where a young man was working on a Rembrandt. "How's it going?" Philip asked.

"Very well, Mr. Rostand. At the moment I'm removing the varnish. It's a slow process. Probably take more than a year," he explained.

"Yes, I know," Philip said, elbowing the young man away from the table, and drawing Cubitt closer. "Rembrandt employed a special technique, mixing his pigments with varnish when he painted. They were so mixed and layered together that it's an art to remove the old varnish without damaging the pigments. That's why all Rembrandts have such an unusual glow to them. Over the centuries, the varnishes and pigments interact chemically to make it seem as though a golden light is emerging from the canvas itself."

Philip ran his finger over the surface of the canvas. "Feel it," he said.

Cubitt touched the painting. "It's very smooth," she said, "like a rock. . . ."

Philip smiled. "Exactly. The pigment of a painting this old has turned almost literally into stone. Ordinary paint thinner or turpentine wouldn't harm it in the slightest."

Cubitt glanced sideways at the young technician and noticed him trying to hide a grin, then followed Philip to a corner of the room where an older man was examining a Léger with a lamp. Books about Fernand Léger and his technique lay on a long table before him. He looked back over his shoulder as Philip and Cubitt approached, then quickly slid off his stool and deferentially said, "Good day, Mr. Rostand." Philip's dark round head nodded aloofly. Never had Cubitt seen a more perfect rendition of the servant-master relationship. No one had told any of these men to act that way, she knew, but the submissiveness of the employees was universal. She wondered what the father was like.

Philip introduced her. "Meet Marco Grimaldi, Miss Keeble. He's one of our most eminent restorers, with an eye for a fake unparalleled in the business. He can read a painting better than an FBI agent can read a fingerprint."

The sloe-eyed Italian smiled broadly, revealing a row of even white teeth. His fine olive features were beautifully set off by wavy black hair heavily streaked with gray. "Mr. Rostand exaggerates," he said, bowing slightly at the waist. The look in his eye, however, suggested that such praise was his due.

"What have you got here, Marco?" Philip inquired, squinting at one of the Légers.

"They were brought in a week ago," Marco replied, "but I have no doubts. They're fakes." He picked up a lamp, illuminating the canvas with ultraviolet light. "I will explain. If there is underpainting it is a good sign that the painting is genuine. A fake is done at one time, and very carefully, usually painted to copy. There is no underpainting showing here, no pentimento."

He picked up another lamp. "This is a fresnel screen," he explained. "It's used basically to detect overpainting, but such instruments are not always that helpful. Some forgers are now using a wonderful substance called luminescent paint which cannot be detected by a lamp. They mix it into their pigments to camouflage the overpainting. The government is supposed to control its sale, but it can be bought, or stolen." He turned to Cubitt and pointed to his eye. "Instruments don't tell everything," he said. "I rely more on the eye. One has it or one doesn't. I look at the brush strokes, the type of paint used, the peculiar style of the artist. All these give a forger away."

Marco went on to explain that the instruments proved that the Légers were forgeries but they revealed nothing as to the forger's identity. To learn that, he had to apply intuition. He described how he looked at the "character" and "quality" of the paintings. The "character" revealed the particular "stamp" of the work: *stamp* meaning its style, brush stroke, the mood and message of the work. *Quality* indicated whether it was "good enough," the way colors merged, the use of line and space. Technically, these forgeries were good enough but they were not quite right. They were too mechanical, too rigid.

He then described a new system of verifying an artist's signature by computer. He used a laser recording device and demonstrated that each signature reflected a unique acceleration, speed of pace in signing, and the direction of the pull of the pen or brush.

Marco stood back from the painting and thought a moment. "It helps, of course, to have a good visual memory bank—like your grandfather," he said, looking at Philip.

"Yes, I wish I had his eye. Father tells me that he was able to recognize the work of an artist as easily as he did the writing of an old friend."

Cubitt, absorbed by the Léger, asked, "Are there that many fakes around?"

"Too many," Marco replied. "We get an average of at least twenty a week. People send us photos and descriptions asking us to authenticate their works. Most I can tell are fakes, just by looking at the photograph. Only once in a while do I have to see the actual painting."

"That's why we must be careful," Philip added. "The market may collapse one day because of the number of fakes and forgeries sold by dealers, knowingly or unknowingly. Collectors of Contemporary painting are particularly vulnerable. For example, a Lichtenstein, a

Warhol or a Jasper Johns can be faked very easily. A painting by
any of them is worth a small fortune, but they can be reproduced
with the simplest of devices. Many Contemporary painters also keep
incomplete records, so that anyone can come along with a good fake
and get away with it."

"Is that the reason why Rostand International doesn't deal in
Contemporary art?" Cubitt asked.

"One of the reasons," Philip replied. "The other reason is that my
father believes Contemporary painting is trash."

"What do you think?"

Philip glanced at Marco and smiled. "To be honest, I wouldn't
collect it myself, but there's money to be made in dealing it."

"The same can be said of Picasso," Marco added. "His drawings
and prints are the easiest thing in the world to fake. It got to the
point before he died that he'd authenticate anything, even a fake, to
keep his market from collapsing."

"Marco's right," Philip interjected. "We had three hundred
Picassos ten years ago; now we have none. My father sold them off
for just that reason." He glanced at his watch, then walked to the
window and looked down on the street below. It was getting dark.
"Speaking of my father, we'd better catch him before he leaves."

VI

"Be careful, dammit! You're straining my trapezius."

The flabby, meaty-faced masseur eased the pressure on Leopold
Marto's neck and muttered, "Sorry, sir."

Marto lay flat out, naked on the padded exercise table, his right
cheek resting on the back of his hands. He grunted, closed his eyes
and gave himself to the rhythm of the massage.

Precisely at one o'clock each weekday, Marto walked through the
swinging doors of the men's baths at the Metropolitan Club of New
York and had a twenty-minute massage, a steam bath, and a lunch of
goat's milk blended with orange juice, yeast powder and two raw eggs.
This ritual, Marco believed, prevented wrinkles, sagging skin and a
poor complexion.

Marto did not believe in growing old. Aging, he believed, could be controlled just like everything else. He celebrated youth. He also loved dogs, attractive women, lapis lazuli, money and art, especially valuable art. He hated cats, warts, meat, homosexuals, the color yellow, the mention of death and, most of all, André Rostand.

Marto's pulse rate quickened, gloating at the memory of the auction the night before. Again and again the satisfying image of Rostand, humiliated in defeat, reappeared. The bidding had gone just as he had predicted. Then, the beautiful denouement. He permitted Rostand the taste of victory, then came that superb denial. Afterward, in celebration, he had allowed himself a few sips of champagne, an intoxicant he despised, though he could appreciate the art of its manufacture.

The masseur applied a thick white glob of rose-scented lanolin between Marto's bony shoulder blades and after flexing his fingers began massaging the sternomastoid muscles at the back of the septuagenarian's sinewy neck. The masseur's hands worked automatically, his great weight pressed down on them. Marto groaned in pleasure. The hands moved upward through the fringe of white hair at the base of Marto's small round skull, back down to the neck, to the shoulder blades, and there they abruptly stopped. The hands shifted to the legs, the masseur's palms pressing and pulling on the mound of gluteal muscle at the back of the thigh.

As the masseur's fingers probed the sciatic nerve, then lingered on the upper thigh, the old man's thoughts shifted accordingly. Marto substituted the memory of the auction with a fantasy of a young girl dressed in a white cotton shirt and shorts. The girl, standing a few yards away from him, unbuttoned her shirt, neatly folding it and placing it at his feet. Marto smiled inwardly. She wore nothing underneath the shirt. Pleasantly sunburned, her fine breasts were full and firm.

The masseur's thumbs splayed each vertebra along his back and the fantasy dissolved. In its place Marto saw the ultramarine blues and fine edges of the Vermeer. The perfection of it. Extraordinary. Its acquisition rivalled any of his past achievements. And there had been many, most of them involving big money.

Marto had made his first million while studying for a Ph.D. in economics at Harvard. There he learned he had little talent for academics, but a natural flair for business. By the time he graduated he had bought a company, asset-stripped it, and sold off its various components for three times what he had paid for the whole thing.

He started on his second million while on a tour of China looking for business opportunities during the chaos of the Chinese civil war. He had heard that a typhus epidemic was ravaging the country. To curry favor with the Kuomintang leadership, he presented them with a surplus army field hospital. The donation of those medical supplies was the first and last generous act in Marto's life, and it paid handsome dividends. He received not only the personal gratitude of Chiang Kai-shek, but also an exclusive contract to supply the Chinese with grain and machinery imported from the United States.

At the time, Chinese currency was nearly worthless, so Marto accepted payment in the form of rare paintings and other art treasures. While the Chinese had no use for the art, Marto did. With a fortune in rare paintings and objects, he returned to New York to open up the first of several art galleries he would eventually own throughout the country.

For fifty-five years, Marto had been dealing in art, and in that time his power and influence had grown enormously. He was considered a taste-maker, a culture baron, with an inventory of Oriental, old, and modern masters that ranked with those possessed by any other firm in the world. Any firm, that is, except Rostand International.

Marto was great. Rostand was preeminent. For years they had vied with each other, but always Rostand had maintained the edge. Rostand. A stab of annoyance came at the very name. At one time his hatred for Rostand had produced enough bile to bring on a case of severe indigestion. But no longer. He had finally maneuvered André Rostand where he wanted him. There was nothing his rival could do now.

Marto felt a tap on his shoulder. He opened his eyes, blinked and rolled over. Through half-closed eyelids he looked up at a bank of six sunlamps. He snapped the fingers of his right hand. The flabby masseur placed two black eye-cups over Marto's eyes, a scanty towel over his genitals. Marto grunted, let out a long shattering yawn, and the mechanism of his emotional clock returned to the vital question of Rostand's final destruction.

VII

The Ark, in St. James's Place, was within walking distance. Alex
Drach left the front entrance of the British Home Office and went
past the Treasury and the War Office. He had reached Whitehall
Place when he sensed he was being followed. He walked another
block, stood on a corner, and waited for the lights to change. Someone, standing quite close to him, was breathing heavily, almost panting, as though he had been running. Alex stood very still and listened
to the labored breathing. He turned and glanced at a heavyset round-
faced man in a gray loden overcoat. Not him, Drach thought: too
close, too bulky, too fat. The stoplight changed. Instead of crossing,
Alex turned left and walked toward the Admiralty, watching from
the corner of his eye to see which of the pedestrians crossed against
the lights with him. At first no one did. Perhaps he was wrong. Then
he spotted a tallish figure, in a black leather knee-length coat, cutting
through the traffic after him. Drach remembered the face, the close-
cropped steel-gray hair, and, though the man was too far away,
Drach knew that he had a silver stud in the lobe of his left ear. The
cleric who had been on the plane from New York was the same
who'd stood chatting in front of the Charles de Gaulle Airport, and
surely one of the shadowy figures in the BMW.

Alex continued walking up Whitehall to Trafalgar Square. The
man in the black leather coat kept pace ten yards behind.

In the rush-hour crowd, Alex knew he had the advantage. He
stopped again for a traffic light. Predictably, Silver Stud drew up
behind. Alex doubted that the man was alone. A second tail had to
be around, probably on the other side of the street. Otherwise, Silver
Stud wouldn't have crossed against the light with him.

At the change of lights, Alex left Admiralty Arch behind him and,
at an even pace, wove through the tangled auto traffic moving slowly
round Trafalgar Square. He sprinted up the steps between Landseer's
lions to Nelson's column. From there he looked back, and a pleased
grin split his face. Caught in the headlights of a double-decker bus, a
short, squat figure in a mackintosh dodged through traffic to join Silver Stud. Flushed out like a brace of pheasants. He didn't give them
very high marks in team surveillance.

Alex looked around Trafalgar Square. His gaze stopped at the entrance to the National Gallery. He loped to the top end of Trafalgar Square and darted through the traffic tied up in Pall Mall. He climbed the front steps of the National Gallery, pulled open the heavy entrance door, and passed through the turnstile. He moved quickly through the rotunda, past stalls selling art books and postcard reproductions. Then he took the staircase to the left, two stairs at a time. He reached the west vestibule and stepped back to look down into the rotunda. They were there, between the two staircases. Silver Stud headed for the stairs leading to the east vestibule. His squat companion moved in the opposite direction, toward the stairs Alex had just taken.

Alex nodded decorously to a blue-uniformed guard, and with his hands clasped behind his back he walked briskly through the gallery's permanent collections of Italian and Florentine Old Masters. It was nearly closing time. Most of the gallery's visitors were trooping in the opposite direction toward the staircase. Alex chose a door to the right where an elegant man with a Vandyke beard stood gazing at Sandro Botticelli's *Venus and Mars*. Drach preferred the circular canvas hanging on the opposite wall, Botticelli's *Adoration of the Kings*. It had more flair, he thought, as he went into the Duveen Room, which was filled with seventeenth-century Dutch Masters. Some day, he'd have to spend more time in that room, but now he darted through a long narrow gallery past a portrait of a very busty woman—no doubt a Rubens—and abruptly stopped, realizing that he was being closely watched by a pinch-faced inquisitive guard.

"Which direction are the amenities?" Alex inquired in a supercilious voice. He hated the word, but on occasion one had to use it.

"Near the main exit," the guard replied impatiently, consulting his watch.

Drach thanked him, and proceeded, almost at a run, in the opposite direction, into a room devoted to Dutch seventeenth-century painters. Instead of turning right, which would have taken him back to the main staircase, he went left into a room full of Rembrandts. He did not have much time. He was not concerned about the man carrying the excess weight. But the leaner, Silver Stud, would cover his side of the gallery quickly. He would be in the Rembrandt Room in no time.

Alex found himself in the last room of the gallery. He acknowledged Rembrandt's *Self-Portrait as an Old Man,* then spotted a door marked "Employees Only." He looked around the room and tried the door. As he expected, it was unlocked. The notice sufficed to keep the law-abiding English public out.

He stepped through the door and descended a narrow flight of wooden stairs, past the ground floor level to the basement. He pushed through a steel door and found three workmen moving a large heavy crate on a trolley. He nodded to them curtly and walked on in the direction of the exit, indicated by a yellow arrow painted on the wall. At the far end of the passageway he came to a door, pushed on its roll bar and walked out into the gallery's loading bay. A delivery van, its driver absent, stood parked in front of wide-open double doors. Alex walked smartly past the van and sprinted up a short driveway into the narrow street which ran along the back of the gallery. There, he inhaled the muggy January air, looked back at the "No Admittance" sign posted on the wall beside the yard doors and made a mental note that some day he would have to offer his services as a security consultant to the National Gallery.

VIII

As the elevator rose to the sixth floor, Cubitt reflected on what she had seen. Rostand International, New York, was no ordinary art gallery. It was an art palace, a museum, a bank all rolled into one. The investment involved was staggering. Art, she'd always thought, was something exalted, rare and beautiful. Her look around the gallery had not changed that opinion, but what she had seen had added a new dimension. She was learning that art was many things. It was glamour. It was prestige. It was truth, revelation and immortality. It was culture. It was class, a symbol of power and achievement. But most of all, she understood now, it was big business.

Suddenly, Cubitt felt good about her prospects with Philip Rostand. Madame Gérard was right. She was going to enjoy herself, and doubtless be well paid for it. She was still feeling good as the doors of the elevator parted and she walked out onto the thick carpet of the sixth floor.

"Don't be put off by the old man," Philip whispered as they headed toward the far end of the hall.

"What's wrong with him?"

"A bit crusty, that's all," he replied.

At the far end of the corridor, they approached a bald man, who, when he stood, was almost a head taller than Philip. Cubitt guessed he might be about forty, but she couldn't be sure. The recession of hair to the right and left of the crown made him look older than he possibly was. Whatever age, he was an intimidating figure. He gave her a frozen smile, and in an English accent offered them a "Good afternoon." Then he moved toward a white paneled door, adding as he grasped the white porcelain knob, "I'll tell him you're here." The door closed behind him.

Cubitt swallowed and prepared herself for what lay ahead. She wondered why she felt so anxious. Perhaps it was because she was tired after the six-hour flight. She shifted her weight to one leg and looked at Philip. A trace of perspiration showed above his upper lip. As the minutes went by she felt embarrassment for his being kept waiting.

"He's a busy man," Philip said uneasily, taking out his pillbox. He had just swallowed a tablet when the white paneled door opened and the bald man reappeared. "Please come in," he said, holding the door open and stepping aside.

Cubitt strode through the door ahead of Philip. As she did so, she took a deep breath, smelling the bald receptionist's exotic cologne. It reminded her of cinnamon and cloves. She stared for a moment at the flames in the fireplace, glanced at the white gardenias and then, for the first time, saw the imposing figure sitting in the straight-back chair behind the desk. She next absorbed the dark eyes, which she knew were already assessing her and, at the same time, felt his presence. Her immediate reaction was to smile, but then she instinctively stopped in the center of the room, waiting for Philip's father to leave the protection of his desk and come forward to meet her.

André Rostand grinned as though he recognized the challenge and stepped around the desk. He glanced at Philip, nodded curtly and went to Cubitt. "My apologies for keeping you waiting," he said, taking Cubitt's outstretched hand and shaking it. "I'm André Rostand."

"Cubitt Keeble." Rostand's handshake was more cordial than she had expected, but there was a coldness in his eyes up close not seen from a distance. Cubitt glanced at the thick gray hair set off by the tanned face and wondered where, in January, he'd been in the sun.

Philip, with the introductions made, angled away from the pair in

the middle of the room and sat on the window ledge to the right of
the fireplace. "I met Miss Keeble in Rome," he said. "I thought she
might like to work for us." His voice had a tremor that Cubitt had
never heard before. It wasn't a tremor of fear, but a soft tremor
suggesting anger coupled with desire for approval. Philip paused, as
if waiting for a response from his father. There was none. He stood.
"Let me tell you a little bit about her."

"Philip . . . ," André said. That was all he said. The name hung
in the air like a note of music that does not end. André turned,
walked slowly back to his desk, and sat down, casually crossing his
legs and adjusting his dark blue pant leg by lifting it slightly at the
kneecap.

Cubitt watched father and son, fascinated by the psychological
duel. There was an unspoken hostility between them. Why, she didn't
know, but it was there. André was trying to humiliate and belittle his
son, as though punishing him for some misdeed. Philip remained
impassive, but still appeared to accept it.

"Philip," André finally said, motioning Cubitt to one of the chairs
in front of his desk, "I'm sure Miss Keeble can tell us about herself."

Cubitt glanced at Philip, smiled reassuringly and took a seat. "I'd
be delighted," she said calmly. She took in Rostand's dark blue suit,
wondrously cut, a style she'd not seen before, the white shirt and
dark silk tie, then fixed on his strong square face. As if playing to an
audience to whom she was introducing a new actress, she began to
speak in the third person. "Cubitt Keeble is twenty-eight years old, a
British subject, born in London of working-class parents. Father: a
docker who had no aspiration other than to drink beer and phi-
lander. Mother: a healthy Saxon woman, love-starved, repressed,
frustrated. Two brothers, two sisters. Miss Keeble has never married
and has no intention at this moment of doing so. Formerly a photographer's model, she has most recently been associated with Madame
Gérard as a highly paid, extremely beautiful, intelligent and sophisticated courtesan. Miss Keeble is . . ."

André Rostand cut in. ". . . A highly paid, extremely beautiful,
intelligent and sophisticated employee of Rostand International." He
was not smiling, but Cubitt saw he was impressed with her honesty.

"You don't want to hear more?" Cubitt asked, her blond eyebrows raised expectantly.

"In time, I'll know much more. Besides, you couldn't have better
credentials than a reference from Madame Gérard. I know, I've . . ."

There was a sharp rap on the door. Rostand's bald aide stepped into the room. "You have another caller, sir, a Monsignor Weiller."

"I don't know the man," Rostand snapped. "Tell him I'm very busy, Harper."

"Yes, sir," Harper intoned, "but before I do, he told me to give you this."

Rostand took the small card Harper handed him and glanced at it. He started to hand it back then looked at it again. His face blanched. He stood abruptly and said, "I'm afraid I'm going to have to see this man. Would you please excuse me?" Then to Philip, "I'll speak with you later." It was a dismissal. Harper opened the door, permitting Cubitt and Philip to pass before him.

As Cubitt left Rostand's office, she saw the man waiting to see André. He looked to be about sixty-five, with fairly close-cut corn-colored hair—the color blond hair turns as it grays. It was combed straight back without a part. The round face was well padded with a thin layer of fat that would have suggested overindulgence, but for the subtle hardness around the thin lips and washed-out blue eyes. On the whole, Cubitt thought, it was not a pleasant face to look at. He was wearing a loose-fitting black suit, black bib and white cleric's collar. Apart from that, there was no identifying characteristic other than a slash of red at the base of the clerical collar. It marked him as a monsignor of the Roman Catholic Church.

The monsignor smiled at her, then bowed slightly at the waist in Philip's direction as Harper held the door open. The monsignor stepped forward to greet André Rostand. Before the door closed, Cubitt had a glimpse of two men staring at each other, saying nothing. To her, they seemed like two disembodied spirits resurrected from the dead.

IX

Nando Pirelli passed the Hotel Pierre and walked through the dec-ades-old wrought-iron portals of the stately mansion that housed the Metropolitan Club. A porter took his name, phoned the baths, and then directed Pirelli past the west lounge and the club library, along an oak-paneled corridor where a phalanx of darkly varnished portraits of past club members stared down on him. He did not know the faces, but he knew the names: Phipps, Carnegie, Frick, Ford, Vanderbilt and the founder of the club, the robber baron, J. P. Morgan.

He found Leopold Marto in the exercise room. The old man was grunting into a situp, leaning forward, forehead to knees, hands clasped behind his sweating neck. "Hello . . . there . . . delighted . . . you . . . are . . . on . . . time . . . ," Marto puffed between situps. The old man stopped for a minute. "I believe that makes seventy-five, Nando. Do you like to exercise?"

"Only in bed," the swarthy Italian replied.

"You should, you know. Lots of exercise, a healthy diet, and moderation in all things. That's why I'm so mentally and physically fit. What age do you make me?"

"Guessing, no more than sixty, and a young sixty," Pirelli flattered.

"Don't trifle with me, young man; you know I'm seventy-nine."

"Yes, I know, born in nineteen hundred. Father a doctor. Made your first million before leaving graduate school. Friend of Chiang Kai-shek, and so on. A man of our time." Marto did not smile. He never smiled. Smiles created wrinkles in the face.

"You're a well-informed young man. I've always admired that about you, especially when it comes to Rostand International."

Pirelli smiled and removed his suit jacket. The air was hot and heavy in the baths. "I try to be helpful."

"Oh, you are, my boy, you are," Marto said, while he did a series of side-straddle-hops. At rest again, he looked at the wall clock. "Well, Nando, are you ready?"

"For what?"

"A steam bath!"

Pirelli's gypsy-dark features blanched. "Frankly, I'd prefer to do business over drinks."

"I never drink," Marto said. "Besides, there are advantages doing business in the steam room. First, one is relaxed, and, of course, more trusting. Second, we can both be certain that our conversation is not monitored or tape-recorded. After all, my friend, what we're doing is quite illegal."

"I'd rather use the word *unethical*," Pirelli said.

"Any word you like, but we still have to be careful."

Pirelli shrugged, and accompanied Marto to a tiled dressing room, where he stripped and wrapped a towel round his waist.

In the steam room the spigots were full open. A swirling white haze eddied around them. Pirelli looked at the temperature gauge on the wall. It registered 110 degrees. He shook his head and sank back on the wooden bench against the white tiled wall. Marto lay down along the opposite wall. His voice, like a disembodied spirit, floated through the mist. "Now then, down to business. What is Art Intrum quoted at on the Exchanges?"

"After last night's sale, it moved a full point to thirty and three-quarters."

"Marvelous!" Marto squeaked. "Now, let's look at the figures. We know that three billion dollars' worth of art changes hands every year. Half of that moves through the auction houses. The other half is handled by roughly five thousand dealers working worldwide. According to our source, Rostand's stake is by far the largest, approximately twenty-five million dollars per year. This year, Art Intrum will only take in half that. However, if we can undermine Rostand's hold on the market, we'll easily double our turnover. There are only two things that could possibly prevent us from doing that: lack of co-operation amongst ourselves, or Rostand himself."

"We saw last night that Rostand's not that strong. You handled him beautifully, Leopold."

Marto's high-pitched laugh came drifting through the steam. "Did you see his face when he left? It looked like a cow's udder that's just been milked." He stood up and walked through the undulating steam to a large wooden bucket filled with cold water. He took a ladle, poured the water over his head and shoulders and shivered. "Good for the heart," he said. "Help yourself."

Pirelli lay flat against the wall, barely breathing. "No thanks. What about the Jannis sale?"

Marto returned to the pine bench. "I was just getting to that. It's terribly important for us to know what Rostand's intentions are. How seriously he's going to press us, how high he's willing to go. We need to know that in order to organize financing." Marto started rubbing his arms and legs vigorously, massaging the sweat from his body. "Will your informant be able to give us that information?"

"There's no question about that," Pirelli replied confidently.

"How can you be so sure, and can we rely on the information?

We're talking about millions of dollars. Financing that kind of deal won't be easy."

"Have we ever been misled? Every time we've needed a tip on Rostand's operations, the names of his best clients, the paintings he's after, we've had the information."

"I'd still feel better if I knew who your informer was."

Marto did not see the grin on Pirelli's face. "That's my leverage, Leopold, that and my organization and knowhow." Pirelli paused. "Besides, I wouldn't jeopardize my source."

"You're shrewd, Pirelli, that's why we brought you in." Marto stood. "Well, that's enough steam, don't you think?" They left the steam bath, grabbing two dry, warm towels from a three-foot stack, and went into the changing room. They dressed, Pirelli donning his blue suit, white shirt, maroon tie, black socks and loafers to match; Marto clothed in brown paper slip-ons and a heavy white terry-cloth bathrobe.

While he ran a comb through his damp black hair, Pirelli realized that he had not asked the most important question. "How are we going to organize the bidding at the Jannis sale?"

"I've thought about that," Marto replied. "Bez will represent us; he'll do the bidding. Duranceau will be there, ostensibly to bid, but he'll monitor Bez and step in if anything happens."

"Good, it's better that way. If we all show up it will be too obvious. Though, God knows, there's no regulation in this business."

"How could they regulate it? Who knows what a work of art is worth? All we're doing is getting our fair markup of what the traffic will bear."

Pirelli laughed. "And then some, doctor!"

A waiter in a starched white jacket appeared in the doorway. He carried a tray on which was set a silver-plated tureen and two large glasses. Marto turned to Pirelli. "Would you join me for lunch?"

The waiter set the tray down on a glass-topped table beside the pool. Marto ladled himself a glassful of the cream-colored liquid. "It's guaranteed to increase longevity," he said, imbibing a mouthful.

Pirelli's nose wrinkled in revulsion and he headed for the door. "You know, Leopold," he said. "There's an old Italian expression. Life is like loving a woman; don't love it too much if you are afraid to lose it."

X

From the British National Gallery, Alex walked up Orange Street to Haymarket, where he quickly lost himself in the crowds of Piccadilly Circus. The rain had become a heavy, hanging mist that softened the brawl of neon and noise through which Drach had to thread his way. Jenner's pub was a few minutes away, and as he hurried along, Alex felt confident that he'd left his two pursuers behind in the elevated company of the Old Masters. Meanwhile, he was caught up in a much more contemporary scene. The corpulent woman in Rubens's painting was certainly a different breed from the trim middle-class women he observed rushing through the streets of London that night. He wondered how Rubens would have reacted to them, caked as they were with makeup, in their knee-length boots, jackets with broadened shoulders, narrow waists and skirts tapered to the hemline.

Drach himself missed the more natural look, the kind of woman who scoffed at cosmetic artifice, wore jeans and insisted on being desired as she was. He hated frizzled hair, six-inch heels, plastic fashion and breasts sloshing about under transparent gowns. The bony sophisticated type held even less fascination for him.

He kept close to the base of the buildings, where movement through the crowd was easier, and where, more importantly, he had to worry about a threat from only one side. He turned into St. James's Place, passed the entrance to the Stafford Hotel, and approached the somber facade of The Ark. He glanced into the pub through the deep-set windows that overlooked the street. The place looked particularly clubby, one of those places where Englishmen were fond of taking lunch, sharing a drink, reading the late evening paper. Alex mounted the steps toward the upper floor, which Deakin had said Jenner preferred. At the top, he pushed open the engraved-glass and mahogany door that carried the flowery Victorian legend "Lounge Bar." Behind the dark bar itself a balding barman was polishing glasses.

"Excuse me," Alex said. "Do you know a Mr. Hugh Jenner?"

"Mr. Jenner?" the barman replied in a heavy Irish accent. "Yes indeed. But he hasn't been in yet this evening."

"I see," Alex said, looking around the spacious room. "Perhaps you would give me a large malt whisky, and I'll wait for him by the fire."

Alex found a comfortable chair in the corner and amused himself watching the varied geriatric population of the pub, muttering to one another.

Drach had always marveled at English tailoring. He wore only English tailored suits himself. But, as he looked at the sprawling figures about the room, he wondered why it was that Englishmen thought it fashionable to reveal so much shiny white skin above their ankle-length socks. An hour later, after a second whisky, he realized that, wherever Hugh Jenner was, he wasn't going to join him, so he walked to the bar and put down two pound notes.

"Could I leave a message for Mr. Jenner?" he asked.

"Indeed. It's very unlike Mr. Jenner to miss an appointment."

"Yes, I've heard that before," Alex said. "Was he here last night?"

"To be sure he was, and I may say looking grand."

"With friends?"

The barman hesitated, glancing down as though the floor had the answer. Back to Drach's face, his eyes twinkled. "Yes, as a matter of fact there was another gentleman with him last night."

"Do you remember what the man looked like?"

The florid-faced barman looked at Drach suspiciously. "And who'd be asking now?"

Drach furtively looked around the room. "Actually I've just arrived from Washington," he said. "We're working on something together. It's rather urgent. You understand?"

The barman leaned toward Drach. "Oh, and indeed I do, sir," he replied. He paused for a moment as though straining to remember. "As I recall, now, the man was blond, rather a large frame, well dressed, but a bit flashy, if you know what I mean. He wore one of them neckerchiefs. One of them French t'ings."

"An ascot, you mean?"

"I don't know the name. But they left together last night about half-seven."

"Do you know where they went?"

"Sorry. Can't help you there. I remember, though, the man had a bag with him. A nice-looking bag it was, too." The barman scratched his head. "He seemed real friendly . . . almost too friendly, even."

Alex asked to use the telephone. He looked up Jenner's number and let the phone ring for several minutes. There was no answer. He left The Ark and hailed a taxi, directing the driver through Knightsbridge to Wilton Place, where he stopped at the new Berkeley Hotel. It was not the kind of hotel a tourist could just walk into and register. An introduction was necessary to be able to stay there. The night clerk recognized Drach and Alex registered, paying for one night. He did not go to his room, however. It was a diversion. Instead, he took another taxi to Dover Street, off Piccadilly, where he registered at Brown's Hotel under the name of Minolta, out of an admiration for Japanese cameras.

Brown's was one of his favorite hotels. It was quiet and comfortable and the service was excellent. An old-fashioned hotel, its rooms were large and high-ceilinged. He called room service, ordered a dinner of turbot Florentine and a Muscadet from the hotel's wine list. At the same time he booked a call to his office in New York and was through almost at once. His assistant, Harry Powalski—Po, for short —reeled off a list of messages, chief among them a request for an appointment with André Rostand at Rostand International.

Curious, Alex thought, he's the one man he most wanted to see in New York. Alex instructed Po to make the appointment.

"The others can wait until Monday."

After dinner, Alex took a long, very hot bath. The white-tiled bathroom rapidly filled with steam. He lay soaking in the deep tub with the hot water tap sufficiently open to maintain the temperature of the water as hot as he could stand it. Slowly, very slowly, the tension and strain of the day ebbed away. A half-hour later, his body glowing from the bath, he wrapped himself in a long white terrycloth bathrobe provided by the hotel, ate dinner, and then, naked, slipped between fresh linen sheets. He would require all the rest he could get between now and his early morning appointment at the Home Office. He freed his mind of any thought that produced anxiety, slowed his breathing and focused on waves breaking on a sunlit seashore. Every jarring thought that floated through his mind, he eased aside. He did allow one image to linger on the unrippled surface of his mind: Minta. She was the last conscious thought he had before he fell into a deep refreshing sleep. He imagined her sitting on a ledge of rock on a deserted beach where the waves broke gently over her legs dangling in the pool below.

XI

Ashen-faced, André stood, his hands clasped behind him, back to the fire. He found himself twisting the gold wedding band on his finger, wondering if the man standing a few feet from him was an apparition, an impostor, or the man himself. He had recovered from the shock of Weiller's entrance to consider all three. He had discarded the first at once. He decided the second unlikely. He would presume it was the third and asked guardedly, "What can I do for you, Monsignor Weiller?"

The prelate smiled politely. "Forgive me for this intrusion, Herr Rostand. I know you are a very busy man, but I thought it best to reintroduce myself this way rather than by letter, telephone or some other indiscreet means of communication."

Montag was enjoying this, André thought. He hadn't changed much over the years. "I repeat, Monsignor Weiller, what is it that I can do for you?"

"Very simply, I'm here to offer you some paintings. They are very beautiful paintings." Montag paused, took a step backward and lowered himself into a chair in front of the desk. "I might also add," he continued, "they are very valuable paintings." Then, with his index finger, he began stroking his right cheek.

André returned to his desk and sat down staring into the face of the man sitting before him. The face had changed. Older yes, but more than that. There was something else, and then he remembered the wine-red birthmark on his right cheek. It had been removed. "Why have you come to me, Montag?" The tone of André's voice was direct and hard.

"Weiller. Monsignor Weiller."

André smiled thinly. "The question stands."

Montag looked down and flicked a white speck from the sleeve of his jacket. "I am a man of modest means. As a man of the cloth, I live very simply. I have few worldly possessions. Those that I have, I don't need. All I require I've found in the bosom of Holy Mother, the Church."

"I'm touched by such a display of faith. Such an interesting transformation."

The monsignor did not respond to Rostand's sarcasm except with a smile. "Surely you are a man I can trust, Herr Rostand. We've done business before. In fact, the paintings I have are the very same ones we discussed the last time we met."

André remembered the night in Monte Carlo, forty years before. It was June and the sirocco was blowing across the Mediterranean from Africa. His stomach tightened as he wrenched himself back to the present. Obviously Montag had prepared this whole performance well in advance. He didn't have time for a performance. "Let's get to the point, Montag. You have some paintings, paintings you've obviously stashed away since the war."

Montag sat back in the chair, his gaze absently wandering about the room. "You're just as direct and to the point as you were then. So shall I be. I have the Drach Collection. And others. I want you to have them." Montag paused. "For a price."

"Now let me be direct and to the point. I am not interested."

"Under any circumstances?"

"There's no point in trying to blackmail or threaten me. You're a war criminal, Montag. Despite the plastic surgery and the spiritual conversion, it's not so easy to wipe the swastikas from your sleeves."

Montag raised his hands in mock horror. "As God is my witness, Herr Rostand, I am not here to blackmail you. I'm in no position to do that, just as you are in no position to expose me." He smiled benignly. "That is, I believe, what the Americans call a Mexican standoff."

"Then there's nothing more to discuss. You have my answer. This time there's no deal. I made one mistake in my life; I don't intend to make another."

"To err is human. To forgive is divine."

Rostand stood. "Forgive me, then, if I say good-bye."

Montag let out a deep sigh. "A pity, I was sure we could come to some sort of arrangement." He shrugged and raised his bulky frame from the chair. "Leopold Marto is hardly a pleasant man, but I'm sure we can do business together."

André returned to his chair. In the silence that followed, he realized that he had no choice. The luxury of honor had once again been denied him. If Marto were to come into possession of the paintings Montag had, the ring would destroy everything he and his father had built. He had to deal with Montag, and the German knew it. "Where are the paintings?" he asked. Montag eased back in his seat, his face taking on a perfectly relaxed character, his hands clasped together as if in prayer. "For the moment that's not important. You may be sure that I have them."

"You won't tell me?"

"Does a magician reveal his sleights of hand?"

"I am not in the business of buying illusions."

"As I am well aware. So from my magician's hat, I shall produce for you, within three days' time, a painting that will convince you. Would Watteau's *Lute Player* suffice?"

Montag couldn't have chosen more astutely. Rostand knew it well. The *Lute Player* had been one of Naomi Drach's most treasured possessions. She always said it held a special magic for her. André, dazed, his stomach churning, envisioned the painting now as clearly as he did the day Naomi had first shown it to him. It was a scene peopled by a group of eighteenth-century ladies and gentlemen on an outing for the afternoon. They had picnic baskets and were listening to a lute player in pink tights. He could almost hear the subtle phrasing of the tenor, surely he was a tenor, blending with the soft voices of the ladies surrounding him. They apparently had no cares, and yet they seemed so sad . . .

"I said, will that suffice?" Montag repeated.

"Is the Drach Collection intact?" André snapped.

"Entirely."

"And the other collections?"

"Also intact."

"Which ones?"

Montag intoned the names. "Rothman, Lévi and Stendhal."

"What about the heirs?"

"There are none. Unfortunately, none survived the war."

"One did."

Montag raised an eyebrow. "You refer to Alex Drach?" he said casually.

André nodded silently. "He has a right to his father's collection."

"I can take care of him."

"Like millions of others during the war?" André said, sardonically.

"Herr Rostand, I beg you. Let us not drag up sins of the past. If we did, you would not fare so well yourself."

André glanced sharply at the German. His brown eyes darkened.

"I'll accept the paintings on one condition. If you refuse you can take them anywhere you like and I will do nothing to stop you."

"I'm not an unreasonable man. What's the condition?"

André leaned forward over the desk, his mouth pursed for a moment, as though he were considering rejecting a thought. Then: "Nothing must happen to Alex Drach. Accidentally or otherwise. If anything—and I mean *anything*—does, I shall hold you personally responsible. Even if it means the absolute destruction of my own reputation, I'll expose you."

Montag's small nostrils wrinkled as though a foul odor had crept into the room. He thought a moment, then said, "What is Drach to you?"

André did not reply. "Once was enough. I've lived for forty years with the memory of Monte Carlo. Nothing can change that. You will agree to my terms or no deal."

"It's clear, my friend, we have need for each other. You have me by the throat, and I have you. If either of us goes, we both go."

"Then you agree?"

"Agreed!"

Montag's face had the look of a contented piglet suckling at a sow's teat. "Agreed!" he repeated. "Drach will be left unharmed. But I warn you, Herr Rostand, he is a threat to both of us."

"Let me worry about that," Rostand said quietly.

"But how will we move the paintings from their, uh, location? He'll learn about them eventually, surely?"

"Rostand International enforces total discretion. Some of my clients have collections hidden away that no one knows about, not even their own families. Anonymity can be assured."

"Then there's nothing to arrange but the method of delivery and the price: inconsequential details, between us."

Rostand allowed the contempt he felt to surface in his voice. "I'll give you fifty percent of their market value on a painting-to-painting basis. As for the method of delivery, I leave that to you. That's your problem."

Montag took on a bubbly cheerfulness. "I hadn't expected such generosity from you, Herr Rostand. I accept!" Montag stood abruptly. "You'll have the Watteau in three days. A courier, Brother Baruch, will bring it to you. When you see it, you'll agree the work is no illusion." Montag walked to the door, opened it, but before leaving, said, "You're a sensible man, Herr Rostand. You always have been." Then he left.

For a moment, André stood motionless behind the desk, without thinking. Then he became conscious of the Quare clock chiming the fifth hour. He looked at the clock, a bar mitzvah gift from his mother on his thirteenth birthday—the day he supposedly became a man—then walked to the table beside the fire, took a cigarette from the silver box and lit it. He had given up smoking years before—thirty-five years to be exact—but he needed something in him now to fill the empty space in his chest. He inhaled deeply, exhaled and watched the smoke rise toward the strapwork ceiling. Then, he walked to the window and watched the passersby, bundled in heavy coats and boots, trundle past the gallery.

He saw Montag too, as he left the building, cross the street and disappear around the corner of Madison Avenue.

He loathed the man! He felt such loathing that it rose inside him like a wave of hot air bursting at his temples.

André puffed on the cigarette. "Be calm," he told himself. There was no other way.

Or was there? He could pull out, risk letting the ring have the paintings and take the consequences. He could go to Interpol. He could tell them what he knew about Montag and let the Nazi spill his guts. But then, the gallery would not survive. That above all was essential. There *was* no other way. Montag had him. Just like the first time, in Monte Carlo, forty years ago.

PART FOUR

---◆---

1940

It began on Friday, May 10, 1940, when the air raid sirens in Paris wailed in earnest. On that day, a force unprecedented in warfare for its size, concentration and fire power swept across the Rhine. Within seven days the German juggernaut reached the channel, cutting off the Allied armies to the north. The Wehrmacht then turned south to launch a massive assault on the Somme. Along a four-hundred-mile front that stretched across France from the channel to the upper Rhine, 143 German divisions faced a weakened and demoralized French force deployed for the final defense of Paris, now ripe for the taking.

That same night, while the German army advanced toward Paris, André Rostand sat in the finely furnished conference room of Rostand et Fils, the family's art gallery, waiting for the members of the Jewish Art Council to arrive. He had agreed to hold the hastily called meeting at the gallery to discuss the German threat.

Outside he could hear armored personnel carriers moving through the streets with the remnants of the French army. It was hopeless. The reserves, consisting mostly of young boys in oversized uniforms, were being marched in ragged columns to board trains that would carry them to slaughter. Jane and Philip were in America and he had cabled them not to return.

Restless and glum, André gazed at an exquisite Fragonard in an elaborate gilt frame that hung on the opposite wall. It was a reminder to him that thirty more Fragonards and thousands of other masterpieces worth millions lay downstairs in the vaults of the cathedral-like gallery. In the forty years since his father had founded Rostand et Fils, the name of "Rostand" had become synonymous with the acquisition and sale of the world's finest art.

With drive, daring and an unerring eye his father, Aaron Rostand, together with his mother, Anna, had parlayed the two-hundred-franc purchase of Vermeer's *Tavern Maid* into a gigantic collection that rivaled even that of the Louvre.

His parents had begun modestly, working side by side. Each had his own desk. On Aaron's large, leather-topped desk there was nothing but a magnifying glass. Everything else was in his head. He never read a book about art. His discerning eye was all that he needed. Anna's desk was smaller. She was the one who began compiling names, locations and provenance of every painting that they saw.

They began buying. They bought everything, whole collections, taking risks that other dealers never contemplated. Often they bought beyond their means. They did not concern themselves with the price of an object. They asked only one queston: was it quality? The Rostands knew, given time and patience—ten or twenty years if necessary —that quality always sold.

By the time André was old enough to go to school, his father's clients numbered amongst the most famous names in Europe and America: David-Weill, the Duke of Gloucester, Rothschild, Rockefeller, Palmer, Gardner, Havemeyer, Morgan, Frick, Rothman, Lévi, Schloss, Mellon and, until the revolution of 1917, the Tsar and Tsarina of Russia.

André was brought up living and breathing art. When most boys his age were playing with tin soldiers, he was trailing after his father making the rounds of museums, galleries and private collections. From childhood, he had a finely developed eye for quality, beauty, taste, the finest in art.

As André grew older, he began working in the gallery. He was given an office adjoining that of his parents and was consulted about the paintings they bought and sold. It was obvious, however, that he had not inherited his father's personality. While Aaron was quiet and sensitive, with an artist's temperament, André was just the opposite: tough, single-minded and pragmatic.

When Aaron was presented with a painting and asked about it, he examined it like a scholar. He would analyze its provenance, the artist who painted it, the period, the quality of the workmanship, the character and ideas it contained.

André, on the other hand, used his eye for a different purpose. He haunted the auction rooms and galleries, assessing the market, learning about important collectors, their habits, and what they preferred to buy. He was always looking for the unappreciated Old Master that could be bought for very little, and later sold for much more to another generation of collectors.

For that reason he had always been an enigma to his parents. While the Rostands had always been a close family, André had remained apart, a loner, a world unto himself. Not even Jane had been able to bridge that gap.

Now, at thirty with his parents dead, he realized sadly how much he had needed them. And how much they had taught him. He remembered his first day of true freedom. It was in 1924, at a sale at the Hôtel Drouot, old and overstuffed even then. André had sat beside his elegant, moustachioed father and listened to him explain the techniques of bidding. He had been entranced by auctions right from the start, the excitement, the competition, and game of it all. That day, the auctioneer was offering a group of Georges Braque's early Cubist paintings. His father, who bought only what he liked, was reluctant to make an offer. Aaron thought very little of Braque.

For that matter, André agreed with his father. The Cubist held no appeal for him either. But he knew, even then, that there would be a market, that a Braque would be a profitable investment. They had argued about that, but his father refused to bid. Finally, in frustration, André started bidding on his own against several well-known dealers. In the end he outbid them all. When the sale was gaveled to a close the Braque was his for two thousand francs. Now, years later, Rostand International still owned that painting and a score more by the same artist. They were worth their weight in gold.

After the sale was closed, father and son walked homeward together. There was a long silence, and then Aaron said, in a voice of great seriousness, "Now that you've bought boldly, let's see if you can sell patiently." André had never forgotten that advice.

By six, the conference room began to fill up. André moved through the room greeting those invited. Great pains had been taken to ensure the secrecy of the meeting. He had requested each man to come alone and on foot. A phalanx of limousines in front of the gallery would have attracted too much attention. There were German spies everywhere.

Those who assembled with him that night were distinguished men of great power and wealth, representatives of some of the most respected Jewish families in France. They were men who carried enormous responsibility and who, by dint of hard work or genius, had acquired great influence in every aspect of French life. Like the Rostands, over a few generations, each man's family had gone from the poverty of the ghetto to the pinnacle of fortune.

The first to arrive had been Marcel Lévi, chief executive of Société Lévi Industrielle, the nation's largest textile manufacturer. A handsome, gray-haired man, Lévi was meticulously dressed and groomed. As soon as he entered the room, he went straight to André and embraced him. "You are standing, my boy, where your father would have stood."

As the others arrived, the ritual was repeated. Each man solemnly paid his respects to André, who stood beside a rosewood table on which a buffet supper was spread. They then gathered in clusters to discuss the latest news from the Northern Front and wait for the meeting to begin.

André knew each of these men well, but he stood alone. Though they respected his brilliance, he did not inspire the same kind of affection or confidence in these men as his father had. For years, they had been Aaron's friends. To them the old man was more than just an art dealer. He was their teacher, their guide through the wondrous mysteries of art.

Minutes later, Paul Drach arrived, the last to walk into the conference room. André noticed expressions of curiosity on the faces of the others. He had warned Paul that this might happen. These were crusty old men, unsure of an outsider. However, André's plan required a man the Germans wouldn't touch. Was there such a man? Who knew?

After general greetings, Paul joined André at the buffet table. "I couldn't help being late," Paul apologized. "Naomi seems strangely worried about leaving for Monte Carlo."

"It's the invasion, the uncertainty."

"I know," said Paul. He looked around the room, then asked, "Is the ship ready?"

André nodded. "I've chartered the *Camargue*. It's due to sail in approximately four weeks. That gives us just enough time." They were interrupted by a waiter with a tray of glasses. André brushed aside the tray and told the waiter to leave the room. Then he turned to Paul. "We must begin the meeting," he whispered. "Stay calm. It isn't going to be easy."

André assumed a pleasant smile and moved to the head of a long mahogany conference table at the side of the room. It was the signal for the meeting to begin.

The others took their places along the length of the table. André began. "I won't waste your time, gentlemen. We all know why we're here. Soon the Germans will be in Paris. Have no illusions. We won't be able to look to the French for protection. We're going to have to protect ourselves." He paused. No one else spoke. Around the table there was a general nod of agreement.

As André was about to continue, Eugène Stendhal broke in, "Before we go any further, I'd like to know what Paul Drach is doing here. He's not one of us."

Drach winced and looked at André. There was a moment of embarrassed silence and then André stood. "I'm the one to explain that. I asked Paul to come. It seems to me each of us has two alternatives, either to hide the collections inside France or ship them out. What you decide is up to each of you. I'll tell you frankly, I have already made arrangements to ship my paintings to America. I have a ship chartered in Marseilles. I can make arrangements for you to share it. On the other hand, if you decide to keep your collections here, you'll need somebody—a Gentile—who can be trusted to take care of them if you yourselves are forced to leave France. Because Paul is not Jewish he may be better able to protect the hidden collections."

There was a buzz of conversation around the table. Marcel Lévi was the first to respond. "I understand that if the Germans occupy France, Jews will have very little mobility, but, how shall I put it, how can we be sure Drach will be any safer a caretaker than we ourselves?"

Paul Drach looked down the table at Lévi and smiled ruefully. Then he stood and addressed the gathering. "I appreciate your misgivings, Monsieur. We're all intelligent enough not to take such remarks personally.

"In these times we can be sure of nothing. My family is also vulnerable to the Nazis in some part. I've already hidden my paintings. My wife, Naomi de Montrose, is a Jew. She will be leaving Paris in a short time. But I choose to stay to help you. Someone must."

André glanced around the table. There were signs of recognition at the name De Montrose.

Paul continued, "Most of you will eventually have to leave. If I understand what is happening in Europe today, you're all in jeopardy. You'll need someone here to look after things, and I shall be happy to do whatever I am asked."

"Of course, gentlemen," André broke in, "you have another option. You can ship your paintings out with the Rostand collection. We're dealers, not collectors, but we would consider buying your art at a reasonable price." From the dark looks on one or two faces, André realized he would not have many takers. He went on at once. "But, for those of you who decide to keep your collections in France, I can say that I've known Paul Drach since he was a boy. He's like a brother to me. I trust him implicitly."

René Cardozo, slim and lively, with quick darting eyes, stood abruptly. "That's good enough for me, if the son of Aaron Rostand says so. I'll keep my paintings here. I'm not going to sell them, nor am I going to see them shot out of the water." There was a murmur of agreement from Braci and Schloss.

"But how are we going to arrange this?" Rothman asked.

André, exchanging a glance with Paul, spoke with authority. "For your protection, each of you must decide where to conceal your collection. Each of you will tell me and Paul. We'll be the only ones to know. We shall tell no one else. Only one man in Europe, and one man in America, will know the secret in a month's time, besides yourself." He paused. There were nods around the table. "The choice is yours. I can think of no better way."

Left alone after the meeting, André and Paul locked up the gallery and walked down the darkened streets of Paris toward Rostand's home. The air was fresh, a perfect spring night except for the ominous tension that enveloped the city.

"You handled it well," Paul said.

André shook his head. "They should have accepted my offer. Their collections would be safer at sea than here, no matter how well we hide them."

"It's too desperate a gesture for them to take. They cannot even conceive that they'll really have to leave. They're still clinging to some imaginary hope that the Nazis won't really harm them."

"They're fools. I've sent Jane and Philip to New York. Your wife is going to Monte Carlo. Anyone with an ounce of sense would leave now."

André, who had inherited his father's cherrywood cane, gripped it as he walked down the Rue de Rivoli toward the Place de la Concorde. He looked at Paul. "Do you think it's safe for you to stay behind? Perhaps you should go with Naomi."

Paul smiled. "They can't hurt me," he scoffed. "But they could destroy you. No, better that you leave things here to me."

André raised his eyes in mock exasperation. "You've always taken care of things, Paul. Ever since I've known you. Remember, at school, the soccer matches we played. You always protected my wing when I couldn't handle the defense."

"Yes, but you were a more clever player than I was."

André laughed. Paul had always been gracious that way. They had met when André was fourteen and Paul sixteen, the fall of 1925.

Both were students at the Lycée Henri Quatre and both were trying out for the school's soccer team.

Issued with a bright red jersey and shorts for the first day's scrimmage, André had walked onto the field just as the other boys were choosing sides. He took his place among the other boys not yet chosen and waited.

One after another, the other boys had been selected while André remained on the sidelines. He had thought that perhaps he was too small, or too young, or not experienced enough. At one point, he had heard a boy on the field say something about the "juif," but André had not known that it had anything to do with him.

Nevertheless, after all the others had been chosen, he was still waiting on the sidelines, alone. The humiliation was unbearable. Inside, he had fumed with shame and indignation. To hide his anger and embarrassment, he had concentrated on the clump of grass he had dug up with the toe of his scuffed shoe.

After both sides had been chosen, the others had directed their attention away from him. They had picked positions and formed a pregame huddle. André, his face burning, had turned his back on them and started to leave the field.

He had reached the far side of the pitch when he suddenly heard his name being called. A tall boy, with blond hair, was waving him back to the field. Back on the playing field, the tall boy had frowned, but in a friendly voice had said, "You're small, but look strong. Play forward!"

André realized that he had not really been needed that afternoon, but he had played, and played well. More than that, he had made a friend, the blond boy named Paul Drach.

From that day, they were inseparable. In almost every way, beginning with their physical appearance, they were different, and yet they always got along well. In contrast to André's dark solidity, Paul was tall, slender, blue-eyed and fair. While André wore dark suits, Paul preferred white flannels. André was intense and distant with others, Paul was sociable and extroverted, drawing his younger friend out, encouraging him to go to parties and meet girls.

Over the years since, in the most natural way, and without a word being spoken, Paul and André had been like brothers.

"Let's not talk about it," Paul said, breaking into André's thoughts. "Have you ever known me to do anything I didn't want to do?"

André shook his head, smiled and then fumbled for his key. He was home. "We'll get together tomorrow to plan the next few weeks. There's a great deal to be done."

Paul nodded, shook André's hand and walked on. As André opened his front door, unnoticed in the shadows across the street was the waiter who had served the canapés and drinks at the meeting. He didn't remain there long. A moment later, he walked back up the street, found a kiosk and placed a call to his immediate superior in the Abwehr.

On the eleventh of June an early morning rain fell over Paris, leaving the streets black and shiny. André Rostand's four-door black Daimler sedan, its rear window shades pulled low and its horn bleating, threaded through the chaotic traffic impeded by refugees streaming south. In the back seat, separated from his driver by a thick glass partition, André once again checked his watch. It was 8:46. He had exactly fourteen minutes to catch the P.L.M. train for Marseilles. Anxiously, he began rubbing his fingers over the gray velour armrest, then caught himself and stopped. Nervous habits in others irritated him. He detested them in himself.

He raised the right window blind, lit a cigarette, and surveyed the snarl of traffic. Since the Germans had broken through at Sedan four weeks ago, the flight from Paris had swollen from an orderly trickle to an uncontrollable flood. Everything with wheels was being used in the exodus: dilapidated jalopies, trucks, fire engines, swarms of bicycles, horse-drawn carriages, even wheelbarrows and baby carriages. The fall of Paris was imminent.

With five minutes to spare, the Daimler rolled to a stop before the Gare de Lyon. André hurriedly left his car and ran into the iron vaulted station. The chauffeur, carrying his suitcases, scurried after him.

André went directly to platform 4, where the Paris-Lyon-Mediterranean train, belching steam and smoke, stood waiting. Pushing through the crowd, he was halfway down the platform when he spotted Naomi and Paul Drach standing next to the first-class coach at the head of the train.

Naomi Drach, clutching a tiny brown dachshund in her arms, waved and came running toward him. "André!" she shouted above the din. "I thought I'd have to leave without you. Thank God, you've arrived."

For the first time in days André smiled. Somehow, Naomi always managed to cheer him. She was wearing a dark green Chanel suit with a beige silk blouse open at the neck. Her skin, smooth and creamy, was the color of bronzed ivory, her hair pitch-black and shiny like ebony. The hair, very long when free, had been fastened tightly around her head with tortoise-shell combs. On her breast was pinned one piece of jewelry, the only one she ever wore, a gold filigree bee with diamonds.

"It's total chaos out there," André said. "We practically crawled here. . . ."

They hurried back down the platform to Paul, who was passing the last of Naomi's cases through an open window in the first-class coach. Inside the compartment, Jocko Corvo had placed the others on the rack above the six empty seats.

"You must have some very good friends somewhere to get a compartment all to yourself," Paul said, shaking André's hand.

"A sympathetic and influential client," André said with a grin. "Of course, I had to buy all six places." He directed his driver, who stood behind him to carry the bags into the compartment, then took an envelope from his pocket and handed it to Paul. "This is the list of repositories."

Paul nodded gravely and tucked the envelope inside his tan double-breasted jacket. Naomi, her green eyes puffy and swollen from crying, looked up at her husband. "I'm frightened, Paul. Please be careful."

Paul embraced her. "Don't worry," he said, "I'll be fine. In the meantime, André will look after you."

Jocko, who had been standing a few feet away, approached Naomi to say good-bye. From behind his back he presented her with a single pink rose. "For you, Madame," he said, in a rough Corsican accent.

"Jocko! How lovely." Naomi's face brightened.

"I grew it myself," Jocko said proudly.

For André, it was a painful exchange. He wondered how Paul had the strength to send her away. She was everything any man could want. And yet, curiously, she had always made André feel uncomfortable and off balance. She was a complex and interesting combination; carefree and almost reckless on the surface, yet underneath, a shrewd and serious woman.

The bell signaling the P.L.M.'s departure rang out. Along the platform, the conductors shouted, *"En voiture,"* and those passengers not yet on the train scrambled to their places.

André and Paul embraced. "Be careful," André said. "No heroics. *D'accord?"* Then to Jocko, "That goes for you too."

Jocko grinned. "I'm not the type, Monsieur."

Paul turned to Naomi. For a few seconds they held each other. The dachshund, still in her arms, struggled between them, then leaped up and started licking Paul's face.

"See, Bonnie wants to stay with you, like me," Naomi said, tears welling in her eyes. She pushed the dog into Paul's arms, turned and boarded the train.

André followed her to the compartment and from the window they both watched as the head conductor waved a green lantern for the "All clear." "Take care of Monsieur Drach," Naomi shouted to Jocko.

The Corsican, standing no taller to Paul than shoulder height, bobbed his head sadly. Everyone's voice was then lost in the blast of the locomotive's whistle. The train jerked forward and slowly began to pull out of the station.

André and Naomi remained at the window of their compartment, waving to the two figures standing side by side on the crowded platform. Jocko, holding Bonnie, was smiling sadly. Paul, his long, lanky body setting him off from the rest of the crowd, doffed his white straw Panama hat in farewell. It would be the last time André would ever see him.

That night, as the train lumbered south toward Marseilles, the compartment was pitch dark. André thought of Naomi stretched out on the upholstered banquette across from him. She was sleeping soundly.

They had arranged themselves in the carriage as if it were a new home. Naomi had packed a large picnic basket with enough food for three days. The run to Marseilles normally took half that time, but the rail lines were in terrible shape and all transport heading for the northern front had the right-of-way.

Earlier in the day, from the corridor they had heard a group of wounded soldiers singing "If Only You Were Here," having already been through "The Jugs Have Ears," and several rounds of "The Marseillaise."

At midday, while the train waited on a siding, they had raised the table from underneath the window and laid out a lunch of pâté, cold roast chicken, cheese, fruit and a bottle of red wine. Were it not for the occasional swooping Messerschmitts André and Naomi would have almost forgotten the war. The small precious bottle of cognac he had brought with him had helped alleviate the tension they both felt about leaving Paris. She had complimented him on his choice of cognac, a fine 1919 Château de Fontipot.

Cognac, he explained, was a passion with him. Only the finest would do. Each year, at Christie's sale of vintage wines, he had an agent in London buy a dozen bottles of Napoleon 1811 brandy for him. He knew, of course, that Napoleon 1811 had absolutely nothing to do with Napoleon or the year 1811. It had actually only been aged in casks since 1903, a fact that he and his agent kept to themselves. Instead of keeping it, however, he distributed most of the cognac to his clients, a select group of collectors who depended on him to provide them with fine paintings as well as fine cognac. As with the art they bought, most of his clients did not savor the taste of the cognac as much as its pedigree.

Naomi listened to all this with a slightly jaundiced look on her face. "Is that how you manage to be such a success, by exploiting other people's sense of their own importance?"

He leaned forward on the banquette and laughed. "It helps," he said. "That's how one survives."

"You've survived very well, André."

"Well enough," he said shrugging his shoulders, feeling a little embarrassed at his own pretentiousness.

As the hours went by, André was surprised to find he was talking abut himself rather intimately. Perhaps because it was wartime, or because of the proximity they shared as travelers. For whatever reasons, reasons he did not then want to analyze, he had spent hours talking about his work, the death of his parents, his son Philip, and the nagging fear he had about losing his collection on the *Camargue*.

While Naomi slept, André left the compartment and picked his way along the corridor through suitcases, satchels and sleeping bodies. At the end of the coach, he opened a door and stepped out onto the tiny space between the two cars. Outside the air was cool and the noise deafening. He withdrew a cigarette from a silver case and cupping his hands, lit it with a black onyx lighter. He was disturbed.

He had been too open, too intimate with Naomi. He liked being with her too much. There was no point in deceiving himself any longer. He wanted her, had always wanted her, ever since he had met her as Paul's wife.

That's what was bothering him, why he had always been so un-comfortable around her, especially when Jane was not present. The fact that they were both married didn't trouble him. Other women had often frequented his bed. As an art dealer, he bought and sold beauty. The possession of anything or anyone was never absolute. Marriage? It was simply a convention.

But the fact that Naomi was married to Paul Drach did matter. No matter what happened, he would have to guard the feelings he har-bored for her.

André returned to the compartment and quietly resumed his place on the banquette. He stared out at the darkness, estimating they were a few hours north of Lyon.

"Is everything all right?" Naomi's voice was soft and deep from sleep.

"Fine. I just went out for a cigarette. Sorry I woke you."

"I slept long enough." There was a brief silence. "Talking in the dark is like talking to yourself. Strange, don't you think?"

"Yes. It's because you don't see the other person's reaction. It's safer."

"Do you ever talk to Jane in the dark?"

André thought he detected more than curiosity in the question. He wondered whether the darkness concealed anything in her face. "Why do you ask?"

"Because today you didn't even mention her name. Not once." There was silence. "You're not happy together, are you?" Naomi asked.

"You're a perceptive woman."

"Not really. It's obvious. You never look at each other, never touch each other. You treat each other like . . ."

"Like strangers?"

Naomi did not respond. Instead she asked, "What do you think of Paul and me?"

André hesitated. He wasn't sure whether he wanted to know the answer. "I can't say," he said casually. "I presume you're very happy together."

"We are, in a way."

He had heard the words she had spoken, but he wasn't sure what they meant. "That's a provocative thing to say," he said.

"It's meant to be."

André let the moment pass. The clatter of the train's wheels filled the void. He found himself remembering the way Paul and Naomi looked together. Nothing indicated a problem in their marriage, nor had Paul ever said anything to him. Had he missed something?

Finally Naomi's answer came. "You're Paul's oldest friend. You know him, perhaps, in some ways better than I. But you're not a woman. Do you understand?"

"Are you telling me that there's something *wrong* with Paul?"

"No. Not that way." She paused. "It's hard to explain. I love him and he loves me, but he treats me like a work of art rather than like a woman. I feel like something hanging on the walls, something he values more than anything else, but still, just one of his objects. Do you know what I'm saying?"

"I don't think I do."

"I didn't really expect you to." Her voice was hard. "I'm sorry I burdened you."

"You haven't. I just never imagined . . ." André didn't want to go further. Already it had gotten out of hand. On impulse, he said, "Perhaps we should get some sleep."

"Is the price of truth too steep?" she asked, sardonically.

"Sometimes, more costly than a lie." Then, in a low voice, he said, "Good night."

Two weeks passed. In that time, Paris had been occupied, an armistice signed, the government of Vichy established and André and Naomi had fallen in love.

It was late afternoon and golden flecks of late afternoon sunlight splashed through the latticed windows of the royal suite in the Pavillon, the Principality of Monaco's most exclusive hotel. André Rostand, halfway between sleep and wakefulness, stretched out across the large double bed and slowly became aware of a flat, officious voice coming from the hotel garden. It was the voice of a Radio Vichy newscaster announcing the latest dispatches from the office of Marshal Henri-Philippe Pétain, the newly installed premier of France.

"The first quarter's trade balance continues to improve despite . . ."

"Last night, in honor of the German High Command, a dinner . . ."

"Today it has been confirmed that representatives of the French and German governments will meet. . . ."

Typical fare these days, André grumbled. France is giving dinner parties for its conquerors. Well, he wasn't going to give anything to the Nazis. His collection was safe, on its way to America. He had personally supervised the loading, had accompanied Naomi to Monte Carlo and would himself soon have to leave via Lisbon for New York. He was getting out while there was still time. He'd be in New York in time to see the unpacking of his treasures.

André stretched. The sensation of his bare skin rubbing across the fresh linen sheets soothed him. He opened his eyes, sat up and blinked into the sunlight. He hadn't felt this good in months.

He rolled out of bed, wrapped himself in a towel and walked out onto the balcony. Looking down, he saw Naomi in the garden. She was drinking a cup of tea while gazing at the harbor two hundred feet below.

André savored the sight of her. With the sun upon her, he could see the line of her hips, her long legs and lovely, full-curved figure through the white batiste dress. Her hair was loose, falling free over her bare shoulders. He wanted to call to her, but decided against it. During the past two weeks they had gone through a great deal together, sharing everything, everything but the splendid pleasure of the bed. That they had avoided, pretending the conversation they'd had on the train had never taken place, yet knowing they wanted each other desperately.

André returned to the room, took a cigarette from a pack on the bedside table, lit it and enjoyed the smoke filling his lungs. He exhaled. The smoke curled upward through the sun streaks. He walked back to the balcony, but Naomi was gone. Probably changing for dinner, he thought.

A few minutes later, there was a soft knock on the door. Assuming it was the chambermaid coming to turn down the bed, André shouted through the door that everything in the room was all right. Again, there was a knock. He put on a dressing gown and opened the door. Naomi was in the hallway.

"Are you going to let me stand out here the entire evening?" she said smiling.

"Of course not," André said, opening the door wide. He stepped aside as she entered the room and closed the door. He knew why she had come, yet he was still unsure what to do. He walked across the room away from her and stubbed out his cigarette in an ashtray resting on the chest of drawers. "Do you want a drink?" he asked.

"No, thank you."

She had changed into a lounging robe of pale green. It accentuated her eyes beautifully, André thought.

"Were you sleeping?" Naomi asked, looking at the rumpled bed.

"Until that radio blasting in the garden woke me. . . . You'd think they'd have more consideration."

"André, you wouldn't be happy if you had nothing to complain about."

He laughed. "You know me too well, Naomi."

"Perhaps," she said playfully. Then, more seriously, she asked, "Do you think you know me very well?"

"Sometimes I think I do. Other times . . ." He broke off and shrugged. She was quiet for a moment. Her face took on a troubled look and then in a sad voice she said, "I wish you didn't have to go away."

This is madness, André thought. He was angry, not at her but at himself. Impulsively, he asked, "Any word from Paul?"

"None."

"That's not good. I expected word from him by now."

"If he were in trouble Jocko knows how to find us."

"Of course, you're right." André smiled. "Is anything else the matter?" he asked.

"On the contrary, I've never felt happier."

"Then why the concerned look?"

"Isn't that evident?" she replied, color running to her cheeks.

The simplicity of the declaration overwhelmed him. He said nothing.

"Do you want me to go?"

André walked toward her. "No, I think . . . I *know* I want you to stay."

He took her hand and led her to the edge of the bed. Slowly, deliberately, he unbuttoned the front of her gown. As it slipped off her shoulders, his gaze shifted from her face to her breasts and down the full line of her body. She reached toward him and pulled at the cord of his dressing gown. He shrugged it off.

They stood looking at each other's bodies, feeling the pleasurable tension grow between them. They smiled and were, in that moment, as close as they had ever been: like two children, in a tent on the beach, undressing for the first time.

André lowered his body onto hers. "You're remarkable," he said.

"I'm frightened."

"Don't be."

She pulled him down. Her lips parted, and as she kissed him he began to feel more relaxed. He began stroking her thighs with the tips of his fingers. He could hardly restrain himself but he waited. Finally, she moved her hips upward, offering herself to him, and as he moved into her, they found each other's rhythm.

Then she pulled back. Sensing her panic, André pressed into her more insistently, assuring her it was all right. And again it was upon them, that spinning dance. She moved her hips up and down, rubbing her breasts against his chest. "No! No!" she cried. "It can't last." She grabbed his forearms and started pushing him away with both hands, but now that they had started he wasn't going to let her stop.

He put his hands under her and grasped the two curves of her bottom. A more intense rush of energy flowed through them. He was losing control. Everything was spinning. The pleasure built and built. They were feeding off each other. And then he felt the spasm between her legs. She moaned, "Give me . . . give me . . ."

He slammed into her, his hands tightening on her buttocks. She moved faster, stroking the hair at the back of his head, then all his weight pressed upon her and he erupted, filling her insides with a hot spurting gush of semen. And then he felt her climax again.

When it was all over, she stared up at him, smiling, her legs still open and drawn back, her knees almost touching her breasts. Then he slipped quietly down beside her, smiled to himself and went to sleep.

An hour later, André woke. He slipped out of Naomi's arms, showered and dressed in a dinner jacket for the evening. He scribbled a note telling her he'd be back to take her to dinner and placed it on the pillow beside her head. He looked down at her. Her face was still and the line of her body beneath the sheets was exquisite. Quietly, he moved to the door and left the room.

It was seven o'clock when he descended the spiral staircase to the hotel's principal gambling room, "La Cuisine." The casino, already crowded, smelled of Havanas and heavy perfumes.

Some months before, in an effort to increase revenues, the Société des Bains-de-Mer had abolished zero from the roulette wheels for a half-hour each night. Predictably, ever since, each evening "La Cuisine" had been packed. The subtle adjustment caused by subtracting the zero had given everyone in Monte Carlo an excuse to gamble.

As André moved through the glittering crowd, he was amused by the fact that a great many Germans and Italians, clearly military, were present in civilian clothes. They may have threatened to occupy Monaco and imprison its prince, but their daring did not extend to violating the casino's prohibition against uniforms. Ordering a glass of champagne from a waiter, the art dealer went to the cashier's desk for plaques amounting to a hundred thousand francs.

A moment later, André found a place at the roulette table beside a moon-faced maharajah who was distributing fifteen green plaques across the checkered velvet. Each plaque represented 20,000 francs.

The silver ball whirled around the polished mahogany wheel, its concave surface reflecting the lights of the crystal chandelier overhead. While the ball stuttered across the notched numbers, André recalled that ten years before, his father had acquired a small Cézanne for less than the amount which the Indian wagered on a single spin. The realization that the Indian could lose many times that amount in the course of an evening, and infinitely more in the space of a week, irritated him. Wealthy himself, André was used to men with fortunes; his father had always brought men of power and wealth into the gallery. But this! This was stupidity!

Rostand placed a 1000-franc plaque on red. Unblinking, the Indian nudged all of his into the black. By now the ball was bouncing crazily.

"Three . . . red," the croupier intoned.

Rostand smiled. "A lucky omen," he thought. The Indian frowned.

For more than an hour, Rostand continued to bet small sums and win, while the Indian countered with massive sums and lost. Although both men were playing against the house, their competition was with each other. André was enjoying the game until a page interrupted the play and handed him an envelope on a silver tray.

Thinking the note to be from Naomi, Rostand opened the envelope and was surprised to find a newspaper clipping. Written in Italian, the item was a paragraph long and the dateline indicated that it was only two days old. It reported that a French freighter, *La Camargue,* had been seized by an Italian gunboat in the vicinity of the Balearic Islands. The ship had been escorted to the Italian port of Civitavecchia and was being held pending a search of its cargo. A diplomatic inquiry was being given "serious consideration" by the

Italian authorities, who would ultimately decide upon the freighter's disposition.

Rostand was stunned. As the page and the maharajah watched, his face flushed and then paled.

"Quite all right, old man?" the maharajah asked, his voice throaty with the tones of Oxford. Looking into the dark and moony face, Rostand was surprised to find concern there.

"Yes. Thank you. I'm fine."

"Shall we continue, then?"

Rostand noticed that the wheel was stilled, the Indian having declined to bet until Rostand did. "I bring you luck," the Indian explained.

Rostand shook his head, apologetically. "I'm sorry," he said. "I seem to be tired."

"Another time, then?"

"Of course." Turning to the waiting page, the art dealer asked who had sent the note. In reply, the boy nodded toward a man with cropped blond hair seated alone at a table near the terrace doors.

"Thank you," André said, handing the boy a fifty-franc plaque. He rose and left the roulette table.

As he approached the table near the terraced doors, the man stood and bowed slightly from the waist. "Hans Montag," he said. *"Bitte.* Sit down, Monsieur Rostand. I can imagine how you feel." André did as Montag instructed. "I've taken the liberty of ordering a cognac for you," Montag said, pushing a snifter across the table toward André.

"Thank you." André raised the glass and inhaled its fruity bouquet. The fumes cleared his head and for the first time he looked at Montag clearly: the pale-blue eyes, the round face, marred by a wine-red birthmark on the right cheek.

"A personal tragedy," Montag said.

For a moment André was confused. Did he mean the birthmark or the *Camargue?* "Yes," André replied. True in either case, he thought.

"But you needn't thank me for the information. You see . . ." Montag paused. He began to massage the birthmark with the tips of his fingers, and then, after a moment, "You see, I was the one responsible for the ship's seizure."

The glass of cognac in André's hand remained suspended at his lips.

"Personally responsible," Montag emphasized.

Still André said nothing. He finished sipping his drink and set the glass down on the immaculate white tablecloth. Across the room, the roulette wheels clattered.

Time, he needed time, he thought. Time to still the fear, to get it under control . . . to think clearly . . . He knew the German wouldn't have come unless he wanted something. What? To gloat? No. Whatever it was, there had to be some way to retrieve the collection. That, no matter what it cost. He remembered something his father had repeated over and over again. When negotiating, always negotiate from strength. Even when you're weak, appear to be strong. It intimidates.

"What do you want?" Rostand demanded.

"Want? I have your paintings, what would I want?"

André sighed, pushed the cognac to the middle of the table, and rose, dropping a blue plaque on the table. "Enjoy them," he said, beginning to walk away.

"Herr Rostand!" Montag called, leaping to his feet. "Herr Rostand, please!"

The art dealer turned and looked at him. "This is a French-speaking country, Monsieur Montag." Glancing around, the German was abashed. A handful of English stared at him with undisguised hostility.

"Could we go to the terrace? Please." Suddenly, the Nazi's voice was abject.

Hesitating for a moment, André walked outside through the doorway to the balcony overlooking the Mediterranean. The night was black and starry. To the east, a small forest fire burned along a mountain ridge, its red light tracing the terrain against the sky. André leaned across the balustrade. A hot, almost suffocating wind, the sirocco, filled his nostrils.

"I asked what you want," he said, looking toward the sea.

The German's tone became businesslike as he tried to conceal his irritation at the Jew's mastery of the situation. "I'm here as the representative of Reichsmarschall Hermann Göring," he said. Unable to see André's face, he could only wonder at the impression this made. "To answer your question, we'd like to make a deal."

André turned and looked at him. "We?"

"The Reichsmarschall would like to make a trade. He doesn't want your paintings."

"Good. Give them back."

"A trade, Herr Rostand. Not philanthropy. As you know, the Führer plans a magnificent museum near his birthplace, at Linz. It will be larger than the Louvre, grander than the Prado. We are talking about a monument to the age."

"A monument to the Führer," André corrected.

"The Führer *is* the age, Herr Rostand." Montag's face was set, but then he smiled faintly. "But this is a business discussion, not a political one. The Reichsmarschall is also interested in art. Very interested. Of course, his interest is tempered by the Führer's own . . . acquisitiveness. It's a delicate matter, but my patron is able to acquire works of importance from time to time."

"Shiploads, even?"

Montag stiffened against his will. "Yes, of course. Which brings me back to the point. If you could help us . . . me locate . . . various collections . . . before Rosenberg does . . ."

"Rosenberg?"

"Reichsleiter Rosenberg is the Führer's envoy in these matters. As you may have gathered, the Führer and the Reichsmarschall have a little competition going between themselves."

"And you're Göring's Rosenberg?"

"That's a way of putting it."

"You mentioned 'various collections' . . ."

"We have certain Paris collections in mind." Hastening over the words, Montag continued, "Old Masters . . . whenever possible. But decadent art, too. The Impressionists, Post-Impressionists. They're useful in obtaining foreign exchange."

"Jewish collections?"

"Yes."

"You realize that I'm Jewish?"

"Yes."

"I see," Rostand said, turning to look at the far-off fire on the mountaintop. There was a long silence before he spoke again. When he did, his voice was tense. "You mentioned what you call 'decadent art'?"

"Yes," Montag said, his voice turning conspiratorial with relief. "You know what I mean."

"I'm not a fool, Monsieur Montag. I know what you mean by 'decadent art.' I was present at the Zurich sale staged by Rosenberg two years ago. I acquired a Picasso there, and a Lautrec as well, for centimes. And I was also present at the bonfire of Impressionists your party members held last year in Stuttgart. Believe me, I know what you like."

"I was hoping we could speak as gentlemen. That you wouldn't get angry."

"I'm not angry."

"But you have no interest in my offer?"

Rostand laughed. "You're a very circumspect man, Herr Montag. Guilt seems to have overcome you. You haven't made an offer."

Becoming irritated by the Jew's sarcasm, Montag spoke icily. "We'll release your collection. . . ."

"The ship."

"We'll release the ship if you help us. We need to know the locations of the following Jewish collections." Taking a list from his pocket, he read the names in a whisper, "Schloss . . . Salomon . . . Arnhold . . . Braun . . . Lévi . . . Bacri Frères . . . Stendhal . . ."

"I have no idea where Salomon's paintings are."

"Société Parisienne Groupe."

"No idea about that either."

"Kalmann. Georges Persiloff."

"I think Kalmann and Persiloff got their paintings out. I don't know where they are."

"But the others?" Montag asked.

"Yes. I know where the others are."

"I have a long list."

"I can see you do."

"It isn't as if these paintings won't be seized, with or without your cooperation, Monsieur Rostand. But you can facilitate matters. It should make no difference to you whether the Reichsmarschall or Rosenberg gets there first. You are safe. You are leaving."

"No difference at all. No."

"Then we have a deal? You'll provide me with the locations?"

"What we're discussing is a collaboration between ourselves," André said.

"*Collaboration* is a harsh word, Herr Rostand."

"Monsieur Montag, as I stand before you, I'm ruined, about to go into exile. At this point in my life, euphemism is a luxury I cannot afford. Clarity is essential. If you and I fail to reach an agreement here, one that is mutually beneficial, neither of us will get anything.

I'll have lost my collection. You, perhaps, will lose your promotion." Montag chuckled, but Rostand cut him off, anger rising in his voice. "You don't expect me to betray my people in the hope that a Nazi will honor an agreement with a Jew, do you? What's to prevent you from seizing *La Camargue* a second time?"

"My word as an S.S. officer."

André smirked. "I need something better than that."

Montag remained silent.

"You mentioned 'decadent art.' How will you sell it? Through what gallery?"

The question nonplussed the German. "We haven't decided yet. We haven't made the confiscations yet."

"Would you be willing to sell them through Rostand et Fils? At a discount, of course. Thirty centimes on the franc, no more. The profits to be divided between ourselves. Let's say you take five percent on each painting sold."

"Yes, but . . . I'm afraid this is impossible, Herr Rostand. You're speaking of Aryanizing the gallery, and the Führer's Decree of 1939 expressly forbids this."

"That, Montag, is a German affair. Surely, somehow, Göring can provide an exemption to the decree, especially in France."

Montag pursed his lips thoughtfully. "I think," he said, "I can persuade the Reichsmarschall to issue an exemption, providing everything else goes as planned. It's only a matter of changing the gallery's ownership on paper, of replacing competent Jews with an approved director, salesmen and so forth."

André glared at Montag. "How very convenient. All right, I have no choice, it seems, except to lose everything. Now, if Rostand et Fils provides an outlet for the paintings you don't want, you'll be more inclined to return the paintings I want, to me."

Montag smiled. "That way everyone benefits, eh, Herr Rostand?"

"Exactly. Now, two more things. Do you have access to a Swiss bank account?"

"It can be arranged."

"Good. You'll need one. Secondly, each of the paintings sold to Rostand et Fils will need proper papers. Their provenance must be clear. Absolutely clear!"

Montag looked at Rostand, surprised.

"Why does that surprise you?" Rostand asked. "Are you so certain of the outcome of the war that you have no regard for what happens after? What do you intend to do, steal from the Jews and simply hand over their treasures to me? I need bills of sale, witnesses. Not a truckful of Gestapo sergeants. You'll have no trouble finding witnesses. Paris is full of ambitious men willing to collaborate."

"What if . . . after the war . . . ?"

"They complain that the sales were forced?" Rostand shrugged. "If the papers are in order, we'll have no problems."

"You're right. I can handle that easily." Montag was excited. The Jew was formidable. No doubt about it.

"As I said," André broke in, "this is an agreement between ourselves. As for Göring, Rosenberg and the others, I have no interest in them except in so far as they're necessary to the agreement you and I make. Now, when I leave here, I don't want to see you again. Ever. You can forward your Swiss account number to me in New York and any necessary communications can be handled through your bank. Understood?"

Montag nodded. André continued, "I assume you can provide safe passage from France for the *Camargue?*"

"Of course. Once you provide me with the locations of the Jewish collections in Paris, the Reichsmarschall will give me considerable authority."

"There is a problem, of course," Rostand continued. "When the collections whose locations I'm about to give you are seized, I don't want the blame! There are very few people who have this information."

Montag smiled. "Like Paul Drach?"

André tried to keep his face impassive, but it was clear that Montag already knew.

"Can you guarantee that no harm will come to anyone?"

"I'm interested only in the art, nothing else!" Montag said, as though offended. "I give you my word as an S.S. officer that no harm will come to anyone."

Both men fell silent, considering the agreement they had made. For André, it was a matter of survival, the family's survival. He was not about to start over again, a refugee in the gutter.

Montag was less philosophical. He anticipated Göring's glee. The agreement they'd reached was a profitable one and, if the Jew had made anything clear, it was that he was a businessman.

While Montag mused, Rostand had been writing. Finally, he

handed the German three small sheets of paper. "Here," he said. "These are the locations."

Montag nodded happily. "I was confident you'd agree. Your ship will be at sea by morning."

The two men looked at each other for some moments, wondering if there was anything else to say. Finally, André shrugged, said "Good-bye," and walked away.

Leaving the terrace without looking behind him, the art dealer walked through "La Cuisine" into the hotel lobby. He climbed the ornate staircase, moving slowly, suddenly tired. Leaning heavily on the polished mahogany banister, he wondered when weakness was considered strength, and strength, weakness. One did, after all, what one had to do. He walked down the long hallway toward his suite, and stopped before a large mirror next to the door. He looked at himself and ran a hand over the side of his head to smooth his ruffled hair. Then he entered the suite.

Naomi, wrapped only in a towel, came toward him. "How did you do?" she asked, smiling.

"I lost everything," he said, his voice hollow.

Naomi looked concerned.

"But I won it all back," he added. "And more."

"I always knew you were a lucky man," she said, letting the towel slip to the floor.

PART FIVE

———◆———

1979

I

Alex breakfasted on grapefruit and black coffee, and lingered over the *International Herald Tribune,* waiting until eleven o'clock before calling the Home Office. When he rang through, neither George Deakin nor Jenner was available; but he was given a message from Deakin that he was to meet him at Jenner's apartment in Albany.

Drach knew about Albany and was surprised to learn that Jenner lived there. He wondered how someone from the Home Office could afford the elegant lodgings there.

Just off Piccadilly, Albany had been built in the late eighteenth century, and converted shortly thereafter into residential chambers for bachelor gentlemen. In the past it had housed such tenants as Gladstone, Macaulay, and Byron.

Albany was no more than ten minutes' walk from Brown's Hotel. Drach made Jenner's apartment in eight. As he approached the four-story edifice, he noticed a police car and ambulance parked at the entrance. With considerable misgivings, he approached the porter, who was chatting with a middle-aged police constable.

The constable stepped forward. "May I have your name, please?"

At that moment Drach knew he would never see Hugh Jenner alive. "Drach," he replied.

"Yes, we've been expecting you. Mr. Deakin is upstairs." Alex accompanied the constable up the two flights to Jenner's apartment.

Deakin, along with several men from the Special Branch, was in the living room. "Ah, Drach, come in," Deakin said. Then nodding to one of the senior inspectors: "This is the man I was telling you about."

The inspector looked up sharply. "I'm Senior Inspector Christopher Stokes. I'd like to ask you a few questions."

Stokes was a short, slight, sand-colored man, with light gingery hair and refined features. Alex thought he was rather young to be an inspector, but then he looked again. Stokes was older than he looked. The fine eyebrows and blond eyelashes gave his face a youthful look, the type that shaved only every other day. "I'm afraid you're too late for your appointment with Mr. Jenner," he said, nodding to a black bag on an ambulance stretcher.

Alex stood still for a moment, then addressed Deakin. "What happened?"

"We're hoping you can tell us," Stokes interjected. "What was your business with Mr. Jenner?"

"Deakin knows," Alex said, abruptly. "Didn't he tell you?"

Stokes withdrew a notepad. "We'd just like to hear it in your own words."

Alex described the telephone conversation he had with Hugh Jenner and explained the purpose of his London visit, to see the painting that had once belonged in his father's collection, Watteau's *Lute Player*.

"Do you see the painting?" Stokes asked.

Alex looked around the room, fascinated for a moment by a painting of a boot graphically crushing a human hand. "It's not in this room. May I have a look around?"

"Deakin knows the painting," Stokes said. "He's inspected the place. The Watteau is missing."

"What happened to it?"

"Damned if I know," Deakin interjected. "It was here a week ago."

"We've alerted Customs and Scotland Yard's Art Squad," Stokes said. "They have a description of the painting. We'll find it. . . ."

". . . If it hasn't already left the country," Drach cut in, unable to hide the cynicism in his voice. He looked at the body-bag. "Natural causes?" he asked.

"Suicide," Stokes replied, jotting something down in his notebook. Then, as an afterthought, he looked up at Drach and said, "Or meant to look that way."

"How was it done?" Alex asked, examining an ivory tusk projecting from the mantelpiece.

"Does it matter?" Stokes asked.

Alex shrugged. "Only to Jenner."

Stokes consulted his notepad. "It was an effective job," he said. "Jenner knew what he was doing. He slashed the tops of both wrists with a razor." Then looking up: "I've seen a lot of botched suicides, all because the poor sods slash the underside of the wrist. It doesn't work very well. No main artery."

Stokes was no fool. Alex wondered if he really thought Jenner was a suicide. He doubted it. "Who found him?" he asked.

Deakin glanced at Stokes. "Go ahead," Stokes said. "We've

checked with Immigration this morning. Drach wasn't in the country when it happened."

Deakin sighed. "When he didn't show up this morning, I phoned. The old boy didn't answer. After that I got on to Stokes."

A detective constable came into the room. "What do I do with the teeth, guv?"

Stokes went across the room and examined the glass containing Jenner's false teeth. "Use the Identikit. The coroner will want to look at them."

Deakin shook his head. "Odd," he said. "Hugh was so vain. I'm surprised he went without his teeth."

"Come in and sit down!" Mrs. Thaw said.

She was a large flabby woman in her mid-fifties seated on a divan, one leg slung across the other, a dimpled elbow resting nonchalantly on the back. She wore a short dress, her chubby legs bare above short white socks and ankle-length boots. Her bright orange hair matched the color of the frosted lipstick covering her mouth.

Alex Drach and George Deakin pulled up chairs in front of a coal fire flickering in the narrow Victorian fireplace. An ornate crystal chandelier overhead dimly lit the room. There was no other light except for the glow cast by flat steel picture lights suspended above a half-dozen paintings around the room.

"I'm terribly sorry to hear about your husband's sudden stroke," Alex said sympathetically. "I very much wanted to speak to him about a painting he sold to a friend of ours."

Mrs. Thaw's heavily made up green eyes frowned. Her gaze wandered to a door behind her. "It couldn't have happened at a worse time."

"Is he very bad?" Deakin asked.

"A vegetable, a bloody vegetable, and we were just beginning to make a go of the business." From a packet of Woodbines, she took a cigarette, inserted it into a thin black holder and lit it. She inhaled deeply on the cigarette and glanced at Alex. "The thing that hurt most, you know, is that he let that painting go for so little. He didn't even know it was a Watteau. He thought it was by one of his followers, Lancret."

"Could you tell us how he acquired it?" Alex asked.

"That was part of it," Mrs. Thaw whined. "A little Italian off the street brought it in. He only wanted a few bob for it. He could hardly speak English. The old fool didn't even bother to have it cleaned."

Alex looked at her intently. "Was it in bad condition?"

"Yellowed, but no flakiness."

"Was it framed when it came in?"

"No, just a stretcher," she replied. Her eyes narrowed. "Why are you asking me all those questions?"

Alex hesitated, then replied, "The painting was stolen." He looked at Deakin and asked, "Anything else?"

Deakin shook his head.

They stood. "One more thing," Alex said. "I wonder if we could see your husband. Just for a minute?"

"Call me Carrot!" She smiled apologetically. "It's a nickname. My hair!"

Drach's eyes widened. "What about it, Carrot?"

"Sure, love, why not. But it won't do much good. He can't speak or, as far as I can tell, understand what's going on around him. He's like a zombie."

Alex and George Deakin followed Carrot through the door at the far end of the room. The darkness inside was total, and they were met by a barrage of odors: must, mildew, body dirt, soiled linen. Carrot stopped and flicked a switch on the door jamb. A watery yellow light wavered overhead. "There he is," she said, pointing to a tiny cadaverous man with unkempt hair sitting in a rocking chair. He did not turn and look at them, he didn't seem to know they were there. He simply rocked, his vacant eyes staring straight ahead.

After a stunned moment Alex walked over to the pathetic creature, bent forward and looked into the man's eyes. "Mr. Thaw," he said. The blankness was absolute.

"God, that was ghastly," Deakin exploded, as they left the gallery on Duke Street. "Two in one day. I need a drink."

"I'd rather be dead," Alex said.

Deakin shivered. "Horrible."

They walked north to Grosvenor Square in bright sunlight. Deakin, his hands clasped behind him, head bowed underneath a bowler hat, was lost in thought. Alex, bareheaded, stuffed his hands into the pockets of his wool-lined trenchcoat and asked, "Tell me more about Jenner. What was he like?"

Deakin chuckled and shook his head. "He was a man who lived in the past. His greatest moments were during the war. He headed a team of Allied Intelligence operators investigating art looting."

"How did he know the Watteau was part of my father's collection?"

"I'm not sure. He just had a phenomenal memory. He saw the painting in the window of Thaw's gallery and recognized it as the Drach Watteau."

"I see," Drach said. "Did he ever mention a man named Montag?"

"Not that I recall."

They were halfway across Grosvenor Square. Alex stopped and walked across the street to where an old man in a tattered ankle-length coat was selling flowers from a pushcart. Selecting a dozen white roses, Alex paid the vendor, then returned to the square and handed them to Deakin. "Here," he said. "I've got to catch a plane. Perhaps you could see that these get to Mrs. Thaw."

II

TWA Flight 703 from London swept over Yankee Stadium, banked steeply, and circled to approach Kennedy Airport from the south. A sudden drop in altitude lifted Alex's stomach disagreeably, causing an unwelcome moment of discomfort that showed on his face. Two rows in front of him, he noticed a pretty blond flight attendant who seemed amused at his distress. Drach smiled weakly, tried to appear blasé, then, with an embarrassed shrug, looked away.

Alex felt a sense of weariness as he glanced about the lounge of the 747. He'd been in the air for more than six hours and felt drained. He had politely refused the dismal meal the stewardess had offered, tried to sleep through an even more dismal film, and finally occupied his time leafing through a stack of depressing news magazines.

The run to Paris was supposed to have been a holiday. Hell of a holiday! He still hadn't fully absorbed the impact of the events of the past two days. Death seemed to be all around him. The horrible agony of his father's suicide—or murder. Jenner's death. Thaw's living death. His own near-miss.

As the 747 touched down, the plane lurched and he received another involuntary jolt to his stomach. At the gate, he stood and took his trenchcoat down from the overhead compartment, then walked to the front of the plane, where he nodded cordially to the pretty blond flight attendant.

"Did you enjoy the flight, sir?"

Drach grinned. "I always like to fly, but not in airplanes," he replied.

The flight attendant looked confused. "Have a good day," she said, automatically. She levered the door open and Alex deplaned into the terminal.

Clearing Customs, he remembered the first time he had landed in New York, when he was fourteen. Jocko had decided that he was to grow up in America under the tutelage of another family, called Rostand.

Alex had hated the thought of leaving the Corvos, but Jocko insisted. Letters had been exchanged and all the necessary documents, immigration visas and passports had been obtained. It had been a difficult decision for Jocko and Louisa to make, but it was an opportunity Alex could not refuse.

Rostand was a man with a "big stomach," meaning, Jocko explained, that he was a very powerful man. Alex would learn what it was like to be an American, to speak another language, to go to school and better himself. Monsieur and Madame Drach would have wanted it that way.

And so on the appointed day, twenty-three years before, Alex Drach left Pigalle. In his coat pocket he carried a letter, written by Jocko Corvo, addressed to André Rostand. In his rough Corsican accent Jocko had read the letter to Alex the night before he left.

Cher Monsieur,

Thank you for your letter and tickets for Alex. He is a very fine boy, always loyal and obedient to Louisa and me.

I feel great sadness in my heart to see Alex go so far away. Although he's a man now, I still feel for him as a boy. As you have said, we know that it is the best thing for him. He will become an American, a citizen of a very rich country, full of great opportunities. Alex is a smart boy and a hard worker. He will not disappoint you.

Madame Corvo and I wish also to give thanks to your wife, Madame Rostand, for her generosity in helping to give Alex a new home.

As I have already written, before she died, Madame Drach spoke highly of you. She was not mistaken in her faith that you would always be willing to help.

In closing, through Alex I extend my hand. May God bless you and your family.

Respectfully,
Jocko Corvo

The day Alex left Jocko and Louisa had been the saddest, most frightening, loneliest day of his life. Since then, he had always measured personal pain in terms of that parting.

Over the years, his relationship with André Rostand had been respectful but distant. He had never felt the kind of affection for Rostand that he had for Jocko.

Alex was met at Idlewild Airport that summer by a thin-faced man with wire-rimmed glasses and a friendly smile. His name was Ray Fuller. After retrieving Alex's two battered leather suitcases, Fuller escorted him to a black Cadillac limousine parked in front of the terminal.

Alex never forgot that drive into Manhattan. The city rose up across the Harlem River like a row of dragon's teeth. Fuller took him by the old Plaza Hotel, pointed out the fountain and the hansom cabs lined up around it. As the late afternoon sun set he was driven through Central Park, past the zoo and through a mass of trees onto Park Avenue and to Rostand International.

There he remembered the cordon of attendants that decorously parted as Fuller led him across the marble floor, into the elevator, and up a number of floors to that first meeting with André Rostand.

For weeks, Alex had dreaded that moment, but when it finally came he was not afraid. He approached the tall elegantly dressed man with large dark eyes and graying hair and was surprised by the way the man spoke such impeccably refined French. For some reason Alex had always imagined Rostand as an American.

Alex remembered André warmly shaking his hand, and then, for a long time it seemed, staring at him. It seemed to him at the time that Rostand was more uncomfortable about the meeting than he was. Then his *patron*—Alex had always viewed Rostand as a *patron*—made the rather unusual gesture of offering the boy a cigar. He declined the cigar, and responded to the usual kind of formal questions. Rostand asked about the Corvos, about the trip and what expectations he had for himself in America. The exchange, which went smoothly enough, ended with Rostand suggesting they leave the gallery and walk to his apartment, where Alex would meet Madame Rostand.

They walked across to Fifth Avenue, and then north a few blocks to Rostand's large fourteen-room apartment overlooking Central Park. Alex had never seen such an opulent home nor had he met such an imposing woman as Jane Rostand. From the moment he met her he knew that he would never get on with her. She received him as an unwelcome house guest, though he never understood why. She explained the rules of the house, what was expected of him, when meals were served, and the way he was to conduct himself with the servants.

Philip Rostand, three years his senior, was a large bulky boy, who immediately struck Alex as being pompous, arrogant and overbearing. He was the kind of boy who insisted on, and usually got, his own way.

During those years with the family, five in all, Alex spent the greater part of the time either at boarding school or summer camp. It was not easy for him at the Fifth Avenue apartment. The resentment Jane felt for him was never openly expressed, but it was there. She avoided him when she could and seemed to spend most of her time playing bridge, talking on the telephone, or organizing the social events she sponsored.

Philip's disposition didn't improve over the years either. He had his own set of friends, tended to stay out late at night, and usually slept late the following morning. Alex saw him only at mealtimes. Apart from that, Philip kept to his own room.

With André Rostand Alex established a distant but mutual respect. Perhaps it was more than respect: Alex was never sure. He sensed there was a bond between them, but it was never expressed, and he actually saw very little of the art dealer, who, preoccupied with his business, rarely spent time in the apartment. There were times, however, after dinner, when Rostand would go to a side cabinet, select two crystal brandy snifters along with a bottle of Calvados, and go to the study. It was understood that Alex was to follow and share an evening listening to Rostand recount anecdotes about his family, the art world, and his business. These were the moments he felt closest to the older man.

* * *

Safely past Customs at Kennedy Airport, Drach scrutinized the crowd. He saw nothing to worry him. The terminal was full of students returning from Christmas holidays. As he watched them, encumbered with books, knapsacks, ski boots and poles, he envied them their frivolity and youth. He was beginning to feel a bit sluggish and wished he'd been skiing. He made a mental note to eat less and exercise more, as he strode through the front exit of the airport, entered the nearest taxi and drove off to Manhattan. He barely had forty minutes to make his appointment with André at Rostand International.

An hour later, as Alex left the taxi, he glanced at his watch and found that it was just after five. The huge mahogany-and-glass doors of Rostand International were locked. He frowned and knocked. The door opened and the face of a guard appeared in the crack. For an instant the face was blank before a smile replaced the frown. The door opened wider and the guard, in a cordial voice, said, "It's Mr. Drach, isn't it?"

Alex nodded, surprised that after so long a time, the guard's memory bank of faces included his own. He hadn't set foot in the gallery in five years.

"It's been a long time, sir," the guard said, leading him to the reception room adjoining the entrance hall.

He nodded to the receptionist, a short, stubby black man who had worked at Rostand International as long as he could remember. "What's new, Jackson?"

"Not much, sir. The same old thing. You're here to see Mr. Rostand."

"Always in the know, eh, Jackson?"

Jackson laughed through a smoker's cough, then lifted a telephone and punched a button.

Alex stood there for a moment, reading the row of buttons on the control panel. Each button had its own cryptic legend. From left to right he associated the individuals with the names he read: "Lbry": that would be Pirrone in the library; "Lab": Grimaldi and company in the lab; "Acct": Fuller, probably still bent over his books in accounting. Alex had known them all, having worked in the gallery during his summer vacations. He particularly liked old Pirrone in the library, and wondered how much longer he'd last. At the far left of this acronymic lineup, the initials of André and Philip Rostand stood out in bold type.

Jackson cupped the receiver. "Can you wait a few minutes? Mr. Rostand has someone with him."

"Certainly," he replied. "Mind if I look at the exhibition?"

Jackson winked. "Don't go stealing anything." He reached under his desk and pressed a hidden switch; the door of the reception room hissed open. Alex hung his coat on a hook as he left the room and walked into the main exhibition room.

He was surprised to see someone else was already there. She had her back to him, and almost simultaneously two thoughts went through Alex's mind. The first was that she was tall, sleek-looking and beautiful even from behind. The other was that he hoped André Rostand would remain occupied a long time.

The woman, her honey-colored hair falling loosely to the base of her neck, stood with her arms folded, gazing at a colorful, delicately painted Monet. As yet, she wasn't conscious of his presence, and so for several moments Alex enjoyed the intricate play of the lines of her body, only half-hidden beneath the loose-fitting dress, juxtaposed to the kaleidoscope of color that surrounded her. After that his curiosity got the better of him and he decided to edge into her perimeter of vision by taking a closer look at the paintings along the wall beside her.

He had reached a Degas painting of a group of ballet dancers when she turned. She looked at him for a moment. Then her mouth turned slightly upward in a token smile. He was not disappointed. She was beautiful, the features perfectly formed around large, ice-green eyes, her pale skin as smooth as stretched silk.

He watched her come toward him, advancing on beige pumps.

He was the first to break the silence. "What do you think of them?"

"What can I say," she replied, looking around the room.

"Say anything."

"Anything."

Alex laughed. She was clearly English, her rounded vowels and the bell-like tones—almost soprano in range—told him that.

"Well, at least I know you don't work here."

She stood motionless, her hands clasped in front of her. "Why do you say that?"

"No one working in the gallery would take its exhibits so lightly."

"And, by process of elimination, you don't work here either."

He looked more directly at her and found himself marveling at the bright, green eyes which seemed even larger up close. Possibly, he thought, because of the way she had set them off with the blues and blue-greens of her eyeshadow.

The eye contact broke. She looked away and Alex noticed a slight flush spread outward from her cheeks. He realized then that he had been staring at her.

He looked at the portrait of a woman by Matisse. The face was painted green, the hair blue and a tree in the background bright orange and pink. "When is the opening?" he asked.

"Monday night."

"Are you coming?"

She looked at him for a fraction of a second, as if afraid of being entangled in his gaze again. "Very likely," she replied, and glanced away again.

"So there you are!" A voice resonated from the other side of the room.

They both turned and saw Philip Rostand striding toward them, his bulky frame at home in a stylishly cut pin-stripe suit carefully tailored to flare in the right places. "I see you two have met." It sounded like an insinuation rather than a statement of fact.

"Not really," Alex replied. "We were too preoccupied." Then, before he could extend his hand in greeting, Philip pointedly veered toward the young woman and kissed her on the cheek.

"Then allow me," Rostand said. "Alex, meet Cubitt Keeble. Cubitt, meet Alex Drach."

As if moving out of Philip's orbit, Cubitt took a step toward Alex and shook his hand. "Hello," she said, smiling softly.

As she smiled it seemed to Alex that her mouth grew more attractive. He wondered how Philip had ever found her, and realized that for the first time in his life he envied the man. He rejected the thought and, knowing how easily Philip could be offended, smiled at him as well.

"How is it, playing detective these days, old man?"

"Quite eventful the past week, in fact." Alex smiled. It wasn't a friendly smile. Other recipients of that smile usually pushed him no farther. The eyes warned them not to. The look was menacing, ominous, almost dangerous. If one looked closely, however, there was also a slight trace of amusement there, as if Alex were enjoying a private joke he shared with no one else.

"Are you really a policeman?" Cubitt said, with a healthy doubt in her voice.

"Not exactly. I . . ."

Philip cut him off. "He's like a bounty hunter, only he hunts for stolen art."

Cubitt looked at Alex for a moment, appraisingly, and said, "Sounds fascinating."

Philip broke in. "I understand you have a meeting with my father this evening," he said to Alex. He took Cubitt by the arm.

"Nice meeting you," she said as she moved to the door on Philip's arm.

"Yes, a pleasure," Alex replied, heading for the reception room.

III

André Rostand's antennae told him that someone was at the door, even before it opened.

It was Ray Fuller. As a matter of policy, Harper never showed Fuller into the room. It was a single honor Rostand afforded no other human being. He knew he couldn't have survived without Fuller. On that level, the most basic one, they were equals.

He watched the tall, thin man advance and once again noticed that his accountant's dress wasn't even remotely fashionable. Fuller was the most nondescript individual he had ever known. Today, as usual, he was dressed in brown: a rusty brown square-looking jacket, a brown knit tie and a white shirt with its collar askew. "Your collar's crooked," André sighed.

"I beg your pardon."

Rostand sighed. "Your collar."

Fuller's hands tugged haphazardly at the collar without improving the effect at all.

André shrugged. "Have you got the dossiers?"

"Yes, Mr. Rostand."

"All of them?"

"Yes, Mr. Rostand."

"Good. Now, in a moment Alex Drach is going to arrive."

Fuller's expression changed. His back straightened and his attention sharpened. ". . . Yes, Mr. Rostand."

"I want you to give him the information you have. I also want you to give Marco Grimaldi a raise."

"How much, sir?"

"A thousand dollars a month."

Fuller cleared his throat, the boldest sign of disapproval the man ever expressed in front of his employer.

"You have an objection, Ray?"

"No, sir, I . . ."

"Tell me, Ray. How is your daughter these days?"

The red rims of Fuller's eyes blinked twice. "My daughter, sir?"

"Yes, Maggie."

"What about her, Mr. Rostand?"

"I was just thinking. She's entering the New York Institute of Fine Arts this year, is she not?" Fuller nodded slowly. "And have I not encouraged that?" Fuller nodded again. "Then I think it appropriate that the gallery sponsor her education with a view that some day she join us!"

Fuller's eyes narrowed. For a moment he said nothing, then: "That's most generous of you, sir. But, if I may ask, what is it you want me to do?"

André did not permit himself to smile, though there was a slight flicker of amusement in his eyes. He and Fuller had a symbiotic relationship. They both understood they needed each other. The equilibrium of their lives depended on that fact. They were like an old married couple. They knew each other's weaknesses and accepted them—for a price.

Rostand looked at Fuller, gauging him. He was dealing with a man who had come to him at the beginning. He'd never threatened him, never intimated that he would use the information he had. All he wanted was his due in return for loyalty. In all those years Fuller had performed admirably. He'd been the perfect accountant: arriving early, working late, scrupulous in every detail, honest and a perfectionist when it came to his records.

There was only one problem. He was, Rostand knew, extremely fond of Alex Drach. "I've something to tell you, Ray. There are some paintings coming in. Some of them may have been stolen during the war. . . ." He paused, watching for Fuller's reaction. As expected, there was none. "It appears that they may be part of the Drach Collection."

Fuller blinked twice, but remained silent.

"One more thing," Rostand continued. "They're in the possession of former S.S. Officer Hans Montag."

Fuller blanched. "Montag? How can that be?"

"I don't know the answer to that question. All I can tell you is that Montag is back and I'm going to buy those paintings to keep them out of circulation. In time they'll either be handed over to the proper authorities, donated to a museum, or returned to the families involved." André paused briefly. "I need to know if I have your co-operation."

Fuller's head slipped to one side, his characteristic gesture when considering a problem. Rostand's question remained hanging in the air. "These paintings, Mr. Rostand, are they important to you?"

"Very important."

"Who else is to know?"

Inside, André relaxed. It was an implied acceptance. "No one but Grimaldi, Philip and yourself."

"You may count on my discretion."

André nodded and picked up the telephone. "Send Drach in."

"Glad you could come," André said, standing and walking forward to greet Alex.

Alex shook Rostand's hand. "Nice to see you again, André." He meant it. Then, he smiled at Fuller, who was standing in front of the desk. "You too, Ray."

Alex gazed at the character lines etched deeply in the older man's face. It had been almost a year since he'd last seen Fuller. The accountant hadn't changed a bit. He'd never really understood the relationship between Fuller and Rostand. They were both extremely private men, but if anyone was Rostand's alter ego it was Ray Fuller.

A silence settled down over the three men as though each was reflecting on the passing of time. Alex glanced about the room and found it hard to believe that more than twenty years had elapsed since the day he had first met André Rostand in this very office. He watched the old man closely now. Perhaps the thick hair was grayer now, the backs of his hands a little more wrinkled. On the whole, however, Rostand's torso was still erect and powerful, remarkable for someone approaching seventy.

Rostand emitted an almost inaudible sigh that Drach was probably not meant to hear. "I've got a problem, Alex."

"I'm listening."

"A *ring*."

Drach looked puzzled. "I'm surprised. With the art market so diverse I would have thought it impossible to organize a ring."

"That depends on what its objectives are," Rostand said, grimly. "In this instance they are out to destroy me."

"Oh?" The monosyllable was not a question, but a comment. For a moment. Alex relived the machine-gun fire, glass shattering around his head. He wondered if there was any connection. If there was, he preferred to keep it to himself.

Rostand continued. "I want Ray to give you a rundown on the ring's operations."

Alex settled back into his chair and looked at Fuller, who, at a nod from André, opened up a thick brown folder. The long, narrow head bent over a series of closely typed sheets. Fuller began: "We are dealing with more than just a ring. Leopold Marto has established an investment fund dealing exclusively in paintings. The fund is a public company which issues shares. It's registered on the international stock exchanges as *Art Intrum*."

Fuller paused, his narrow eyes glancing over his spectacles at Drach. Alex noted that as Ray grew older his nose seemed to become more knifelike, its tip hanging slightly over his thin-lipped mouth. Fuller's eyes returned to the folder.

"Art Intrum is registered in Panama. Its main offices are in Geneva, with branch galleries in London, New York and Buenos Aires. It quotes prices in dollars, and shares are negotiated in Swiss francs. The Panamanian registration is useful because, under present registration in Panama, the fund is not subject to corporate taxation.

"The board of directors is made up of eleven private dealers, bankers and other investors, backed by a panel of art scholars who are of no importance to us. Their purchases in the last year include Picasso, Léger, Soutine, Pollock, de Kooning and"—Fuller looked up at Rostand—"the Vermeer. I have also provided a statistical breakdown showing the proportions of each period and school they've acquired." He handed Alex a copy of the list. "You see, for example, French Realism forms three tenths percent of current holdings. The Contemporary school represents thirty-three point eight percent. Old Masters comprise forty percent of the collection and so on. . . ."

He paused. "Now for the more vital statistics . . . As of today, Art Intrum is trading at thirty-one fifty dollars a share, with five million shares outstanding. Current holdings are estimated to be worth approximately one hundred and twenty-five million dollars. It's . . ."

"Fine, Ray," Rostand interrupted. "That's a good overview. Now, could you get on with the individuals involved?"

"Yes, of course, Mr. Rostand. . . ." Fuller proceeded for the next half-hour to give a detailed description of the key members of Art Intrum, not only its board of directors but those "independent" art dealers working with Marto, who would be counted members of the ring: Bez, Duranceau, Kellerman, Feigan and Pirelli. Pirelli alone of the group was not a member of Art Intrum's Board. Fuller did not know the reason why.

His report completed, Fuller handed the folder to Rostand. "Thanks, Ray, that'll be all," André said.

As the door closed behind Fuller, André Rostand stood, stepped behind his chair and pressed a small, almost invisible button recessed in the paneled wall. The paneling slid open discreetly, revealing a well-stocked bar. There were several bottles of liquor and wine, together with a dozen glasses and an ice bucket. "A drink, Alex?"

"Please, I could do with one."

"Glenfiddich, isn't it?"

Drach smiled. "You remembered."

"It's a habit. Some people remember telephone numbers; I remember a man's drink, especially if he's a man I admire."

Drach accepted his drink without responding to the compliment, took a sip and then set the glass down on the edge of the desk. He watched Rostand pour his own and settle back into his chair. "Ray's report was quite thorough."

"As usual," André said setting his glass aside. He leaned forward over the edge of his desk and looked down at the backs of his hands, blotchy with age. "There's more to it, however."

"I thought so. You've got the resources to deal with Art Intrum. Why did you really call me?"

"You're right," André replied, looking directly at Alex. "The problem is not the ring. I can handle that myself. I've got another problem. Inside the gallery. A leak."

"Marto's got someone on the inside?"

André nodded grimly. "You've always been a quick study. That's why I've called you in. I need someone on the outside I can trust. I know you don't like working for me. Under normal circumstances I wouldn't ask, but I am now. I trust you. You know that. You also know that I've always hoped you'd come back and work for me, take a position here, even, someday, take charge."

Alex paused, took a sip of his drink, and weighed the proposition. The summers he had worked for Rostand were interesting and pleasant enough but he always felt uncomfortable being on Rostand's payroll. Besides that, over the years he'd seen things he didn't like, the artifice, the phony intrigues, the manipulation of the art market. He preferred his independence.

Nevertheless, he owed the man a great deal. And Rostand had never come to him this way before. "I'll do what I can," he said quietly.

Rostand pushed the dossier across the desk toward Alex. "You can take this along with a list of my employees and their various functions. You can also have access to our personnel files."

Alex reached for the folder and opened it. His gunmetal-blue eyes quickly scanned the first page. Then he closed it with a sharp slap and pushed it away from him. "I think I'll get at it from the other side first," he said, "starting with the members of the ring and working back. There are fewer of them."

Rostand smiled for the first time since they'd met that evening. "That's sensible."

"I'll try and get back within a week."

"Excellent," Rostand said. He took a drink and his gaze appeared to wander aimlessly around the room as though he were preoccupied with something else. Then, focusing on Drach, he politely asked, "How are things with you?"

"Coincidentally, I've got a problem I'd like to talk to you about, André."

Rostand leaned forward, the complex network of ridges and lines on his face softening. "I'm moved that you would honor me by discussing your problems with me."

Alex, unsure exactly how to respond, fell back on a cordial but formal reply. "That's very gracious of you." He paused. "I want to ask you about the Drach Collection."

The muscles in Rostand's face tightened. "What about it?"

"One of the paintings from it has surfaced."

Rostand sat perfectly still for a moment and then nodded twice. "I see," he said.

"It showed up in London, recently, then mysteriously disappeared."

"You're sure?"

"Positive."

"Which one?"

Alex had the distinct impression that Rostand knew something, but he couldn't be sure. The old man was framing the questions as if he already knew the answers. "Watteau's *Lute Player*," Alex slowly replied, watching Rostand closely now.

André sipped his drink, now mostly melted icewater, and leaned back in his chair. If Alex could detect any kind of reaction, it was one of concern. Had he known anything, he was wily enough to conceal it. The old man was schooled in masking his real responses.

"I remember it well," he said. "It was your mother's favorite."

"I didn't know that."

Rostand nodded.

"If you hear of anything, I'd like you to let me know about it?"

"Of course I will."

Alex reached for his glass. "I'm learning a lot about my parents these days," he said, lifting the glass halfway to his mouth. "I've never spoken to you about my father, but during the past week I've had occasion to hear several stories about him. I was wondering"—he paused briefly—"what was your opinion of him?" The glass completed its arc and Alex sipped the Glenfiddich.

"What stories?"

"That he collaborated."

Rostand glanced down at the palms of his hands, as if trying to read in the pink flesh an answer to the question. "I never knew a finer man than your father," he said slowly. "I find it very hard to believe that he collaborated. But then you must realize a man shouldn't be held responsible for what he says and does in the hands of the Gestapo." He took another sip of the iced water. "Sometimes we do things under pressure that are completely out of character."

"I can understand that."

"Can you?" It was a question implying a negative answer.

Alex did not respond. He finished his drink and rose from his chair, preparing to leave.

Rostand left his chair and walked with Alex toward the door. "It might be a good idea if you come to the opening of our exhibition on

Monday night. It'd give you a chance to meet some of our employees."

Alex smiled. "I'll be there. You can count on it," he said, thinking of Cubitt. Then, as he reached the door, he turned to Rostand. "One more thing. Do you know anything about a man named Montag?"

"Who?"

"Hans Montag. He was an officer in the S.S."

"Montag?" André said, his eyes looking downward toward his hands, then up toward the ceiling, and only then looking Alex directly in the eyes. "Montag? No, the name means nothing to me."

IV

Cubitt was high on music and marijuana. Studio 54, a television studio reconverted into Manhattan's most fashionable discothèque, was jammed. The staccato beat of the music pulsated through speakers the size of movie screens. The dance floor reeked of hot human scent. The music, blended with the sweet acrid smell of amyl nitrite and the musky pungence of marijuana was enough to give everyone on the floor a contact high.

Caught in the flickering strobe lights, the dancers in front of Cubitt appeared frozen, their nostrils flared, eyes gleaming, wild and catlike in the impulsive madness of the dance. The scene made her think of a Roman amphitheater filled with dancing gladiators, coupling and uncoupling in a combat of debauchery.

She took another sip of champagne and glanced along the banquette where she sat with Philip and a group of his friends. Everyone was shouting to be heard over the pulsing thump of the music. Philip was doing his best to charm Andy Stabler, the Master of Hype and Pop Art, drawing out the painter, trying to learn something about the trends in the contemporary art scene. They had met Stabler, along with several others, at Le Relais, where they had eaten dinner. After midnight, the group had taxied to the disco on West Fifty-fourth Street, pushed through the noisy crowd clamoring for admittance and found an unoccupied banquette on the edge of the dance floor.

Stabler, who never danced, was seated with his arms folded across his chest, staring blankly at the dancers, reminding Cubitt of a white squid. Every once in a while he nodded at a point Philip made, but it was obvious that he was bored with the conversation.

Someone passed Cubitt a joint. She took a hit and passed the thick reefer to Philip. "Good stuff," he said, inhaling deeply. "It's sin-semilla."

Cubitt, holding the smoke in her lungs, flashed her eyebrows in agreement. It was good grass, and it helped. Normally, she wouldn't have smoked in public, but tonight she was a bit bored. She was being ignored and she didn't like it. After a few puffs on the reefer the evening definitely improved. The colored lights were brighter and the music took on an added dimension, as though there was no distance between it and her.

Suddenly she decided to dance. She nudged Philip, but he was too deeply engrossed in conversation to notice. She tossed her head in a shrug and left the banquette. She stepped onto the dance floor, edged closer to the speakers, and began to dance alone. Next to her, a dark-haired man in a brown leotard undulated voluptuously with a young girl whose dress was cut to expose one bare breast, the rosy nipple of which stood out hard and stiff. Another man, wearing nothing but a pair of tight-fitting silk shorts, gyrated his pelvis in parallel with his partner, a shriveled old woman who looked up at him with a rapturous smile on her face. Beside them, two attractive slim-hipped men twirled in each other's arms, one sucking continuously on his friend's collar. Lots of them did that at Studio, she knew. Even from where she was, she caught the smell of the ethyl chloride. Dancers soaked their collars, cuffs or handkerchiefs in the anesthetic chemical and then sucked at it through the evening for an instant rush.

In the middle of the floor a bare-chested, brown-skinned man, wearing a red towel around his waist, stood stock-still, moving only his hands up and down to the beat of the music, chanting an indecipherable mantra. Cubitt watched him, amused at the attempt he was making to achieve astral projection. Then she closed her eyes and gave herself to the music, letting the beat carry her along.

When she opened her eyes, a tall attractive woman was dancing in front of her. Legs planted apart, back arched, the woman was dancing with her waist-tied halter dress hoisted to midthigh. She looked at Cubitt but said nothing. They continued to dance.

Cubitt had noticed the woman earlier that night, when she had strolled by the banquette and pointedly smiled at her. Now, with a cajoling look on her face, she was here again and, Cubitt thought, danced beautifully. Her body produced an extraordinary effect: a female proclaiming all the power and heat of her sex.

Cubitt was also struck by the similarity of their looks. Both of them were blond and long-limbed. The woman's eyes were blue, however, rather than her own glistening green. She also wore a darker shade of lipstick and smoky eyeshadow, which gave her an exotic look. The woman glided closer. They began to synchronize the movement of their bodies. "You're not an American, are you?" She spoke with a strong French accent.

"What makes you say that?"

"Americans sway and tilt. You don't. You float."

Cubitt laughed. "I didn't realize."

"Where are you from?"

"London," Cubitt replied. "And you?"

"Paris," she said, making eye contact with Cubitt and holding it. Then, looking away: "I prefer it here."

"Don't they have discos in Paris?"

"Not like this," she replied.

The tempo of the music changed. One number faded while another swelled to life. Cubitt smiled. "Nice talking to you." She turned and started back to the banquette.

A hand on her waist stopped her. "Why go back there?"

Cubitt didn't reply.

"They're obviously very boring."

"What's the alternative?" Cubitt asked.

"Why don't we go someplace else?"

"To dance?"

The woman looked coyly at Cubitt. "Have you ever been with a woman?"

"No," she replied, honestly; though she'd had plenty of opportunities, she'd never gone that way.

"Only a woman can understand another woman."

Cubitt said nothing. She glanced in the direction of the banquette.

Philip had left it and was walking toward them. As he approached the woman took Cubitt's hand and whispered, *"Viens, ma chère.* Come with me." But then it was too late.

"Anyone I should know?" Philip asked, his arm circling Cubitt's waist.

"Je m'appelle Solange," the woman said.

"Enchanté," Philip said, bending slightly at the waist.

"Solange just invited me for a drink," Cubitt said.

Philip put his other arm around Solange. "Join us," he said. "My place is just across town."

Solange looked at Cubitt. For a moment, Cubitt said nothing, though she was pleased. Physically, she wasn't attracted to the woman, at least not in a sexual way; but aesthetically, Solange was special. Besides, if it pleased Philip, why not? "Please do," she finally said cordially. "I'm sure we have a lot in common."

Philip Rostand's six-room Manhattan high-rise apartment provided a spectacular view of the East River. Through curvilinear windows it was like a capsule floating in space. The walls were upholstered in vinyl suede with bands of shiny stainless steel edged along the ceilings and floors. The sofa and chairs were upholstered in beige velvet, with succulents and cacti taking root in Cartier gold pots strategically placed about the apartment.

The front room was large enough to accommodate three couches, several armchairs, a desk, a backgammon game the size of a card table, and a well-stocked bar.

When Cubitt, Solange and Philip entered the room, a wizened old man approached them, took their coats and hung them in a large mirrored closet in the hallway.

"Where are the dogs, Samuel?"

"In the back, sir!"

"You can let them out now."

"Who's the little man?" Cubitt asked, as the spare figure disappeared down a stainless steel corridor.

"That's Samuel," Philip replied. He walked to the bar. "He's my valet."

Cubitt laughed. "Do you really need one?"

"He helps out, does the laundry, that sort of thing. He's like a piece of furniture. After a while you don't even notice him."

Solange looked about the room. "It's quite elaborate, Philip."

Philip shrugged. "It's home." He stepped behind the bar. "What'll you have, Solange?"

"Any champagne?"

"Only if you like Pol Roger," Philip replied, opening a compact refrigerator built into the wall. "How about you, Cubitt?"

"I'd love some."

Rostand poured three glasses of champagne, set them on a tray and carried them to a coffee table made of cream-colored onyx. He handed each woman a glass, then took his own and raised it in a toast. "To friendship." They all smiled and sipped in unison. "Come on, I'll show you around," Philip said, walking through a large bronze door.

He led them into the master bedroom, which contained a king-size bed encased in bronze Plexiglas. From there they went into a large bathroom.

"*Mon Dieu*," Solange exclaimed. "It's fantastic." In the middle of the room was a vast, free-standing Jacuzzi, constructed of stainless steel and redwood. Solange stepped up onto the redwood platform and dipped her finger into steamy hot water.

"Takes hours to fill," Philip said, setting down his drink and removing his jacket. He went over to a cabinet, where, after a moment's hesitation, he selected a bright orange packet from among the bottles and tubes lining the shelf. He poured the contents of the packet into the Jacuzzi, then turned on the water, testing the temperature. He made a slight adjustment of the knob and continued to sprinkle the orange powder under the gushing faucet. "It holds a thousand gallons of water," he said, gazing over his shoulder at Cubitt. "I keep it ready for just this kind of occasion."

Cubitt smiled, but not at the remark. She was struck at how muscular Philip was. He was even thick, though there wasn't an ounce of fat on him. She giggled as he leaned over the steaming bath, his tie dangling precariously an inch above the water, fussing with bath powder.

Cubitt took another sip of champagne and set her glass down on the Jacuzzi's platform. With a quick movement she undid the strap at the back of her neck and let the bareback gold lamé dress fall to the floor.

Solange looked at her and smiled. There was admiration in her eyes. The French woman hooked her shawl over the edge of the towel rack, slipped out of her shoes, lifted her dress and removed her panty-hose.

Cubitt watched her graceful movements; even under the dress she could see that her body was flawless. She judged her to be about twenty-three or twenty-four.

Philip too was watching Solange as she sat down on the edge of the Jacuzzi, letting her legs dangle in the water. They were soon covered by the rapidly rising foam. Then she drew her dress over her head, exposing her naked breasts. "You're beautiful," Philip remarked.

He was right, Cubitt thought. She was beautiful. Every curve was right: the breasts high and firm, the stomach a slight oval before trailing away to the honey-colored triangle between her legs, and nice round buttocks.

Solange looked up at Cubitt. "What do you think?"

"I agree with him; you're lovely."

Solange's face brightened. "Yes, I see you do," she said, slowly stroking Cubitt's thigh with the tips of her fingers. "But beauty is wasted unless it's used the right way," she added.

A moment later Philip was undressed. His muscles rippled as he lowered himself into the hot, steamy Jacuzzi. Cubitt and Solange followed him. "Not bad, is it?" Philip said, floating next to Cubitt.

"Umm. Wonderful," she said.

He leaned over and kissed her on the lips.

She didn't draw away. He moved closer, and slipped his hand between her legs. Cubitt twisted away.

"What's the matter?" he asked.

"Nothing. I'd just like to relax a little."

There was a flash of resentment in Philip's eyes. He said nothing.

Cubitt looked at Solange. She was floating on her back, her hair wet, her breasts rising out of the foam like red-tipped mounds. The women smiled at each other. "Want to play?" Cubitt asked.

"It depends on the game," Solange replied, laughing.

"Anything you like," Philip interjected.

They left the Jacuzzi, dried themselves, and went into the master bedroom. While Cubitt and Solange lounged on top of the red velvet bedspread, Philip opened a lacquered Chinese chest. From it, he took a vial filled with white powder. A tiny spoon was attached to the lid of the vial by a fine gold chain.

Philip opened the vial, extracted a spoonful of the white powder and snorted it into each nostril. He filled the spoon again, and this time held it under Cubitt's nose.

She sniffed the spoon clean, and almost immediately felt the cocaine numb the membranes of her nostrils. Then the explosion came. "Christ, that's something," she whispered.

"Now you," Philip said, holding the spoon out for Solange.

"I'm fine," she said. "Champagne's enough for me."

"Sniff it," he said coldly. He grabbed her by the arm and held the spoon under her nose.

"No, thanks," she said, slapping his hand away. White powder floated down onto the blood-red bedspread.

"Fucking bitch!" He grabbed her by her wet hair, yanked her head back and shoved the vial into her nostril. "Snort, I said."

Solange gasped and powder was drawn up into her nose. Philip put the vial to the other nostril. "Again," he said.

Cubitt sprang at Philip. "Let her go, you bastard," she shouted and struck him across the face.

He shoved Solange away, then wrestled Cubitt flat onto the bed. "Playtime," he grunted looking into her eyes. "You'll like this." He tipped the rest of the coke onto his fingertips, then thrust two of them deep into her. It was so swift and unexpected that before she could react to the pain, her genitals exploded with agonizing pleasure. Rapidly he began to move his fingers in and out, while his thumb kneaded her clitoris. She moaned, writhing under his hand. Then her insides burst again. She had never come like that before. Never.

Solange, as though in a trance, watched them. Philip glanced at her. "Get your ass over here," he commanded, grabbing her arm and pulling her with his free hand. He put her head to Cubitt's breast. "You wanted her, now take her."

Solange cupped Cubitt's breasts in her hands and alternatively pinched and licked her nipples. After a moment Cubitt could hear herself whimpering with pleasure. She reached for Philip's phallus. It was thick and hard. She jack-knifed her legs, drew him around so that he straddled her and then guided him inside her.

As he pushed, she caught her breath. She was afraid he might rip her apart. Her nails dug into his buttocks and slowly, she drew him deeper into her. Then he was all the way inside, and for a moment lay still. Gently then he began to move with short smooth strokes. Again she started spiraling toward orgasm.

Suddenly, Solange shifted and while continuing to caress Cubitt's breasts, positioned her thighs on either side of Cubitt's face. "Love me," she whispered to Cubitt.

Cubitt began to massage the two breasts hanging pendulously in front of her. Then her tongue found Solange's clitoris.

"Oui, oui, ma chère," Solange murmured, swaying rhythmically over the loving mouth.

Cubitt's muscles tensed. Sensation was everywhere. She concentrated on the yellow spiral hairs, lapping at them, then on the cock inside her, moving faster now like a trip-hammer. "Please, I can't stand it. No more," she wailed. She arched her back. "Please . . ." And then she forgot everything but the unbearably exciting spasms that engulfed her, as she, Philip and Solange came together.

The next thing she knew, they were all on the bed laughing.

The next morning, her eyes wide open, Cubitt stared at the sunlight through a screen of Mylar blinds. The glare bothered her as she reluctantly surveyed a scene of elegant devastation. Glasses and bottles were everywhere. Overturned and overflowing ashtrays littered the floor.

They had made love all night long, and each time they became different people. They were soft and thrilling one moment, then quick and brutally demanding the next. Finally, in the early hours of the morning, they had all fallen into a deep, exhausted sleep.

Cubitt listened to the soft breathing next to her. She looked across Philip's chest at Solange and wondered what made some women so different. She couldn't imagine what it would be like to love another woman totally. She'd never found a man she could give herself to completely, either, but for her, being with a woman wasn't the answer.

Suddenly the alarm clock buzzed. Philip's dogs, two Great Danes, padded across the carpeted floor to the night table. They sniffed the clock, then flopped into their customary position at the end of the bed.

Philip, groaning, reached across Solange. His hand slapped the clock. The buzzing stopped. Oblivious of Cubitt's gaze, he picked up a tightly rolled hundred-dollar bill, sniffed the residue of cocaine from it, then slumped onto his pillow and drifted back to sleep.

Cubitt got out of bed and walked into the bathroom. She passed the Jacuzzi, smiled wryly to herself, then turned on the shower. While she waited for the water to run hot, she looked at herself in the mirror. She'd always been told that she had a good figure, but to be honest, her hips were a little too heavy. She would have preferred to have a more boyish line. She palmed her breasts as if they were two pieces of fruit. They were all right, nicely pear-shaped, but they weren't as beautiful as Solange's.

She felt her belly. It had lost the flatness it once had when she was young, those days when she was a photographer's model. Now, though still firm, her stomach was rounder, not so adolescent. She reached lower to touch the patch of the down between her legs. She probed deeper. She was sore.

She thought again of the night before. She was physically sated from the lovemaking, but there had been little emotional satisfaction. Sex was entertaining enough, and fun, but it led nowhere. None of it. And why should it? She never expected it to.

She shrugged and stepped under the needle-point spray of the shower and let the drumming of the water jets on her scalp drown her melancholy thoughts. The mirrored walls of the large shower cubicle began to blur with billowing steam. It reminded her of the condensed vapor that dripped from the cracked plaster ceiling whenever she took a bath as a child. The bathroom of her mother's home in London was always damp—even in summer—and freezing cold in winter.

Her attention drifted to the different soaps and gels stacked neatly on the shelf above the shower. She experimented with several of them, lathering and rinsing her body. She alternated the water from hot to ice cold, and slowly the feeling of fatigue left her. She turned off the water and stepped from the shower stall, wide awake. She grabbed a thick terry-cloth towel, dried herself and ran a comb through her wet hair. After dressing she went into the master bedroom. Solange and Philip were still asleep.

In slumber he looked so innocent. Men were all the same. They were so preoccupied with themselves they didn't bother to find out what a woman felt. Philip regarded her as no more than an accessory to him. Some men were gladly used by women, others were blind to it, and then there were the few rich enough not to care. Philip was none of these. He used women.

Philip's eyes flickered and focused on Cubitt. "What are you doing?" he asked.

"Thinking."

"About what?"

Cubitt bent over, kissed Philip on the cheek and whispered, "Fucking you."

V

Alex Drach, about to leave for his office, answered his home phone. The caller was a woman friend, and the conversation flirtatious. He was not so carried away, however, to delay his departure too long.

Alex cradled the receiver and walked across the expanse of his Gramercy Park loft. He made sure the bolt lock on the iron door leading to the stairway was secure. Then he went to the kitchen area and rummaged around for something to eat. His inspection of the refrigerator rewarded him with a dried-up English muffin and a shriveled grapefruit. This gastronomic tragedy he took to the part of the loft which had been converted into a dining area, and there he sat on a stool beside an old farmer's workbench, which he used for a table.

Drach's loft, retaining its original rafters and beamed ceiling, rough walls and wide wood planked floors, was his sanctuary. He loved the place, which, because of its size and space, allowed him any number of unrestrained indulgences. The enormous sweep of the three-story-high ceiling had great advantages. Chairs, tables, large comfortable sofas and a score of track-lights conformed to the large space and appealed to his sense of independence.

Alex looked past the double stairway leading to the bedrooms, at the skylight overhead. Warm sunlight had melted the snow. He walked to the coatrack, selected a camel-hair overcoat and pushed the elevator button. As he left the loft he punched the dimmer switch extinguishing the lights, and stepped into the elevator.

Outside in the sunlit dazzle children were making snowmen in the park. A little five-year-old girl named Alexandra saw Alex walking toward Park Avenue and waved from atop the snowman. They always kidded each other about having the same name. Alex formed a pistol with his index finger and thumb and shot at the girl, who fell tumbling from the snowman clutching at her chest. He hoped no one was taking a bead on him. The squeal of her laughter followed him down the street.

The day had turned unseasonably warm, somewhere in the low fifties, and the snow was fast becoming slush, running in gray rivulets along the curbs to the gaping mouths of the sewers. The air felt clean

as he inhaled it. Though it was Monday morning there were few vehicles headed uptown. The heavy snowfall had discouraged the normal flow of commuter traffic.

On Park Avenue Alex flagged a taxi and was driven the twenty
blocks north to his offices in the Pan Am building. He left the cab
but before entering the building, watched as an immense dump truck
shifted rubble behind a gray painted fence that surrounded the site of
the old Hotel Commodore, now being renovated.

Alex never got used to the destruction, the constant tearing down
and building up of the property developers. That was the one saving
grace of the art market. At least it preserved the heritage of the
civilized past.

He waited there as another truck left the construction site, then
turned and walked through the revolving doors into the vast black
marbled interior of the Pan Am building. As he strode down the corridor to the elevator bank he sighed. He could imagine what his appointment book looked like. He would have to squeeze in time for
the Rostand job, and God knows when he'd be able to see Sol Stern.
Stern. If anyone could help him now, it was Sol. He made a mental
note to call him at the first opportunity. Then he thought of Cubitt
Keeble. He wondered if she would be at the reception at Rostand International that night.

As he waited for the elevator he looked at the withdrawn worried
faces of people hurrying to work, their eyes empty, mouths tightened,
foreheads wrinkled, a universal Monday morning look. Any one of
them could be an assassin.

Alex flexed his shoulders. The tension of the last few days had left
the cords of his neck knotted. He breathed deeply, exhaled, but the
lump of fear remained in the pit of his stomach. He remembered the
feeling. He'd felt it all through the war in Vietnam, ten years before.
He recalled the days when the Marine Corps unit he had commanded
moved through Hue on the bomb-pitted road to the sea, probing the
ruins through Vietcong-held territory. Any moment might have been
his last, every man, woman and child a potential enemy. It was a
strange, almost buoyant, feeling that at any second he could die.

The elevator doors opened. Alex stepped into the car. Several
others, a bespectacled businessman type and two rather dumpy-look-
ing women, followed. The door slid shut and Alex felt the lift in his
chest as the elevator ascended.

In his office, for the first time in four days Alex went through the ritual of greeting his unattractive, astringent-looking secretary Miss Goodyear.

"You're looking especially lovely this morning, Miss Goodyear."

Miss Goodyear glanced up warily, then returned to her typewriter. "Your messages are on the desk," she said. "Mr. Franklin is in the waiting room."

"Well done, Miss Goodyear." Alex examined the messages and checked the appointment book. He glanced down at the head of strawlike red hair. "Tell Mr. Franklin I'll be with him in a moment. I want to see Po first."

Alex walked through Miss Goodyear's office into the office of Harry Powalski, his assistant.

"Ah, at last you've acceded to be with us," Po said, his face beaming. He was sitting on the edge of his desk leafing through a sheaf of papers. Short and stocky, Po had pale skin and sandy brown hair, which he parted down the middle. He prided himself on his handlebar moustache, and the long sideburns which he kept carefully squared off at the base of the ear. He was also a very accomplished lock-and-pick man.

Alex liked him immensely. They had been friends ever since they had met in the Marine Corps. Even then Harry had been a troublemaker. He would try to get away with anything. Though other officers thought him insubordinate, Alex accepted him as a good soldier, unconventional but effective.

The story of Harry's induction was typical. At eighteen, with no chance of getting into college, he was drafted. Determined not to go, however, Harry read the army regulations and discovered that for his height he had to weigh at least one hundred and ten pounds to qualify. At the time he weighed 160 lbs., so for weeks he starved himself. He existed on a daily diet of Tiger's Milk, castor oil, brewer's yeast and a half-cup of orange juice. This he drank with a handful of vitamin pills. In the end he looked like a skeleton, but he was elated. To ensure that he was below the weight requirement, Harry went to the barber and had his head shaved. He even clipped his fingernails. And just before the weigh-in, he made sure he had gone to the bathroom. On his way into the induction center, he spat twice on the sidewalk just for good measure. Finally, as he nervously approached the scale, he ran in place for two minutes. The needle jumped to 105. For Po it was a miracle.

Two weeks later he received notification from the Surgeon General that he had been certified I–Y. But the deferment was granted for three months only, and to Harry it was obvious that he couldn't go on starving himself four times each year. He wouldn't survive.

At this point, Po's only recourse was to fail the mental aptitude test. He figured out the right answer to every question and then responded incorrectly. There was only one problem with this procedure. Po scored a perfect zero, which was a statistical impossibility. Later he learned that a baboon taking the test and marking the various boxes at random would have scored at least 25 percent of the answers correctly.

The psychiatrist at the induction center pointed this out to Harry and then maliciously threatened that unless he retook the test, he'd recommend special psychiatric treatment at a local mental hospital. Harry demurred, took the test and scored what was the first 100 percent mark the induction center had yet recorded. Only then did Harry "Po" Powalski capitulate and enlist in the United States Marine Corps.

Alex smiled at Po's stilted English; he had a gift for malapropisms. "How are you at leaks?" he asked.

"I'd be reluctant to reply to that question until I have further information like, for example, am I plugging or creating them?"

"Plugging."

"What's the S.O.P.?"

"First thing that I want you to do is rent a one-room apartment somewhere in the East Sixties. Then telephone the New York Telephone Company's central business office." Alex handed Po a list of six names, the members of the ring. "Identify yourself, first by phone number, and then by name, as one of these art dealers about to change the location of your gallery. Tell the phone company you want to have your phone bill sent to another address."

"I know. To the address of the apartment I'm going to engage."

"Clever fellow, but try and use the English language a little more correctly when you make those calls."

The intercom buzzed. Po flicked the switch. "Reading you . . ."

"Mr. Powalski," Miss Goodyear's nasal voice came over the speaker. "Please remind Mr. Drach that Mr. Franklin is waiting."

Alex leaned over the desk. "I'll be right there, Miss Goodyear."

Alex crossed the suite of offices to the waiting room, where he shook hands with an old man in a wheelchair. "Sorry to keep you waiting, Mr. Franklin. Please come into my office."

A female attendant in a tailored suit of gabardine stationed herself behind the wheelchair. As she steered the chair into his office, Alex wondered where the old man had found her. She was unusual-looking, with wide cheekbones, short, black bangs, thick lips, a bosom that more than filled the tight jacket, ample hips, sturdy legs and bulbous ankles. A pair of brown brogues covered her feet, but Alex presumed her toes were ample as well.

Alex took a seat behind his desk while Franklin's extraordinary companion moved discreetly to the corner of the room and remained standing. "What can I do for you, Mr. Franklin?" Drach asked.

"I have a collection," Franklin replied, looking around. "Tibetan and Chinese antiquities, mostly. Some odds and ends. I was hoping you might pay us a visit one day and recommend a . . ."

"A security system?" Drach interjected.

"Yes, you come very highly recommended."

"I think I could do that," Alex cut in. "Tibetan and Chinese antiquities, you say. They're difficult items to protect. Any losses?"

"No, never. The house is very secure."

"Have you catalogued the collection?"

Franklin, obviously not wishing to deal directly with the question, hedged. "Well, we do have most of it photographed. Two pieces are on loan to the Asia Society," he added unnecessarily.

"I'd love to see it," Drach said. "I spent quite a bit of time in the Orient; I never tire of its art."

"I've been fortunate to have acquired many superb pieces."

"Are you a collector, Mr. Franklin? Or an art investor?" The question seemed to puzzle Franklin momentarily. Alex had known it would. It always did. An art investor, according to the IRS, must document certain expenses, and as Alex had found, was always the better client. Franklin might be a serious collector, but without investor status he was not as likely to want, or be able to afford, his services.

"In this day and age, I certainly hope that the collection offers some hedge against inflation. But I don't trade or deal my pieces. I only collect."

"I can offer you a bit of curbstone advice, Mr. Franklin. Tibetan and Chinese antiquities are a very marketable commodity on the black market. If you are going to be away for the summer, I would suggest that you take a long, hard look at making this collection secure. There are many ways to go about it. And please, don't misunderstand me, but a 'very secure house' is exactly what the art thief of today drools over."

"That's somewhat disheartening, Mr. Drach. Specifically what do you suggest?"

"Ah, now we're getting beyond the curbstone. I can tell you this. No one particular device is necessarily going to protect your collection. Many factors are involved. First, I'd like to do a threat analysis, and check out the present alarm system." Alex paused. "You do have an alarm system?"

"Yes, of course," Franklin frowned. "It comes with the house."

"Yes, I see. But this isn't the place to talk. Give me a call and arrange for me to pay you a visit some time next week."

"That would be fine. I'll send Maeve in to pick you up with the car," Franklin said, nodding in the direction of the woman standing in the corner.

Alex shivered inwardly. "That's kind of you, Mr. Franklin. I'll need my own car."

While Alex busied himself with his clients, Po spent the morning talking to the New York Telephone Company. For each member of the ring, he dialed 3–4–8 and then the first four digits of their office telephone number. A service representative for the area in which each gallery was located answered.

Under the pretext that he was moving to a new office, Po requested that his telephone account be sent to the new address. He also asked for a list of the long-distance calls made during the past year.

The service representative explained that the phone company maintained a record of its users' calls for the previous month only.

Po thanked the representative for the assistance and provided the address of his apartment for future billings. He was assured the accounts would be there within a week. This procedure he followed for every member of the ring.

VI

Georgette's Salon in Manhattan caters to women who want to keep their skin young, smooth and wrinkle-free. Prices vary from the average thirty-dollar one-hour facial, to the more complete treatment, which runs to one hundred fifty dollars. Jane Rostand always had the complete treatment.

In a supine position, she lay back, her legs covered with a blue and white Paisley quilt. A white-jacketed cosmetologist cleaned her skin with unscented lotion. As the thick fingers of the attendant moved in circles over the firm surface of her face, Jane, only half conscious of her thoughts, dreamed of a man. One in particular. He was standing at the foot of her French canopied bed. She was wearing a simple white bed jacket, delicately embroidered. Unfastened, it had fallen open to reveal her long graceful neck and tiny well-shaped breasts. She lay against a mass of fluffy white pillows, backed by a white satin headboard.

He smiled at her as he moved to the head of the bed. His dark finger traced a line down her neck to the cleavage of her breasts. Then he was kissing her, arousing her, thrusting deeply into her. It had been years since she had felt that way.

". . . Now, Mrs. Rostand, are you ready for the lubricant?" the voice of the cosmetologist broke in.

Drowsily, Jane opened her eyes. "What was that?"

"The lubricant . . ."

"Sorry, Lisa, of course. Go right ahead."

The cosmetologist applied a treatment cream containing live cells from a sheep's placenta, believed to retard aging. She applied the cream with a small hot iron to soften the pores.

"We feel this process is terribly important what with the new décolleté fashion. We also have to care more for our backs, shoulders and so on."

"Indeed," Jane said. "Changes in temperature shock the skin, especially in winter. The cold gives me a blotchy look."

The body treatment took place in a partially darkened quiet room with comfortable furniture, a fireplace and soft music. The attendant now focused on Jane's thighs, arms, elbows and feet. She used a hot towel to remove the lotion, then applied a vegetable cream that lifted off dead cells and activated circulation within a few minutes. Later, after an antiwrinkle body massage, Jane was wrapped in gauze soaked with Theraffin, which formed a cast.

Jane drifted back to her daydream. Now, instead of her lover, the lips that brushed her milk-white cheek belonged to André. Once, in the beginning, they had been so close, so alive to each other's touch.

She was twenty-three when they met in Palm Beach, the winter of 1935. She was dancing at the Flamingo Ball, the highlight of the social season that year, when she saw André walk into the Palm Beach Country Club. He was in white tie and tails, and stood by the orchestra, watching the dancers "pepper shake" around the Grand Ballroom. She was conscious of his eyes on her and she was flattered. She wore a green chiffon dress and a topaz necklace that set off her tanned honey-colored skin.

As soon as the dance ended, he walked to the edge of the floor, where she was talking to her escort, a limpid-looking fellow with a clear, translucent face, baby-pink with no rigidity, line or texture to it. André stepped before them, nodded at her partner and asked her for the next dance.

She looked at him, surprised. "I don't believe we've met," she said.

André was about to speak when the man who had been dancing with her interjected: "She's already booked for the evening. Terribly sorry . . ."

André ignored the comment and waited for her to reply. On impulse she decided to play hard to get. As the next dance began and the sound of "Melody Time" floated across the floor, without a word she turned with open arms to her partner and danced off with him, leaving André standing alone.

Minutes later, the master of ceremonies announced that the next dance would be a Paul Jones. To the rumble of drums, two circles, men on the outside, women on the inside, were formed. The orchestra struck up "The Virginia Traveler." The men and women faced each other and the two circles slip-stepped in opposite directions. Jane, in the inner circle, watched as the faces of the men flew past her. When the music stopped she was astonished to find André in front of her.

"Seems as though fate has brought us together after all," he said, smiling broadly. "Shall we dance?"

The music was slow and romantic. André took her in his arms and led her smoothly around the room. She noticed that she was as tall as he was. Her long legs were able to stay perfectly in step with his.

"I'm delighted fate arranged that we should meet," he said, looking into her eyes.

"That's nice of you," she said. "And yet, how curious."

He pulled her closer to him. "Perhaps it's destiny."

She nudged him away, gently edging her forearm between them. "You're not an American, are you?"

"No."

"Italian?"

"French."

"France! I was there last summer."

"Did you enjoy it?"

"I adored it. It was so quaint. The food . . ."

She was interrupted as the music stopped. They parted and the circles re-formed. The orchestra broke into another round of "The Virginia Traveler." Twice, she and André passed each other. Each time she smiled at him, but when the music stopped again and they were face to face, she frowned.

"Don't tell me this is fate, too," she said as she slipped into his arms for another dance.

"Don't talk," he said. "Just dance."

He put his right hand in the small of her back and pulled her to him so that her hips pressed tightly against him. They danced slowly in time with the music and after a few moments her body began to relax. She draped an arm around his neck and rested her head against his. Their hips and thighs rubbed together and she felt him getting hard.

When the music stopped and they parted, Jane looked at him knowingly. "Will our luck hold the next time around?"

André shrugged. "You never know," he said innocently.

Their luck held again and as they danced she told André the basics about herself: schooled in Switzerland, burned in the Bahamas, frozen in St. Moritz, finished at Duchesne in New York. Her parents were divorced. Both had since remarried and now she lived with her father, who had made a fortune in real estate during the postwar boom. The man she was with that night was her "steady," though she certainly made a point of letting André know that she wasn't "serious."

By the time the dance ended, Jane was certain that he was the man she wanted, even though she knew nothing about him. He was terribly attractive, not because of the way he looked but because of the aura he created. She sensed that he was a man who knew himself. The attraction was impetuous, but instinctive.

As the music ended, André led her across the room to a corner table, where they sat and talked. The waiters were frantic with orders for drinks, but André solved that problem by waving a twenty-dollar bill in the air. Minutes later, a bottle of Moët et Chandon champagne sat in a silver ice bucket beside their table.

"That's an expensive way to get a drink," she said. She realized then that André had paid the leader of the orchestra to stop the music at the precise moment they were opposite each other. He was obviously a man who left nothing to chance. "Do you always arrange things like that?" she asked.

"Sometimes," André replied, smiling casually. He lifted his glass. "To the prettiest girl in Palm Beach."

She laughed. "Do you know them all?"

"Enough," he said. "Here and there."

She looked at him questioningly. "What are you doing so far from home?"

"I'm selling art."

"What?"

"Art. You know, paintings, drawings . . ."

She nodded appreciatively and glanced about the room. "I think I'd better be getting back to my date."

"Don't go. We're just beginning to get to know each other."

"What do you mean? I don't even know your name."

"You're Jane Thompson. That, I already know," André said. "For my part, I can remedy that easily." He withdrew a card from his wallet and handed it to her.

She glanced at it. "André Rostand. Rostand et Fils. 3 Rue de la Boétie. Paris huitième," she read aloud. "Rostand. That's easy to remember." She sipped her champagne and added, "It's a nice-sounding name."

"I'm glad you like it," he said. "Because it's going to be yours."

She looked at him wide-eyed. "You're crazy."

"No, I'm not. You're going to marry me."

She laughed and halfheartedly wondered if she had any option. "You're quite a clown."

"I've never been more serious. We'll start by having a swim and breakfast in the morning."

"You are mad," she said, emptying her glass and trying to convince herself that this was really happening.

"We'll see."

When, the following week, André told his father he planned to marry, his father had tried to dissuade him. Jane's father also objected to the match and made it clear he did so because he didn't want his daughter to marry a Jew. None of this mattered to either of them, and despite all the protests from their families, they married in a civil ceremony in New York that spring.

André took Jane back to Paris, where their first two years together were blissfully happy. Wherever in the world he traveled she went with him. On the rare occasions when he went alone, she was faithful to him. There were no other men in her life. They bought a house on the Riviera, where they spent their first summer together. She studied French with a tutor and soon spoke the language fluently. In the fall they returned to Paris, a city Jane had come to love. It was vital, alive, effervescent, full of interesting and exciting people. And she had the money to enjoy it. Everything was idyllic: their love, their home, their marriage, their life together.

Everything changed when she became pregnant. She felt morose and sullen, lost her appetite and hated the morning sickness that plagued her. She also refused her husband further access to her bed.

She tried to explain to him what she felt, though she was unable to explain to him why she felt that way. The basic problem, she knew, was fear. She was abnormally afraid of pain, not only for herself, but for any human being or animal. She had never been able to stand the sight of blood, even in the movies. Childbirth was contemplated with horror. She had heard so many stories of torture from other women that the notion of having a child herself was terrifying. André listened and seemed to understand. He did not try to fight her fears, telling her that after the birth of the baby things would return to normal.

As the time for her confinement approached, Jane knew her behavior became increasingly irrational. She was desperate and even considered suicide. She shouted at the servants, ate very little and refused to leave her room. She felt like an animal caught in a trap from which there was no escape.

The contractions began one night in bed. She felt a vague feeling of pain in her pelvis and then noticed that the sheets were wet. She called André, and when he came into the room, a more painful contraction came. Her pelvis tightened and then the pain went away. André began massaging her lower abdomen. Fifteen minutes later, there was another contraction, less painful than the last. After that, the contractions followed more closely, every ten, and then every five minutes.

André called the midwife and a half-hour later, they left for the hospital. In the car, she had two more contractions, made more painful by the bumps and jolts along the way.

She arrived at the hospital in a state of uncontrolled panic, was rushed into the labor ward and examined by the midwife on duty. Inexplicably, the contractions stopped and the midwife explained that she was only in the first stages of labor. The birth would not take place until the next day. André was told to go home and return in the morning.

Jane was given a private room and there, alone and frightened, she waited.

Four hours later, the contractions began again, this time more intensely. She began screaming and had to be held down by an attendant as the midwife examined her. She was two fingers dilated.

The doctor was called. He gave her an injection of Spasmalgine to relax the pelvis area. A mask was placed over her nose and she was given nitrous oxide and oxygen to calm her. Nothing helped. For ten hours she labored. The anesthetic, Demerol, stopped working, and underneath the mask, Jane felt trapped and claustrophobic. She screamed continuously, pleading with the midwife to do something, anything to stop the pain. The midwife's response was always the same. "Be calm. Breathe in . . . breathe out . . . Everything will be fine. . . ."

The pain, especially in the back, was constant and became stronger with each contraction. She was in agony. As if to echo her, the sound of inhuman screams came from the adjoining rooms. The lights dazzled her eyes. The stirrups left her helpless. On top of it all, she was exhausted. She hadn't the strength to push anymore.

When she actually delivered the baby, she was only vaguely aware of what was happening. The words the doctor said seemed to come from someone very far away. "Breathe in . . . breathe out . . . Stop . . . Push . . . Again . . . Again . . . Again . . ." She felt the tissues stretch painfully. She was being torn apart.

She glanced down through a haze to see what the doctor was doing. She saw two gigantic spoons that looked like fruit salad servers being put into her. "It hurts," she cried. Then she felt the baby moving out of her.

The doctor's calm voice recorded its progress. "The head has reached the perineum. The hair is brown. . . . The head . . . The forehead . . . The eyes . . . The first shoulder . . . Push now . . . again for the other shoulder."

She felt warmth on her thigh. In her delirium Jane looked down and saw the bluish-pink creature lying between her legs. Afterward, she would never tell anyone, not even her mother, how she felt at that moment. Only occasionally had she even admitted it to herself. She knew it was horrible, that there was something wrong with her, but she could do nothing about it. She had never been so repulsed by anything in her life.

She knew it wasn't André's fault, but she couldn't bear the thought of ever having sex with him again. Something inside her had snapped.

The next morning when André returned to the clinic and rushed into the room to see his son, Philip, she told him. She saw the euphoria leave his face; only in his eyes did she see any reaction. They registered a bitter dismay. But she repeated it because she meant it. "Never again."

Now, forty years later, she felt like a girl again. In spite of herself, she was in love with a man and she couldn't wait to see him again. It was silly, that longing ache, but she was defenseless, she ruefully admitted.

He was intelligent, strong and had an old-fashioned gentleness about him that she'd almost forgotten existed in men. And yet, deep down, she knew very little about him. In time that would change, she was certain. At last she had someone to look beautiful for. The face ironing, seaweed facial, manual and deep-pore cleansing, the tightening mask, all of it was for him.

Jane smiled to herself. He was the kind of man who would appreciate it.

VII

"But the designs have already been completed!" Philip exclaimed to his father.

The two men were sitting in André Rostand's office that same Monday morning. André's heavily lined face darkened, as he listened to Philip's protestations about the suspension of work on his twelve-meter yacht. From the breast pocket of his suit coat he took out the pair of heavy tortoise-shell glasses he increasingly used these days, though he never wore them in public. He slipped on the glasses and through them studied his son's face. As always, he found both resentment and stubbornness there.

"What is it that I've done," André said, barely able to control himself, "that's made you so foolish? Don't you recognize the threat the ring represents?"

"You're overreacting. So Marto got the Vermeer; there are plenty of other paintings around. We could start dealing in the Contemporary market."

"You don't know what you're talking about. We're dealers in the old tradition. We buy and sell quality. We're not junk peddlers."

Philip wagged his head from side to side, barely concealing a smirk. "If Marto's so powerful, why don't we make a deal with him? Between us, we'd dominate the market."

André removed his glasses and put them back in the inner pocket of his gray flannel suit. He had heard enough to realize that Philip had no understanding of his own legacy. "No other gallery in the world stretches over three generations. We have always bought and sold quality. I don't intend to change. Rostands will never descend to the level of Marto and his crowd. I'll handle the ring. You curtail your spending."

"But I've incurred obligations that . . ."

"The only obligation you have is to the gallery."

Philip glared at his father. "All right, what do you want me to do?"

"That's better." The baron stood and walked to the fireplace. "I've had an offer of several very valuable collections of paintings," he said, grasping the shaft of the cherrywood cane. He stroked the silver knob and continued. "The paintings are now in the possession of a Monsignor Weiller. I intend to buy them."

Philip stood and faced his father. "But . . . I thought there was a moratorium on spending?"

"This is a unique situation. It's essential we have those paintings."

"What's so essential about them?"

"They're worth a fortune."

"So! You'll pay a fortune."

"No, I won't." André hesitated a moment, tapping the head of the cane in his open hand. "They're being offered for half of what they're worth. The paintings were stolen during the war, looted by the Nazis. They're just surfacing now."

Philip leaned back against the edge of the desk, smiling sardonically. "Is this part of the grand tradition you were talking about?"

"Philip, don't be an ass," André snapped. "These paintings are on the market. Marto would snap them up if he had the chance, then use them to destroy us."

"Yes, even I can see that," Philip said, a hint of sarcasm in his voice.

"Good, because I need your help. When they're ready for delivery, I want you to handle it."

"Have I ever let you down?"

André looked at his son. He understood the question. It was Philip's price for his support. "No," André said softly. "That's why I'm counting on you now."

Philip, a pleased look on his face, walked behind André's desk and pushed the button that opened the paneled door to the bar. "Who's this Monsignor Weiller?" he asked, fixing himself a scotch and water. "How did he get hold of the paintings?"

"He's an old acquaintance," André replied, setting the cane down on the mantel and walking to the window. "We met briefly during the war. All I know is that he's in possession of them and wants us to take them off his hands. They'll be coming from somewhere in Europe; the first one arrives tonight."

"Tonight!"

André turned toward his son and nodded.

"Are you certain you want to get into something like this?" Philip asked. "You're playing a dangerous game."

"I have no choice."

"Who owned the paintings originally?"

"They're all dead."

"All of them?" Philip asked, a smile beginning to spread across his face.

"All but one."

Philip's smile faded. "Who's the lucky one?" he asked, taking a sip from his drink.

"Alex Drach."

"Alex Drach!" Philip shouted, a look of amazement on his face. He walked toward his father. "The Drach Collection? It wasn't destroyed?"

André shook his head.

"I see!" Philip exclaimed.

"No, you don't," André said quietly. "Furthermore, you'll keep your mouth shut. Only Grimaldi, Fuller and you are to know about this."

"Don't worry about me. Worry about Drach."

"Do your part," André said curtly. "That's all I ask."

Philip shook his head excitedly. "It's insane. What if he finds out?"

"He won't, at least not until I'm ready to tell him." André paused, walked toward his desk and added, "When I've dealt with the ring. Once that's done, the Drach paintings will go to Alex."

"You mean to tell me we're going to buy these paintings, then give them away?"

"That's my affair," André replied firmly.

"I didn't know you were a philanthropist."

"I'm not. Nor am I a thief. And neither are you. A terrible injustice was done to the owners of those collections, Drach especially."

"That's not our business."

"We differ on that, Philip. If I can help repair that damage, I intend to. Can you understand that?"

Philip sipped the last of his drink, then looked at his father. "All right. I sympathize with them, but where's the profit?"

"There will be profit enough for everyone. Just do your part and I'll do mine." It was a dismissal.

As Philip left, André started pacing the office. Philip was right. He was playing a dangerous game. It was the only intelligent thing he'd said all afternoon. André looked at the tips of his highly polished black shoes, imagining he was walking a tightrope. The question was how far could he get? The precariousness of the situation was unnerving. On the one hand, he had to protect the secret of his collaboration, especially from Alex Drach. At the same time he had to keep the Drach Collection and the other paintings out of circulation until he had neutralized the ring. Then, there was the leak.

He considered telling Alex about the paintings, but if he did, young Drach would surely discover the truth about his collaboration. He couldn't level with him. Better to secure the paintings and keep Drach close to him, both to protect and to monitor him. After that, he'd settle with the ring, and then, at last, with Montag.

VIII

Alex sat back in the taxi, absorbing the jolts as the driver swerved and bumped over the uneven, potholed streets. He'd spent the entire day in nauseating conferences with gallery owners, collectors, and the usual crowd of art patrons that streamed through his office. Few of them were truly appreciative of art; most of them were mere possessors of it. *"La honte, le remords, les sanglots, les ennuis,* the fuckers . . . ," he muttered to himself, expressing both facets of his personality—the educated intellectual and the street-tutored swag hunter.

He breathed deeply and focused on the problem at hand. He looked forward to seeing Sol Stern again. A victim of the Nazi concentration camps, an old eccentric and an authority on stolen art, Stern had devoted his life tracing art looted by the Germans during the war. Over the years they had spent long hours together sharing information about the thieves, rogues and con men they had to deal with in the course of their work.

The taxi nosedived to a stop and Alex paid the driver in front of a large, somewhat rundown apartment building in New York's Upper West Side. He walked through a large marble lobby, empty of the usual furnishings, took the creaking elevator to the sixth floor, and then walked down a narrow tiled corridor to a heavily locked door. He rang the bell sharply, waited for a minute, and then rang the bell again. Finally, he heard the door's interior peephole cover move aside, and through the closed door a rasping voice asked, "Drach, is that you?"

"Yes, Sol. Sorry I'm late."

"Just a moment." Chains rattled and locks turned. The door swung open and an aging man with a brittle-boned head peered around the edge of the door. "The burdens of security, eh, my friend?"

"My life story . . . ," Alex said, stepping into a room whose walls were lined with filing cabinets.

Sol Stern's thin face beamed in a halo of gray ovine hair. He gestured towards a cluttered table, beside which stood two straight chairs. "Take a seat," he said, then excused himself and disappeared into the next room.

The old man apparently lived an extremely simple life alone. Alex only had a few seconds to survey the room, devoid of furniture except for the table, chairs and filing cabinets, before Stern returned with two tumblers and a decanter filled with a golden-colored liquid.

"Sherry?" Stern proffered the decanter.

Alex nodded once, unsure whether to accept. "A pleasure," he said weakly, noticing a layer of dust in the bottom of each glass.

"You're in for a treat, young man. It's home-made."

Alex smiled, amused by the old rabbinical-looking character. In his baggy trousers and knee-length coat, Stern reminded him of a cross between an ancient scholar and an Irish tinker. He sipped the sherry, winced and said, "First rate!"

Stern lifted his own glass and said, *"L'chaim!"*

Stern knocked back his drink, set the glass on the floor and looked at Alex with an evaluative squint from beneath his bushy gray eyebrows. "Now, what can I do for you?"

"It's about the Drach Collection."

"Your father's?"

"Yes."

"Pity about that. It contained some beautiful paintings. Mostly Impressionist, if I'm not mistaken."

"Do you know anything more about it?"

"Only that it was destroyed during the war."

"I don't think so."

Stern's craggy brow wrinkled. "Why do you say that?"

Alex's voice took on the tone of a witness in court as he explained the circumstances surrounding the tragic end of Hugh Jenner. When informed of the attempt on Alex's life and the appearance of the Watteau, Stern's eyes widened in disbelief.

"Incredible," he murmured. "But then again, it makes sense. . . ."

"Why do you say that?"

"Well, for one thing no one actually ever saw the Drach Collection destroyed. It was rumored to be in Rome. If it's still around, now's the time to bring it out."

"What do you mean?"

"It's complicated, but it has to do with the law of adverse possession, which limits the rights of previous owners. Lawyers argue about it, but generally speaking, if a painting is in someone's possession, say for thirty years, and no one claims it in that time, title passes to him."

"Even stolen property?"

"In some cases, yes. Moreover, the statute of limitations expires not only on a particular property involved but even on prosecution of the crime itself. For art theft there are several time limits: six years in New York, five in France. In fact, there are only two crimes that have no statute of limitations attached. War crimes and murder."

"So you're telling me that once these paintings surface they can be sold legitimately on the open market."

"Yes, if there are no heirs remaining."

"I see," Alex said. "If the Drach Collection *is* about to surface, I'm in the way. . . ."

"People are killed for much less." Stern reached for the decanter. "More sherry?"

Alex declined. "Do you know anything about an S.S. Officer named Hans Montag?"

"Montag! Of course. He worked for Göring. One of the key people around in those days. Montag was responsible for most of the 'requisitions' that took place in Paris."

"Tell me more."

For an hour Alex listened spellbound as the old man described how, like the Romans of ancient times, the Nazis pillaged, looted and hoarded the artistic treasures of the people they conquered. "They had units devoted to nothing but confiscating art. When the Wehrmacht moved into a city, behind them came the looters with their lists already prepared. They knew exactly what they wanted. Rare paintings, tapestries, silver, gold, everything of value. They loaded the loot on trucks or special trains and shipped it back to Germany. Then the top boys would scramble for the spoils. It was the greatest burglary in history.

"Take Göring," Sol said. "He was a fanatic about art. By the end of the war he had amassed the largest art collection any one individual has ever possessed. Just to give you an idea, he once traded a hundred and seventy-five paintings for a Rubens. . . ."

"I heard he had a weakness for pulpy nudes."

"More than that. He had a hawk's eye for any masterpiece. No matter where it was hidden, he would use any tactic to get his hands on one." Stern's albescent fingers grasped the decanter and he poured himself another drink. "Hitler, on the other hand, never really appreciated the pictures that came into his possession. He looked at them, had them stored and forgot about them. To him they were only part of a collection that bore his name."

"But why the fascination with art?" Alex asked.

Stern turned his head in the direction of his files. "I take it you don't know much about Nazi Germany, young man." Stern's hand fluttered. "The thing you have to remember is that Hitler not only wanted to conquer his enemies militarily, he also intended to reshape their culture. Art was the prime target in that effort. He viewed Van Gogh, Matisse, Cézanne and most modern artists as psychologically warped misfits. He wanted all their paintings burned or banned. Of course, any work of art produced by a Jew or a Bolshevik, anything showing Jewish themes—even if painted by non-Jews—anything depicting exploitation or social misery, anything glorifying the African or the Negro race, was considered degenerate. Hitler wanted patriotic, inspiring art, works that supported his idea of a master race. He even made elaborate plans for a museum to be built in Linz, his birthplace, which was to house the greatest collection of art in Europe. Linz was to be the cultural center of a new civilization built on the concept of Aryan supremacy."

Alex was impressed but persistent. "Whatever happened to Montag?"

The old man sat back, glass in hand, and rubbed his aquiline nose. He thought for a moment. "I believe he was killed in Rome when the Americans took the city. Though there was a rumor that he may have survived the war."

"Only a rumor?"

Stern shook his head. "It's hard to sort these things out. One also hears rumors that some of the looted art is being used to support . . ."

"War criminals?"

"The rumors are more adventurous. They say there is some vast collection . . . hundreds of paintings . . . that will be used to support a Neo-Nazi network that runs through Europe and Latin America. I give it no credence."

"Neither do I," Drach said. "Anything else?"

"I haven't got anything on Montag, but you might try the O.S.S.* files in the National Archives. Washington has declassified them this year. Check through the material compiled by the Allied Intelligence Art Looting Unit. You might find a lead there."

Alex rose to leave.

"Sorry I couldn't do more for you," Stern said.

"You're always helpful," Alex said, moving to the door.

At the door the old man grabbed Alex's arm. "Don't chase shadows, son. This won't redeem your father. . . ."

"I know that," Alex said curtly. "I'm not interested in redeeming my father. I'm interested in the collection. More than that, I want to find out who's been trying to kill me."

"Of course. I apologize. You'll be going to Washington, then?"

Alex nodded. "In a couple of weeks. I've just got back. The backlog of work is overwhelming."

"Well, when you get down there, be careful. D.C.'s not what it used to be. You know, the junkies . . ."

"Thanks for the sherry, Sol."

IX

The exhibition at Rostand International that night reminded Alex of a film première, with the added cachet that the art opening had intellectual snob appeal.

Alex, in black tie and dinner jacket, moved through the stylish crowd. He estimated it at roughly seven or eight hundred. Few

* Office of Strategic Services, the wartime predecessor to the CIA.

guests, of course, were there to see what was hanging on the walls. The paintings were only a backdrop to the fashionable gathering of beautiful people dressed in couturier-designed clothes. Attended by waiters serving champagne and canapés, the entire crowd was also being carefully watched by Rostand's security guards, who were as formally dressed as the guests they observed.

Rostand International was not downtown Soho, where anything could happen. Bizarre and shocking happenings were out of the question here. This was a solid-core, blue-chip audience, where names symbolized more than family and good breeding. Those invited were walking institutions, bearing names that dominated financial and industrial empires that spanned the globe.

As Alex walked into the crowded vestibule, the heady scent of musky perfumes, cigar smoke and the tinkle of laughter enveloped him. He glanced around the gallery. Another typical opening, he said to himself, regretting his decision to attend. There was nothing to gain by coming; he wasn't going to discover the source of the leak this way. He was also disappointed because he didn't see Cubitt Keeble. His eyes became hostile gray slits as he moved through the crowd, listening to snatches of conversation.

A tall, distinguished-looking man acknowledged Drach's set smile as he explained to a young woman that paintings were a better investment than Ginza real estate!

Elsewhere, a sophisticated matron was discussing the Vermeer sale at Sotheby's, wondering aloud whether Rostand International was on the decline.

"He's really not up to it, anymore."

"Who?"

"Rostand."

"Why do you say that?"

"In the old days he'd never let a painting like that slip through his fingers."

Another woman interrupted. "Don't count him out, darling. He's a very shrewd man."

Further on, a cluster of guests was celebrity spotting, pointing out the new arrivals. "Christ," someone remarked, "if they bombed this place the DOW would have a heart attack."

"If who bombed this place?"

"I don't know . . . anyone. The Arabs, I suppose."

Irritated, Alex decided to leave. As he pushed his way through the hallway leading to the front exit, he encountered André Rostand. Rostand was standing with Jane Rostand, who was engrossed in conversation with a female sculptor. They shared an interest in, and affection for, Shintoism.

Jane wore a slip of a dress. Black velvet, it was backless and fitted her body snugly. Over her shoulders was draped a black silk shawl. The only ostentation was a pair of hoop diamond earrings. She was, as always, beautiful.

Alex approached the group and Jane looked at him, smiled coldly, then immediately returned her attention to the sculptor.

Alex ignored the slight, and greeted André Rostand. The two men shook hands formally, as if meeting for the first time.

"Any progress?" André asked.

"None yet," Alex replied, sensing a weariness in Rostand.

André avoided Drach's eyes and seemed out of sorts. "I'm on my way to Zurich tonight. If you have any news, get in touch with Fuller. Tell him you want to speak to me, but don't explain why. He's been instructed to tell you where I can be reached." André looked across the room. A flicker of disapproval crossed his face.

Alex followed the line of Rostand's gaze to Philip, who stood surrounded by a throng of attractive women. Philip looked bored. The women around him were typically New York, attracted to a man they knew would treat them badly. Like moths around a flame, they had to be burned in order to feel.

"He's smashed," André said, bitterly.

"Just enjoying himself."

"The future of Rostand International," André muttered sarcastically.

Alex remained silent; there was nothing to say. The old man had always resented his son. It was the one reason Alex tolerated Philip. He could understand: Philip was a father-wounded son. It was not easy to exorcise the grief of a man love-starved for a father. Alex knew that so well.

For several moments the two men stood in silence. Alex found himself listening to Jane's conversation with the sculptor.

"Did you hear about Johnston?" the sculptor inquired.

"The critic?" Jane responded in a puzzled voice.

"Yes. He's doing obits now. That series killed him."

"What series?" Jane asked. "I never read the papers."

"Well, what do you read? I mean, if you don't read the papers."

"Women's Wear Daily, Vogue, things like that."

"Well . . . as I was saying . . . It was a series about the art world's underbelly."

"Did you say 'belly'?"

André, who had been listening as well, smiled ruefully and shook his head.

Jane turned to André as if asking for help. "Do you know about the series?"

"Yes. I think it had to do with the practice of some museum curators accepting paintings from the artists they're showing. It tends to make their selection more assured."

"Well, don't you think gratitude is essential . . . I mean, in the world today?"

"Sometimes," André replied, amusement in his eyes. "Sometimes."

Alex excused himself, hastening to get away from the conversation. He started for the door, then stopped. Cubitt Keeble, standing an inch or two taller than the crowd, was staring directly at him. She was smiling as though for him alone. Alex was in trouble. As he inched through the crowd to be closer to her, her jade-green eyes once again stunned him. "Have you been here all evening?" he asked when he reached her. The question was guarded, and yet he knew at once that the worst thing between a man and a woman was too much caution.

Her reaction was direct and simple. "Long enough. I'm glad you're here."

"Are you enjoying yourself?"

She raised a glass of champagne to her lips and surveyed the crowd. "I'm bored."

"I know what you mean. There isn't one person in the room looking at the walls. They're all standing around looking at each other."

"Forced appreciation."

After that neither of them said anything. Alex wondered what she was thinking. He had to admit that he wasn't there to look at the paintings either. He was there to see her.

Suddenly they both began speaking, almost at the same time. Alex stopped. "I'm sorry."

"No, go ahead."

Alex hesitated for a moment, then said, "It's just that the last time we met I didn't have the opportunity to ask what it is exactly that you do."

"I work for the Rostands."

"Doing what?"

"I'm another set of eyes."

"Green eyes. They're lucky."

Cubitt smiled, and her face softened.

"Are you based in New York?" Alex asked.

"For the time being. I'm staying at the Carlyle."

"A nice place to stay." Another guarded response.

"It's handy."

Suddenly Philip pushed between them. "Enjoying?"

Cubitt flashed her eyes at him, unsmiling. "The crowd's a bit dull, but the champagne is good."

"Well at least you have Alex here," Philip said, sounding annoyed.

Alex didn't react on the surface, but the air between him and Philip was charged with instant hostility. Philip had always enjoyed being rude to him, but there was more than that in Philip's voice this time. Alex made as if to move on.

"Wait a minute," Cubitt said, detaining him with a tug at the lapel of his dinner jacket.

He felt the long, dark red fingernail of her index finger scrape the black silk.

Philip scowled. A deep flush spread upward from his shirt collar. "We'd better be going," he said to Cubitt. "I have to drive Father to the airport. I'll take you home first."

Cubitt grimaced. "I've just arrived. I can see myself home."

Alex could see that Philip was beginning to perspire heavily. Cubitt was pressing him hard.

"Suit yourself," Philip said harshly. He broke away from them and pushed through the crowds toward the door.

"Moody guy," Alex said.

"Don't worry. I'll smooth things out later." She lowered her eyes. "Do you have a car?"

"I have taxi fare."

"May I share it?"

Alex looked around the gallery. The crowd had thinned considerably. He reminded himself to be careful. His warning system was in high gear now, though he didn't hesitate. "Of course you may."

X

An hour later, Baruch stood at the Customs counter in New York's Kennedy International Airport, while an inspector studied the canvas he had brought from Rome. The official, a weary man, wore a wrinkled blue shirt stained with sweat.

Nearby, a young man with explosive red hair waited nervously as another Customs man picked delicately through a tattered yellow knapsack.

Baruch, relaxed as though he were going to a movie, sniffed his carnation and watched the inspector leaf through a large book. Baruch noticed with annoyance that the flower had lost its bloom. He removed it from his lapel and tossed it in a neat arc toward a nearby wastepaper basket.

"You a basketball player?"

Baruch smiled. "Football."

"I played a little myself a long time ago."

Baruch nodded. "The game's changed."

"You betcher ass it's changed. Niggers took it over." Baruch nodded again as the Customs man continued. "Just like they're takin' over everything else." Baruch nodded a third time. Finally, looking up from his book, the Customs man regarded the painting. "What is that, anyway? Paris?"

"Yes. Do you like it?"

"Well . . . modern art. I'm not much up on that sort of stuff." The Customs man gestured toward a younger fellow down the line. "Freddie? C'mere a minute and take a look at this." As Freddie walked toward them, the Customs man said, in a confidential voice, "Freddie's an art student . . . a *graduate* student." He was obviously impressed by the fact, but took care to add: "A little, uhhh . . ." and his hand wiggled from side to side. Baruch nodded, understanding. "Fruit," the Customs man explained, unnecessarily.

As Freddie approached the two, he regarded the canvas with a look of boredom.

"Paris," the Customs man offered, helpfully.

Freddie turned to Baruch: "A souvenir?"

"Yes. Striking, don't you think?"

"How much did you pay for it?" Freddie asked in a condescending voice.

"Four hundred." He shrugged. "Four hundred and change."

Freddie smiled, as though he regarded Baruch as a fool. "Okay," he said to the inspector.

The Customs official chalked the painting's back and then, pointing to Baruch's leather shoulder bag, asked, "What'ya got in there?"

"My insulin," Baruch replied, opening the bag.

The inspector pulled out a vial of clear white liquid along with several encapsuled syringes. "What's it for?" he asked.

"I'm a diabetic."

"Oh, must be rough." He replaced the insulin and syringes, rummaged through the case, flipped it closed and buckled the leather strap. "Have a good day," he said, turning to his computer to punch in Baruch's clearance.

Baruch picked up the shoulder bag, then the painting and walked through the swinging doors into the airport. There, he noticed a Hare Krishna girl, went over to her and accepted the carnation she pinned to his lapel. He handed her a dollar, and with the brown paper parcel secure under his arm, walked outside the terminal.

Parked a few yards from the front entrance, a black Cadillac limousine nudged slowly forward. Its front headlights blinked twice.

Baruch smiled, and walked toward it.

Through the lowered rear window of the limousine Philip Rostand peered at him. "The carnation says you're Brother Baruch."

Baruch nodded, fingering the carnation. "You must be Rostand International."

"Welcome to the Big Apple," Philip said. The door swung open and Baruch bent to enter.

In the rear of the limousine Baruch positioned himself on the jump seat facing André and Philip Rostand. André Rostand, his face partly concealed by the brim of a black homburg hat set squarely on his head, pressed a button on the armrest. "The gallery," he said curtly. The limousine slid away from the curb and sped off toward Manhattan.

"Meet my father, Brother Baruch, André Rostand. My name's Philip."

Baruch's blond head bowed slightly. "Forgive the rumpled appearance of my suit. It was a long flight."

"I know what you mean; I just did the same run myself. It's . . ."

"Any trouble?" André asked, cutting him off.

"None." The monosyllabic reply implied professional pride. "The overpainting worked perfectly. There were no problems with the declaration. So long as we stay under five hundred dollars, there will be nothing to worry about. No inspections. No problems!"

"Good," Philip said. "We'll clean the painting tonight at the gallery. If it's genuine . . ."

"I presume it's in good condition," André interrupted again. "If so, the funds will be deposited in the Monsignor's account within three days."

"I'm sure you'll be pleased," Baruch said, watching Philip closely. Tiny beads of perspiration had suddenly begun to form on Philip's forehead.

XI

Alex and Cubitt strolled north along Madison Avenue toward the Carlyle Hotel. It was nearly ten o'clock. The streets were thinly blanketed with an icy dust blown by the freezing winds off the Hudson River. Walking along the silent empty streets, Cubitt leaned on Alex's arm.

"Isn't it beautiful?" she said. "It reminds me of a white desert."

"It reminds me of frost."

"You're not the romantic type, are you?"

"Not when I'm freezing."

They walked briskly for a few more blocks to the Carlyle, and, once inside the entrance, stopped.

"Thanks for seeing me home," Cubitt said, unbuttoning her fur coat. Until then Alex had concentrated on her face but now, as the coat fell away, it was impossible for him not to look at her body. She smiled as though reading his thoughts. "Where do you live?" she asked.

"Gramercy Park."

"You've come out of your way."

"Not really."

Cubitt laid her hand on his arm. "Would you like a drink before you go? It'd warm you up."

Alex smiled. "I'm romantic enough for that."

They took an elevator to the eleventh floor and walked in silence down the long corridor to Cubitt's suite. She unlocked the door and passed on ahead of him through several rooms, turning on lights as she went.

"Is there no end to it?" he asked.

"Don't worry! Only another half-mile to go before we reach the bar."

"At least you don't have traffic problems."

Cubitt led him into a room with an Oriental flavor. A subtle glow from a lantern lamp reflected off the Chinese tea-papered ceiling. She draped her coat over a black-lacquered armchair and busied herself fixing drinks. Alex sat on a hard Japanese sofa framed in ebony, brass and mother-of-pearl. Next to him an orchid-filled bowl rested solidly on an ivory inlaid chest. Cubitt, carrying a glass of Martinique rum in each hand, sat down beside him.

"I'm afraid the furniture isn't very comfortable in here," she said, handing him the drink. "It's not exactly my taste."

"Nothing's more contagious than bad taste. It's the disease of our time."

She looked at him quizzically. "Like the art scene?"

"Exactly. I go to openings regularly. It's amazing. Everyone knows the stuff on the walls is a hype, but people still flock to them."

Cubitt sipped her rum. "Then why do they go?"

"I guess they just like being stroked." As a finale to his lecture, Alex raised his glass. "Cheers." He sipped the rum. "Nelson's Blood."

"Rhum St. James, to be exact."

Alex glanced at her over the rim of his glass. Her eyes were softer now from the effect of the rum, and he found her extremely attractive. Yet only an hour ago he was thinking how dangerous she could be. That was part of her appeal. He noticed that her face contained the same elements. From the front her features were soft and alluring while in profile they were much more severe.

She returned his long gaze. "What are you thinking about?"

He shrugged. "Living on the edge."

"What's that?"

"Right here."

A slight smile played across her lips. "You have a nice accent," she said changing the subject. "It's sort of nondescript. You're not American, are you?"

"I am, but I grew up in France."

"How did you come to be here?"

"The same way you did; Rostand. I was adopted by the old man when I was fourteen."

"Strange. Philip didn't tell me that. But it explains why."

"Why what?"

"Why Philip's so antagonistic toward you. . . . Sibling rivalry."

"That's part of it, I suppose."

Alex stood up, walked to the bar and set his empty glass down. He remembered Philip's darkened face earlier that night at the gallery. "If you knew that, why did you provoke him?" he asked.

Cubitt shrugged and using her long, delicate fingers like a comb, swept her hair away from her face. "I didn't provoke him."

"Of course you did. And you knew perfectly well that you were doing it. We both know that. You were making him angry so he'd come back for more."

"I didn't know you were a psychiatrist."

Alex smiled, vaguely amused. "I'm not," he said, "but I know a button-pusher when I see one."

Cubitt shifted on the sofa. She kicked off her shoes and tucked her legs underneath her. "What"—she stressed the word—"is a button-pusher?"

"Every man has a button, his weak spot. Once you know where it is, all you have to do is push it to set him off."

Cubitt's eyes narrowed. "Now you've pressed mine," she said, her voice taking on a hard edge. She stood up, went to the window and looked out in silence. For a time she fidgeted with the drapes. Finally, she turned and looked at him speculatively. "Where's your button?"

"Can't you tell?" he asked, an amused grin on his face. He set his glass down and reached for his coat. "Thanks for the rum. It was warming." He walked toward the door, adding, "I can let myself out. . . ."

XII

André Rostand stood alone in the mahogany-paneled elevator, watching the buttons light up as it took him to the fifth floor of Rostand International.

Exhibition . . . Library . . . Viewing . . . flashed as the elevator passed each floor.

At the floor marked "Laboratory," the elevator's doors slid open and Rostand stepped out. A security guard stepped forward, touched his cap and said, "They're still at it, Mr. Rostand."

Wordlessly, André walked past the guard, moved through the space created by the noiseless parting of the electric doors and entered the laboratory. Inside, Marco Grimaldi was at work, flanked by Baruch, Ray Fuller and Philip, all watching him patiently.

"Is it coming through?" André asked as he approached them.

"Yes, sir," Marco replied. *The Lute Player.* It's perfect." He continued to work, dipping cotton into a pan of hydrocarbon solution and with exquisite slowness and care removed the remnants of Montag's clumsy overpainting. The removal was a complicated process based on oxidation. While paint dries physically in a few weeks, it takes at least a hundred and twenty-five years to dry chemically. By that time the surface of a painting, in a molecular sense, turns rocklike, chemically insoluble to any medium, including a hydrocarbon solvent. Thus the recently applied paint could be carefully removed without damaging the original.

"When will it be ready?" Philip asked.

Preoccupied with his task, Marco shrugged his shoulders. "Patience, Mr. Rostand." Moving his hand in delicate, circular arcs across the Parisian scene, he continued to reveal the hidden Watteau masterpiece beneath. After a pause, he added, "I can have it for you in a few days. Chemically, it's dry underneath. There'll be no damage."

"Good," said Philip, delighted with the gallery's newest acquisition. "We won't have any problem finding a buyer for this." Then, turning to Baruch, he added, "The rest of the collection should bring a fortune."

Fuller looked at André, as if struck in the stomach, his eyes reflecting shock and dismay.

André noticed Fuller's reaction, frowned, but said nothing. He glanced at his watch. "I'll leave you to it, Marco," he said. "I have to get back to the airport. The flight plan has been set for a midnight departure." Then, turning to Baruch, he added, "Will you be in town long?"

"A few weeks," Baruch replied. "I've got a number of things to take care of."

"Perhaps we'll see each other again."

"Anytime, Mr. Rostand. I'll leave my number with Philip."

"Fine," André said.

"Glad to be of service!"

The slow swirls of Marco's hand continued.

XIII

Jane Rostand pulled back the loose velour sleeve of her dressing gown and looked at her watch. Only a few more minutes. For a moment she sat without moving and relished the anticipation of the night ahead. All day she hardly had been able to contain herself, waiting for this hour. André's absence made it easier, though it wouldn't have mattered. He never noticed her comings and goings these days, anyway.

She ground out the orange Sobranie cigarette she had permitted herself to smoke to its gold filter. The occasion called for it. Then she got out of bed, and in front of the mirror, let her gown drop to the floor. She was pleased. Physically, she looked the same as she did twenty years ago. Perhaps her breasts were a little less firm, but they still had the muscle tone of youth.

She dressed quickly, having carefully chosen her dress and accessories earlier. She had just finished dressing when the house phone buzzed. Her taxi was waiting. She hurried through a long hallway lined with Rouault lithographs and put on a hooded mink coat on her way out the door.

Outside the apartment she pulled the coat more tightly around her and stepped into the cab. The air was freezing cold, though the wind that had buffeted Manhattan throughout the day had dropped. The taxi sped south on Fifth Avenue and entered Central Park at Sixty-sixth Street. Five minutes later it was on Central Park West, traveling north until it reached the Dakota, a magnificent Gothic apartment house overlooking the park.

A doorman in a heavy overcoat and cap hovered inside the porter's lodge. As Jane left the cab, he opened the heavy glass and iron door and tipped his cap. He smiled in recognition and said, "Good evening."

Jane smiled nervously and rushed on through the Dakota's ornate lobby, where she pushed the elevator button. The wait seemed interminable. "Ironic," she thought. Once she and André thought about buying an apartment in the Dakota. Its high ceilings and splendid architectural detailing reminded them of a Parisian apartment house. Built when the Upper West Side of New York was open country, dirt roads and farms, the building was so far out of town, the sophisticates of the day had quipped, that it was in Indian country. Thus the name, Dakota.

Now it was one of the most fashionable residences in Manhattan. In the end that was what dissuaded André. It was too trendy for his liking. He preferred the quiet elegance of their apartment on Fifth Avenue. He also found the Upper West Side too literary, too culturally self-conscious, too bohemian.

The elevator doors opened and Jane stepped inside. As always when she got this far, she felt a tightness in her chest that seemed to spread upward to her throat. She closed her eyes trying to control the dizzying sensation. She would never get used to it.

The affair had begun in early October, at Christie's, where she had gone to preview a sale of Old Master paintings. He had walked up to her and introduced himself. They chatted amiably about the sale and he had suggested lunch. She accepted, and they met two days later at a tiny Italian bistro in the West Village.

That lunch was a turning point. They sat across from each other and ordered veal piccata and red wine. She especially remembered the way he had dipped his thumb into the wine and then, cupping her face with his fingers, rubbed the crimson liquid back and forth across her lips. Finally, his thumb had pried open her mouth and come to rest on her tongue. Without thinking, she began to suck it. The taste of salt and wine lingered with her the rest of the afternoon.

A week later they met again and that time, after dinner, taxied to the Dakota. They opened a bottle of wine but left it unfinished while they made love hastily with most of their clothes on. Then they had taken a shower together, wrapped themselves in towels and talked for hours. The first time the lovemaking was neither as good as she hoped it might be, nor as bad as it could have been. But then they made love again and that time it was wonderful. When she returned home, she felt better, physically and mentally, than she had in forty years.

Through the fall and winter, they had continued to meet sporadically, both during the day and at night, the latter when André was out of town.

As the months went by she became more and more obsessed by him. She began to live for their meetings. Week by week, the love affair became her reason for living. Her life had split in two, like day and night. The time without him was fantasy, the time with him, reality. Still, she knew it wouldn't last. It was foolish to think it would. For the moment, however, she was enjoying herself, uninhibitedly, and so, she hoped, was he. He had made her come alive again. Everything had become more meaningful, more beautiful, since they had met. Even art, which she had never really cared about, now stimulated her. Amazingly, she found herself talking about the art world for hours with him. He was so unlike André in that respect.

The elevator doors opened and Jane stepped into a large foyer. A bright red and yellow Poliakoff painting provided a welcoming backdrop to the rich mahogany walls and dark-stained floors. She had always found it a very masculine apartment, and as soon as she stepped into it she began to relax. It was as though the place itself took her by the hand and caressed her.

As usual, he wasn't in the entrance hall to greet her. It was part of the little game they played. She laid her fur across the hall table and followed the long corridor through the penthouse to the master bedroom.

The light in his room was on. As she entered the room, his back was to her. He was reading, stretched out on a leather-covered Barcelona chair. She knew he was aware of her presence but he didn't turn. She walked across the reddish-brown carpet to where he was sitting, leaned over the back of the chair and draped her arms over his shoulders. "Hello, darling," she murmured.

Nando Pirelli looked up, his darkly tanned face breaking into a welcoming smile. He kissed the palm of her hand and led her around to face him.

"Wonderful. You look wonderful," he said, looking up at her. "Can I fix you a drink?" Without waiting for her reply, he stood and went to the bar. "White, or red, darling?"

"White . . ."

While Pirelli uncorked a bottle of white wine, Jane strolled around the study, her arms folded, every muscle in her body awash with desire.

"Will he be gone long?" Pirelli asked.

Jane turned and smiled. "Three or four days, this time."

"London?"

"Yes. The Jannis sale is this week."

"I know." Pirelli eased the cork from the bottle. "I'd be there myself, but the opportunity to be with you . . ." He looked down, boyishly unable to complete the sentiment.

Jane went to him. "I'm glad you didn't go."

He handed her a glass of wine. "Of course, for André, the sale is very important."

"So important he couldn't even trust Philip to handle it," Jane said.

Pirelli took her hand and led her to the couch. He took her glass and set it next to his on the side table, then, pulling her down to him, he slipped his hand underneath her dress and started to move it languidly across her inner thigh.

"What do you think he's likely to bid on?" he asked, smiling amiably at her.

XIV

The Lear jet taxied along the northern perimeter of London's Heathrow Airport, passing among the 747s and 707s like a sparrow among crows. It came to rest at Terminal Number Three. The aircraft's rear door opened and André Rostand, carrying his cherrywood cane and all the luggage he had—a hand grip—deplaned and went into the terminal. About a dozen Immigration officers lounged about, along with a score of policemen. It was, evidently, a slack time for them. There were no other passengers in the special section for private flights.

A self-effacing immigration official handed him a yellow card, which André hastily filled out, giving "business" as the purpose of his visit. He went through Passport Control, keeping half an eye on the policemen leaning against the walls, and started through Customs. He had nothing to declare, so he quickly headed for the exit on the green side.

A curt gesture from a Customs officer stopped him. He instructed André to put his grip on the stainless steel table, and the officer then began to go through it, carefully checking the contents of the case: two suits, three ties, several shirts, pairs of socks and a change of underwear. He opened André's shaving kit, spotted the electric razor, removed it from its case and examined it. Then with an apologetic look, he returned it to its proper place and said, "Sorry, sir, just doing my job."

André said nothing. He snapped the grip shut, picked it up and left the airport terminal. Two minutes later, he walked through the rain, the airport traffic swishing past him, and spotted the Rolls-Royce parked adjacent to the car park entrance. He slipped into the back seat and said one word: "Claridge's."

Claridge's, traditionally housing Britain's oldest families and numbers of visiting royalty, protected its clientèle from unwanted publicity. For that reason André Rostand always stayed there.

He emerged from the Rolls as the rear door was opened by a black-uniformed commissionaire, who, on accepting the fifty-pence piece André handed him, tipped a black felt top hat and walked ahead of him to open Claridge's front door.

It was on the dot of half past nine. Michael Koenig was seated, smoking a cigarette in the front lobby. While the porter took André's bag to the reception desk, André angled off and shook hands with Koenig.

"I appreciate your being here, Michael. I have a room where we can talk."

Koenig, tall and well dressed—a bit too dapper by Rostand's standards—picked up a leather briefcase and followed André to the reception desk.

The desk clerk greeted André with a smile. "It's a pleasure to have you back, Mr. Rostand. Your usual suite is ready."

Claridge's had two hundred and nine apartments, all with private bathrooms, fifty-seven suites and a staff of over five hundred. There was no set price for the privilege of staying there. The cost was a personal matter between each guest and the manager. André had never seen a bill, though he knew, to maintain his suite, Ray Fuller was paying a small fortune.

Rostand and Koenig followed the reception clerk through the front hall to the wrought-iron staircase that serpentined upward from the ground floor.

In Rostand's suite, flower arrangements were set in every corner of the room and a log fire crackled in the open grate. Period furniture rested upon deep lilac carpeting, and a collection of prints lined the dove-colored walls.

The clerk backed toward the door and inquired, "Is everything satisfactory, sir?"

Rostand absently handed him a five-pound note. "Perhaps we could have some coffee sent up?" he said. As the clerk left, Rostand motioned Koenig to the armchair in the front room.

André decided to remain standing and went directly to the point. "Today I want you to open an account with two brokerage firms," he explained. "One at M. J. H. Nightingale and Company, Limited, the other at Galloway and Pearson. Say that you are a private investor with considerable funds at your disposal, that you will be investing heavily on the London Stock Exchange. Do not be specific as to the amount, only that it's a substantial sum." André paused, thought for a moment, and then continued. "I also want you to explain to them that you travel a great deal and that most of your communication with them will be by Telex. As a result you'll have to arrange some kind of code to use whenever you buy or sell shares."

"Any code in particular?" Koenig asked.

"That's the right question!" He handed Koenig an index card. On it in capital letters the first three initials of Koenig's surname, "KOE," were typed out, followed by his date of birth, in reverse order.

Koenig read it and nodded. "I understand," he said with an amused expression on his face.

"I open the account," he said, "set up a code, and the funds are transferred by Telex directly to the brokerage house. I'm actually a blind for you."

"My money, my game," André said.

"You realize, of course, that the money you're investing will be subject to Exchange Control regulations?"

"I know that," Rostand replied, "but there will be ways of moving the funds out of the country after our business is concluded."

"What guarantee do you have that once the money is deposited in the account I won't simply close it and abscond?"

There was amusement in Rostand's dark eyes. "Read this," he said. He presented Koenig with two copies of a letter giving André Rostand power of attorney, duly authorized and witnessed, to operate the accounts in Koenig's name. "You won't need to worry about this at all, Michael. The funds won't even pass through your hands."

"I see you've thought of everything."

"Perhaps," he said. "I'll need your signature on that."

He waited a moment as Koenig read the paper again, paused, then signed it.

"You'll have to sign these as well." André handed Koenig two application forms for numbered accounts at the Swiss Credit Bank in Zurich. "I believe each of them has been filled out correctly," he said.

Koenig took the forms and read them. One was made out in Koenig's own name, street address and profession. The other was in the name of a Charles Stuart-Hunt, with a different address, and listing his profession as "Publisher."

Koenig absorbed the information without moving a muscle. There was a momentary look of confusion. "Why two cards?"

"Because you're opening two accounts. In Britain we're governed by the very strict laws regarding the buying and selling of shares."

André explained that under British law, any individual acquiring ten percent or more of the shares of a public company was obliged to notify directors of that company within fourteen working days. The law was meant to guarantee the public's right to know who owned a given percentage of any publicly traded company.

"I see," Koenig said.

There was a knock on the door, and a maid entered with a silver tray on which was balanced a steaming pot of coffee and a plate of croissants covered with a pink napkin. She set it down on the table in front of them and quickly left the room.

Rostand poured two cups. "Cream?" he asked.

"Black, no sugar."

André handed Koenig a cup. "That's why you're going to open two accounts, each under a different name."

"That's no problem," Koenig said casually. "My profession lends itself to that sort of role-playing."

"I know. That's why I picked you. You'll also be protected, of course, because the funds will be untraceable. There is no way the brokerage house can learn their source."

"One final question," Koenig said. "What am I getting out of it?"

André sipped his coffee. The question reaffirmed his judgment. Koenig was the right man for the job. Beneath the veneer of affection, he had the morals of a riverboat gambler. "Would ten thousand pounds suffice?"

"A nice weekend in Acapulco," Koenig said, smiling happily.

Before Koenig left, André told him that he would receive further instructions by Telex. Koenig, in turn, was to inform him at once if anything went wrong at either of the two brokerage houses. Finally, André withdrew five hundred pounds in cash and handed it to the theater producer. "I want you to use cash to open the accounts. It's safer and quicker! No paper trails!"

Their meeting concluded, Koenig left. André took a long, hot bath, ordered an Amontillado to be sent up from the Causerie, the hotel's bar and grill, then changed into a fresh suit of clothes.

While André bathed, Koenig took a taxi to the City and entered the gilt and glass front doors of M. J. H. Nightingale & Co., Ltd. Inside, he introduced himself to the head of the Personal Accounts section, a Mr. Simpson, explaining that he wanted to open an account with a deposit of two hundred and fifty pounds sterling, in cash.

Mr. Simpson frowned and suggested that Koenig would receive better service at his local bank, where clients with fewer funds at their disposal were more acceptable.

Mr. Simpson's demeanor changed considerably, however, when Koenig informed him that a sum of twenty-five thousand pounds, in the form of a transfer from Switzerland, would be deposited in his name within three days.

In an instant, Koenig was seated at Simpson's desk, where the producer signed the necessary papers to open an account, including an indemnity form protecting the brokerage house, should he buy or sell shares under false pretenses. With Simpson, Koenig also established a guarantee that he would be able to buy on margin once the funds from Switzerland were lodged and cleared through the Central Bank.

Finally, Koenig suggested that, due to his constant travels—he spent more time abroad than he did on English soil—he would like to use a Telex code to buy and sell his shares.

Simpson agreed that it would be a good idea and readily accepted the code André had given Koenig earlier in the day.

By noon Koenig was on his way to Galloway and Pearson in Cornhill. There, he followed the same procedure, employing the pseudonym of Charles Stuart-Hunt. He then ate a pleasant lunch of game pie and green salad at Corts Wine Bar, near the Old Bailey, before returning to his work at the Drury Lane Theatre.

At 12:35 the phone rang in André Rostand's suite. He lifted the receiver. The rapid beeps of a public phone box pipped at the other end. He heard a coin drop and Blandford Donahue's voice came through on the suite's private line. André glanced at his watch. He was surprised. Donahue was early.

"You must be hungry," he said. "How about some lunch, Blandford?"

Donahue expressed his delight, and fifteen minutes later, they met in Claridge's spacious restaurant. While a Hungarian orchestra played gently in the background, the two men enjoyed a lunch of asparagus vol-au-vent, jugged hare and a bottle of Château Margaux 1970.

Blandford Donahue, a jowly, pink-faced man with a Churchillian aura about him, had a healthy appetite. His watery blue eyes sparked with appreciation at the sight of the first course. His pale, thin lips widened in an excited smile as the second was set before him, and by the time he had finished the wine, along with biscuits and Stilton cheese, his face showed all the signs of soporific gratification and, most important of all to André, an obvious diminution of moral judgement.

The first sign of that was when, over coffee, Donahue was relaxed enough to inquire whether André was attending the Jannis sale that afternoon, a question the auctioneer would normally never ask. Donahue was renowned for his reluctance to talk about art outside the auction room. André's lunch had had its effect.

"That's why I'm here, Blandford. I thought I'd bid on a few items."

Donahue smiled. "Glad you're coming," he said as a waiter arrived with a box of Punch Corona cigars. André had ordered them especially because he knew they were the auctioneer's favorite. He also realized that Donahue was clever enough to recognize such attention to detail.

Donahue held the cigar at a right angle to the light, rolled it gently in his fingertips, then ran the cigar underneath his thin, aristocratic nose.

An odd silence settled over the two men. André wondered how he'd handle the subject. He decided to approach the problem obliquely. "How do you think the bidding will go today?"

Donahue stopped smoking. He sat back in his chair, his eyes fixed on Rostand. After a moment he sucked at his cigar, but made no effort to respond to the question. At last he said, "Why do you ask?"

"Because I want you to push the bids as high as you can."

Donahue looked around the room. "That's my job," he quipped.

"Yes, I realize that, Blandford, but I want you to push them higher than you normally would."

"What are you driving at, Rostand?"

"I mean I want you to chandelier-bid, take the bidding up on your own. Pull them out of the air."

Donahue looked stunned. "That's unethical!"

"But you *can* do it!"

"I *can,* but I won't," Donahue said bluntly. Again, a silence enveloped them.

André drew a folded piece of paper from his inside jacket pocket. "I really don't know what to say," he said, his voice edged with embarrassment, "but I am aware of the eminent position you hold with the Workers' Pension Fund. You're their chief consultant on art investment, are you not?"

Donahue nodded cautiously.

"Your recommendations carry a lot of weight, do they not?"

Donahue nodded again. "I have some influence," he said quietly.

"I know this is indiscreet of me, Blandford, but I also know you recommend works of art to them in which you have a personal interest. I'll go further than that. Occasionally you are the secret owner of the paintings you suggest they buy!"

Donahue blanched. "Come now, Rostand. That's absurd."

"I don't think so, Blandford. I think it's an accurate description. As chief auctioneer, you, along with several department heads, divert items that would normally go to auction, to yourselves. You and your colleagues also accept kickbacks from collectors who sell to the

Pension Fund on your recommendation. It may sound absurd, but it's true, and you know it!"

Donahue, nervously plucking at a gold cufflink, began to sweat. "You can't prove that."

André's eyes lifted. "I think I can." He poured Donahue another cup of coffee. "Or would you rather have a brandy?" he offered sympathetically, fingering the paper he still held.

Donahue puffed rapidly on the cigar and was visibly beginning to squirm. "Wherever did you hear such scurrilous things about me?"

"That's of no importance, Blandford. This is what's important."

André passed the paper across to Donahue, who read it. It was a list of paintings Donahue had secretly acquired and sold, on his own recommendation, to the Workers' Pension Fund. The figures involved, including a list of kickbacks from numerous collectors, were also given.

Donahue looked up. His face took on a vaporous expression of disbelief. "I see," he said softly.

André's hand reached across the table and rested on the auctioneer's forearms. "Now, Blandford, how about that brandy? I recommend the Château Fontipot. . . ."

The long-awaited sale of the Stanley Jannis Collection began spectacularly when a Dürer watercolor sold for £600,000.

André Rostand, seated in the sixth row center, participated in the indecent spectacle with poker-faced amusement. He particularly enjoyed the view he had of Bertram Bez.

The Iranian was dressed in a rumpled brown suit which tried to do justice to his figure. Bez had a passion for sweets, especially Moravian chocolates, which he was then sampling from a small box tucked in his right coat pocket. At an angle to Bez, André was in a perfect position to gauge his reactions as the bidding continued.

In the auctioneer's stand, portly, bland and apparently calm, Blandford Donahue went through the motions of selling the Dürer with a pained but professional air of a monarch about to abdicate his throne. His voice, sacerdotal in tone, responded to the bids in a rapid cadence. "Two hundred thousand, three hundred thousand?"

The perspiration on Donahue's brow was highlighted by television lights that glared from every corner of the salesroom. Beneath the glitter board he scanned the jam-packed room. The board, resembling the scoreboard at the Olympics, converted pounds sterling into half a dozen different foreign currencies. To the left of the auctioneer's box, a bank of telephones linked the salesroom with bidders from as far away as Los Angeles and Tokyo, where the fact that it was four in the morning did not seem to deter them.

Crowded into cushioned salon chairs around André, elegant-looking men and women sat immobile as the astronomical bids tumbled from Donahue's lips. To most of those in attendance, the game being played was incomprehensible. To André, however, it was a beautiful display of craftsmanship on the auctioneer's part. From out of the chaos Donahue imposed order with a firm voice and converted the jumble of signals, symbols and gestures into the nexus of hard, cold cash.

André had bid on the Dürer, touching his pearl tiepin half a dozen times, jump-bidding Bez and forcing the prices ever higher. At the £500,000 mark, however, he withdrew. Today, he wasn't buying; he was setting them up.

After that the bidding continued between Bez and an anonymous bidder, actually chandelier bids by Donahue. The price soared in increments of ten thousand pounds a bid. Donahue was pushing the Iranian nicely. Finally, Bez took the Dürer, but only after looking about the room in amazement, trying to decipher who his anonymous opponent was.

For André, it was an exquisite moment. He relished the spectacle of Bez, his powerful frame weighing over three hundred pounds, shifting uncomfortably in his seat while overbidding on an item whose provenance was, to say the least, hazy. During the course of the bidding, Bez's dark-complexioned face occasionally turned in Duranceau's direction. The Iranian obviously suspected something, but the black eyes above the scimitar-like nose revealed nothing. The only indication that he was agitated was the frequency with which he delved into his right coat pocket for a Moravian chocolate.

Against the seventy lots that came later, the sale of the Dürer was the merest clink of small change. A Perugino Madonna went for £900,000. An eighteenth-century enamel miniature, described in the catalogue as "probably" from the collection of Louis XVI, was sold in ninety seconds for £1,100,000.

Minutes later, a bluish-green medallion, six inches in diameter, "attributed" to the thirteenth-century craftsman Robert of Nye, went for £1,500,000.

For Bertram Bez, it proved to be an exhilarating, but very expensive afternoon. He and Charles Duranceau, the chameleon-like French dealer, were responsible for sales amounting to £6,000,000, including the doubtful Dürer, the Perugino Madonna, the eighteenth-century miniature and Robert of Nye's medallion.

André Rostand left the salesroom empty-handed but elated. As he watched Bez moving at top speed—approximately two miles per hour, with the dignity of a hippopotamus—he smiled to himself and stood graciously aside as the reporters crowded around the disgruntled Iranian.

"And your age, Mr. Bez?" one reporter shouted.

"Does it matter?" the Iranian snapped.

XV

The Jannis sale ended at half-past five that afternoon. By eight o'clock the same evening, André Rostand had left Claridge's, driven to Heathrow Airport, checked through Immigration, boarded his Lear jet and flown to Paris.

He was met at the airport by Leon Decroix, director of Rostand International, Paris. Decroix, one of his oldest employees, greeted André like a visiting potentate. Such visits by Rostand were rare. He had an aversion to the city of his birth and especially to the Paris branch.

Now, chauffeured by Decroix, André stared at the late evening traffic, exhausted. He had been up all night, had two intense meetings with Koenig and Donahue, not to mention the tensions engendered by the auction, and now there was Villot to see. He groaned inwardly.

Decroix smoothly wheeled his somber black Mercedes 600 around the Place de la Concorde and parked in front of the Hôtel Crillon.

The Crillon, once an eighteenth-century ducal palace, was not a very sympathetic place to André. He didn't like the hotel. Too many bellboys, too many chambermaids, too many valets, altogether too much traffic. He would have preferred a quieter location. It was, however, convenient for what he had to do.

He said goodnight to Decroix, having arranged to meet him early the following morning, then walked through the Crillon's open iron gates into the bustling atmosphere of the hotel's front lobby. He acknowledged a deferential salute from the bellboy, handed him his suitcase, registered and then strode across the blue and green arabesque carpet into the bar.

He sat down in the shadows of one of the booths and waited. Across from him, two Japanese businessmen were talking quietly over their whisky and ginger wine. The drink was a ghastly combination, André thought, but he made a mental note to check up on the operations of Rostand International in Tokyo.

It was then that Edouard Villot came into the bar. André raised his arm to catch his attention. The Frenchman nodded, came forward and shook the art baron's hand. It was not the fishlike handshake so common among the French. Villot's handshake was firm and forthright, another reason why André liked him.

Villot took a seat in the booth. "A drink, *mon ami?*" André asked, speaking in French. He signaled to the waiter and ordered two cognacs.

Villot offered André a cigarette, which he refused.

"How's life treating you?" André asked.

Villot replied, puffing on a Gauloise, "A bit hectic at the moment. My mistress is demanding I marry her. My son is high on marijuana most of the time, and my daughter has just informed me she's in love with her dance instructor. I wouldn't mind, only her teacher is a woman."

The drinks arrived. André signed for them and raised his glass. "*Salut,* Edouard! To the burdens of fatherhood."

Villot shook his head and sighed. The two men exchanged gossip for a time, and then André leaned across the table and asked, "Have you had time to consider my proposition?"

"I've thought about it."

"And?"

"I will, of course, help in any way I can."

"*Bien,*" André said, relieved. "Tomorrow morning I'd like you to open a personal account with a reputable brokerage firm. Potin et Frères will do. Explain that you spend a considerable time outside of France and would therefore like to establish a code to trade by Telex . . ."

Villot continued to listen intently as André explained what he wanted him to do.

Fortunately, in France André was not burdened with the strict rules that applied on the London Stock Exchange. The Paris Bourse permitted an individual to buy as many shares as he wished without identifying himself. His use of Villot as a nominee was therefore a less complicated procedure.

Within a quarter of an hour, agreement had been reached. Villot signed two copies of a letter giving Rostand power of attorney over the account he was about to open. He also signed an application form for a numbered account at the Swiss Credit Bank. With a specimen signature on both forms, their business was concluded.

André handed Villot two thousand five hundred francs, which was to be used to open the account the following day, and moments later, the two men left the Crillon bar. They shook hands and went their separate ways.

Villot, leaving the Crillon, smiled to himself. In his mind's eye he was already picturing his mistress's curvaceous bottom lifting toward him at a convenient angle.

André, on the other hand, took the white-and-gold paneled elevator to his suite on the sixth floor, where he looked forward to spending an hour in a softly padded chair, with a heavy book in his lap and a light supper on the table beside him.

The alarm call came through the following morning at half-past eight. André woke up and groaned. He reached for the phone, listened to the operator's high-pitched voice repeat the noxious phrase, *"Bonjour, M'sieur . . . ,"* and acknowledged it with a mumbled *"Bonjour, Madame . . ."* Then he replaced the receiver.

He left the bed and padded across the room to the large windows overlooking the Place de la Concorde. The drapes pulled, he observed the bright, hospitable light rising over the Louvre. It occurred to him that his father had witnessed the same view each morning from his rooms above the Rue de Rivoli as a student in Paris during the 1890s. He wondered if he would have time to get to the cemetery where he was buried, then discarded the idea as impractical.

As he dressed in a pale blue shirt, mauve tie and dark gray suit, the room brightened and flickered to the play of the sunbeams. A preordered breakfast arrived, which he enjoyed along with a copy of *Le Figaro*.

Fifteen minutes later he left the Crillon and stepped into the front seat of Decroix's waiting Mercedes. They drove past the American Embassy and the rear of the Elysée Palace on the Rue Gabriel, across the Rond-Point des Champs-Elysées to the Place de l'Alma and finally to the Place du Trocadéro. There, Rostand told Decroix to wait as he stepped out of the car and walked into the Trocadéro Tower.

The Tower, a gigantic complex built sixty-five years ago, housed Sogegarde, Europe's largest storehouse of precious art works. Cylindrical in shape, and unseen except from the top of the Eiffel Tower, the Tower was a triangular-shaped building, surrounded by a moat complete with drawbridge. The two-hundred-and-forty-foot Tower was made of concrete and topped with a six-hundred-ton cupola. There was only one entrance, through a series of steel doors that could be opened only from within. If any of the multiple alarm systems went off, every door would have slammed shut.

To leave at night, the guards locked the doors from the inside and left through a narrow tunnel, which afterward was flooded with water. The following morning, the passage was drained to permit the guards to return. On the extraordinary chance that someone did penetrate the Tower's defenses at night, a gas was released, which, while doing no harm to the works of art stored there, asphyxiated any intruder.

Rostand, along with such comparable institutions as the Louvre, the Jeu de Paume, the Prado and the Tate, used the Tower as an art repository.

As André walked toward the entrance of Sogegarde, he was perfectly aware that from somewhere within, he was being watched on closed-circuit television. At the entrance, he pushed a button set into the wall and spoke into the microphone recessed into the outer wall. *"Numéro six-cent cinquante-neuf. À voir Monsieur le Directeur, s'il vous plaît."*

André knew there would be a wait before his account number was checked with his photograph in the files. Idly, he glanced up the Avenue Kléber and wondered how Villot was getting on. The trees along the avenue were stark and withered from the January cold. He knew he was still being watched and felt conspicuous. He would have liked to have looked into the camera, but avoided doing so.

Suddenly the door buzzed open and he walked into the second anteroom, where another camera focused on him. He repeated his number into another microphone and again had a minute's wait before the second door slid open. He walked into a third anteroom. There, he confronted a two-inch clear Lexan barrier, behind which stood the director of Sogegarde, Monsieur Jean Rey.

Rey, a squat, pallid man, tended to treat his visitors with the condescension of a governess shopping at the local *épicerie*. He stepped forward and peered at André through the bulletproof glass, then nodded in the direction of a hidden guardroom. He then lifted his fingers in some sort of signal and the final barrier disappeared into the marble floor.

"Forgive the delay," Rey said, extending a thin, limp hand to André. "You know how it is."

"Certainly," André said cordially. "That's why I've used the Tower for so many years."

Rey led André into a small, windowless office. He sat on a couch and directed André to a comfortable chair across from him. There was a pause.

For André it was an uncomfortable situation. While the director, of course, knew him, he would never refer to him by name, only by number, a system identical to that used in Swiss banks.

"How can I be of service to you, M'sieur?"

"I'm here to make arrangements for my bank's representative to enter the repository and make an appraisal of the paintings I have stored here."

"That poses no problem," Rey said. "For the sake of security, however, I would, of course, require some means of identification and code."

André nodded. "I understand."

"And the duration of the visit? Will it be a morning? An afternoon? All day?"

"At least two days," André replied, knowing that the director already knew the extent of his inventory. It was a subtle, but ineffective display. As for a means of identification, André suggested that his banker use his own account number, prefixed by the word *Cellini*.

"That would be suitable," Rey agreed. "Can you give me an approximate date?"

André, palms upward, replied, "Within the week, I presume."

"I'll make a note of that in your file."

That settled, André stood up and walked toward the door. He felt slightly awkward, as though he were a prisoner in the custody of a gnomish warden. "It's good to see you looking so well, M'sieur Rey," he said.

The little man stood, shook André's hand and led him into the chamber with the Lexan barrier. Again, the director nodded in the direction of the guardroom, signaled with his fingers. The barrier receded automatically.

André walked across the room to the exit, then turned and saw Jean Rey waving at him through the transparent screen. André waved back. He pitied Rey. The unreal surroundings in which he lived were in many ways similar to his own. Each of them was trapped in a vacuum of self-imposed isolation. He shivered and walked out of the impervious art-infested mausoleum.

While André was entombed in the Trocadéro Tower, Edouard Villot had had a busy morning. Having satisfied his mistress for the third time, he breakfasted on croissants, unsalted butter and raspberry jam, drank three cups of coffee and then taxied to the main offices of Potin et Frères, where he opened a margin account in his own name. Like Koenig, he left a small deposit in cash and informed the brokerage officer who interviewed him, that a balance of five hundred thousand francs would be transferred, by Telex, within the week.

He also explained that he spent a great deal of time outside the country and arranged to negotiate the purchase or sale of his shares by code, using the first initials of his last name followed by his date of birth in reverse. The account executive agreed to this only on the condition that Villot sign a detailed contract that freed the firm from any liability in the event of Villot's death or disappearance.

Before he signed, Villot thought of arguing the point, but then decided against it. It wouldn't really matter to him what happened to Rostand's money if, God forbid, he wasn't around to dispute the point.

XVI

André returned to the Crillon with Decroix, checked out of the hotel and drove to Le Bourget airport, where his plane was fueled and ready to depart. Two hours later, he landed in Zurich, cleared Immigration, passed unhindered through Customs and taxied to the Hotel Baur-au-Lac.

The Baur-au-Lac, a late Renaissance building on the edge of Lake Zurich, was majestic. The stone facade, three stories high, with intricate sculptured design around the gates, doors and windows lent the hotel an almost medieval effect. It was an impressive structure. It had to be, for the prices they charged him for staying there.

André Rostand arrived at the hotel just after lunch. He regretted his late arrival. The cuisine and ambiance were the finest to be found in Zurich. It was here that he had brought Jane on their honeymoon, another reason why he attached a sentimental value to its romantic surroundings.

Refusing the doorman's attempt to take his luggage, he mounted the wide oak stairs to the main reception room. Suddenly, a spasm in his chest lifted him onto his toes. He dropped his cane, crumpled and clutched himself as if attacked by an unseen foe. His bag slipped from his fingers and he leaned forward from the waist, clutching the banister. The floor seemed to rise up in front of him, its ocher planks glowing from the application of years of wax polish.

The bellboy ran across the foyer and applied a commanding pressure to André's elbow, steadying him.

"*Mein Herr,* are you all right?"

André inhaled deeply and nodded.

"Do you need a doctor?"

André shook his head, rejecting the suggestion with a double sideways wag of his index finger. His face was still white but the pain had eased. He straightened slightly, pointed in the direction of his bag and made his way to the reception desk.

As he signed the register he felt a hand touch his shoulder.

"Herr Rostand?"

André turned and his eyes, unblinking, stared up into the dry, marbled face of George Asher. His head shook as if trying to dislodge something. Asher's face blurred and then came into focus again.

"George," he said weakly. "For a moment I didn't recognize you."

"You look ill, Herr Rostand."

André smiled. It was the most sincere expression of feeling he'd ever heard from Asher.

Asher's hazel eyes softened. "Shall we sit down?"

For some reason the word *Todtentanz* kept running through André's mind. Death dance. It was not a good omen. He forced himself to stand erect, clasped Asher's right hand with both of his and said, "Let's get down to business."

Asher's face brightened. It was the kind of language he understood.

The two men walked into the hotel's front lounge, where, before a huge log fire, they settled themselves into comfortable, low-slung armchairs. André glanced at Asher, a thin, tall man, well over six feet, with a narrow unlined face that did not show his age.

"You're looking fine," André said.

"I'm afraid I can't say the same for you, Herr Rostand."

"Good," André said feebly. "You're not a liar, then."

"Perhaps, Herr Rostand, but one doesn't make friends telling the truth."

Rostand understood the subtlety of Asher's remark. The lawyer was a descendant of one of Zurich's oldest merchant families. His father had been burgomeister of the city and a member of the Federal Council. His great-grandfather had been one of the founders of the Crédit Banque Suisse.

Until recently, Asher's family had stood at the very top of the social pyramid of Switzerland. Now, after his failure as an art dealer and other financial disasters, his family had been reduced to more modest circumstances.

André felt for the man. In Switzerland, the loss of a family fortune was social disaster. Only one thing entitled a family to prominence, one thing made it aristocratic, elevated it to the ruling class. That was money.

As with Koenig and Villot, André detailed for Asher what he wanted the Swiss lawyer to do. In Switzerland, where there were four thousand banks—one for every thirteen hundred people—the trading of stocks and securities was done through the banks.

That was all the better for André, since the purchasing of shares had to be done anonymously, using the facade of the bank's protective screen. Although the Swiss banking system was custom-tailored to his needs and he could have traded on his own, he had contacted Asher because he wanted the insurance of an extra buffer between himself and the operation he had planned.

André instructed Asher to open a trading account with the Union Bank of Switzerland. Asher, known personally to the directors of the bank, would have no trouble acting on his behalf. Again André handed his Swiss surrogate two copies of a letter giving him power of attorney to operate Asher's account. He also handed him an application form with which he would open a numbered account, on André's behalf, at the Swiss Credit Bank.

Asher read the letter and, with a knowing look, signed all three documents. He looked up. "It's all quite straightforward," he said. "I've done the same thing for numerous other clients."

"You'll have no problems, then?" André said, rubbing his septum with the tip of his thumb.

"Not at all. It's quite a common practice here. No need to worry."

André looked in the direction of the waiter hovering in the background. "Drink, George?"

"Not especially. A cup of coffee would do fine."

André looked up at the waiter. "Two, please." He turned back to Asher. Now that the business was done, he began to relax.

Asher leaned forward and gave André one of his rare smiles. "I'm glad you came to me."

"So am I, George."

"I look forward to hearing how things work out."

"I'm sure you'll hear about it," André said confidently.

"I quite agree," Asher said. "My father felt exactly the same way." He tugged at his trouser leg and crossed one leg over the other. "I remember once, my father held a few coins in the palm of his hand. He threw them on the carpet and then asked me what I heard. I, of course, said, 'Nothing.' He told me to pick them up, which I did, and handed them back to him. Then he told me to listen again. He threw them on a stone floor and asked me what I heard that time. They had naturally made a loud clatter. Then he looked at me and smiled. 'My boy,' he said, 'always put your money where it can be heard.'"

André laughed. "Your father was a wise man."

"He was," Asher agreed. "Unfortunately for me, it hasn't worked out that way."

The Swiss Credit Bank, one of the three largest banks in Switzerland, was almost empty shortly before five that afternoon. André approached the doors of the imposing building at the corner of Bahnhofstrasse and was ushered respectfully into the banking hall by a uniformed security guard. Five minutes later, after having glanced through several business magazines without reading them, he was led into the third-floor office of Bertrand Keller.

The two men were not strangers. They had known each other for years, and during that time, Keller had acted anonymously for André in various financial deals.

There was one further important aspect to their relationship. Their fathers had grown up in the same little Swiss village of Endingen, in the Canton of Aargau. They had not known this until a few years ago when, by chance, André had mentioned his intention to visit the village on one of his business trips, which frequently took him to nearby Basel. They compared notes and discovered that Aaron Rostand, André's father, had once courted Sophie Keller, Bertrand Keller's aunt. That had sealed their friendship.

Keller, who stood six foot three inches, was anything but gnomish. He was a modern-day, effective banker who had worked his way up the hard way, spending years on grinding business trips in the Middle East. Apart from his business, Keller had two other passions: the four St. Bernards he raised, and his ten-speed racing bike, on which he pedaled to work each day.

The banker rose to shake hands and offered André a seat in a highbacked armchair in front of his desk.

André felt at ease there. The office was large but unostentatious, the desk uncluttered except for a large screen, which flashed the latest financial data from around the world.

Keller offered André a cigar, and in an unusual gesture, brought out a bottle of Tomatin, a Scotch whisky. André declined the cigar, but accepted the Tomatin. Keller poured two glasses from the hourglass-shaped bottle, then, glancing from time to time at the computer screen, listened as André outlined his business.

"Over the next two weeks I'll be investing heavily in shares throughout Europe," André explained. "Specifically, I'll be buying on the London, Paris and Zurich exchanges. At first, I'll be trading actively and speculating in a wide variety of stocks. There is, however, one company which will absorb most of my funds. At the moment I cannot give you its name, but I can assure you that it's very solid."

Bertrand Keller grinned knowingly as André continued.

"To start with, the trades will involve meager sums. Later, they will become more substantial, so much so that the impact may attract public attention, especially in the financial press. For this reason, among others, I intend to act anonymously."

There was no need for André to explain to Keller his reasons for coming. Swiss bankers took it for granted that their clients desired anonymity.

Keller nodded, opened his desk drawer and withdrew a large note-pad. He began taking notes.

"In order to execute these trades," André continued, "I've enlisted the cooperation of four partners. Each of them has opened a margin account through which the trades will be made. They will, however, be trading on my behalf. They have also asked me to open numbered accounts in their names."

Keller leaned forward and made a note. He didn't have to be told that André's four partners were no more than fronts for his opera-tion. But so long as no Swiss law was broken, there was no need to question his client's actions. What British or French laws were bro-ken was of no concern to him.

"This can be done," he said nonchalantly. "Of course, I must meet your associates."

André sipped his drink, set the glass down on top of the desk and reached for a leather portfolio he had with him. "Unfortunately, my associates are preoccupied with other matters. They've delegated me to present, on their behalf, the appropriate application forms."

André took out the four application forms and handed them across the desk. "It's more efficient this way, don't you think?"

Keller perused the forms, then read the names aloud. "Charles Stuart-Hunt, Michael Koenig, Edouard Villot and George Asher." As he read the last name he raised his eyebrows in recognition, but said nothing. He looked up at André. "I presume you have some means of protecting yourself against embezzlement?"

André pulled out the copies of the letters each man had signed granting him power of attorney over their accounts. He handed them to Keller. "You'll find the signatures match those on the application forms."

"Of course."

"To finance these trades," André said carefully, "I wish to arrange a loan."

Keller set the papers aside, glanced at the computer screen, then back at his notepad. "How much will you need?"

André leaned back, clasping his hands in front of him, one thumb over the other. "In all, I've estimated that I'll be investing approximately ninety million dollars on various exchanges. Since I'll be buying on margin, I'll need roughly sixty million dollars in liquid capital. I can put up half of that myself."

Keller continued to make notes.

"The rest," André continued, "I'll need from you."

The Swiss looked at Rostand. "Thirty million," he said, his face paling slightly.

André nodded slowly. He waited for Keller to make the appropriate remark. He did.

"As to the matter of financing . . ."

André cut in, "You mean collateral?"

"Exactly."

For the third time André reached for the leather portfolio and withdrew several sheets of heavy paper containing lists of his paintings stored in the Trocadéro Tower.

Keller was scarcely able to contain his impassivity. The list of masterworks before him represented an incalculable fortune. "It's a bit unusual—borrowing money on paintings—but I don't think it presents a problem. There will, of course, have to be the formality of an appraisal, certificates of authenticity and provenance, and a statement from you to the effect that none of the paintings can be removed from the Trocadéro without the express consent of the Crédit Banque Suisse."

"The papers will be on your desk in the morning," André said curtly. "One of them will have the code which will give the bank's representative access to the Trocadéro Tower."

"Excellent. As always, André, you've come prepared."

André did not respond to the flattery. He stood and picked up his portfolio from the desk. "Then I'll be in touch, Bertrand."

They shook hands and André was shown to the elevator. He took the ornate, highly varnished cage to the ground floor and walked into the freezing air of the wealthiest of all Swiss cities. He strolled along the shore of Lake Zurich and gazed into the distance at the wooded slopes of the Glarus Alps.

The city's church bells began to chime harmoniously. It was six o'clock.

On Limmatkai, he stepped into a waiting taxi and directed the driver to the Baur-au-Lac. He would eat a good meal, retire early and the following morning, take the train to Endingen. His hand

went to his chest. It was time, he thought. He might not have another chance to visit the birthplace of his father, and his grandfather
before him.

The following afternoon, when André reached the long curve of
the riverbank road that bordered the Swiss village of Endingen, he
asked the taxi driver to slow down. The Jewish cemetery, he had
been told, lay half a mile outside the village. Up a small rise the
driver pulled in alongside a cut-stone wall. André emerged from the
back seat and, with his hands in his pockets, walked the few feet to
the entrance of the graveyard. He stepped over an old rusty link
chain that hung across the entrance and began walking between the
lichen-covered headstones, blackened with age.

The cemetery hadn't witnessed a burial in forty years. The Jewish
population of Endingen, once forced to bury their dead outside the
village walls, now shared the same earth as their Gentile neighbors.

André walked faster now, feeling the cold north wind penetrating
the light camel-hair coat he wore. He had walked perhaps a hundred
yards before he saw a headstone with the simple inscription: "Benjamin Rostand, 1826–1897." Next to it, he noticed another headstone. He walked over to it. Hoarfrost, like a beard, covered whatever inscription was carved in it. With a stick, he scraped away the
frost to reveal the words "Rebecca, wife of Benjamin, 1847–1870."
His grandparents.

He stood now, hunched over between the two graves. After so
many years, he thought, he had come back home. Then he thought
about death. He had thought about it for many years. At first he had
dreaded the notion. Not because life was sacred. He wasn't a religious man in that sense. For him it was simpler than that. He took it
for granted that being healthy was better than being sick, and that
being sick, even infirm and helpless, was better than being dead. That
was when he was younger.

Now, his view of the end had changed. He was getting tired. Life,
in some ways, had become a prison for him. Death, he could see,
might be a release. He could understand how a man could want to
die, as once he might have craved a woman, power or prestige. He
thought about it. Freedom in death wasn't so much a conscious
desire as it was an impulse, like a bird that instinctively knew when it
was time to migrate.

Then he remembered his father. The image of the lean dark face consoled him. "Strange," he murmured to himself, how close he felt to him in this place.

He visualized his father standing in the exact same spot and tried to imagine what he would have been thinking about. Somehow, he knew his father would have thought about new life, about the ivy that covered the graves in the spring, about the future. His father had been like that.

PART SIX

———◆———

1894

His name was Aaron Rostand. He was twenty-four and he was an artist.

At the age of seven he had known that, ever since the evening he sat in his father's rocker alone in the house in Endingen. The sun was setting, the front room fading into shadow. He thought about lighting one of the oil lamps, but noticed that the dusky light had created strange shapes on the far wall. He imagined figures forming, fading and reforming as the light from the setting sun inched across the wall.

He went to the fireplace, found a piece of charcoal and began tracing the forms he saw on paper. He didn't think about what he was doing, letting his hand work naturally, moving almost by itself to re-create the patterns made by the changing light.

He heard the door bang and his father's voice ask, "Son, what are you doing in the dark?"

Aaron didn't look up. "Drawing, Papa, just drawing," he said absently. He continued to draw with the charcoal, and from that day on, pieces of charcoal were never far from his reach.

Now, on a bright September day in 1894, he was seated in the second-class train compartment with his father, Benjamin Rostand, watching the line of horse-drawn carts and wagons ambling along the dirt roads leading into Paris. From the speeding train, the carriages and landaus seemed to be standing still. Nearer Paris, he could make out the tip of an iron tower constructed by a man named Eiffel in commemoration of the Exposition Universelle of 1889. He had read about it in the newspapers back home, in the Swiss mountain village where he and his father had been born.

"Papa!" he said, nudging his father. "La Tour Eiffel!"

Benjamin peered into the distance through his new spectacles. At sixty-eight, Aaron's father was a strong, solid man with deep brown eyes, set in thick features that matched his bulky frame. He had an uncommonly large head that grayed gently above the temples. His hair, receding slightly to the right and left of his forehead, fell back wild and long to the nape of the neck.

"I see it," he said. "The black lacy thing . . ."

Aaron shook his head. "Imagine, Papa. Fifteen million francs. Such a sum, just for a monument."

Aaron moved closer to the edge of his seat, mesmerized by the paved roads and sidewalks full of people. He had never seen such congestion and, for a moment, almost forgot the reason he had come to Paris. As if to remind himself, he clutched the brown leather valise tightly under his arm. He had worked on its contents for two years, a series of drawings he would present to André-Louis Sabatini, the great *maître* and teacher at the most important art school in Paris, the École des Beaux-Arts. What Sabatini thought would determine everything: his qualification for admission to the school, his worth as an artist, his future.

The train pulled into the Gare d'Austerlitz, and in the ear-splitting din of clanging wheels and hissing steam, Aaron and Benjamin had to shout to be heard.

"How do you feel?" Benjamin asked.

"Nervous!" Aaron replied. "How do you feel?"

"The same!"

They both laughed.

Dressed in the finely tailored suit his father had made him especially for this journey, Aaron pushed and shoved along the platform to the carriage rank in front of the station. They hired a horse-drawn fiacre and sat back as the carriage lurched over the cobblestoned streets toward the heart of the Latin Quarter. Aaron was amazed to see so many lights. Gas lamps lit every street and *quai,* and in some of the newer buildings light was produced by electricity.

Never in his wildest dreams had he envisioned anything like Paris. Zurich and Lausanne, which he had visited as a young boy, were villages compared to this. It was hard to believe that only twenty-four years ago Paris had been bombarded by the Prussians and that the proud, self-indulgent Parisians had scurried about like a ragged army cutting down trees on the Champs Elysées for firewood.

The Beaux-Arts was on the Quai Malaquais near the Pont des Arts in the section of Paris which had been the heart of French scholarship since the Middle Ages, when Latin, from which the quarter derived its name, had been the common language spoken by students and teachers.

The school was a strikingly impressive series of eighteenth-century buildings flanked on one side by the Seine, on the others by the Rue Jacob, the Rue des St.-Pères and the Rue Bonaparte. As Aaron approached the front portal, he stared at the heavy iron gates and imposing statues on either side of the entrance. The statues, the columns, the fluted arches overwhelmed him with their size, solidity and grandeur.

Benjamin looked at his son. Not every father had such an opportunity. He had always been a religious man, especially after his wife, Rebecca's, death in childbirth. More than in the Talmud, more than in his faith, he had sought consolation for her death in Aaron.

From the time Aaron was born, father and son had been especially close. Whenever Benjamin was able to get away from his tailor shop, he and the boy would take long expeditions into the country. In summer, they fished together in the river that flowed beneath the bridge near their house on the riverbank, picked apples that hung fat and red in the orchard, and ran together down the green hills past the speckled cows that grazed lazily in the pastures. In winter the two climbed the steep, snowy slopes above the town, carrying the heavy wooden skis Benjamin had fashioned, then swooped down through the mountain trails cut through the deep woods.

When Aaron told him of his wish to be an artist, Benjamin tried to dissuade his son. He didn't want his son leaving home and going to Paris. He hoped that Aaron would become his apprentice and be a help to him in his old age. But the young man's heart was set on his dream, and finally he had given Aaron his blessing. Who knows, he thought, perhaps his son would be another Rembrandt, or better yet, a Rostand. So now Benjamin dreamed his son's dream. What more could he do?

Benjamin put his arm around Aaron's shoulders. They were the same height now. His son had started to fill out. Aaron's hair was longer than he usually wore it, perhaps for the style of the Latin Quarter, but he still combed it straight back. His moustache had grown and was now a fine black line on his upper lip.

The porter conducted them past the vestibule, along a large corridor with high ceilings and stained-glass windows. The windows opened on an enclosed courtyard. Clusters of students dressed in top hats, frock coats and trousers tapering to the ankle stood about talking animatedly. At the end of the corridor, Aaron and Benjamin were left alone in a large studio, its walls covered with charcoal drawings tacked up haphazardly, in some places three in a vertical row.

At the front of the room, dominating the entire space, was an elevated platform. On it rested a huge desk and a lectern. In the center of the room was a four-foot-square dais covered with a red felt drape. Around the dais, forty high straight-backed chairs stood empty, facing as many easels, waiting for paper or canvas, paint, brush or charcoal.

Suddenly a door flew open and a fragile-looking man holding a silver-topped cane walked into the room. He was impeccably dressed. A pince-nez on a fine gold chain dangled around his neck. *"Bonjour, Messieurs,"* he said curtly. "I am Sabatini. I believe you've come about some drawings?"

Aaron wondered how such a frail, fastidious man could possess so powerful a voice. He felt the man's presence immediately. Sabatini was obviously a blunt man who didn't waste time. Since the *maître* had addressed his father, Aaron remained silent.

"We're grateful for your precious time, Monsieur. For my son and me this is a great privilege, but"—Benjamin paused and looked briefly at Aaron—"it's more than drawings we've come to see you about. My son, Aaron, hopes to enter the Beaux-Arts. He wants to study. Under your direction, of course."

Sabatini gazed intently at Aaron. The eyes of the *maître* seemed to bore through him, but, surprisingly, he felt less intimidated than at first. Then he noticed Sabatini's hand, fiddling with the pince-nez. The hands were astonishingly delicate, yet strong, sinewy and darkly veined.

"What have you done?"

"Drawings. Would you . . . ?"

"On what?" Sabatini pointed at him with the cane.

"On paper, Maître. Or whatever was available."

"What do you draw with?"

"Usually, charcoal. Once in a while, pencil."

"Nothing in color? Watercolor or oils?"

"No, Maître."

"Do you have sufficient funds?" Sabatini glanced at Benjamin, as if gauging him.

Benjamin stepped forward. "We have the means," he said. The tone of his voice ruled out further discussion on the subject.

Sabatini nodded at Benjamin, then walked to one of the windows at the far side of the room. He stood looking out at the students in the courtyard. "Every young man who can draw a straight line comes to me," he said, his back to the Rostands. "They all want to be artists. Few of them, very few, really are." He turned and looked at Aaron, pointing at the drawings around the room with the top of the cane. "I'm not interested in a student who can draw a straight line. I'm not even interested in a student who can draw perfectly. I don't care how well you can duplicate what you see in front of you, or how well you can copy. No matter how exactly you reproduce nature, it is not enough. Copying reality itself reveals nothing. What I want is the inner being. You must be able to *see. Comprenez?*"

"I'm not certain," Aaron said.

"Well, at least you're not a buffoon. You can ask an honest question." Sabatini went to one of the easels, pulled a drawing from it and handed it to Aaron. "That is a drawing of a nude woman. It's competent, accurate, a faithful imitation of the model. But it's not art. The student who did that is not an artist. He is not *seeing* what he's drawing. He's only imitating."

Sabatini flipped the drawing onto a desk. "To begin, an artist sees from here," he continued, pointing to his eyes. "Then, from here," he added, clutching his chest. "You must be able to see in the end from your soul, and that, no one can teach you."

Abruptly, Sabatini pointed to a nearby easel and said, "Take a seat and draw my face!"

Aaron looked at his father, startled. Benjamin lifted a shaggy eyebrow in the direction of an easel.

Aaron selected a chair, a sheet of paper, and a narrow piece of black charcoal. His mouth was dry and his fingertips moist with perspiration. He looked up at Sabatini. He remembered the way he felt about the man when he walked into the room: fastidious and frail. He began to work by instinct. First he sketched an outline of the head in swift, deft strokes.

Aaron felt that Sabatini's features were too small for the space occupied by the face. The frailty was there. Sabatini had a large face, set on a small round head. While each feature was quite perfect in itself, the overall impression conveyed was of refinement, a finicky and petty character. The mouth was small, too small. The nose was average-sized, while the eyes were relatively tiny.

As the lines and planes took shape beneath Aaron's fingertips, André-Louis Sabatini's face began to emerge on the paper, a face that Aaron thought did not particulary flatter the great *maître*. He was about to add a bit more strength to the line of the jaw when Sabatini suddenly walked to the easel and grabbed the drawing. "I'm not finished," Aaron objected.

"No matter," Sabatini said. He went to the windows and examined the portrait, then glanced at Benjamin. "Your son does not think too highly of me," he said.

"Perhaps, Monsieur Sabatini, it's the way he sees you."

Sabatini returned to the easel and handed the drawing to Aaron. "Is that really me?" he asked.

"To me, Maître, yes."

Sabatini looked puzzled. "So delicate and gaunt?"

"It's what I saw. I'm sorry you don't like it."

"But not sorry you did it that way?"

Aaron flinched. He had made a terrible mistake, but he had to be honest. "No, Maître."

"I'm glad of that," Sabatini said smiling. "It's good."

Aaron took a deep breath. "You think so?"

Sabatini nodded. Aaron looked at his father, who showed the beginnings of a smile.

"You may start in the morning," Sabatini said, "in the last rank. Your place is by the wall there." He pointed to the far corner of the room. "I call that corner the sphere of fire. From Dante. Every student begins there, hopeful to reach the sphere of the angels on the other side. In time, if you're good enough, you may move around to the windows. It's up to you."

Sabatini shook Benjamin's hand and then told them to wait in the studio for a moment. He left by the door he had entered earlier and a few minutes later returned with a pale young man who dwarfed the slight, frail Sabatini.

"Rostand, this is Matisse, Henri Matisse, one of my students," he said. "He's agreed to help you get settled."

The two young men looked at each other and smiled. Aaron liked Matisse at once. He had a moustache and a short beard and looked every bit the image of a young artist: rough shoes, sloppy attire, frock coat and hands splotched with color.

Sabatini nodded to Benjamin, and said, "I'm sure he'll give you all the gossip about the school, Rostand. Matisse loves to talk. Happily, he can paint as well."

The week that Aaron Rostand enrolled at the Beaux-Arts, what seemed to be a totally irrelevant act on the part of a cleaning woman, working in the German Embassy in Paris, led to a series of events that altered the course of French history and with it, an aftershock which affected forever the course of Aaron Rostand's life.

As she did at the end of every working day, Petra Reichard, mop and dustcloth in hand, moved through the Embassy cleaning the floors and emptying watebaskets. Once inside the office of the German Ambassador, however, she rescued a few bits of paper from the basket and tucked them carefully into a tiny leather pouch she wore concealed underneath her dress.

The next day, through a series of anonymous hands, those same bits of paper found their way to the desk of Major Léon Henry, head of the French Army's Bureau of Counterintelligence.

Pieced together, the papers presented a detailed account of the French army's state of readiness in the event of war with Germany. Only an officer serving at General Staff Headquarters could have written it. Major Henry was looking for a spy, and there could be only one officer responsible, Captain Alfred Dreyfus.

Major Henry had no concrete proof that Captain Dreyfus was the spy. The handwriting on the document did not match the Captain's, nor was there any evidence that Dreyfus had any contact with the German Embassy. There was one salient fact, however, that convinced the rabidly anti-Semitic Major Henry. Dreyfus, from a wealthy, Alsatian textile-manufacturing family, was a Jew.

Alfred Dreyfus was arrested and ordered to stand before a court martial. The court martial that followed, against a backdrop of national hysteria, was held in secret. The case was crude but effective, and Dreyfus was found guilty. Still proclaiming his innocence, Dreyfus was publicly degraded, his officer's epaulettes ripped from his shoulders, his sword broken. He was sentenced for life to solitary confinement in the tropical hell of Devil's Island.

For the next year the arrest, trial and sentence of Alfred Dreyfus dominated the national headlines, and Aaron watched apprehensively as a wave of mass hysteria and anti-Semitism swept France. The cry of Judas echoed in the streets of Paris. In the papers, columnists called for a repeal of the law that allowed Jews French citizenship. In the cafés and cabarets, there was talk of expelling all Jews from the Republic. Mobs began to attack synagogues, and anti-Jewish riots broke out all over the country.

During that year, Aaron concentrated on his studies. Never had he worked so hard or learned as much. Sabatini's classes began promptly at half past eight in the morning and continued, with brief intermissions, throughout the day, a schedule enforced with iron discipline.

Each morning, André-Louis Sabatini strode from his chamber at the side of the room, mounted the rostrum and began the class with an exercise. He placed a canvas on an easel in front of the rostrum, gave his students three minutes to examine it, then had them draw it from memory.

"Today, I want you to look at a Boucher. Train your eye. Concentrate. You're not here to like or dislike the picture, to approve or disapprove. You're here to learn to 'see.'"

Aaron had never looked at anything so intently in his life. He took in every coil of line, every slash of Boucher's brush. Later, he would learn that the painting was one of Boucher's most famous works and that Sabatini had been given permission to borrow it from the Louvre. Entitled *Bath of Diana,* it presented two female figures bathing. The painting was all fresh pinks and blues, a pretty picture, Aaron thought, but artificial and candied. Nevertheless, he would remember every swirl, every puff of cloud the rest of his life.

A minute later a porter removed the painting and the class began to sketch the Boucher from memory. Half an hour later, Sabatini approached Aaron's place in the corner. He pulled the sketchpad from Rostand's hands and gazed at the drawing through his pince-nez. Aaron felt as though he were on trial again. Was this going to go on every day? He didn't know if he could stand it.

"Correct, Rostand, quite correct," Sabatini commented. "Good detail. For a start. But it's too rigid. Relax, give it some life."

"Oui, Maître." Sabatini smiled and moved on.

During the following intermission, Aaron met some of the other students. One of them, Georges Rouault, had a quiet dignity that Aaron liked at once. "Rouault works part-time in a stained-glass atelier making church windows," Henry Matisse explained.

Jean LaRoque, a third-year student standing nearby, heard Matisse. "Rouault spends a lot of time in church as well," he said. He turned to Aaron. "Do you?"

Aaron looked at LaRoque's long thin face and the arrogant, churlish smile spread across it. He had met this kind of bully before in school in Endingen. "Not really," Aaron replied with a casual smile.

"No, of course not," LaRoque's voice was silky. "Pardon me. I realize now that you're a Jew."

Aaron held his temper and walked away.

Watching Sabatini day after day, Aaron tried to find some clue to the *maître*'s inner life. Aaron wondered what went on inside, but Sabatini remained a mystery to him, just as he had remained an enigma to his other students for years.

Sabatini's private life was the subject of endless speculation at the Beaux-Arts, but no one had added much to what little was known about him. He lived alone and was rarely seen in public. So far as anyone could tell, his life was totally devoted to his teaching and his students.

Sometimes, though, when Sabatini looked out at the class, Aaron thought he detected a hidden anguish in the *maître*'s eyes, a painful sadness in the lined face. At such times Sabatini would say something harsh, almost cruel, as if to protect himself. "Only one in a hundred of you will ever amount to anything," he repeated often. It was as if he understood what it was to be young and full of hopes and dreams, and then to discover that most often, such dreams never came true. Aaron sensed that Sabatini understood his students, and realized that he couldn't help them. Your pain is your own, he tried to tell them. Without it, you'll never be artists. Even more, without pain, you'll never become men.

When the New Year's holidays came, Aaron returned to Endingen. He hadn't seen his father in over a year. In that time, much had changed. The Dreyfus Affair had brought hatred and mistrust to Endingen.

"Things have changed," Benjamin explained the first night of Aaron's return. "The people here are as divided over Dreyfus as the French are. The reaction is ugly, but, so far, it's mostly talk. Some want to expel the Jews from Switzerland, take away our land and return to the old days."

Aaron tried to calm his father's fears. "It's just politics, Papa."

"It's more than that, Aaron. Once or twice small gangs of thugs have been over to this side of the river and have stoned Jewish homes. There have even been a few clashes in the neighborhood. Nothing serious yet . . ."

The next week, helping his father in the shop, Aaron set down a bolt of cloth, went out, bought a *Kirschtorte* and returned to make tea. He brought the torte in and set it down next to his father's worktable.

Benjamin set his work aside and clapped his hands, then pointed to a shelf on the opposite side of the crowded counter. On it were a jumble of plates, cups and cutlery. "You know where everything is. . . ."

Aaron was preparing tea when a brick crashed through the shop window. He was not fully aware of what had happened until shards of glass and the brick clattered on the floor. Aaron rushed into the alley where he expected to see a few urchins running toward the marketplace. Instead, he saw a group of older boys, well dressed, smoking cigarettes, lounging several hundred feet away. They appeared to take no notice of him.

"Did any of you see who threw the brick through our window?" Aaron demanded, walking toward them.

One of them, a tall lanky boy, looked around at the others. "Anyone see a brick thrown?"

"What brick?" one of the others responded, smothering a snigger. The lanky boy stepped forward. "The only brick I've seen around here is the one between your shoulders."

His eyes burning with anger, Aaron walked up to the bigger boy. "Would you like to try and knock it off?"

The boys jeered. "A tough kike, eh? Trying to be a hero, he is . . . insulting us like that."

The boy Aaron had challenged said nothing more. He glared back and slowly wiped his nose with the back of his hand. Close to him, Aaron saw that he was an albino with large, protruding eyes.

Then, from behind, he heard Benjamin call out, "Leave him be!" Aaron turned to calm his father and then, from the corner of his eye, caught a blurred glimpse of a dark shape moving toward his face. He started to duck away, but wasn't quick enough. Fire burst in his head, blinding him. Then, the albino's knuckles smashed into his nose, while at the same instant, another fist, Aaron did not know whose, sank brutally into his stomach. He fell forward onto his knees, gasping for breath, shaking his head groggily, trying to clear his brain. The cobblestones wobbled in and out of focus as he knelt.

His head reeling, Aaron got up again. He lashed out and hurtled himself forward toward the albino. Somehow, his fist grazed the boy's face, leaving a dark red weal in its wake. As they met head-to-

head, Aaron and the albino started mauling each other, pushing each
other toward the end of the alley. Both of them fell over a cart shaft
and tumbled to the ground. Then, several of the others joined the
fight. Aaron felt hands grab him. He was separated from the albino
and thrown to the ground. He managed to squint through one eye
and saw the hatred in their faces. He wished fervently that someone
would help him. And then, deliberately and methodically, they put
the boot to him: in the groin, in the stomach, in the back. An agonizing blow to the back of the head finally ended it. After that Aaron
felt nothing, not even the snow that had begun to fall.

Hours later, Aaron regained consciousness. He felt fresh bed-linen
against his skin and smelled tincture of violet. Then he heard his father's voice and through one swollen eye recognized his own bedroom.

"You're safe now," Benjamin said, his voice breaking.

Aaron could feel his father's hand, but the voice sounded so far
away. He remembered everything now. He had been hurt. "Papa?"
he whispered.

Benjamin leaned closer. "I wasn't hurt, Aaron; don't worry. I attacked them, but they knocked me down and ran away. The gen-
darmes took a report, but they say it was you who started the fight."
Benjamin's eyes welled with tears. The big man slipped his hand underneath Aaron's back and gathered him into his arms.

Aaron tried hard to ignore the pain in his shoulder. "What else did
they say, Papa?"

"Nothing, Aaron, nothing. The witnesses all tell the same story.
You started the fight, then fell over the cart shaft and struck your
head."

"It's as you always said, Papa. We're not Swiss. We're Jews." The
effort to talk tired him and he slumped back onto the pillows. He
was in pain everywhere, but apparently nothing was broken. Then he
noticed something peculiar about his right arm. He couldn't move it.
"Papa?"

"Yes, Aaron."

"My arm . . ."

Aaron looked down at his right hand. He couldn't feel the woolen
fiber of the blanket. He tried to move his fingers, but he could not
translate the command from his brain. He attempted to lift his arm.
No sensation, no movement. "Papa, help me lift my arm. The right

one." Benjamin lifted Aaron's arm, a concerned look on his face. "Let it go," Aaron said. As Benjamin released it, the arm fell limply to the bed.

Benjamin started to rub the arm. "Do you feel anything now?" Aaron shook his head. Benjamin continued to move his hands up and down the arm, pressing, massaging with his fingers. Aaron kept shaking his head. They both knew it before Aaron said it: "The arm is paralyzed."

During the weeks that followed, Aaron remained in his room, refusing to talk to anyone. His physical condition slowly improved, but his arm remained useless. He neglected the food his father proffered, stopped taking care of himself, grew increasingly morbid and lost track of time. He slept during the days and remained awake, pacing his room, at night.

Benjamin watched his son isolate himself, but felt helpless. What he feared most was that Aaron might be losing his mind.

Then one evening, just before dusk, Aaron heard a footstep on the landing. He knew it was a man climbing the staircase, but he did not know who. The doctor? No. This step was firm and brisk. Probably a different doctor, this time to check out his head. The stranger stopped at his door and lightly knocked. A second knock, this time louder. Aaron stirred himself, fumbled with the latch, and opened the door. When the light struck his eyes, he was, at first, unable to see his visitor, but something about the man was familiar, the frail stature, the fine, well-groomed head. As he grew accustomed to the light, he gasped. "Maître. It's you!"

"Hello, Rostand," Sabatini said, pushing the door open with the head of his cane.

Aaron swallowed, then asked guardedly, "What do you want?"

Sabatini shrugged. "I was just on my way to Basel for a conference. I heard about your trouble and thought I'd pass by to see how you were getting along. Do you object?"

Aaron was not certain how he felt. His relationship with Sabatini had once meant everything to him. "No, no, come in."

"Do you mind if I open the shutters, Rostand? There's still a little light." Sabatini went to the window and pulled open the shutters. He glanced at Aaron, scrutinizing him as intently as he had on the day they first met. Aaron felt a surge of resentment. He turned his right side away from Sabatini so that his helpless arm was not visible.

"What do you expect to see, a lunatic, a cripple?"

"I see what I see, Rostand, nothing more, nothing less."

"And what do you see?"

"A young man with promise and pain. An artist who may never draw again. A little boy full of loathing and self-pity." Sabatini drew himself up on his toes. "Do I 'see' correctly, Rostand?"

Aaron stiffened. "*Merci,* Maître. Your analysis of my character is so perfect. Perhaps you'd like to draw me?" Sabatini remained silent. His hands calmly toyed with the gold fittings of his pince-nez. Aaron looked down at the floor and then slumped onto the bed. "I didn't mean to offend you, Maître; I . . ."

"You didn't offend me, Rostand. You are no longer my student, you are no longer even obliged to listen to me. It is I who am the intruder here." Sabatini set the cane on the bed, clasped his hands behind his back and strode to the window. For a time he was silent, then he said quietly, "Do you realize that you and I have much in common?"

"We do?"

"I was an artist too. Once. I studied at the Beaux-Arts. My professor, the great Ingres, used to say that only a few of us would ever amount to anything. I, like you, believed that I would certainly be one of them. So I gave up everything: material rewards, the love of a woman, a family. Sabatini would not only be another Fragonard or David, he would be the great Sabatini." He paused, continued to look out of the window at the pink haze of the winter sunset. His voice took on a hard edge. "One day, Ingres came to me. He said, 'Sabatini, what would you rather be, a mediocre painter or a great teacher?' "

"I see," Aaron murmured.

Sabatini took a handkerchief from his vest pocket and carefully wiped the lenses of his pince-nez. "I could have continued painting, but once he said that . . ."

"Yes, Maître, but I never had the chance to find out."

Sabatini turned to face Aaron. His eyes were warm. "I could stand here and tell you the same thing Ingres told me. But I can't. You were good." Sabatini went to his briefcase and pulled out a dozen drawings and looked at them for a moment. "You have a great 'eye,' Rostand. You know what art is. You have genius that way. Don't let it go! Use it!"

"What can I do?" Aaron lifted his paralyzed arm with his good one, then let it drop limply to his side.

"Overdo it, Rostand, and no one will care."

Aaron's eyes ignited with anger.

"Self-pity disgusts me, Rostand. Your life isn't over. You still have your eyes. From now on they will be your talent. You're young. You have a gift. Go where you can use it."

"And what do you suggest?"

"First I suggest you clean yourself up. You stink, Rostand. Then use your head. Art is your life. That will never change. Go on studying and learning about it."

"To what purpose? So that I can teach?" Aaron asked sardonically.

Sabatini ignored the malice. "You're not the type, somehow," he said quietly. "I was thinking more crassly. I suggest dealing."

"Dealing?"

"Exactly." Sabatini smiled for the first time.

"An art merchant? Never. You yourself call them frauds."

"The very reason I suggested it." Sabatini's face lit up. He began to speak more rapidly. "The true artists are desperate. Manet and Fantin have been smeared, Degas turned into a misanthrope, Cézanne ridiculed. . . . Meanwhile the likes of Meissonier and Bougereau sell by the square yard. . . ."

"What am I supposed to do? Save French art?"

"I wasn't thinking of French art. I was thinking about you. Most art merchants are fools. They wouldn't know a great work of art if it were shoved under their noses. With your eye and your taste you could make a good living. Besides, you understand the art of the future."

"I haven't got a sou."

"That's your problem. But there are ways. You have an 'eye,' which is the most important thing. You love art, which is second. And you are an artist. . . ."

"I was. . . ."

". . . were an artist. You have a respect for what it means." Sabatini crossed the room, lifted the latch and opened the door. "Think about what I said." He set his pince-nez firmly on his nose and peered at Aaron. "Someday when you're feeling better, come visit me. I'd like to know how things turn out for you." He started to leave.

"Your cane, Maître!" Aaron picked up the cherrywood walking stick from the bed and handed it to Sabatini.

Sabatini smiled. "Keep it, Rostand. It may come in handy, someday."

The latch fell and Sabatini was gone.

A week later, Aaron left Endingen for Paris. A cart waited to take him to the train. He had asked the family not to accompany him to the station. He loathed long good-byes.

"I'm sorry I couldn't give you more money," Benjamin said. "You've got enough there for a few months in Paris."

Benjamin smiled weakly, and reached out for his son. They held each other for several moments, then Benjamin clapped Aaron on the back and said, "Keep safe."

Aaron held the straight dark cherrywood shaft in his left hand. He could think of nothing more to say. He stepped up into the front seat, nodded to the driver, and the cart lumbered off down the road to the station. A cold north wind began to blow.

Six months later, seated before a dusty-yellow Pernod and water, at a crowded café on the Rue de la Paix, Aaron Rostand savored the sparkling atmosphere of Paris on a cloudless autumn afternoon. Considering everything, affairs had gone well for him.

He had been living on the money his father had given him when he left Switzerland; his days settled into a carefully organized routine. In the mornings he continued to school himself at the Louvre. In the afternoons, when the art stalls and galleries opened, he scoured Paris to familiarize himself with the inventories of the art houses and the nuances of the marketplace.

What struck him in his rounds was the paucity of new talent offered the French public. The art dealers of Paris were, with few exceptions, shortsighted. They had no eye to the future. They rejected the younger artists of the time—Matisse, Vuillard, Bonnard—as irrelevant. Even Cézanne was not yet widely recognized for the genius he was. Innovation and genius were suspect. The galleries sold what the fashionable establishment of the day considered to be great art— which Aaron considered imitative and conventional.

Seated at the café that afternoon, he began to jot down notes on the squalor he had seen on his previous week's tour. "The Big Names," he wrote. "Jean Louis Meissonier: unimaginative but highly honored hack . . . heroic portraits of Napoleon on horseback, high prices . . . Gabriel Descamps: uninteresting, sterile, but a sense of humor . . . Émile Vernet: traditional, dry, turgid . . . François Heim: conventionally violent . . . Adolphe Bougereau: pretentious painter of pious subjects . . ."

Nevertheless, Paris at the turn of the century *was* the art capital of the world. Collectors descended on the city like locusts. From all over Europe they had come, acquiring their Rubenses, Rembrandts, or Raphaels. From Moscow the Tsar and Tsarina had come, and behind them flocked the Russian nobility: the Stroganoffs, Bolkonskys, and Yousupoffs. From Vienna came the Bendas, the Liechtensteins, and the Reitzes. No season would have been complete without the arrival of the Prince of Bulgaria, although this year he was selling, not buying.

Of course they found it convenient to buy a few jewels, some ladies' gowns, stay at the Ritz, dine at Maxim's. But there were other capitals with other great hotels and fine restaurants. Only Paris had Art.

Aaron's problem was acquiring it. A few big firms, roughly fifteen, controlled the right connections and made the important purchases and sales. Smaller dealers did not have much chance and were forced to conduct business from hand to mouth.

It would be hard to begin and even harder to survive. He had to find works of exceptional value that could somehow be bought for very little and sold at a considerable profit. He had an eye, he knew that. Still, he needed luck, the right painting, and the right opportunity to purchase it. Such opportunities would not occur often. What thrilled Aaron, as he lifted his glass and took his next-to-last sip of Pernod, was that opportunity, that first lucky moment, seemed on the point of arriving. He need only wait until the auction rooms at the Hôtel Drouot opened for the day.

Aaron paused and, putting down his notebook, reached for his watch. It was time to make his last reconnaissance of the Hôtel Drouot. For the past three days he had been visiting the auction house, examining a small painting from every angle, hoping that no one would discover his find and buy it before he could be sure that it was genuinely by the great master, Vermeer. In the mornings he had consulted every library, every scholarly source he could find on the techniques and materials used by Vermeer and the other painters of his time. He was sure he had discovered a treasure.

Aaron drained his Pernod, left money and a tip in the saucer on his table, and, taking his cherrywood cane in his left hand, set out for the dusty and dilapidated Hôtel Drouot, the largest and most active auction house in Paris. He entered the portals. Good. Very few visitors as yet, the halls were almost empty. He entered the room where the Vermeer hung, and stopped short. For the first time in three days, there was someone looking at it, at his painting. A woman.

Very circumspectly, affecting a boulevardier's hauteur and indifference, he circled gradually around the room to get a good look at the woman studying the tiny, two-foot-square painting. She was tall: most Frenchwomen tended to be short. Her carriage, even standing still, was arresting. She held her head erect under the large hat she wore at an angle, concealing her features.

She looked as though she engaged in some sort of professional work, though he could not guess what. She wore a high-necked white blouse, the collar set off by a band of narrow black velvet. A neatly fitted beige coat with long sleeves and an ankle-length black skirt completed her dress. As Aaron studied her, he saw from behind that the black band around her throat was fastened with a silver clasp.

He circled around to the other side so that he could see the face beneath the hat. The lines of her face were not precisely classical, but the blend of curves was almost perfect. She would have been ideal for one of Raphael's madonnas, if it were not for the strong, even stubborn, line that ran from her jaw to her chin. He saw a willfulness there that he wasn't sure he wanted to test.

As if she had read his mind, the woman looked up and caught Aaron's glance. He did not look away. She looked directly at him, but without warmth or interest. It was Anna Lerner's first encounter with Aaron Rostand.

Anna, at thirty, had made her own way ever since she had moved to Paris from her native Strasbourg. She had been a governess, a companion to the Countess Villebranche and, finally, assistant manager of an antique shop in the Rue Saint-Honoré. She took from each what she needed, and moved on. It was not until she began to deal in art and with artists that she felt both independent and contented. She had always loved beautiful things. As an art dealer, she had found a profession that suited her perfectly.

Although she could not afford to buy much, Anna liked to visit the Hôtel Drouot. There she ferreted out choice objects she thought would go well in her little apartment in the Rue Monsieur-le-Prince.

She browsed without the benefit of a catalogue. There was never time for much of a preview before lots were sold, anyway.

That afternoon Anna spotted a painting that she thought she might buy. She knew nothing about it except that it held special magic for her.

The luminescent portrait showed a plump tavern maid pouring ale into a white porcelain pitcher. She was clothed in a dress the color of lapis lazuli. The moment was timeless, as the maid stood there, pouring the ale. What serenity, Anna thought, and yet what movement! The ambiguity of the work fascinated her.

Anna's gaze dropped to the floor, where she noticed a pair of shiny black shoes, the shiniest she had ever seen. Her glance traveled upward along the line of neatly pressed black trousers to a black frock coat, and then to the face of a tall, spare man with a pointed Vandyke beard, piercing black eyes and a slightly quizzical smile, the same man who'd been staring at her a moment before. Again, he was looking directly at her. After a long pause, he leaned toward her, his left hand resting on a silver-topped cherrywood cane. "Do you like it?" he asked. Anna felt as though she were a student being addressed by a professor.

"It interests me."

"Are you going to buy it?"

Without really thinking, she replied, honestly, "I had considered it."

"I wouldn't," he said. "The painting is a fake."

This man was disparaging an extraordinary work of art. "How interesting, Monsieur, you should say that," she said, sarcastically. "I'm delighted to have . . ."

"Vermeer. Supposed to be, anyway. That's what the forger wanted you to think."

She became angry and impatient. "And why, Monsieur, do you say that?"

"Quite simple, Mademoiselle. It's all wrong. Take, for instance, the colors. What color dominates this painting?"

Anna looked closely at the painting. "Blue. Yes, I'd say a deep, dark blue, like lapis lazuli."

"Precisely. But Vermeer's blues were lighter, airlike. And for a reason. He believed he was painting light, not darkness." The man leaned closer to the canvas, examining the surface of the painting. He nodded to himself and looked at Anna. "And you, Mademoiselle, of all people, should have noticed something else. Look," he said, using his cane to point to the maid's dress, "the fold, here, it rises rather than falls."

"I'm afraid I don't quite follow."

"Surely Vermeer would never have been so clumsy. A painter paints what he sees. The forger of this work couldn't see what he was painting. Then look here, at the shoes. The style is all wrong. The fashion of the day was the slipper, not a laced shoe. Laces came in much later."

He was getting carried away, Anna thought. One met strange people at auctions.

"Here," he said. "Hold this." He shoved his cane into her hand and lifted the painting off its hook on the wall. He turned it around, held it under his right arm, and with his left hand ripped the brown backing paper away from the frame. "Do you see this?" he said, folding the paper so that Anna could examine the back of the canvas. "There, that proves this was the work of a Frenchman."

"Frenchman? I'm astonished. Why do you say that?"

"The canvas. Dutch artists like Vermeer painted on linen because it was finer. The Dutch of Vermeer's time were prosperous. This, however, is jute. The French used jute because it was cheap and easier to get!" He replaced the painting on the wall and took back the cane from Anna. "Yes," he said, looking at the painting, "clearly a forgery, and not a very clever one at that."

Anna was more than a bit bewildered.

"*Bonjour, Mademoiselle.*" He dipped his head slightly, turned on his heel and walked away.

Anna felt as though she had just dropped a precious vase. He was probably right and the painting was a fake. She continued to walk around the room, gazing at other paintings, but could not concentrate. She felt depressed. She noticed a porter sweeping the floor and went up to him. "*Pardon, Monsieur.*"

"*Oui, Mademoiselle?*"

"The gentleman who just left. He was examining the painting, there. Did you notice him?"

The porter's eyes lit up in recognition. "The one pulling the backing off? I noticed, but there is really nothing I can do about it. People complain all the time. . . ."

"No, no. I just want to know who the man is. Does he come here often?"

The porter plucked his chin with his fingers. "Yes, I know him quite well. Everyone here knows Monsieur Aaron Rostand. He comes almost every day."

"He's not demented is he? I mean . . ." Anna touched the side of her head.

He shrugged. *"Comme les autres. . . ."*

Several days later Anna returned to the Hôtel Drouot. She went to the desk of the *commissionnaire,* the clerk responsible for the records of sales, and inquired about the painting of the *Tavern Maid.*

"Let me see, Mademoiselle." He checked his ledger. "Ah, yes. It went for two hundred francs," he replied.

She smiled ruefully. She turned to leave and then it occurred to her to ask another question. "Will you tell me, Monsieur, who was the purchaser?"

The *commissionnaire*'s lips pursed. "Ah, Mademoiselle. That is impossible. You know, we are not allowed . . ."

"Of course, Monsieur, I understand." She reached into her purse. "Your commission on the sale, I believe, was ten percent. That's twenty francs. Would ten more francs do?"

The *commissionnaire* smiled broadly. *"À votre service, Mademoiselle."* He opened the ledger and ran a nicotine-stained finger down the handwritten columns. He stopped. "Ah, yes, Madame, here it is. Monsieur Aaron Rostand."

For Aaron, Paris had radiated more than sunlight that day. A fresh rose in his lapel, cane in hand, he sauntered back from the Hôtel Drouot to his clean furnished room on the Rue Rivoli. Pressed against his body, under his bad arm, was the Vermeer he had just purchased for next to nothing. He was on his way at last.

Two weeks later, the Vermeer cleaned and reframed, he began the rounds of the half-dozen most prominent and prosperous art galleries. In the end, it was Armand Baumont who bought the painting.

Baumont ran a flourishing art gallery on the Champs-Elysées. When Aaron brought him the painting, the dealer's eyes glittered. After some bickering he offered Aaron fifteen thousand francs.

Aaron smiled thinly. "The price is twenty thousand," he said.

Baumont pressed the tops of his fingers under his chin and let his gaze wander around the gallery. Finally he said, "Sixteen thousand, then. After all, Vermeer, while undoubtedly a master, is not all that much in favor these days."

The man thinks I'm just a young courier, Aaron thought. He remembered his father's favorite expression, *Buy boldly; sell patiently.* "The price still remains at twenty thousand, Monsieur. . . ."

The negotiations were interrupted by Baumont's male secretary, who brought four o'clock tea and then several letters for Baumont to sign. After more than an hour, Baumont yielded, but with the stipulation that he pay five thousand francs in deposit, and the balance in ten days. "Our usual terms," he announced firmly.

Aaron studied Baumont's face. "Very well, Monsieur. You will provide a bill of sale?"

Baumont glared at him. "Young man, in the world of Paris art, Armand Baumont's word is enough." Aaron's impulse was to pick up the painting and walk out. But it was late in the day, his arm ached, and no other dealer had come near his price. He would be trading with Baumont again, he thought, and he should not offend him. "Very well, Monsieur, we have a deal," he said.

Baumont smiled, went to a wall safe and withdrew five thousand francs in cash. "I hope this method of payment is satisfactory."

"Of course," Aaron replied as he placed the notes in his *porte-monnaie.*

Aaron left the Galerie Baumont and walked down the Champs-Elysées. When he passed a newspaper kiosk, he bought a newspaper, *Le Figaro.* Ordinarily, he would not have stopped, but the headline startled him. "DREYFUS CASE REOPENED," he read. "CLEMENCEAU AND ZOLA RALLY THE DREYFUSARDS." The report detailed how the new director of French counterespionage told the head of the General Staff that he had strong suspicions that the real culprit was a French officer of Hungarian descent, not Dreyfus. Dreyfus, it was clear, was innocent.

How ironic, Aaron thought. Like Dreyfus, he had almost been destroyed, his career ruined. And like Dreyfus, today he had been given another chance. He would have to celebrate with Matisse tonight.

Ten days later, Aaron returned to Baumont's gallery, where the dealer greeted him as if he were a client about to buy a painting. "What is it I can do for you?" Baumont said unctuously.

"I came, Monsieur, for my money."

Baumont looked blankly at Aaron. "What money?"

Aaron's stomach knotted. "The money for the Vermeer you purchased from me ten days ago."

"You're mistaken, Monsieur, I never bought a painting from you. In fact," he continued, "I've never seen you before."

Aaron understood at once. He'd been a fool. He'd received payment for the painting in cash and stupidly neglected to obtain a receipt. He could never prove that the Vermeer had changed hands here. He had no appeal. "Is this the way you always conduct your business, Monsieur Baumont?" he said, white-lipped with rage.

"I'm afraid I don't know what you're talking about, Monsieur. Now, if you'll excuse me . . ."

Aaron controlled himself. He wanted to leap at the man's throat. "You've not heard the last of me," he said as he turned on his heel and walked out.

Over the next few days Aaron made and discarded several plans to recover his money or the painting. The police would be no help. He could not sue. Nor was he a thief. On the other hand, he was no sacrificial lamb. On the fourth day, at closing time, he entered the gallery again, this time without his cane, but with a five-liter jug in his hand. He set the jug down near the front door of the gallery and pulled the cork. Next he picked up the jug by its ear, tilted it slightly and strolled about the gallery letting its contents spill over the floor. A strong smell of kerosene immediately filled the air.

Baumont, who had been in his office, rushed toward Aaron. "My God, what are you doing, you fool!"

Aaron said nothing. He put the jug down, reached in his pocket and pulled out a small box of matches. Then he said, "You have a choice, Monsieur, give me the painting, or the balance you owe. If not . . ."

"You wouldn't dare."

Aaron smiled. He looked into Baumont's eyes, and caught the glint of fear.

"Be reasonable," Baumont pleaded.

"Negotiations are over," Aaron said coldly. He moved as if to strike the match.

"Wait! . . . Wait! I remember now. You did sell me a painting. I have the money. Let me fetch it from the safe."

Aaron returned the matches to his pocket, his hand trembling slightly. Within a minute, Baumont returned with the money, and shoved it into Aaron's hand. "Count it," he said. "It's all there."

"Surely you wouldn't try to cheat *me*." Aaron smiled. It was a menacing smile, a smile that implied a threat. Yet it also contained a faint element of amusement, as though it were all a private joke. He turned, and with fifteen thousand francs in his pocket, walked slowly out of the gallery.

With the 20,000 francs from the Vermeer Aaron opened Rostand Fine Arts in a shop near the Hôtel Drouot and made himself an immediate reputation as one of the most astute and knowledgeable dealers in Paris. He bought boldly but wisely, and never made a mistake. He had an unerring eye, which his rivals envied and his clients trusted. But quick success did not change his character. He led a frugal disciplined life, and put all the profits back into the business.

Every morning he made the rounds of the auction houses, moving quickly and yet deliberately, making careful mental notes, which he later dictated to a secretary. In this way, he managed to keep a complete file on every painting he saw. It was almost redundant, however, for he remembered every piece of art, in every detail.

One afternoon he found in his mail a formal letter from Léon Fabre, arms manufacturer and one of the most important art collectors in France. The letter asked Rostand "to evaluate the Fabre Collection for its eventual sale, either at public auction or by private contract." The date of the evaluation at the Château Listrac would be on Monday, March 21, 1897.

When he boarded the Paris-Listrac train the following Sunday evening, Aaron was in high spirits, for he expected to conclude a major purchase the following morning. He settled himself in his second-class compartment, opened a newspaper and began to read. Just before the train left, two other passengers entered the compartment. Aaron looked up and his spirits plummeted. One of the passengers was Pierre Breton, a tall blond man in a bright tweed cap and a loose, raglan-sleeved overcoat to match. A clever dealer, he and Aaron had become fierce competitors for choice items at the Hôtel Drouot. On Breton's arm, wearing a dark green woolen coat, a sealskin toque and shoulder cape, was Anna Lerner.

Aaron stood to greet them both, forcing himself to observe protocol. In the stilted conversation that followed, all three carefully avoided mention of their final destination. Aaron, resuming his seat by the window, was doubly depressed. Not only was he up against a formidable competitor for the Fabre Collection, but Anna was snub-

bing him. She took her place in the farthest corner of the compartment and was soon absorbed in a book.

Two hours later, the train pulled into Listrac. When they reached
the platform, the three of them shared the only fiacre available and
found they had all reserved rooms in the same inn.

Aaron was relieved to learn that Anna and Breton had separate
rooms. Perhaps they were working together, he thought, but at least
they weren't sleeping together. Aaron and Breton wished each other a
perfunctory goodnight. Anna smiled at Breton and said goodnight to
him. She continued to ignore Aaron.

The next morning, Anna arose early, opened the door and took in
her freshly polished black high-buttoned boots. She glanced down
the hallway and was pleased to see that Aaron's glistening shoes were
still in the corridor outside his door. She dressed, quietly went down
the hallway to Breton's room, and tapped lightly on his door. Breton
opened the door, fully dressed, and the two went downstairs.

"Rostand seems to be a late sleeper," Breton said, adding tritely,
"The early bird catches the worm."

"Then let's hope he sleeps all morning," Anna replied as she
poured herself another cup of coffee.

An hour later, Anna and Breton's hired carriage leisurely pulled
into the courtyard of the Fabre château, stopping directly behind another rig opposite the front door. Breton descended from the carriage
and offered his hand to Anna. As they moved toward the entrance,
the oak door opened to reveal Léon Fabre and Aaron shaking hands,
smiling. Then Anna and Breton watched dumbfounded as Aaron
walked toward his carriage and lifted his left arm in greeting. In his
fist he held what was, obviously, a contract. They watched him climb
into his rig. The last thing they saw of him was his feet, clattering up
the carriage steps in *sabots,* a pair of scruffy, mudcaked wooden
peasant shoes.

The next time Aaron Rostand saw Anna was on a cloudless Friday morning, several months later. The boxes under the street-floor
windows of the Hôtel were full of brightly colored flowers. Pink, yellow and white blooms enlivened the classic gray facade of the most
exclusive hotel in Europe.

When Aaron mounted the shallow steps leading to the main lobby,
he heard through the swinging glass doors a babble of voices. The
morning's mob of art dealers was already in place. The siege had

begun. They were waiting to see the man they called "The Menace," the international financier and banker, the American multimillionaire, J. Pierpont Morgan.

Of all the world's art collectors, J. P. Morgan was the wealthiest. For years he had ransacked Europe for every kind of treasure. In every capital dealers hungered for a Morgan buying spree. News of the objects of his desire spread like flames. With eleven billion dollars at his disposal, the titan snapped up every major collection he could find, one by one. His fondest saying was, "What's the good of buying one piece, if you can have them all?"

As Aaron made his way through the crowd of dealers, he felt their feverish desperation. Many of them clutched bulky, odd-shaped bundles, obviously containing statues, porcelains, jewels, odd bits of treasure and paintings. It was comical. Morgan must think them a pack of peddlers. No wonder the great man had sealed himself off on the second floor.

Every major dealer was there: the wily Joseph Duveen, Seligman, Gimpel, that fool Baumont and Pierre Breton. But the one who interested Aaron most was Anna Lerner. As usual, he couldn't take his eyes off her. She moved around the lobby, nodding to acquaintances, wearing a tailored blouse and skirt of violet and white striped cotton. What was it about her that attracted him? She was cold, hostile, ambitious, and apparently indifferent. Yet his original feeling for her had not changed. She fascinated him. No matter. He had other things to think about, principally his scheduled meeting with Morgan.

He was about to have a cup of coffee when he was stopped by the sound of a woman's voice behind him. "Must we always compete?" she asked.

He turned, amazed to see Anna smiling at him.

"I didn't know we did," he replied with a grin.

"Of course we did, and I've always been the loser."

He was bewildered. This was the last thing he'd expected.

He laughed. "Is this a peace pact, Mademoiselle Lerner?"

"At least a temporary truce, Monsieur Rostand."

They both broke into laughter. At that moment, Aaron heard himself paged. He signaled to the boy with his cane and replaced the single white envelope on a silver tray with a one-franc piece. Tucking the cane under his arm he deftly opened the envelope. "It's from Morgan," he said.

Anna blinked. "How did you do that?"

Aaron shrugged with a gleam in his eye. "Through a little connection I made in Listrac," he said, moving toward the wide rococo stairway leading to the second floor.

"Don't wear sabots this time," Anna teased.

From the landing Aaron looked down at her. She was still watching him. He tipped his cane and smiled. It was a very special day.

When a secretary ushered Aaron into the gilded salon of Morgan's personal suite, the financier was seated at a marquetry table playing solitaire. Morgan stood, and a fluffy Pekingese scrambled down his trouser leg to the floor.

"Fabre spoke highly of you, Rostand," Morgan said, his authoritative voice given added dimension by his commanding six-foot figure. But it was the big square face that Aaron found extraordinary: snapping black eyes, a walrus moustache, and a huge puffy nose, enormously swollen by disease and covered with strawberry-purple pimplings.

"There is no need to tell you how highly I think of your collection," Aaron said.

"You think I'm an astute buyer, then?"

Aaron detected amusement in Morgan's voice. "One of the best."

"Well then," the big man said, "I have something to show you." He motioned Aaron to follow him to the far end of the room. There, on three separate pedestals, stood three porcelain figurines. "I'm going to buy one of these, but I'm not quite certain which one." Morgan looked quizzically at Aaron. "I'm partial to one of them. Which one do you like?"

Aaron looked at the figurines. One was an eighteenth-century Dresden shepherd, all pinks and blues. Beside it stood a Chelsea peacock on an elaborate baroque base. The last figure was Sèvres porcelain, a seated white cat.

Aaron glanced quickly at Morgan. He knew that for the eccentric collector this was a test, and that their future relationship would depend on his making the right choice. He moved closer to the mantel and examined each of the china figures closely. He knew nothing about porcelains, but he instinctively had a feeling about the Chelsea peacock.

He chose and in the same instant raised his silver-topped cane. With two deft strokes he smashed the Dresden shepherd on the left, and then the Sèvres cat on the right, leaving the Chelsea peacock standing.

He looked back at Morgan. "That, sir, is the one you want," he said, pointing to the peacock. "The others are not worthy of your collection. They were obviously fakes!"

Morgan pushed aside one of the china shards on the carpet with his foot. "I think, young man, you and I will do a great deal of business together."

1979

PART SEVEN

---◆---

1979

I

The morning after his visit to Endingen, André Rostand's Lear jet awaited takeoff clearance from the Zurich airport. The pilot turned his head back to him.

"We're next in line, sir. It won't be long now . . ."

André nodded. His mind was elsewhere.

In Endingen, he had spent the night in the house that his father had grown up in. It was still the family home, though no one had lived there in years. André had bought sausage, goat cheese and a few bottles of ginger beer, taken them back to the house on the riverbank and eaten a solitary meal by the fire.

After dinner, he had walked through the rooms of the old wooden house, now devoid of furniture, and thought about the last visit he had made to Endingen. He was sixteen at the time and had come with his father. They had taken the train from Paris, arrived in the little village and then climbed the hills surrounding the town. He remembered how his father had talked about how things had changed. The house, once isolated on the riverbank, was hidden among a score of new holiday homes built by strangers. The roads were all paved and the old Jewish quarter had disappeared.

André's mind continued to race over the past. Memories of Aaron and his mother, Anna, came back to him for the first time in years. His parents had made a good marriage, much better than his own had been. As his mother grew older, she had become heavier and more robust. The Anna his father had married—slim, ambitious and eager—had changed. A calm, quiet woman took her place. She had always been self-assured, but the self-assurance was tempered by time. Her face, once so beautifully defined, became softer and more serene. Only on rare occasions did the fiery Anna return, when André did not do so well in school or antagonized her in some other way.

He remembered his mother's dying. During those last days, Aaron never left her side. His father had not wept, nor openly expressed his grief. His feelings were so strong that he couldn't. He simply watched her slowly and quietly slip further and further away. André knew that when his mother died, the most important part of his father died with her.

Finally, André thought of Sabatini, the man his father had named him after. Once, in his old age, the *maître* had visited the gallery, tottering in, dried out like an old wrinkled apple. The visit had taken Aaron by surprise.

"Did you think I was dead?" Sabatini shouted.

"Working, Maître," his father had replied.

Sabatini chortled. "Working indeed!"

André followed the two men as they walked arm in arm through the gallery, examining the masterpieces hanging there. They had descended to the vaults, and there Sabatini gasped with awe. For a long time the old man stood there, saying nothing.

Afterward, they all stood in front of the gallery waiting for the car that would drive the *maître* home. Then the two men embraced and said good-bye for the last time.

André never forgot the last words Sabatini had said to his father. "You were a gifted artist, Rostand, but you're a great dealer."

Abruptly, the pilot's voice broke André's reminiscing. "Comfortable, Mr. Rostand?"

André nodded, his face grim and tight. He didn't like flying, especially the long flight across the Atlantic. It took too much out of him.

"It's a beautiful day, sir."

André didn't reply. Small talk wasn't going to make it any better. He reached for his portfolio and withdrew a batch of newspapers containing reports about the Jannis sale, brought the day before by a courier from his London Gallery. The lead column on the arts page of the *Daily Telegraph* reported that an all-time record had been broken at public auction, when the Jannis Collection sold for £15,750,000.

The article went on to note that the majority of the lots sold went to the powerful consortium, Art Intrum, headed by Dr. Leopold Marto. Art Intrum had faced stiff competition from an anonymous bidder, thought to be from Los Angeles. Nevertheless, the article pointed out, the Marto group had dominated the sale and in only a few months had become one of the world's major art consortiums, even rivaling Rostand International, conspicuous in not having bought a single lot.

Another article, in the *Guardian,* itemized the astronomical prices of the sale, then alluded to its philistine aspect. The prices brought into the salesroom, it noted, bore little relationship to reality, and could be described only as staggering. The Jannis sale provided an alarmingly clear portrait of some of the most persistent vanities and foibles of our times.

André was particularly pleased to read the next line. "In fact, the sale was in many respects unhealthy, brought sharply into relief when objects of such poor quality could have been bought from private dealers for a fraction of the price paid under the glare of the television lights."

The critics were right, of course, André thought, but for the wrong reason. Certainly art was a commodity, inversely cheapened as prices for it rose. He had always known that. Only now, instead of blasé aristocrats, the auction rooms were filled with businessmen wearing dark glasses accompanied by bored, hardfaced, bejeweled blondes.

He shrugged. And why not? If they were willing to pay the prices, he was willing to sell them the goods.

He pulled out his notebook, flipped it open and went over the checklist he had made earlier in the week. He had installed his runners and briefed them fully. The accounts with the brokerage firms had been opened and the codes established for their use. The loan of thirty million dollars had been granted, and the first hundred thousand dollars telexed into each account. The Jannis sale would have overextended the financial resources of Art Intrum and left them vulnerable. At last, everything was in readiness.

In the morning, a series of coded messages would be sent through the Swiss Credit Bank instructing the brokers to begin trading on behalf of Messrs. Stuart-Hunt, Koenig, Villot and Asher.

It didn't really matter what happened to the initial funds invested. If lost, they would be replaced. The only important thing was that each "investor" established a good track record with his brokerage house. It was imperative that the brokers perceived their "clients" as investors, not speculators, for when he began to move against the ring, his instructions would have to be executed without question.

By three o'clock that afternoon, André was back in New York, in his leather armchair at Rostand International. He glanced once again at the columns of figures in front of him and murmured to himself, "At last, it begins . . ." No one was present to hear him.

He had already worked out the calculations a dozen times. There were five million shares outstanding of Art Intrum stock, which were, at the moment, being quoted at approximately thirty-one dollars a share. He intended to acquire thirty percent of them, 1,600,000 shares, at a cost that he estimated would be upward of at least $50,000,000. In all, he gave himself no more than ten business days to pull it off.

It was fast, but he had no other choice. He had to buy an average of 160,000 shares of A.I. stock each day. In the beginning the price would stabilize, but as he traded, the market makers would force the price upward. The cost of the shares would begin to rise and, fueled daily, the rise would become a rush. André estimated that by the end of the tenth day, each share would be worth almost a third more than its present value, about forty dollars per share.

He hoped that Marto would attribute the interest in Art Intrum shares to his phenomenal "success" in the auction rooms over the past few weeks. By the time his rival realized what was happening, it would be too late.

He stepped from behind the broad, flat-topped desk, crossed the room to the fireplace, and reached for the cherrywood cane. Holding the cane in both hands, he walked to the Georgian windows over-looking the corner of Madison Avenue and gazed down at the heart of New York's art world. To most of those who scurried past window after window filled with paintings, antiques and sculptures, the galleries lining Madison Avenue were probably mere places of employment, trading in objects that, while colorful and pleasant, were essentially decorative though uninteresting. For others—the trendy and fashionable—the Madison Avenue art galleries represented the epitome of social grace, affluence, wealth, all that money could buy. To the serious-minded students, the romantics, Madison Avenue was, no doubt, a repository for the world's most beautiful and precious objects, the finest of man's cultural heritage. Of course, to the dealers themselves, the street was no more than a marketplace. From where André Rostand stood, the avenue was all of these, a kingdom where all these worlds came together, and in it he had always been the monarch. Today he intended to make certain he remained so.

He returned to his desk, on his way returning the cane to its place on the mantelpiece, and placed a call to Bertrand Keller.

Two minutes later, Harper had Keller on the line. André spoke quickly and in code. He ordered the Swiss banker to place an order, on his behalf, for 40,000 shares of A.I. stock with each brokerage house. Every day, as long as things went according to plan, he would ring through and repeat the same order, until he owned 1,600,000 shares of Art Intrum stock. Then the fun would begin.

II

Two weeks later, André walked into his office at a quarter past nine in the morning, to find Ray Fuller waiting for him.

"I've got some things for you to do," André said, passing Fuller and going to his desk.

Fuller opened his portfolio and waited as André flicked through the notebook he pulled from the inside pocket of his jacket. His instructions were simple. Fuller was to issue a set of coded instructions to Keller to sell another 100,000 shares of Art Intrum stock.

As usual, the shares were to be sold in odd lots, first in Zurich, through Asher's account. The Paris account would be unloaded next. After that, a ripple effect would be created when the London accounts were cleared a few hours later.

During the past week, André had unloaded a million shares of Art Intrum stock on the market. On the first day, he flooded the market with 400,000 shares. The price of the shares fell on the Paris, London and New York exchanges, but not as severely as it did in Zurich, where the price dropped from $37 to $32 per share.

The second day, he unloaded another 300,000 shares, the price continuing to drop to a closing of $26 per share. At that point, André had anticipated Marto's response. Art Intrum, low on capital after the demands of the Jannis sale, fought back with what funds it could muster, but it wasn't nearly enough. On the third day, with Rostand selling another 200,000 shares, despite Marto's support, A.I. stock plummeted to close at $20 per share. On day four, another 100,000 shares were dropped. By then the panic André had hoped for finally set in. Art Intrum stock fell disastrously to $15, down twenty-two points from the week's opening quotation.

André knew, of course, that he had taken a beating himself, suffering a loss of approximately $6,000,000, having bought his shares at an average price of $33 a share and sold into a down market, recouping roughly an average of $29 a share. He still had six million shares in his various accounts, but the final blow to Marto wouldn't necessitate selling all of them. As for the loss of the six million dollars, that would come back over time. Besides, Marto's losses would be infinitely greater. André wondered how Marto was taking it.

He glanced up at Fuller. "Report back to me as soon as you know the market quotations for the day."

"Yes, sir."

"Quite good timing, don't you think, Ray?"

"Yes, sir. It will coincide nicely with the Art Dealers' Association dinner this evening."

André's face brightened into a grin. "I understand there's to be a special ceremony in honor of Dr. Marto?"

"That's correct, sir. Marto's been selected to receive the Association's Special Award this year, for his contributions to the profession."

"It should be an interesting evening," André said. "I'm looking forward to the presentation."

III

Alex Drach passed through the front entrance of the National Archives, its bronze doors eleven inches thick and forty feet high. Located midway between the Capitol and the White House, the massive twenty-two-story building was the repository of the Republic's most treasured records.

As he went through the front portico he read an inscription, chiseled in stone. "Study the Past," it read, and then he remembered Shakespeare's line, "What's past is prologue."

The pressure of work had delayed his trip to Washington by almost two weeks. The problem, as usual, was an overanxious client. The chairman of a major television network had recently returned to his estate in Westchester to find the walls of his mansion stripped of several million dollars' worth of Impressionist paintings. For reasons of his own, the chairman decided not to report the loss to either his insurance company or the police. Instead, he called Alex Drach.

He consulted Alex because the recovery of his canvases required special talents. The paintings first had to be located, then identified as not being fakes or forgeries.

For Alex, the hard part had been to find the paintings. From a mental file of contacts, names never committed to paper, he had finally found an ex-convict who, for the right price, produced the address of a warehouse where the art was hidden. The rest was routine. Aware of his client's need for secrecy, Alex had only one recourse—to recover the paintings the same way they had disappeared. He simply stole them back.

When he returned the paintings, his client expressed his appreciation by giving him a landscape by Monet, an offhand gesture worth roughly a quarter of a million dollars.

Unfortunately, the job did have one tragic aspect. The warehouse Drach emptied was the main repository for a syndicate fencing stolen art. When they discovered their loss, the syndicate took it very unkindly and held those in charge of the warehouse personally responsible. Alex was not happy, therefore, to learn that in the frozen ground of the Forest Hills Cemetery, three former warehouse guards lay buried, all victims of an untimely accident, and all with broken necks.

In the Great Hall of Archives, Alex took a moment to glance at the original copy of the Declaration of Independence, sealed in its case of glass and bronze. The case, a plaque informed him, contained inert helium and measured amounts of water vapor to prevent the national treasure from deteriorating. Light filters protected the document against fading. He also learned that every night the documents were lowered into a vault twenty feet below the chamber. As a security consultant, he was intrigued by such trivia.

Drach signed the register kept by the guard at the entrance to the central research room, and was directed to the office of the archivist in charge of all the O.S.S. files. He took the elevator to the seventh floor and followed the corridor to Room 712. There he introduced himself to a quiet, serious-looking man, whose straight gray hair fell to his collar.

John Temple, who for more than thirty years had been the archivist in charge of O.S.S. records, offered Alex a chair and listened to his request.

"I'm researching a novel," Alex explained, "about World War Two. It's about a collaborator, a Frenchman, who was an art collector. He collaborated with the Nazis, then committed suicide. I'd like to know more about what it was like in France at the time, and about what happened to collections that were looted by the Nazis."

Temple smiled. There were many requests for O.S.S. records. "In this building we've got one-point-three million cubic feet of records. Do you know how many pages of material there are in a cubic foot?"

Alex looked bewildered. "I haven't quite worked that one out yet."

"Well, I'll tell you. On an average, twenty-five hundred pages. Just in terms of the O.S.S.," Temple continued, "we've stored eight hundred cubic feet of documents. Could you be a little more specific?"

"I'm interested in the Allied Intelligence Art Looting Unit."

Temple nodded. "That'd be Record Group Two-Three-Nine." He reached down and pulled open the bottom drawer of his desk. His gray head disappeared for a moment as he thumbed through a series of notebooks. He extracted one of them, then sat back and leafed through its pages, peering over them every once in a while at Alex.

Alex felt himself growing increasingly impatient. Here was Temple, a walking vault of secrets, holding what perhaps might be the key to his past.

Temple looked up. "We have roughly sixty-five boxes of material relating to art looting. Take this index and tell me the ones you want."

Alex accepted the index and scanned its contents: "Box Six—London file, British element, C.C.; Box Eleven—Axis victims; Box Twenty-three—List of Personnel, Einsatzstab Rosenberg, Hitler's art squad; Box Thirty—Interrogation reports, Göring, Haberstock, Rosenberg; Box Fifty-five—Orion, the Drach Affair." His eyes stopped. It was as though his father had come back and whispered to him. Below the last entry he read, "Box Sixty-five—Special report on the firm of Rostand International." He closed his eyes.

"Are you all right, Mr. Drach?"

Alex opened his eyes. "Fine," he said. "Can I see this material?"

"Of course, if it's not classified," Temple replied. He reached across his desk, picked up several reference service slips and handed the forms to Alex. "Fill these out. It should take about forty-five minutes for the request to be processed. They'll bring them to you in the Central Research Room."

An hour later, seated next to the cart on which the boxes had been delivered, Alex looked for Box 55, the one containing material on the Drach Affair. The box wasn't there. Nor was Box 65, containing the report on Rostand International. He rechecked, then went to

the phone and dialed Temple's extension. He told the archivist about
the missing files.

"I'm afraid those files are still classified," explained Temple apologetically. "If you still need them, I suggest you demand them under
the Freedom of Information Act."

Drach pleaded that he didn't have the time, but Temple could only
apologize.

"I understand," Alex said thoughtfully. "What record group was
that you mentioned?"

"R.G. Two-three-nine . . . fifteenth floor."

Alex thanked Temple and replaced the receiver. He left the Central Research Room and took the elevator to the fifteenth floor. He
walked to the right down a long corridor, flanked on either side by
thick wire mesh. Every few feet he stopped to check the numbering
on the stacks. Halfway down he found the appropriate stack. On it
he could see the two gray file boxes he wanted, not ten feet apart.
Above his head the sign on the mesh read: "Authorized Personnel
Only." It occurred to him that he might pick the lock, but there were
too many people around. He glanced through the stacks and saw a
young woman placing files onto the shelves from a cart she pulled
along beside her. Calling to her, Alex waved and asked her to direct
him to the State Department archives.

The young woman looked at him and came forward to give him
the complicated instructions to Record Group 33L, the State Department files.

As she pointed him in the right direction, he studied her I.D.
badge, remembering her name: Beverly Sanchez.

Alex left the archives, crossed the street to the florist and bought
two dozen long-stemmed red roses. Returning to the archives, he
went to the fifteenth floor, turned to the left, and approached the female receptionist to ask if he could see Beverly Sanchez.

"I'm afraid she's in the stacks. Is it important?"

Alex smiled demurely. "It's her birthday today. I just wanted to
surprise her with these roses."

"How thoughtful, but I'm afraid . . ."

"Just for a minute." He glanced at his watch. "I'm just on my way
to see the Chief Archivist, Mr. Lloyd. I'm the new man in Modern
Military."

The receptionist nodded knowingly. "Just for a moment, then,"
she said.

Alex thanked her and was buzzed through the gate.

With his flowers he proceeded directly to the shelf containing File Box Number 55. He removed it, setting the roses on the floor. Hurriedly he thumbed his way through the manila folders, looking for the one labeled "Orion." It was the last one in the box. He took out the sheaf of papers, replaced the folder and returned the box to the shelf. Then he moved a few feet farther on and extracted File Box Number 65 from its place on the shelf. He rummaged through the box. There were nine folders in the box, none of them labeled "Rostand International." He checked again. Nothing. He began to sweat, then cursed under his breath.

He replaced the box and started going through the boxes on either side of it, hoping there'd been some mistake. Interrogation reports, lists of looted paintings, personnel files and other documents flicked through his fingers. Still nothing.

Suddenly he heard a clicking sound coming toward him from the other side of the stacks. Quickly he shoved the boxes back in place, unbuttoned his jacket, then his shirt-front, and stuffed the papers inside his shirt. While buttoning his shirt and adjusting his tie, he started walking back to the entrance of the stacks. *"Merde,"* he muttered angrily to himself. He turned on his heel and ran back to retrieve the roses, just in time to see Beverly Sanchez advancing toward him.

"Miss Sanchez?"

She watched him for a moment, stunned. "Yes?" she asked in a nervous voice.

Alex wondered what he was going to do next. The first thing was to put her at ease. He stood stock still, extending his arm, holding the roses out toward her. He hoped she wouldn't think he was crazy. "Happy Birthday."

"But it's not my birthday." She looked as though she were expecting trouble. Her dark eyes looked at him.

"Of course it isn't, but how else could I meet you?"

A faint flush spread upward to her tiny dimpled cheeks. She hesitated a moment, obviously trying to recover her composure. "You're not supposed to be in here."

"There was no other way."

"But you don't even know me."

"I know; I'm just new here. I'm in Modern Military," he said, feeling a drop of sweat run down his side. "You know, Temple's department."

She nodded and her black curls shook slightly. "Where is your identification badge?"

"Oh, that. It hasn't been issued yet. You know, Personnel is a long way behind."

She smiled. "Yes, I know. It took a week to get mine."

He glanced at her badge. "That photo doesn't do you justice."

She looked away, embarrassed.

"Do you have time for coffee?" he asked tentatively.

She glanced at her watch, then back at him, hesitated for a moment, pondering the question. "I suppose Margaret can fill in for me," she said, accepting the roses.

"There's a place across the street," he said as they walked toward the entrance gate.

They passed the desk of the smiling receptionist and Alex smiled back at her, hoping that neither she nor Beverly heard the slight crackling sound that emanated from his shirt-front.

IV

Again Alex read the memorandum and still the impact of its contents stunned him.

. . . LONDON, ENGLAND
8 JANUARY 1946
SUBJECT: ORION

FROM: HUGH JENNER, WING COMMANDER
            SPECIAL INVESTIGATION SERVICE (S.I.S.)
            SUPREME HEADQUARTERS ALLIED EXPEDITIONARY FORCE
            LONDON, ENGLAND

TO: MAJOR RAY J. FULLER
            ART LOOTING INVESTIGATION UNIT (A.L.I.U.)
            OFFICE OF STRATEGIC SERVICES
            WASHINGTON D.C.

Complying with Allied Intelligence Directive A-42191, a special report on the major incidences of German looting of Jewish-owned art collections in Paris during the Occupation is issued this date. I have focused on the major confiscations beginning 1 July 1940, oth-

erwise known as the "Drach Affair." Allied Intelligence has put together a chronology of the events based on original documents captured from the GERMAN HIGH COMMAND at Berchtesgaden, and
field investigations by the O.S.S. in Paris, Monte Carlo and Rome.

The Collaboration of Paul Drach

1. Prior to the German Occupation of Paris, the heads of many
prominent Jewish families secretly met and arranged to hide their
valuable art treasures in various locations throughout France.

2. PAUL DRACH, the French industrialist, although not Jewish but
married to the Jewish heiress NAOMI DE MONTROSE, was entrusted
with the names and locations of these repositories.

3. DRACH was arrested by the GESTAPO at 1140 hours, 18 June
1940. He was taken to Gestapo Headquarters at No. 74 Avenue
Foch, Paris, and there interrogated by S.S. CAPTAIN HANS
MONTAG, the special representative of REICHSMARSCHALL HER-
MANN GÖRING. Two weeks later, according to testimony received,
DRACH accompanied the S.S. on a series of confiscations of the hidden Jewish repositories around the Paris area. Five major art collections, including those of the WEILL, STENDHAL and ROTHMAN
families, were requisitioned by MONTAG on behalf of GÖRING. Later,
four additional collections, including that of the DRACH family, were
appropriated by MONTAG and his subordinates. (See Appendix: Dep-
osition, Tab A.)

4. The value of these last four collections can be conservatively
estimated to be one hundred million dollars. A detailed list of the
items looted and their value is attached. (See the Appendix: Inventory, Tab B.)

5. According to the household staff working in the DRACH household at the time, PAUL DRACH was released by the GESTAPO and
returned to his home. The very day he returned, Drach committed
suicide. Testimony from JOCKO CORVO, housekeeper who found
DRACH's body, established death by hanging. He noted also that
when DRACH returned home, he appeared to have been beaten.
Witnesses to the confiscations also commented on his bruised appearance.

6. We conclude, therefore, that PAUL DRACH collaborated with
the GESTAPO under duress, revealing the locations of the secret
repositories, and then committed suicide. While it is a matter of con-
jecture, it appears likely that guilt and remorse motivated him to this
act.

The Disappearance of Hans Montag

1. Enquiries concerning the whereabouts of MONTAG today have provided no new information. As in previous reports, our conclusion is that MONTAG was killed by Allied troops entering Rome in June 1944. German records list a Major Hans Montag as "Missing in Action." Posthumously, he was awarded the Iron Cross for his services to the Reich.

The Collections

1. The first five collections requisitioned on behalf of GÖRING have been located and recovered by our unit, the most important find being a cache of 3000 paintings and other works of art discovered in Niederleining Castle outside Berchtesgaden, Germany. The others, including the DRACH COLLECTION, have not been recovered. These paintings were last traced to a Roman warehouse, where MONTAG was reported to have stored them in 1943. MONTAG, promoted to Major, was then serving as GÖRING's personal liaison to the Vatican. We surmise there is a connection between MONTAG's presence in Rome and the collections stored there. Field inquiries, however, indicate that the Roman warehouse was destroyed by Allied bombing and the paintings lost. (See Appendix: A.L.I.U. Report, Rome, Tab D.)

Classification

We have asked for a "Secret" classification of this report in order to minimize embarrassment to the families involved, especially the DRACH family. Such a classification also protects data in which we have a continuing interest. We request that the O.S.S. keep London informed through S.I.S. concerning any development with regard to these matters.

Signed

JENNER (WNG. CMDR.)
LONDON

Alex returned the papers to his briefcase and stared out the window of the Eastern Airlines shuttle circling Manhattan. The plane was an hour late into La Guardia. There was nothing he could do but sit and wait.

He cursed the weather. He cursed the airlines. And then, he cursed André Rostand.

While Jenner's memorandum confirmed his father's collaboration, it also suggested that Rostand knew more than he had let on. The fact that the recipient of Jenner's report had been Ray Fuller and that Fuller now worked for Rostand, and had done so since the war, had to be more than coincidence. What the association was, what had passed between Fuller and Rostand, he didn't know, but he was determined to find out.

Since reading the documents he had taken from the Archives that afternoon, he had thought about Fuller incessantly. He could understand Rostand's duplicity, but Fuller's had wounded him. He had always known that Fuller was basically amoral. But this . . . this was beyond comprehension. He wouldn't have credited Fuller with that kind of nerve.

The other documents in the file were interesting but inconsequential. There were several official German reports relating to the confiscations that took place in Paris during the war. One or two items, the orders issued by Göring to his subordinates, chief among them the one for S.S. Major Hans Montag, were illuminating, but it was the Jenner memorandum that was extraordinary.

Alex's thoughts were interrupted by the saccharine-sweet voice of the stewardess apologizing for the delay and assuring passengers that they would be at the gate within a few moments.

The delay over the city had been unpleasant but it also had been beneficial. He had been allowed time to think about his course of action during the next few days. His anger had not dissipated, but it had been more effectively channeled.

There was a crowd around the arrival gate, but Po wasn't hard to find. He was conspicuous in his black beret, dark glasses and olive-green field jacket. Alex thought, however, that in early February, the clogs he wore were a little out of place.

"Why the disguise?" Alex inquired as the two of them left the terminal and walked toward Po's beat-up 1969 Ford.

"I don't want to be recognized in your company."

"I'd have thought it would be the other way around."

"Christ, that's sang-froid." Po pronounced *froid* like *freud*.

Alex smiled at the mutilation and asked, "What's wrong?"

"Your attitude for getting into trouble."

"You mean aptitude?"

"Yeah, aptitude. Between the gooks in Paris and the mob here, my life's not worth a Gypsy's promise."

They got into the car and drove off. Po down-clutched his psychedelically painted Ford and took the final curve out of La Guardia, pressing his foot to the floor and accelerating into the rush-hour traffic. They headed into the city.

"What did you excavate in Washington?" Po asked, wiping the condensation from the windshield.

"Nothing much," Alex replied.

"Don't jive me. You're as tight as a camel's ass in a sandstorm."

Alex grinned. "You'd be that way too if you'd just spent an hour circling over Manhattan."

"Okay, okay. So don't tell me. I've got news for you. The toll slips came through for everyone but Bez. He hasn't gotta phone in Manhattan."

"Have you checked them out yet?" Alex asked.

"Not yet. I was waiting for you to share the load."

Po punched the button on the glove compartment. It fell open and he pulled out a stack of New York Telephone Company bills. He handed them to Alex. "They're all here," he said.

In the dim light Alex flipped through them. The bills listed the date, time and number of every long-distance call each dealer had made in the past month. Alex was pleased. He looked across at Po.

"What are you doing this evening?"

"Playing pool with my girlfriend. Why?"

"Have you got time to go to the library with me?"

Po moaned. "Kee-rist! Tonight?"

"Why not? We've got the slips. Let's check 'em out."

In Manhattan, Po parked the car in a garage on Forty-fourth Street. Then he and Alex plunged into the cold night air and walked the two blocks to the New York Public Library on Fifth Avenue and Forty-second Street. On the corner of Forty-second Street they paused and waited for the streetlight to change.

"The burdens of our profession, eh, Po?"

Po grunted.

Alex felt a little ashamed at taking Po into the Public Library. He felt as though he were walking with a deranged Cuban espionage agent. Then he realized that it was the other way around. More likely, in the New York Public Library, he'd be the one oddly dressed.

They mounted the steps of the library and entered on the Fifth

Avenue side, taking the only working elevator of six to the third floor and entering the main reading room. In alcove number seven, they found the Haines Telekey Directories. Indexed by city, the Haines Directories list over two hundred million telephone numbers in the United States. Following each number, the Directories provide the street address, occupation, type of business and name of each subscriber. Each Directory is serial numbered and supposed to be leased only to corporations for the purpose of soliciting business. For Alex, however, the Haines Directories provided a very useful tool of investigation.

Alex and Po divided the slips between them, and using the Manhattan Telekey, began matching every long-distance call with a name and address. The process was a long and tedious one. Each toll slip had an average of thirty telephone numbers. Alex began with Marto and found, not surprisingly, that most of his calls had been made to women. He was also able to determine where Marto had traveled during the past month, as the toll slips provided the origin of each call.

Meanwhile Po worked on Kellerman, Feigan and Duranceau. An hour later, it was Alex who found the key call, and for the second time that day he was stunned. "Pirelli," he cried out. "He's made a call from Los Angeles . . . incoming, no, not one, several, and they're all to the same number: two-five-four-seven-six-eight-one."

"Who the hell is that?" Po asked.

"You're not going to believe this, Po. It's André Rostand's home number."

Po retreated into his gentle, gormless smile. "That's an impasse," he said gawking at Alex. "What kind of game is this guy playing?"

Alex frowned and continued to look through Pirelli's toll slips, checking off the number of times he had called the number. During January he counted six. He made a note of the date, time and duration of the call, then slammed the directory shut and looked up at Po. "It's not André Rostand who's been talking to Pirelli. He was out of the country when most of those calls were received."

"It's wild, man!"

"Yes, Po," Alex said, "but do you know who it is?"

"Not yet," he said, scratching his head. "Give me a moment." Suddenly his face lit up. "Jane Rostand?"

"Well done, Po. Now you can go play pool."

V

The next morning Alex Drach emerged from his loft feeling thoroughly miserable. Not only was this one of the worst colds that had ever plagued him, but the thought of what lay ahead of him that day made his mood even gloomier. Fuller and Rostand would have to be forced out. Until now he had been the one reacting to events. It was time they reacted instead.

In a card shop on the main floor of the Pan-Am Building, he stopped and bought a St. Valentine's Day card, then crossed the lobby and took the elevator to his office on the thirty-first floor. He ignored Miss Goodyear, his dour secretary, and went directly into his office.

It was just after ten o'clock when he phoned André Rostand. Harper came on the line and a few moments later he was connected with André.

"Alex?"

"Yes, André. . . . How are you?"

"Fine. . . . Have you got something for me . . . ?"

"I've got your leaker."

There was a pause at the other end of the line. "Shall we talk about it?"

"Any time."

"Would this afternoon at three o'clock suit you?"

"I'll be there."

"Excellent." André sounded pleased.

"One more thing," Alex said nonchalantly. "Could you transfer me to Ray Fuller?"

Alex tried to visualize André's face. He knew the question would shake the old man.

"Of course. Hang on a moment," Rostand replied.

There was a click and as Alex waited, he penned a note on the Valentine card he had bought. He slipped it into the envelope, addressed it and set it aside to mail to Minta Corvo later that day.

Almost simultaneously, Ray Fuller's voice came through. "Yes, Alex. What is it?"

"Just one question, Ray. It's to do with an O.S.S. report I came across in the Archives yesterday. It's a memorandum to you from Hugh Jenner. Do you recall it?"

"Well . . . Jenner. . . . Offhand the name doesn't mean anything to me."

"Shall I read you some of it to refresh your memory? It starts . . ."

"No, no," Fuller broke in. "Perhaps we should talk about this some other time."

Alex smiled into the receiver. "I didn't know you were with the O.S.S., Ray?"

Fuller was silent. "Do you think we could meet sometime?" he said, avoiding the question. "I can't talk now."

"Certainly. When and where?"

"I'll call you at your place about nine-thirty tonight."

"Fine. I'll wait for your call. We'll have a drink together." Alex said good-bye and hung up.

VI

An hour after Alex phoned, André acknowledged a knock on the door of his office.

Harper stepped into the room. "It's Mr. Philip, sir."

André didn't have a chance to reply. Philip pushed through the door and, brushing past Harper, said, "Security sent this up. I think it's important."

André turned slowly in the leather armchair, his eyes narrowing on Philip.

Philip handed him a small cassette tape. André accepted it, looked at Harper, signaling him to leave the room. Then he stood and with an icy voice said to Philip, "Never, ever come into my office like that again."

Philip glared at his father. "Listen to it," he said, nodding at the tape in André's hand.

Rostand opened the bottom drawer of his desk and slipped the cassette into a Uher tape recorder. He pushed the "play" button, sat down again in his armchair and waited.

There was a click. Ray Fuller's voice came through. "Yes, Alex, what is it?"

"Just one question, Ray. It's to do with an O.S.S. report I came across in the Archives yesterday. It's a memorandum. . ."

André snapped the machine off and sighed. "I've heard it," he said.

"What's it all about?" Philip said, still excited.

"It's nothing," André responded calmly.

"Drach knows something."

"Apparently."

"He's dangerous."

André shrugged. "We'll see. There's no point in getting overexcited about it."

Philip started pacing the floor in front of his father's desk. "There's every reason to get excited. What's all this about Fuller and the O.S.S.? And what is the Jenner Report?"

André sighed. His son, visibly nervous and upset, was unable to control himself. It was time to face the issue. He motioned Philip to a chair. "Take a seat and stop acting like a schoolboy. I want to talk to you."

Philip settled his bulky frame into an armchair and listened as André briefly explained to him how he and Ray Fuller had met.

It had been shortly after the war, in Washington, when Rostand was working with a study group investigating art looting and collaboration during the war. Fuller, as head of a unit set up by the O.S.S. to recover art looted by the Nazis, was a member of the same group.

"One day," André continued, "in the late spring of 1946, Fuller came to me with copies of some documents, which, had they been made public at the time, would have been extremely embarrassing."

Philip, now on the edge of his seat, asked, "What kind of documents?"

"Compromising documents. They disclosed that during the war I had been forced to make certain arrangements with a network of agents working on behalf of Hermann Göring."

Philip smiled and leaned back in his chair. "Let's be blunt, Father. The word is *collaboration,* not *certain arrangements.*"

André barely controlled himself. His lips tightened, but he saw no reason to soften the explanation. Philip was right; he had to face that squarely. "Don't judge me, Philip." It was a warning, not a plea. "You wouldn't understand what it was like then. I've never viewed the world as a Frenchman, nor as an American, and certainly not as a Jew. I'm a survivor. I owe allegiance to no one but to my family and the gallery, which is more than I can say for you."

For a split second André thought of Paul and Naomi Drach, and then of Alex. The image faded and he focused on his son.

Philip stood and leaned over his father's desk. "In that case," he said bitterly, "think about what you're doing. You just told me that for forty years Fuller's held a knife at your throat. He . . ."

"It wasn't that way," André shouted, leaping to his feet. "We understand one another. He's protected me and never asked for more than I've been willing to give."

"He's still a threat, a threat to me, if not to you! And so is that bastard, Drach."

"Shut your mouth," André said slamming his fist onto the desk. His contorted face was scarlet with anger. "I'll handle this. I'm still in charge here."

Philip stepped back, looked at his father for a moment, and then said, "I'm afraid you've lost touch with reality, Father. You're getting senile!"

André stood erect and walked around to the front of his desk, reached back and struck his son across the mouth with the back of his hand.

Philip staggered back, his hand clutching his face. "That was your second mistake," he muttered, visibly trembling. He strode around his father, flung the door open and disappeared down the hallway.

Philip walked down the flight of stairs to his fifth-floor office and let himself in through his private entrance. The spacious room was in shadows from the gray light of the cold winter morning. He punched a wall switch and the recessed lighting in the ceiling brightened the office. He walked to the liquor cabinet on the other side of the room. He poured a glass of Perrier water and went to the window. The passersby outside hurried along on the street below, huddled into themselves seeking warmth from the winter cold. He stood watching them for a moment, then went back to his desk and sat down.

He knew he shouldn't, but he reached into his pocket and took another phenobarbital. The pain in his temples throbbed. He put the base of his glass to the side of his head. His father was insane to trust Fuller, but there was little he could do. Drach too. What was between them? He leaned back in his chair and felt the sedating effect of the barbiturate begin to work on his system. Shrinks were all right; pills were better. Suddenly, the intercom buzzed. Philip flicked the switch down, and his secretary's voice answered. "There's a Mr. Baruch on the line, sir."

"Put him through. . . ."

The phone rang. Philip picked it up. "Baruch?"

"Yes, Mr. Rostand."

"What is it?"

"I'd like to suggest a meeting. There are one or two things my superiors would like to discuss with you."

Philip hesitated. "Any problems with the shipments?"

"None at all. Would this afternoon suit you? The Oyster Bar at Grand Central . . . ?"

"What time?"

"Five o'clock."

"I'll be there," Philip said and hung up. He lay back in his chair, curious now about what Baruch wanted to tell him. He wondered if he should inform his father about the phone call, then decided against it. "Relax," he told himself. "Keep calm and everything will be all right." He thought then of Cubitt and suddenly an idea struck him.

He reached across the desk, picked up the telephone receiver and dialed. As the line on the other end rang, the faint sound of a police siren wailed outside. The ringing continued and he was about to replace the receiver when Cubitt's voice answered.

"Hello?"

"Cubitt, it's Philip. I want to talk to you. . . ."

VII

Early that afternoon, a yellow pool of light cast by the green-shaded reading lamp splashed down on a notepad on Alex's desk. He stared at his notes. Rostand. The key to it was Rostand.

Like the spokes from the axis of a wheel, Alex drew lines out from Rostand's name. One he traced to Jane and, underneath her name, Pirelli.

That one was obvious. How long the affair had gone on, he didn't know, nor did he know who initiated it. Jane would certainly have had her reasons. Her marriage was anything but blissful. He'd lived in the Rostand household long enough to know that. Still, he was surprised. If he had to bet on it he'd have put his money on Pirelli. The affair—and that's what it must be—had to be a setup. He wondered how André would react.

Then there was the Jenner-Fuller connection. André Rostand had to know that he knew about that by now. There was no doubt in his mind that between the time Rostand hung up and Fuller came on the line, Security had been alerted and his conversation monitored. The next move was up to Rostand.

Then Alex drew a broken line from Rostand's name to Montag. He was not certain there was a link, but he was suspicious. If there was only some way he could get inside the gallery.

Alex moved the pencil idly across the pad. He'd give anything for a glimpse of Rostand's stockbook, the only place where everything that was bought and sold at Rostand International was itemized. If Montag was still around and Rostand dealing for him, the connection would be there.

Alex drew a square and underneath it wrote "Rostand International." Then he made a list beginning with the words *Alarm Systems*. The column ended with *Proprietory Console*. He stared at the pad: it could be done. But there were other problems. He would need backup.

The telephone rang. "Hello?"

The familiar English voice sounded in his ear.

"Alex?"

"Yes, Cubitt."

"What are you doing?"

"Thinking," he answered.

"Do you have time for dinner?"

"Are you all right? You sound strange."

"I'm fine." She sounded uneasy. "If I'm disturbing you . . ."

"Not at all. I'm glad you phoned. What time?"

"Whatever suits you."

"Let's make it early. I'm expecting a phone call tonight at my place."

"Half past six?"

"At the Carlyle?"

"Perfect. See you then."

The phone clicked abruptly as she hung up. He looked at the receiver a moment, cradled it, then punched the intercom for Po.

"Po here."

"Po, what have you got on Sam Kell?"

"Very little," Po replied.

"Can you find him?"

"Tough detail, Alex. He's disappeared."

"Give it a try, anyway."

"I'm on it," Po said. The intercom went dead.

Alex checked the time. He had fifteen minutes to get to Rostand International.

Fuller walked across André Rostand's office. "I'm worried," he said. "I don't know what to tell him."

"Don't worry about it," André said from behind his desk. "All he's seen is the Jenner Report. If he knew more he wouldn't have phoned you. He'd have come directly to me."

"You're right, sir. He's like that."

The intercom buzzed. Rostand pressed down the switch. "Yes," he said, annoyed at the interruption.

It was Harper. "Security just phoned. Alex Drach just walked in."

"Fine. Show him in as soon as he gets up here."

Rostand left his desk and walked around to Fuller. "It's late in the day, Ray. I think it would be better if you're not here when he comes. Phone him tonight and arrange the meeting on your own. I know I can trust you to handle it."

"Yes, Mr. Rostand," Fuller said as he backed out of the door.

Alex arrived a few minutes after Fuller's departure.

"Sit down, Alex," André said. "I'm waiting for some calls to come through from Paris. I hope you understand if we're interrupted."

It was, Alex knew, a subtle rebuff just to let him know where he stood. The man was going to play hardball.

Alex took a chair in front of the desk. The two men glanced uneasily at each other.

"All right," André said. "Tell me! Who is it?"

Alex reached into his dark blue suit jacket and withdrew an envelope. He handed it to André.

André took the envelope. It was unsealed. He opened it and pulled out a newspaper clipping. He read it quickly, then looked at Alex.

"What's this?" he asked.

"It's Hugh Jenner's obituary," Alex replied. "It was sent to me from London the other day. I thought you might like to see it."

"What's it got to do with me?"

"I'm not sure. Why don't you tell me?"

"I don't know anything about him."

"How about Hans Montag?"

André was silent for a moment, gazing at Alex. "I told you, I don't know anything about him, never heard of him."

"Fuller does."

"I wouldn't know."

"When did you and Ray meet?"

André got to his feet and walked to the window. "What is this all about, Alex?"

"My father's collection. His death. Jenner's death. An attempt to hit me."

André turned to face Alex. "Someone tried to kill you?"

"Last week . . ." Alex briefly described the incident in Paris and the events in London.

André, the facial lines in his face hardened, asked, "And since then?"

"Nothing, at least nothing I can confirm, although I think I'm being watched." Alex hesitated, then added, "That's why I asked about Montag, and why I'm curious about Fuller. When did you first meet him?"

"If it's any help, I'll tell you. We met after the war. I was called upon to give evidence about several art dealers who collaborated with the Nazis. Fuller was head of the O.S.S. unit investigating the charges. We got on and I hired him as soon as he left the army."

Alex joined André by the window. It was snowing outside. "Fuller never told you about his work, never talked to you about my father's death?"

"Briefly," André replied. "But I didn't want to talk about it. What's past is past."

Alex remembered Shakespeare's line chiseled in stone over the front portico of the National Archives. "What's past is prologue, André."

"I hope you haven't drawn the wrong conclusions."

"It's hard not to. How do I know you're not lying to me right now?"

"You don't. You'll just have to accept my word for it."

Alex smiled. It wasn't a pleasant smile. "I'll do more than that, André. I'll find out whether you've lied to me or told me the truth."

They stood face-to-face, staring at each other coldly. It was André who then broke the silence. "I'm sorry this has come between us. When you verify what I've told you, I hope we can be friends again."

"I hope it works out that way," Alex said.

André smiled. "Now, what about my leaker? What's his name?"

"It's not a 'he'!" Alex said. "It's a woman."

"You're sure?"

"Positive."

André's eyes opened in astonishment. "I don't employ women. Except for Cubitt Keeble."

Alex sighed. "This woman doesn't work for you."

André's eyes were uncomprehending.

Alex hesitated a moment, then said evenly, "It's Jane. . . ."

VIII

Philip Rostand walked hurriedly through Grand Central Station and down a set of steps into the Oyster Bar. It was just past five o'clock and as he moved along the space by the crowded bar, his eyes scanned the tables in the back of the room. Baruch, dressed in a sober gray suit, black tie and white shirt, was at the last one. He stood gracefully as Philip sat down across from him.

"Mr. Rostand. What'll you have?"

"Lime and Perrier water, please. I'm off the booze these days."

"I'll join you. I don't drink myself." Baruch walked to the bar and a few minutes later came back with the drinks, set one in front of Rostand, and sat down.

"I'm glad we could meet," Baruch said. "We've got a slight problem."

Philip relaxed and crossed his legs. He reached for the glass and squeezed the juice of the lime into it. "I'm listening," he said.

"It's Drach."

Philip frowned. "What about him?"

"He's been to Washington, digging around about the Drach Collection."

"So . . ."

"So, we think he's an obstacle to any further dealings we might have with Rostand International."

"He hasn't learned about the Watteau, has he?"

Baruch smiled. "Not yet, but you know as well as I do he's onto something. He's meeting Fuller tonight."

Philip sat up. "How do you know that?"

"We have ways."

"Am I talking to God?"

"His servant," Baruch said, unctuously. He removed the carnation from his lapel and started twirling it in his long, veined fingers. "We suggest that the meeting between Drach and Fuller not take place."

"I quite agree, but their actions remain the responsibility of my father."

"Don't you think it's time to act in your own interest, Mr. Rostand?"

Philip began to perspire, anger rising in him. "What do you recommend?" he asked irritably.

Baruch sipped his Perrier water. "Your father may no longer be in control of the situation. His emotions are clouding his reason."

Philip glared at Baruch. "I'm not here to discuss my father's emotions with you." He paused. "I'll repeat the question. What do you recommend?"

"You ask such unnecessary questions, Mr. Rostand. All we want to do is solve this problem so that we can all continue to do business."

Philip looked around the Oyster Bar and for several moments said nothing. Finally, he looked at Baruch. "I understand. I'm as anxious about this situation as you and your superiors are. As for Drach and Fuller, I leave it to you to handle them."

"Yes, Mr. Rostand. That can be arranged. I presume you represent Rostand International."

"In this case, I do."

"I can convey this to my superiors?"

"You can tell them anything you want. Just handle it."

"It won't take long. A matter of hours," Baruch said, signaling for the check.

"When can you get back to me?"

"Don't worry," Baruch replied. "You'll be informed. I'll know where to find you."

Two hours later Ray Fuller was oblivious to Baruch, who was walking a few steps behind him. The emaciated accountant was thinking about his daughter, Maggie. Her twenty-first birthday was two days away and he was still trying to decide what to get her.

He walked through the IRT subway turnstile, quickening his pace to catch the rush-hour train arriving below. He trotted down the stairs and entered the Lexington Avenue, north-bound train, just as the doors began to close.

Still unnoticed, an instep behind him, Baruch shoved his arm between the closing doors, and, as if parting a curtain, flung them open. He stepped aboard the densely packed train and moved to a place directly behind Fuller. The doors slammed shut.

The train swept out of the station and rattled off into the darkness. As it pitched along, Baruch contemplated a young man seated nearby.

The man, lean, with a small moustache and close-cropped brown hair, noticed Baruch's attention and seemed flattered by it. He smiled. So did Baruch, before he looked away.

The car's interior was noisy and jammed with rush-hour commuters, staring in boredom at advertisements for Marlboros and Levy's rye bread. Baruch studied a sign which read: "I got MY job through the *Times* Classified!" The man beside him glanced through a fresh copy of the *Daily News*.

The train shrieked round a curve, its lights blinking on and off, its wheels shrilling painfully. With another playful glance at the seated man, Baruch put his hand into his suit pocket. As he did so, the end of a hypodermic needle emerged, protruding two inches through the expensive weave of his jacket. Then, leaning forward as the train swayed, Baruch pressed gently against Fuller. The wheels of the train shrieked even louder, smothering Fuller's gasp.

The needle Baruch wielded usually contained his insulin. This evening, however, it held Triftazine, a drug employed in the mental wards of the Soviet Union. A one-percent, sterile solution of purified sulfur in peach oil, mixed with a quantity of haloperidol, Triftazine had several effects, depending on the dosage. In small amounts, it could be used for punishment, enervating a patient to an extreme degree and causing intolerable nervousness. In larger doses, it sent a person's temperature soaring to 104 degrees, creating spasms in the throat, making speech impossible. In still larger doses, comparable to those used by Baruch from time to time, it turned a man into a vegetable, an effective, undetectable way to silence him forever.

As Fuller turned around and recognized Baruch, his eyes widened, then glazed. The last thing Fuller would ever comprehend was the bored faces of his fellow commuters.

No one but Baruch noticed Fuller lose consciousness. The train, entering the station, slowed to a stop and, as the passengers around him moved to the exit, Fuller sank to his knees. The door opened and Baruch made his exit as a middle-aged black woman in a nurse's uniform shouted behind him, "A man's had a heart attack! Give him room!"

IX

The evening began with a gala cocktail reception at the Metropolitan Museum of Art. Lit by candlelight, in the rooms set aside to display art treasures of the Middle Ages, the elite of the art world, buyers and sellers, dealers, collectors and museum curators, gathered to dine and compliment one another.

André Rostand in black tie, accompanied by Jane in a full-length halter-neck evening dress, mingled with hundreds of others attending the dinner, sponsored each year by the Art Dealers Association of America.

"There's an awful lot on display," Jane whispered to André, as they entered the Byzantine Room.

André nodded. "More than chalices, gold crosses and tapestries."

"The jewels on that woman are blinding," Jane whispered.

The woman Jane referred to was Muriel Postman, a taffy-haired thirty-five-year-old Southern belle, with expensive tastes and a studied air of wide-eyed naïveté. She and her husband were considered one of the most poorly matched couples in the New York art world.

Muriel's husband, Stanley Postman, was a small but important dealer in the international Old Masters market. He was a quiet, soft-spoken introvert, who spent most of his time fishing, cooking and writing poetry. He hated socializing and, for that reason, was not in attendance tonight.

For Muriel, on the other hand, glamorous dinner parties represented the pinnacle of a Big Rock Candy Mountain. She came rushing up to the Rostands.

"It's just duhvine, seeing you again, Jane, honey." She reached up and pecked at Jane's cheek, leaving a tiny smudge of crimson.

"I love your dress," Jane said, bestowing a frozen smile as she removed her compact case from her purse.

Muriel flicked a limp wrist in the air. "It's nothing, really. A Cardin I bought in London," she said. "I dragged it out to go with this aquamarine my husband just bought me."

The ring—a massive lump of stone—the glittery dress and the orange ostrich feathers she wore around her neck like a boa constrictor were too much for André.

Muriel flicked her hand into his face. "Isn't it duhvine?"

"Spectacular," he replied with a grimace. "Actually, though, I'm more interested in the chalices." He took Jane by the elbow and maneuvered his wife toward a display case.

This was the first A.D.A. dinner André had attended in seven years. He had never joined the association, preferring not to test his popularity with the board of directors, who selected the membership. He knew other dealers disliked him, not least because one of his employees had been discovered installing a wiretap on the telephone of a rival dealer. It had cost him four million dollars, two million to his employee and two million to the offended dealer, though every dealer in the city knew the story within a matter of weeks. He regretted it. He was younger, and inexperienced, then.

The furor in the art world, as a result, had cost him a few of his old-fashioned clients. But as he looked around the room tonight, André thought that very few of his colleagues had cause to be so self-righteous. They all spied on one another. It was standard business procedure.

Ivan Lasky, a dapper, diminutive dealer, waved and started toward the Rostands. Lasky, who owned the largest contemporary art gallery in SoHo, was a former shirt manufacturer and vaudeville hoofer. He could often be seen on the dance floor of the Roseland Ballroom cutting his usual figure doing such Latin-American specialities as the samba and the tango.

André didn't like the art Lasky sold. He ran his gallery like a supermarket, but he did like the little round man himself. Though Lasky was an incessant talker and an egomaniac, he did have a sense of humor, which, in the art world, was his saving grace. André offered Lasky a drink.

"God, I could use one! I've had a hell of a day. This morning I stepped out of the gallery and saw someone being shot a yard away from me!"

"Who did it?" André asked, wide-eyed.

"I have no idea. I immediately dove into a snowbank."

André and Jane enjoyed Lasky's company until dinner was served. Then they walked into a huge, two-story-high hall where more than one hundred tables, with twelve settings each, were artfully draped with sparkling white tablecloths emblazoned with the A.D.A. crest.

André and Leopold Marto were placed at the same table. The two antagonists glanced at each other, nodded cordially, and sat down at opposite sides of the large round table.

As the hors d'oeuvre—an avocado filled with large chunks of shrimp—was served, conversation at the table was light and oblique. The Vermeer was never mentioned, though there were one or two congratulatory comments subtly directed in Marto's direction.

The woman on André's right carried on a continuous chatter with the skill of a geisha, giving both the dealer on her right and André plenty of opportunity to display tact, diplomacy and charm.

While the rest of the table dined on shrimps and filet mignon, Marto consumed a series of dishes featuring grainy, colorless substances that looked totally unappetizing. Instead of the wine the rest of the table enjoyed, he drank carrot juice. As if to make up for his pallid diet, however, he put on a great display of wit. He titillated the company with a series of ribald stories, dominating the conversation at the table as though he were enthroned on a slightly elevated chair, the Art Baron for the night.

To the others at the table, André supposed he seemed retiring and placid, even diminished by Marto's exuberance. Indeed, why should it appear to be otherwise? For all they knew, he was a man of the past, while the tide ran with Marto.

Compared to Marto, the other dealers were like unleavened bread. André respected only one other dealer at the table, eighty-five-year-old Sam Sloane. Sloane was an old-fashioned private dealer who had sold paintings for fifty-eight years. Before that he had been a painter himself in Paris, with Picasso, Bonnard and Vuillard.

In many ways André envied Sam. As a private dealer he didn't have to worry about a large staff, overhead costs, the encumbrances of displays and the demands of exhibitions. He bought and sold his paintings quietly, only to clients he liked, which, when one came down to it, was the only way pictures should be sold.

Sloane hated the way the art world had changed, especially the rise in the importance of the auction house. "No important painting is sold publicly these days," Sloane was saying. "Take your gallery, André. It's about the only old-fashioned establishment around. Today the art world is changing. It isn't the same anymore." Sloane glanced in Marto's direction.

"All things change, Sam. We'll have to go with it."

"Not me," Sam protested. "The new people are too crass and crude. They treat paintings like a pair of shoes. They really don't care what they're buying or selling. I've even sold works for less than I've bought them for, just because I appreciated the client's reaction to the work."

André nodded, then sat back as a waiter bent obsequiously to serve him a wedge of baked Alaska. There were very few around like Sam Sloane. The world *was* changing. To survive today an art dealer had to run a shopping center, and tailor his market to the masses. That meant computers, media promotion, new systems of inventory, new kinds of advertising, public relations and a better understanding of what art "value" was. There would be a larger market, but fewer and fewer great works of art to sell.

He shrugged. Happily, he wouldn't be around to see it. That was Philip's world and he could have it.

André looked across the table at Jane. She'd been seated two places removed from Marto and thus far she had totally ignored him. Obviously, she had other things on her mind. Nando Pirelli was at table six. Jane had told him that from the number of times she had swiveled in her seat to look in Pirelli's direction.

When Alex had told him about Jane and the Italian, he had been astonished. At first he doubted whether they were actually having an affair. It was so out of character for the woman he had married. But now, observing the sidelong glances that passed discreetly between them, André was sure that he had been wrong.

Surprisingly, he wasn't angry. The information she had provided Pirelli was passed innocently. Of that he was certain. As for the affair, it was probably good for her and for that he was happy. Whatever psychosis had driven her from his bed years ago, it had been as hard on her as it had been on him. Harder perhaps. Since then, he had been in love a score of times, and many more women than that had frequented his bed. For her, he knew, there had been no one at all, until now. There was, however, one thing he could never forgive her for. He had accepted her frigidity years ago—what he never accepted was her unwillingness to have another child.

He watched the baked Alaska ooze over his plate like a deflated balloon and weighed his alternatives. He could confront her, but that would achieve nothing. He could ignore the whole situation, and let them carry on, even manipulate the relationship, using it to convey misleading information to Marto. That held some appeal, though in truth, it was no longer necessary. No, he'd protect her, but in another way.

At that moment, there was a sharp rap of a gavel from the speaker's platform. A throat cleared into the mike and there was a rustle of papers before the voice of Henry Gelding, the newly appointed head of the President's National Commission on the Arts, echoed throughout the hall.

"Ladies and gentlemen . . . It gives me great pleasure tonight . . ." Gelding, a short, amply padded figure of a man, was a flamboyant character, a major power in the art world because he controlled the enormous amount of public money flowing out of Washington. His job was to get public attention for the arts and offer more and larger grants to those who produced it.

Gelding's pale eyes, behind wire-rimmed glasses, gazed over the audience looking up at him. He smiled through a thick, grizzled beard, a beard that compensated for the lack of hair on his domelike forehead, and started his oration.

"As Mondrian was wont to say, 'Art is not made for anybody and is, at the same time, for everybody.' To those out there in the vast heartland of America, we must send this message: To the art collector, collecting is an art. . . ."

André raised his eyebrows beneath the hand on which his forehead rested. He was staring at the table, vowing that he would never attend another one of these appalling dinners.

Gelding droned on. "As collectors and dealers, we know that buying a work of art is an adventure. While some do it for profit, most do it purely for pleasure and appreciation."

André looked about the room. He wondered how many of those in attendance really believed what Gelding was saying.

"The country must recognize the large cultural contribution the art dealer makes to society. His role is both delicate and uncelebrated. He offers to his clients confidential information, personal contacts and trusted advice. Most of all he is providing a service, his 'eye,' which for the great ones is both enduring and prophetic. . . ."

André glanced at Marto. The cretin understood one basic thing, André decided. Appearance was most important. Marto sat solemnly listening to every word Gelding spoke, a look of rapt attention on his face.

Suddenly André saw a man tiptoe between the tables and approach Marto. He bent over the old dealer and began a long whispered conversation. The top of Marto's skull moved gently back and forth as he listened, alternatively asking a question while gesturing with his hands.

André didn't have to mind-read to know what it was they were discussing. Marto was clearly being briefed by his aide about the further precipitous decline in the price of Art Intrum stock. After flooding the market with another 100,000 shares that day, the stock had dipped $2.75 to $12.25 a share.

Marto, his eyes staring off into space, seemed staggered. André guessed that he would issue instructions to his aide to try and sell whatever holdings they had, including the Vermeer, to acquire the capital they needed to support the price. When that happened it would only make matters worse. Through his informants, André already knew that Art Intrum shareholders were panicking. Several large blocks had found their way to the market in addition to his own.

All the awards in the world would not help Marto now. However boring the dinner had been, to see Marto's face at this moment had made the long evening worth while.

Marto seemed to be collapsing from within. He looked helplessly up at his aide and then suddenly straightened in his chair as the piercing glare of the spotlight shone down on his face. Gelding was introducing him.

". . . Altogether fitting and proper that tonight we honor a man who, when the history of collecting and selling art in the twentieth century is written, will be remembered as one of the greats. We honor him tonight with the presentation of the Art Dealers Association of America Award. This man, shoulder-to-shoulder with all of us, has improved the stature and status of the fine arts business, and helped to enhance the confidence of the public in responsible fine arts dealers. It gives me great pleasure to summon forth Dr. Leopold Marto."

Marto rose to the sound of applause echoing throughout the vast hall. He walked to the dais jostled by a crowd of well-wishers and friends clapping him on the back. He waved back at the audience, a broad grin on his face as he moved to the microphone.

"Thank you, Henry," Marto said, nodding in Gelding's direction. "That was a pleasant and concise introduction," he added, winking at the audience. After allowing for a moment of laughter, chair-scraping and throat-clearing, Marto settled down to a twenty-minute acceptance speech. Long before he had finished there were two vacant places at his table.

André and Jane Rostand had threaded their way between a seemingly endless number of tables, reached a side door and walked into the cool welcoming darkness outside.

X

Alex and Cubitt had ordered two glasses of Calvados after a pleasant meal at a candlelit table in the back room of Harvey's Chelsea Bar, an out-of-the-way restaurant on the Lower West Side. They were in a relaxed mood and Alex thought they had gotten on surprisingly well.

After their last discussion at the Carlyle, he hadn't expected to see her again. He had picked her up at her hotel, but instead of staying up on the stuffy East Side, he had suggested the little restaurant he frequented closer to his own neighborhood.

Cubitt had enjoyed the meal. She had eaten everything on her plate and sampled portions of his. He was again intrigued by the changeability of her face. He had discovered something new—a mischievous streak in her character. She had poked fun at the way he'd insisted on sampling the wine twice before finally accepting it from the waiter, then chided him for being too serious-minded. Her bottle-green eyes changed, too, one minute expressive, hinting at laughter, the next playfully sympathetic.

Cubitt took a sip of Calvados and then, as she often did, ran her fingers through her hair, pushing it away from her forehead.

"I like your face," she said. "It's rugged."

"Oh?"

"The eyes bother me, though!"

"In what way?"

She leaned closer to him and peered into his eyes as though she were an optician. "I can't tell whether they're blue or gray."

"Try blue-gray."

She nodded, still eyeing him professionally. Her gaze disconcerted him, but secretly he enjoyed the attention.

"The difficulty is," she said, "I don't know what you're thinking. The expression in them never changes. I can't tell whether you're happy, angry or sad."

"Time to change the subject," he said. "I was just thinking the opposite about your eyes."

She leaned back, smiling. "Do you like them?"

"I think they're expressive."

"I know. Windows to the soul."

"Yes, I've heard." He sipped from the glass, and for a minute they sat in silence. Then he recalled her analysis of his eyes. "By the way, when did you ever see me angry?"

"With Philip."

"Oh, yes. Back to him."

"What do you mean?" she asked.

"We talked about him last time."

"Yes, I remember. What is it between you? Why does he hate you so?"

Alex sat back. He didn't like Philip. He never had. Right from the beginning they'd been enemies. "I remember when I arrived in New York, I was very young at the time, and it was difficult to take. Philip pressed a lot and then one day he called me out in the playground. He said I was a 'frog' and started pushing me around. Then we began fighting. He was much older and bigger than I was, and kept knocking me down."

As he described the story, Alex's face became more intense. Vulnerability and a memory of isolation came into his voice as he relived the memory of facing the older boy on alien ground.

Philip had maneuvered him against the garden wall and continued to pummel him. He was helplessly overpowered, but he kept getting up and going for more. Each time he attacked Philip he wound up on the ground.

He hadn't realized it at the time, but from a window André Rostand had been watching them. The fight must have gone on for half an hour or more. Finally, panting heavily, Philip had quit and walked back into the house. Alex followed him and went to the bathroom to wipe the blood from his face. His nose was bleeding.

Suddenly, the bathroom door opened, and André walked in. He handed him a silver dollar and told him that he had taught Philip a lesson that day. That no matter how much bigger and stronger he was, and no matter how many times he knocked someone down, if he kept coming back at him, he knew if he ever fought him again, he would be in for a long battle. It was a lesson very few boys ever learned.

Alex fell silent. He stared at the frosted partition between the restaurant and the bar, remembering that day. Cubitt's voice broke through to him.

". . . and the silver dollar?"

"What were you saying?"

"What about the silver dollar?"

"Oh, that," he said. "I still have it. Not because of the value, but because of the sentiment behind it."

She smiled, this time a genuinely sympathetic smile. "Have you ever really needed anyone, Alex? Or loved anyone?"

Normally, an impenetrable curtain descended whenever he was confronted this way by a woman, especially the kind of woman he sensed Cubitt to be. Somehow, though, he didn't mind this time.

"*Need* and *love* are hard words to define. Sometimes we mix them up. We all keep making choices that draw us together or keep us apart, for good reasons, or maybe bad ones. However, we still make the choice. The trick is to know why we choose the way we do."

"Maybe it's because we have wounds that don't show."

Alex saw the look on her face and realized that her wounds went deep. "Tell you what," he said. "Let's change the subject. I'd like to get out of here."

Cubitt relaxed and smiled easily. "What are we going to do? Or shouldn't I ask such a leading question?" A mocking glint twinkled in her eyes.

Alex shrugged, pretending innocence. He slipped $40 onto the table to cover the bill and they left the restaurant, walking arm in arm into the cold. They strolled east, along Eighteenth Street to Park Avenue, then north to Gramercy Park. It was nearly nine-thirty.

On the corner of Eighteenth and Park, Alex took Cubitt in his arms and kissed her. Pressing against her, he tasted the fiery apple taste of the Calvados on her breath. They clung to each other in the freezing air. He liked this woman, he thought. He liked her a lot.

"Would you like to go to my loft?" he asked.

"I don't know. . . . What's your sign?"

"My sign?" He looked at her quizzically. "Does it matter?"

"Of course it does! When were you born?"

"May fifth," he said. "Nineteen forty-one."

"You're a Taurus, then. That's good. I'm a Sagittarian."

"Great. Now I know. Are we compatible?"

"Wait'll we get to your place. I'll show you how compatible."

XI

"My father used to revile me for being a plaything of the rich. He believed in the Catholic Church and Labor."

Philip Rostand, seated in a banquette at a corner table at "21" smiled at the unattractive brunette seated down the table from him. He thought she was an idiot, but as a staff member of the Old Master department at the Metropolitan Museum of Art, she was a very important contact. Seated in the club's inner room with him were several other friends, all connected with the art world.

"I believe in neither," the brunette's male companion, a young pseudointellectual and avid collector of Magritte's surrealistic paintings, rejoined. "I believe only in the very rich."

There was laughter around the table. This time Philip joined in.

He reminded himself that he had to humor her. She had provided him with a great deal of inside information.

The woman next to Philip, an elderly matron, a grande dame of New York society and one of his best clients, leaned over to him. "Smartass, isn't he?"

Philip smiled and agreed.

"The young are so vulgar. They're misshapen and lack harmony. That's why I love my paintings."

"Which reminds me," Philip interrupted. "We have a marvelous Cézanne that might interest you."

A waiter arrived with two bottles of champagne, set them down and left.

"I'd love to see it," she said. "When?"

"I'm going to Rome this week, but I'll give you a ring when I get back."

"Wonderful."

Across from Philip two of his closest friends who bred horses were carrying on a more interesting conversation. One had just returned from the bloodstock sales at Tattersalls, Newmarket, where he had acquired two new yearlings at the nominal price of £140,000.

Philip leaned across the table and listened intently. The discussion about horses animated him much more than ones about paintings. "You should have seen them, Philip. There was some beautiful horseflesh there. I'm surprised you've never invested in horses yourself."

"Actually, I'm quite interested in horses, always have been." Philip became excited—he'd always wanted to own a stud farm with air-conditioned stables and a string of racehorses running at Ascot, Longchamp and Belmont, all at the same time.

He poured a round of champagne for everyone. A waiter brought a telephone and plugged it into the wall behind Philip's head. He leaned over and whispered, "A phone call for you, sir."

Philip nodded gloomily and picked up the instrument. It was Baruch.

"I just thought you should know, Mr. Rostand. Unfortunately, Mr. Fuller has been taken very ill this evening."

"I'm sorry to hear that," Philip said, shaking his head sympathetically. He cupped the receiver with the palm of his hand. "Our accountant," he explained to the others, "taken ill."

There were frowns and clucking around the table.

"Thank you for telling me," he said into the telephone.

"We'll talk again," Baruch said.

"Fine."

"Glad to be of service," Baruch added. Then there was a click at the other end.

Minutes later, Baruch's phone rang. "Yes?"

"Baruch?"

"Yes, what is it?"

"Just thought you'd like to know they're still at Drach's place. Looks like an all-nighter."

"Anything unusual?"

"Nothing."

"Good. Get some sleep and pick him up in the morning."

"Right. Good night, Baruch."

There was a click, then silence at the other end of the line.

XII

"And then what did you do?" Cubitt asked excitedly. She was sitting on the floor, her back against the couch, flanked by Alex's legs. Her neck, bent forward, tingled to the touch of his fingers. The violins of Johann Pachelbel's Kanon drenched the spaces of Alex's loft. The champagne he'd given her, and the waves of music, formed a smooth and appropriate accompaniment to the gentle play of his fingers over her skin.

He told her. "Po picked the padlock on the warehouse door and there they were."

"All of them?"

"Easily three million dollars' worth!"

"And what did the chairman say when you returned them?"

"He looked at them and then in that deep resonant voice of his said, 'Quite an accomplishment, young man.' "

Cubitt laughed, then bent her head back until it rested between his thighs. She looked up at him, a serious expression on her face. "I worry about you. Someday you're going to run into trouble."

"There's nothing to be concerned about."

She locked her fingers in his hand. "Don't you frighten?"

Alex shrugged. "I don't really think about it," he said. "It's part of existence. Everybody's afraid." He thought a moment. "I like to think I'm pragmatic about it. Channeled properly, fear can be very useful."

"As a spur, you mean?"

"As a warning signal," he said, smiling.

"Let's change the subject again."

"Fine," he said, "but first I have to make a phone call."

He walked to the far end of the loft and up a set of oakwood stairs to his bedroom. It was nearly ten o'clock. He dialed Fuller's number and waited. There was no response.

He hung up the phone and returned to Cubitt, wondering what had happened. Maggie, Fuller's daughter, was an invalid, and certainly she would be home. He wondered if he should go over to Fuller's place, but then, looking at Cubitt, thought better of it. There had to be some ordinary explanation.

He bent over and pulled her up.

"You look worried," she said.

"We all do at times."

"Can I help?"

"Sure, come on," he said, taking her hand. He led her back across the loft and up the double stairway to the large bedroom overlooking the body of the loft.

Alex's bedroom was dominated by three-arched windows that faced north. They framed the glittering portrait of midtown Manhattan. At the other end of the room, against the wall, was a large double bed. Opposite that was an alcove with a fireplace, and to the left, a large door leading to a dressing room and off that, the bathroom.

"Would you like some more champagne?" Alex asked.

"Not right now." She put her arms around him and kissed him. A delicious warmth eddied through his body and he felt himself growing hard.

She drew away. "I'll be right back," she said, heading for the bathroom.

Alex watched her disappear into the dressing room. He had wanted this to happen, but he was afraid where it was going to lead. He stood there, thinking about her and then began taking off his clothes.

In the dressing room, Cubitt took off her shoes and panty hose, then went into the bathroom. She ran the water and then sat on the toilet, trying not to think. But she was thinking. She was turned on. This wasn't supposed to happen. What she had to do, she sighed, was part of the job.

She looked around the bathroom. There wasn't much to look at. It was a large, high-ceilinged room with a wooden floor and white bare walls. To get to the shower, she had to walk up three more steps. This man liked height, she thought.

She left the toilet and walked back to his dressing room, where she picked up his Mason-Pearson hairbrush and started running it through her hair. The dressing room was as plain and austere as the bathroom. Again the walls were white, without even a colorful print to brighten things up.

Then she realized that with the exception of the Monet hanging on the chimney breast, she hadn't seen a single work of art in the entire loft.

She put the brush down and walked to the tall mirrored wardrobe. It had ornate brass handles. She pulled on the right-hand one. The door creaked loudly as it opened. She stood rigid, wondering if he heard it through the closed door. She listened. The undulating strains of Pachelbel were just audible through the heavy oak door.

She couldn't resist going through the wardrobe. It was somehow more intimate than what they were about to do. There were six deep shelves above an inlaid chest of drawers. The top shelf, which was just above her head, contained a heavily scuffed leather suitcase and two tennis racquets, their handles wrapped with sweat-stained tape.

Below that, a shelf held a heavy white reinforced cotton karate *gi*, together with several athletic supporters and one black belt. Stacks of shirts lined the third shelf; whites and light blues predominated. Most of them showed signs of fraying at the collar, and all, she suspected, were victims of a Chinese laundry.

She resisted opening the drawers but took a quick peep into the other side of the wardrobe, where at least a dozen suits and sports jackets hung neatly on wooden hangers. She liked the way he looked in a suit, especially the dark blue one he had worn the first afternoon they met.

The ones in the wardrobe were either heavy flannel or wool, his winter ones. Somewhere in the spacious loft, his light-weight summer suits were stored away. She was certain there wasn't a seersucker one among them. She eased the wardrobe doors shut, took off her dress, bra and underpants and, with a towel wrapped around her, returned to the bedroom.

He wasn't there. She went over to the bed, pulled back the spread and crawled between the sheets.

A few minutes later Alex came into the room. He was carrying two glasses of champagne. He came to her. He handed her one of them, lowered his own and they touched glasses. He sipped from the glass, then set it on the bedside table. He removed his terry cloth robe, flipped it into a nearby chair and slipped into the bed beside her.

"Where have you been?" she asked.

"On the telephone," he said.

"Who to?"

"There was no reply."

She looked at him, puzzled, and was about to ask him something else, when he put one hand over her lips while the other began to move down her body, gently cupping her breasts, then stroking her stomach and finally the soft mound between her legs. Her whole being focused on that part of her body.

She put her arms around him and pulled him down beside her. Her lips parted and her tongue moved in tiny circles around his mouth. She began stroking him. His body was extraordinarily strong and smooth, almost like ivory.

The trembling she felt inside rapidly spread through her body. Her knees began to quiver. Once she had seen a mare about to be mounted by a stallion. She understood now what that trembling animal had felt. She visualized the stallion with its huge pink organ prodding into the mare, ripping into her, and now felt the power of that moment in the deepest part of her.

His tongue moved to her ear, to her neck and steadily down to dab at her nipples, then around in tiny brushstrokes under her armpits, again at the nipples, down her torso, flicking over her stomach, her navel, always downward. Finally, he was there. She pulled her legs back, every muscle in her body taut, and then she exploded. The orgasms began.

He broke from her and suddenly she was afraid. She opened up her eyes, reaching out for him. He was there. She smiled up at him, and was glad, so glad to feel the hardness of him slip gently into her. It was all so easy, so right. He understood what it was all about. She hadn't thought he would, but what lay behind those eyes was much more than she had discerned.

She shuddered and heard herself moan as he plunged deeper inside her. She looked up into his eyes. They were intensely blue now, the pupils large black spheres. They engulfed her. She wallowed in them. No one had ever made her flow like this before.

And then with one last sporadic thrust it was over.

Afterward, she lay very still in his arms as the trembling slowly ebbed away. He, too, was silent, idly running his fingers through the strands of her hair. She wondered what he was thinking. Surely, no human being could trigger such feelings in another and remain insensitive to it. She thought about it, then vowed she would never, ever, let herself fall too deeply in love with this man.

That night, as Cubitt fell asleep, Alex sat propped up against the pillows gazing out of the windows at the skyline of Manhattan. He was troubled by something. As the clock on the Madison Park Tower neared midnight, he still felt something nagging at him. Finally he rolled over, turned out the light and went to sleep.

Toward morning he dreamed he was in the French army in a cavalry division stationed in a forest. He glanced up at a cloud-bank rolling in from the east. A gray mass hung heavily above the misty forest, suggesting rain. In the distance, he thought he also heard the rumble of thunder, though there was neither wind nor the sweet smell of moist air that usually preceded a storm.

Sallow and leaden after a long night's patrol, he desperately looked forward to the luxury of a dry, warm bed, when the rains came. He hated the forest. A gray mist permanently shrouded him, and a knifelike chill constantly penetrated the heavy brown greatcoat he wore over his slender back and shoulders. He seemed to be waiting. Waiting for nothing. If the enemy did come, it wouldn't be through his sector. Not through the forest with its rough and irregular terrain and the hundreds of streams cutting through the hills and the clefts, its muddy paths and perpetual mists rising from its bogs.

He dreamed he was smiling to himself, buoyed by the thought that he was safe. He started off walking through the endless forest, and never fully comprehended what happened next. Suddenly he heard the rumbling and whine of an engine, the grind of steel treads, the crack of snapping trees and then a sound like popping corn.

He never saw the tank which spearheaded the assault under cover of heavy fog. He was only aware of a sudden stab of pain in his back, like the lash of a birch rod as the spray of a dozen rounds from a turret gun caught him from behind. For one agonizing moment he recognized himself, assuming the classic posture of crucifixion. His head and shoulders were flung backward, his arms outstretched and his fingers extended. He could make no cry, nor after the initial slash, did he feel pain. He was conscious only of the flight of his body drifting through the air.

The force of the blast threw him forward, hurtling him against the base of a nearby tree. He settled there, a torn, bleeding figure, face down at the edge of a bog. The shreds of his brown army overcoat soaked red now, fluttered in the wind.

In the moment or two of life he had left, Alex listened to the gargling in his lungs, and through a red haze heard the sound of grunting German soldiers running past him. He knew they were German because he smelled the stink of urine-soaked leather. The Germans used urine to soften their heavy black combat boots.

With a start, Alex woke up. He looked around the room, not realizing where he was. His body was soaked with sweat. He looked across the bed, saw Cubitt asleep, and gazed at the lights of the city below.

Suddenly, he remembered words they had exchanged earlier that evening.

"My sign? Does it matter?"

"Of course it does! When were you born?" she had remarked.

Alex slipped out of bed, went to the small desk in the corner of the bedroom and from the middle drawer pulled out the sealed envelope. He ripped it open and withdrew the Jenner report, turning it to the second page. He scanned it, looking for something. Then he found it. His finger underlined the date of his father's arrest by the Gestapo: 18 June 1940. After a pause, he muttered, "It's impossible. . . ."

For a long time he stood at the arched window, staring into space. Paul Drach was not his father. He couldn't have been if his birthday was the fifth of May, nearly eleven months after Paul's arrest. Unless his mother and Paul Drach were reunited somehow before Drach died? But Jocko had made no mention of that. Where was his mother during that time? What had Jocko said? Paul had closed the house and let the staff go because Naomi had been sent to Monte Carlo. What else did Jocko know? What was he hiding? Who was his real father?

Numb, Alex returned to the desk, folded the onionskin report and put it back into the envelope, trying to absorb the inconsistency of the story Jocko had told him.

He sealed the envelope and returned it to the middle drawer. Nothing seemed to make sense anymore. Nothing was certain. Reality was like water running through his fingers. He returned to his bed and lay down next to Cubitt. She was fast asleep. He watched her for a while, wondering how real she was, what her true feelings for him were, then rolled over, knowing that he wasn't going to sleep much that night at all.

XIII

Hans Montag and a priest representing the Vatican's Commissione di Archeologia Sacra, approached the Catacombs of Monte Verde from the Via Portuense. The entrance was in the garden of an ancient Roman villa, on each side of which was a small chamber. The one on the right, Montag explained, was the Schola, or meeting place of the faithful, where the deceased were honored before being carried below. The one on the left housed the guardian of the catacomb.

Just inside the entrance, a system of pulleys which operated a large number of retractable wires had been installed. "These," Montag explained to the priest, "ensure our safety below. Without them, we would never find our way out. The catacomb is a labyrinth of corridors and chambers that run underground for miles. In some places we'll be descending a half-mile through a network of passages a yard or so wide and no more than six feet high. Without the line of wire, we'd probably starve or die of thirst before finding the right corridor to the surface."

The priest paled slightly and murmured: "Perhaps it would be better just to have a written report, Monsignor Weiller?"

"Nothing to worry about, really," Montag said, handing a canvas harness to the priest. "Here. Strap this on. The wire is hooked onto the back of the harness to ensure your safety. We've yet to lose a visitor." Montag was amused at the priest's discomfort.

They descended a pathway that sloped gradually for a short distance, then fell away steeply down a well-worn stone staircase.

Both men carried flashlights, and as they walked on, darkness closed in behind them. As they made their way deeper into the catacomb, Montag expounded on the salient facts of Monte Verde. It was dug in the first century by Christians languishing under Roman rule. Roman law forbade burial within populated areas and stipulated that the dead were to be cremated, the ashes placed in urns and deposited in mausoleums on the large thoroughfares that led out of the city.

Jews and Christians alike refused to cremate their dead and so resorted to underground caves, which, in time, were linked together by a network of passages. To save space, the passages were constantly widened with graves dug into the sides, one on top of another.

Montag added that there were now forty-five catacombs known to exist and that if their passages were extended end to end, a line would run from the foot of the Alps to the base of Sicily, a distance of nine hundred miles. Only a very small number of these passages had been explored, and the knowledge of the full extent of these was minimal. It was estimated that at least seven million bodies were buried in these underground chambers.

The nature of the soil in the Roman countryside provided the perfect conditions for creating these subterranean cities. The low hills surrounding Rome were composed of tufa, a soft clay that became as hard as stone when it dried. Porous and dry, the soil had been excavated by "Fossores," a guild of gravediggers who were minor Christian clergy.

Gradually, Montag could see, the young priest was losing his fear. "Feeling more comfortable, Father?"

"A little," the priest replied.

"One gets used to it."

They plodded on for another half-mile until they reached the excavation site. A group of four workmen, outfitted in dark blue overalls, hobnailed boots and miners' helmets, toiled painstakingly, removing rubble from the entrance of a chamber.

"Making any progress, Brother Rolf?"

Rolf, holding a shovel which was dwarfed in a pair of huge, broad hands, stood erect. "We should be through within a week, Monsignor."

"Excellent, Brother."

A fat, jowly brother, chewing gum, looked up from the entrance to the chamber where he was digging. "We're having a bit of a problem, Monsignor. The lights seem to be flickering quite a bit." He rolled the gum over his tongue, his jaws oscillating like a cow chewing its cud.

Montag sighed deeply, then spoke slowly as though lecturing a backward child. "I'll check the condenser switches, Brother." He turned to the priest.

"Inadequate equipment, you know," he said, exasperated.

"I know."

"It's a big operation."

"For a good cause, Monsignor."

Montag put his arm around the priest's shoulders and directed him back up the passageway, toward the entrance, the spring-fed wires retracting as he went.

"An odd crew you have there," the priest remarked as they reached the entrance to the catacombs. "It's rather unusual, isn't it, for a brother to be wearing an earring?"

"Brother Rolf came to us several years ago. He comes from an ancient line of Gypsies. Tradition, you understand."

The priest nodded knowingly. They emerged into the sunlight.

"I don't know what in the world we'd do without you, Monsignor Weiller."

"Whatever we do, we do it for the greater glory of our Holy Mother, the Church."

The priest climbed into the back seat of a black Fiat sedan. He rolled down the window and peered up at Montag. "The Bishop will be pleased, Monsignor."

Montag smiled benignly. "Do give him my humble regards."

The priest nodded and the Fiat drove off.

As Montag stood watching the car drive down the hill toward Via Portuense, a double amputee, bedraggled and perched upon a roller-board, came to a halt at his feet. Suddenly he felt a tug at his trouser leg. He looked down and saw the beggar's beseeching face, a gnarled hand gripping at the hem of his cassock.

Montag stared into the amputee's face and began trembling. He tried to pull away, but he was paralyzed. His right hand went to his face. Rapidly he began rubbing his cheek with his index finger, as the memory of Lodz returned in all its force.

PART EIGHT

———◆———

1940

A sunless pall hung over the ancient Polish city of Lodz. In a barren lot outside the city walls, a large pit, forty feet on each side and twenty feet deep, had been dug. To the staccato sound of automatic gunfire and the drone of a bulldozer, hundreds of naked men, women and children were being led to their mass grave.

Allgemeine S.S. Captain Hans Heinrich Montag, clutching a riding whip, stood on the brink of the pit and cautiously peered down. The smell of rotting flesh wafted up at him. Effective, but hardly efficient, he thought, holding his nose.

He turned and watched the procession of prisoners. The path to the pit was well worn now, and dust from thousands of shuffling feet rose high above the ground. Five at a time, they were ordered forward, halted and told to kneel at the edge of the pit. There was a burst of machine-gun fire and they disappeared over the edge.

Montag's physical proximity to these executions gave him a peculiar perspective, since he stood only a few yards from the row of victims. At first, the work had been difficult. The stench, the faces, the suppliant looks. Even when he didn't see the faces, the necks, as the heads bent forward, tended to take on individual characteristics: frightened, defiant, broad, thin, hairy or smooth. But after a time, standing day after day, rigid and impeccable in his black uniform, Montag became bored by it all.

Once, watching the naked men and women trying to retain some shred of modesty by covering themselves with a hand or an arm, he had been amused. Now even that futile gesture had ceased to entertain. He recorded the scenes passing before him but no longer reacted to them. Like a blind man, Montag's eyes gazed out, but saw nothing.

Everything about Montag, the son of a bank clerk, had been mediocre until he joined the S.S. He had gone to several good schools, including the University of Berlin, but indifference, coupled with a stubborn streak of laziness, kept him permanently at the bottom of his class. Colorless, unable to attract the attention of the girls he wanted, inept at sports, Hans managed to survive only by ingratiating himself with the school authorities. He never made a misstep when it came to rules and regulations, and in this way he advanced from year to year. He may not have been brilliant, but he was crafty and shrewd.

Finally, at the end of his first year at the university, Montag's scholastic ineptitude caught up with him. He failed his comprehensive examinations and was forced to look for work. Through a friend, his father found him a job that required little effort—as an assistant to an art dealer in Munich.

The dealer soon realized his assistant's inadequacies and would have let him go but for the fact that Montag had joined the Nazi Party. The dealer realized he might be useful in other ways. Montag suspected this, and the revelation led him to discover his true destiny.

His career began one night in a beerhall when he brawled with a student poking fun at the Führer. Both he and the student were arrested, but while the student was prosecuted for the incident, Montag was quietly asked to join the S.S. and allowed to go.

When he left the jail that night, Montag was jubilant. At last his talents had been recognized. He was determined to show the Party how right they had been to place their confidence in him.

In the S.S., Montag rose quickly through the ranks. Eventually, he was assigned to the Gestapo's Vice Department, where he exercised considerable power under the pretext of fighting immorality and homosexuality within the Party ranks. His superiors understood that Montag was one of them.

Not that Montag was a dedicated Nazi. He wasn't. He simply understood the uses of power. For him, the notion of good and evil had no meaning. An act most men might consider evil, he would regard as a supreme good, if it served his interests. He was neither moral nor immoral, but rather an amoral man.

When war came in September 1939, Montag was transferred to head a Special Action unit. His job was to move in behind the German army and implement Nazi ideology in occupied territories. Captain Hans Montag understood perfectly what this meant. His real job was to eliminate the Jews of Europe.

Now, from the top layer of the death pit a naked old man looked up at Montag, his eyes pleading for mercy. Too weak to talk, the old man stretched out his clawlike hands and grabbed the S.S. captain's shiny black boot.

Montag shook his leg, but could not free himself of the old man's desperate grasp. For a second, Montag was afraid that he would lose his footing and fall into the pit, but the old man was dying and his fingers slipped away.

Although freed, the heavy-set S.S. captain remained paralyzed at the edge of the pit. He began to tremble. His black-gloved forefinger stroked, almost reflectively, a wine-red birthmark on the right cheek of his round cherubic face.

From behind Montag, a thick-necked S.S. sergeant, a cigarette dangling from his lips, stepped forward. He unslung his rifle and bent forward, smashing the old man in the face. The corpse rolled down a hillside of bodies.

Still shaken, Montag retreated from the edge of the pit and stationed himself at the spot where the prisoners were ordered to undress. There, he observed a group of twenty Poles of all ages taking their clothes off. One of them was a young girl with long blond hair, holding an infant in her arms. The infant cooed with delight while its parents looked on with tears in their eyes.

Montag ordered the group to hurry along. There were others waiting behind them.

There were no cries for mercy, as the prisoners placed their possessions, shoes, jewelry, undergarments, coats in separate piles. When the intended victims were ordered to move to the pit, the young blond girl passed close to Montag. She pointed to herself and said in Polish, "Fourteen years old."

Montag hesitated briefly, then beckoned her to him. "What's your name?" he asked.

"Lena," she said. "Lena Kolarska."

Such an innocent little thing, he thought. Montag looked at her with admiration. He patted the infant gently on the head, ordered a soldier standing nearby to return the baby to its mother and, as an afterthought, to have the girl removed to an empty truck. "Find a blanket for her," he barked over his shoulder as he returned to the pits.

The girl struggled desperately to break away from the soldier to rejoin her family, but it was futile. As she was led away, she looked back and saw her parents and baby brother disappear over the edge of the pit.

Lena was thrown into the truck to the sound of a long burst of machine-gun fire. She huddled in a corner, her face like a stone.

* * *

That night Lena stood waiting beside the tub as Montag bathed. He was talking to her, but she was not listening. She felt nothing but hate. She would never forget what he had done to her. Her account with life had been settled. She expected nothing from it. No love. No children. No home. She would live, but only for one act of vengeance. One day, Hans Montag would suffer horribly, just as he made her suffer.

"Do you know what it means for an S.S. to give his word?" Montag was saying. "Do you know how valuable that is?"

She nodded, looking at him without seeing him.

"Good. Because it's important for you to understand. If you do as you're told, behave, and appreciate what I've done for you, I promise that you'll leave here a healthy and happy girl. I give you my solemn word as an S.S." Montag looked up at her and smiled. "Well, what do you say?"

"I'll do as I'm told," she said, pronouncing each word slowly in a dull, wooden voice.

"Good. Now, the towel." He stepped out of the bath and, as he ordered, she handed him a towel. Naked, he was round and white, except for the horrible pink thing dangling between his legs.

He stepped out of the tub, his eyes gleaming, holding his penis, growing larger now, in his hand. "Do you like it, girl? Have you ever seen one before?"

She turned away, her arms involuntarily locking across her chest.

Montag walked over to her and slapped her across the face. "This is the last time I will hit you," he said coldly. "The next time you displease me, I'll have you shot."

She lowered her eyes. "I understand," she said in a low voice.

He grunted, walked to the door, locked it and turned to her. "Come here," he commanded.

She went to him and he took her in his arms. His breath smelled of stale beer. She turned her head as he directed her hand to his erection.

He smiled at her clumsy virginal effort to fondle him. "Take your dress off," he said.

She was wearing a brown muslin shirtdress with buttons that ran the length of the front. She turned away from him and began undoing the buttons one by one. Her hand trembled as she gripped the last button, squeezing it so tightly that it came off in her hand. The dress fell from her shoulders to the floor. She was naked. They had given her no undergarments.

She flung herself, face down, onto the bed and buried her head in her arms. In that position, she felt Montag lower himself on her from behind.

"Your body was made to please," he said. "Don't be afraid."

He straddled her, fondling her small, round buttocks, her back and, reaching around in front, her breasts. She felt a dull ache inside her. She ground her teeth and forced herself to lie still. She dared not look at him. If she did, she wouldn't be able to go through with it.

He was gripping her buttocks now, raising her and pushing the two half-moons apart. With his left hand he pushed her back, downward. The right hand held her in position while his penis stabbed at the opening between her legs.

"Look at it. Isn't it beautiful." He was talking to himself. "So fresh. It wants to live. It wants me. . . ."

She felt the hard thing prod her, then start to push into her. He was ripping her apart. She screamed with pain, twisted and tried to wriggle free.

"No," she cried out. She slipped away.

Montag grasped her shoulders and pulled her back. Again he heaved his body up over her, and with his knees, spread her legs apart. He gasped. He clutched her breasts and started squeezing with all his might.

She shrieked and tried to move out from under him, but he held her and then, as though he were piercing some wall deep within her, he was all the way in. He grunted and she felt him lunge forward. Once. Twice. And then it was over. He was still. Underneath her, the sheets were wet. There was blood on them.

A moment later, he withdrew from her body and rolled beside her. Without meaning to, she glanced at him. He was checking his watch. After that, he slept. She lay there, hardly breathing.

It was midnight when a knock on the door awakened Montag from a deep sleep. His aide handed him a dispatch from Luftwaffe headquarters, Berlin. It ordered him to leave at once and report to Reichsmarschall Hermann Göring.

He left her in bed and hurriedly began dressing.

"I knew it. I knew it," he mumbled to himself. "Great things lay ahead."

He looked at her. "Right, girl?"

She nodded, dazed.

Five minutes later he stood before a mirror and examined his appearance. He looked quite pleased with himself. His black boots were shined, his breeches pressed, and his shirt tucked and pleated properly at the sides.

He faced her, tightening his belt with the silver buckle. Inscribed on the buckle was the S.S. motto, "My Honor Is Loyalty." He picked up his cap, placed it squarely on his head, and then, in the mirror, made certain that the death's head insignia was centered.

He grabbed his bag, opened the door and climbed into the open black Mercedes requisitioned to take him to the airfield.

Montag's aide, standing in the doorway, gestured in her direction, "What do you want done with her?" he said.

Montag shrugged and grinned. "Whatever belongs to me belongs to my men," he said, amused at his show of benevolence. "Take the little sow. She's yours."

The Junker trimotor transport with black swastikas on its wings bumped along the silky runway of the Berlin airport and came to an abrupt stop. Hans Montag deplaned and strutted rapidly toward a waiting Horch convertible.

Two hours later, the car hurtled through the misty forest surrounding Reichsmarschall Hermann Göring's ten-thousand-acre estate. Montag, in the back seat, nervously stroked his cheek. In a short time, he would meet the Reichsmarschall, head of the Luftwaffe and second in importance only to the Führer himself. He wondered why he had been summoned. His orders had been unusually cryptic.

Göring's estate, named after his dead wife, Karin, was set in a clearing dotted with small evergreens. It looked like a Bavarian mountain lodge. Built of stone and timber, it had a roof of false thatch and sets of deer antlers attached to the facade. The entire estate, Montag noted, was surrounded by a fence of barbed wire punctuated by machine-gun emplacements and sentry towers. It reminded him, distastefully, of a concentration camp.

At the front entrance, a young Luftwaffe lieutenant in jackboots and gray-blue uniform, stretched his right arm stiffly in the Nazi salute.

"Heil Hitler," Montag snapped in response.

The lieutenant, named Kropp, led him through the heavy oak

doors down a long corridor lined with huge glass cases displaying
gold and silver mementoes, cups, trays, batons, medals and all sorts
of other gifts from heads of state presented to the Reichsmarschall.

The sound of boots striking the highly polished dark wood floor
echoed throughout the hallway. Montag knew that Karinhall was
only one of eight the Reichsmarschall owned. There was a Berlin
townhouse, a sixteenth-century castle near Bayreuth, a model farm
and a country house near Berlin, another hunting lodge on the Prussian border and still another small farm near Hitler's house in
Berchtesgaden.

At the end of the corridor, he followed Kropp up a wooden staircase to the second floor. "These are your quarters for the night,"
Kropp said, opening a door to a room that overlooked the dark forest. Before leaving, the lieutenant added, "The Reichsmarschall ex-
pects you at his reception and dinner in honor of General von Manstein, the architect of our great victory in France. It begins promptly
at eight in the Great Hall."

"*Jawohl!* Heil Hitler," Montag replied, saluting smartly. Montag
was delighted. Manstein was one of Germany's most celebrated war
heroes. It was his plan that Hitler brilliantly executed to annihilate
the Allied armies in France and the Low Countries. Still, Montag
could not understand why he had been invited to the reception. He
was eager to make the most of it, however. He bathed, put on a
fresh uniform and, at eight sharp, descended Karinhall's great staircase to the vaulted timber banquet hall. Huge logs burned in a stone
fireplace, set in a wall hung with hunting trophies.

Oil paintings, in elaborate gold frames, hung in tiers of three like
postage stamps on the other walls. Montag, a glass of champagne in
his hand, gaped at the canvases. He recognized a Dürer. That alone
was worth two million deutschmarks. Next to that was a Brueghel.
Another fortune. A Cranach. From every side, works by the great
masters looked down on him.

The party was in full swing. Fieldmarshals, generals, admirals, and
other high-ranking officers in dress uniform, with gold braid and
rows of medals, flirted with women in elaborate evening gowns and
twinkling jewels. The air smelled of pomade, perfume, wood smoke
and roasted lamb, stag and boar then being served at a buffet by a
phalanx of white-capped chefs.

In front of the fireplace stood the guest of honor, young, brilliant
General Erich von Manstein, cordially receiving congratulations

from several high-ranking officers of the General Staff. Around him, Montag recognized the thin-lipped General von Brauchitsch, the newly appointed commander-in-chief of the army; balding Jodl, head of Operations; Keitel, chief of the High Command and Admiral Canaris, head of the Abwehr or German Intelligence.

Suddenly, near the doorway, there was a movement as if a scythe had swept the room. The crowd cleared a path, and Reichsmarschall Hermann Göring entered the banquet hall. This evening, he wore a snow white uniform with pale-blue facings and five rows of medals, the most important of which was the "Blue Max," Pour le Mérite. It hung from his neck on a black, white and red-striped ribbon. As Hermann Göring moved through the crowd, he paused and jovially greeted Reichsleiter Alfred Rosenberg, the Nazi Party's leading ideologue and long-time confidant of Adolf Hitler.

Rosenberg, in contrast to the uniforms in the room, wore an ill-fitting, double-breasted, tan suit. His hair unkempt, his skin sallow, he peered with a dour expression through rimless spectacles.

Montag, knowing that Göring and Rosenberg despised each other, moved closer. He wanted very much to overhear this. "Ah, Reichsleiter," Göring blustered, addressing Rosenberg, "we'll be in Paris soon."

Inclining his head a fraction, Rosenberg replied, "This is a momentous time for the Reich, Herr Reichsmarschall. The Luftwaffe has performed brilliantly."

Göring, a pudgy hand on his hip, eyes narrowing, said, "No doubt your staff has readied itself?"

Rosenberg edged away slightly. "We estimate that between twenty and thirty thousand works of art will pass through our hands within a few months. The finest objects, of course, will go to the Führer, for his Linz museum."

"*Natürlich,*" Göring beamed. "Nothing but the best for our Führer." He clapped Rosenberg on the shoulder and lumbered on.

There was no doubt in Montag's mind that the brief exchange between Göring and Rosenberg was not as harmless as it seemed.

It was quite different when Göring greeted Manstein and the other army officers standing near the fireplace. With the military, Göring, at forty-seven, was the most popular of the Nazi Party leaders. Although he was mockingly referred to as *der Dicke,* the Fat One, the two-hundred-and-eighty-pound Göring was the object of considerable affection. Despite his foppish clothes, his constant changes of uniform, emerald tie-clips and diamond rings, the German military accepted him as a great flyer, an ace in World War One who had earned the right to lead them.

A string quartet began Haydn, and, on a signal from Göring, the guests moved to the table. Montag, as befitted his rank, was seated far away from his host, whom he noticed leaving the room as soon as dinner was served.

Montag's plate had barely been set down before him when Lieutenant Kropp appeared at his right shoulder and whispered, *"Bitte,* Captain. Follow me."

Kropp led Montag quickly through a maze of corridors. They passed several doorways, guarded by Luftwaffe sentries who snapped to attention as they approached. The guards had a uniform look. They were young, blond, blue-eyed, and pink-complexioned.

The pair stopped before a large oak door adorned with a gold eagle and swastika. Kropp opened the door, allowing Montag to pass before him.

The S.S. officer stepped into a dimly lit room and saluted. Animal skins covered the floor. Animal heads dotted the walls, and the musty smell of stuffed animals filled the room.

Hermann Göring, already changed into a fresh sky-blue uniform, sat in a huge armchair. "Sit there, Captain Montag," Göring said, pointing to an easy chair opposite him.

Montag sat nervously on the edge of his seat. He had to control his anxiety when he saw his name on the cover of a folder on Göring's knee.

"Your record indicates that you know something about art, Captain."

"Something, Reichsmarschall. . . ."

"Good. You also show a talent for handling unpleasant jobs."

Montag, tensing a little, replied, "I do my best."

Göring stood up. He crossed the room to his desk, opened the left-hand drawer and withdrew a small bottle of white tablets. Montag had heard about the Reichsmarschall's drug addiction. Whether he was taking a diet pill to control his insatiable appetite, or sleeping pills to conquer his insomnia, or one of the thirty paracodeine tablets he took daily for energy, Göring was known to be an addict.

Montag thought it best to avert his eyes. He fixed his glance on the only painting in the room, a religious scene.

Returning to his chair, Göring remarked, "You've noticed my favorite picture, Captain."

"It's a beautiful work, Reichsmarschall. Astonishing!"

"A Vermeer," Göring boasted, pursing his lips. "It's called *Woman Taken In Adultery*," he added. "I paid a great deal for it, two hundred paintings in trade. But it's worth it, don't you think, Captain?"

Montag nodded appreciatively.

Göring paused and unfastened the top button of his tunic. He crossed his legs and began to swing a foot. "I have a job for you."

"It would be an honor," Montag said firmly. Inwardly he glowed.

"What I say from now on is to be kept in strictest confidence."

"Of course, Reichsmarschall." The words leaped from Montag's mouth.

"Before the end of the month, we'll be in Paris. There's a fortune in art there for the taking. There is, however, a slight problem. Rosenberg wants it all. He has lists of everything." Göring's eyes narrowed. "And so have I." Göring paused, and Montag nodded. "The S.S. will be in charge of the confiscations, of course. That's where you come in. I want you to see that certain items are directed to me. *Verstehen Sie?* Do you understand?"

"Yes, Reichsmarschall," Montag replied. "How do you want me to proceed?"

"My agents in France have informed me that the Jew-birds are fleeing the coop. Some of the best collections have already been moved out of Paris. They're being shipped out of the country. Others are being hidden. We haven't traced them yet, but we've located the Rostand Collection. You can start with that."

Göring rose again and returned to his desk. He unlocked the center drawer and withdrew two pieces of paper from a sheaf of documents. "You'll find these useful," he said, handing the papers to Montag.

"You can depend on me," Montag said, rising to his feet. "Am I to assume that I can use my own methods in this matter?"

Göring unfastened two more gold buttons. "Do as you like, but remember at all times what you do for me is unofficial. This is personal business, not state policy."

"I understand completely," Montag said.

"As for the Jews, I have nothing against them personally. You may find it's more profitable to do business with them than to kill them. I'm not a fanatic. Like Rosenberg."

Montag remained outwardly impassive, but he could not share the Reichsmarschall's views. The Führer was right. Jews were the principal enemy. But, of course, the Reichsmarschall's sympathies were his own business. Montag knew that Göring protected several Jews who worked for him. He had also heard rumors circulating about the racial impurity of the Reichsmarschall's lineage, that he was the son of a Jew. "I understand, *mein Kommandant*," Montag said.

"Good, Major. Fanatics don't survive."

Montag stood and saluted smartly, his eyes widening. Had he said "Major"?

"Yes, *Major* Montag. Your papers will come through within the week. With the promotion, I'm sure you'll perform far more effectively for me. That'll be all!"

Montag was in Paris on the day following its capitulation.

Three days later, he set in motion a plan he had worked out prior to his arrival. His agents had informed him that the most valuable Jewish art collections had been hidden throughout the city. Their locations were known only to two men: Paul Drach and André Rostand.

Drach was arrested and, under Montag's orders, taken to Gestapo Headquarters, where two days later he was drag-stepped up a flight of stairs into a stark, white-tiled room.

Montag, together with S.S. Sergeant Horst Schlenker, waited for him. Drach was led across the room to a pulley and chain suspended from the ceiling. One guard wrenched his arms down in front. Another handcuffed him. While he strained, a third guard slipped a hook through the handcuffs and hoisted him into the air.

Montag, his hands clasped behind his back, stared up into Drach's face. The prisoner's attention seemed to wander, his eyes fixed on the floor. Montag waited until the dangling man focused on him. It was like that with most of them, Montag thought. After a while they longed to touch the floor. It became an obsession, enough to make any man talk. He turned his back on Drach and beckoned Schlenker to him. "Talk to him," he said crisply. "You know what I want."

Schlenker's lips curled tightly, his bloated face flattened with eager anticipation. Well over six feet tall and almost a yard wide, he had the eyes of a fanatic.

Schlenker approached Drach, his thick arms crossed over his muscular frame, a riding crop held tightly in one hand. The S.S. sergeant handed his riding crop to the guard, removed his gray uniform jacket, and rolled up his sleeves. Then he addressed Drach in the dry clipped voice of a man obsessed. "You know why they've sent you to me. Just tell me what you know and you'll be fine. You'll remain handsome. You have such a good face. An Aryan face. A fine nose, bright blue eyes, straight blond hair. You could be a German!"

Drach remained silent and bowed his head.

Schlenker cupped Drach's chin in his left hand. "I said, I liked your face. Don't you know how to respond to a compliment?" Then he slapped Drach across the face. The blow left a large red welt. Schlenker smiled and struck him again.

Drach screamed. "You bastard, I'll tell you nothing!"

Schlenker shrugged. "A pity," he said. He turned to one of the guards and nodded. "Now."

The guard, in black breeches and top boots, stepped forward and ripped Drach's shirt from his back. Then he stripped him of his pants and stepped back, leaving Drach naked except for the gumboots he wore.

Schlenker extended his hand and the guard gave him the riding crop.

Montag watched with interest. It was his first Gestapo interrogation. The first stroke exploded nicely across the man's buttocks. Surprisingly Drach didn't scream. When the whip whistled again, Montag could almost see the pain shoot up Drach's back into his brain.

Drach clenched his teeth but again he didn't scream. The third stroke was decisive. Drach screamed and kept screaming until Montag thought he would tear his vocal cords into shreds. As the whip sang again and again, Drach began twitching, like a fish caught on a line. He twisted and turned, trying to avoid the blows.

Montag noticed the wrists had swelled and were fast turning blue. Then the capillaries burst, pumping purplish fluid onto the hands and fingers.

The interrogation continued for several hours. Drach was disappointingly uncommunicative. Montag stopped Schlenker from time to time and tried to speak kindly to his prisoner. He tried to explain that he didn't like to have the rough fellows hurting him. It was a shame. It could all be over, if only he would tell him a few small secrets. Where were the collections? What had he done with them? He owed nothing to the Jewish swine. He was not one of them.

Montag continued to be disappointed. He really couldn't understand why Drach would want to protect such scum with his silence.

Finally, Schlenker suggested a more effective instrument of persuasion. Montag nodded and stepped back. The guards lowered Drach to the floor and strapped him into a straight-backed wooden chair.

Montag watched, fascinated, as a pair of copper clamps were fastened over Drach's testicles. A larger clamp was fitted onto his head.

Half-conscious now, Drach could only gaze vapidly as Schlenker asked him for the information one more time.

Drach shook his head but there were tears rolling down his face. Schlenker looked down at him sympathetically, while his hand moved over a dial.

Drach screamed as the electricity surged through his genitals.

Schlenker asked again. Again Drach shook his head. Another scream; this time blood was coming from his mouth. Drach had bitten off part of his tongue. His hands were white, gripping the arms of the chair.

The electricity continued to surge. Drach's legs jerked convulsively and he began to smash the back of his head against the wooden frame. Then, at last, he went unconscious.

"An obstinate prisoner," Schlenker said, in a bewildered tone.

Montag shrugged. "Don't be concerned, *Hauptsturmführer*. There are other ways. Take him back to his cell."

Two weeks later, after the trip to Monte Carlo and with the list André Rostand had given him, S.S. Major Hans Montag strode into Gestapo Headquarters on the Avenue Foch. He issued orders for Paul Drach to be cleaned up, shaved and brought to him.

That afternoon, dazed and still barely able to walk, Drach was led through a series of corridors into a glass-encased guardroom. Montag, smiling cheerfully, behind a large wooden desk, greeted him. "How do you feel?"

"You'll get nothing from me," he said indistinctly, his mouth swollen.

"That's right, nothing. I want absolutely nothing from you, Monsieur. I'm afraid there's been a mistake." Montag leaned across the desk, his entire body a gesture of concern. "Is there anything I can do for you?" The question was like a verbal embrace.

"You can let me go."

Montag's face beamed. "With or without your paintings?"

Drach glanced at Montag, unamused. "With, of course."

"There was a small matter about false documents."

Drach remained silent.

"After all, it was a criminal act," Montag added.

"What do you want?"

"I told you. Nothing." Montag began rubbing his cheek. "Everything has been arranged for your release. You'll see the streets of Paris again, I guarantee it. On my word as an S.S."

Drach looked at Montag skeptically. "When?" he asked guardedly.

"Immediately! My car is waiting." Montag stood, clapped Drach on the back and smiled. "Shall we go?"

Drach limped along with Montag to the front of the prison. There, his personal belongings were returned to him and a release paper typed up and handed to him to sign. Montag handed him a pen. Drach put his signature on the paper and handed the pen back to Montag. "Keep it," the German said. "A memento."

"A perfect day for a drive," Montag said expansively, as the two men walked out into midafternoon sunlight. He put his arm around Drach's shoulder. "You'd best be careful not to exert yourself the first few days. You took a lot of punishment back there."

Unsmiling, Drach climbed into the back seat of Montag's black eight-cylinder Horch sedan. Two burly S.S. guards flanked him. With Montag in the front seat, they drove out of the prison into the streets of Paris.

Montag turned to Drach. "Since you're the guest on this trip, you can pick the route."

"Any way you like," Drach replied. "Just as long as I get home."

"Would you object if I make a few stops first? I've got a few things to pick up along the way."

"Not at all," Drach said, sounding almost grateful.

"Fine," Montag said, nodding to his driver. "Let's go."

The Horch accelerated past the Trocadéro, down the Avenue du Président Wilson to the Place de l'Alma. There it swung across the bridge to the Left Bank, where a German military convoy stood waiting. One by one, a dozen trucks, each carrying a squad of German soldiers, filed in line behind the Horch.

Drach peered through the rear window. "Looks like a parade, Major."

Montag laughed. "No parade, Drach. House calls!"

Minutes later, the Horch, followed by the convoy, turned past a pair of gateposts. On the iron grillwork that formed an arch overhead was inscribed "L'Église du Père Orgail." It was one of the central Jewish art repositories.

Without hesitating, Drach leapt for Montag's throat. The two guards lunged at him, grappling for his arms, trying to break his hold on Montag's neck. The driver, taken by complete surprise, slammed the brakes with such force that the Horch lurched sideways, throwing Montag, Drach and the two guards forward inches from the windshield. The tires screeched, gravel spun up from the wheels and the Horch skidded diagonally through the gates, coming to a stop in the drains that ran along the side of the entranceway.

"Get him off me," Montag choked.

A blow from one of the guard's revolvers broke Drach's grip. The two guards converged, held him and twisted his arms behind his back.

Montag, swallowing repeatedly to catch his breath, blurted out, "Don't kill him. Just handcuff him."

Still struggling, Drach cried out, "Lies. Lies. All lies."

Montag rubbed his throat, and barely above a whisper spoke with venom. "I've not got the time to debate ethics with you." He stepped out of the Horch and signaled to the first truck behind to proceed on ahead. He walked around the car, looked at the damage to the front bumper, then motioned to the driver to back off the drains. Moments later they were at the doors of the church rectory.

While Drach remained in the back seat, pinioned between the two guards, Montag went to work. He swept past the priest who opened the door and went directly to the doors leading to the rectory's cellar. There were two master padlocks on the door. Montag motioned to a soldier standing behind him. "Shoot them off," he said.

The soldier leveled his weapon and fired several rounds. The padlocks sprung, the steel hasps were severed in half.

The door swung open. Inside were more than three hundred cases with the Rothman family's coat of arms inscribed on each. A squad of soldiers began to remove them. They carried the cases to the loading door of the first truck and passed them to two soldiers, who stacked them in the van.

Drach watched from the back seat, his eyes vacant. In the rectory, one of the priests recognized him and with several other observers started shouting, *"Collabo . . ."*

Several guards moved toward the chanting Frenchmen, their weapons drawn. Montag, standing on the front porch of the rectory, called them back. "It's nothing," he said. "They're understandably upset with him. Hard feelings."

That afternoon, one after another, five other collections were seized, with Montag directing his troops to various hiding places. At each location it was the same. Drach, prominently displayed in his civilian clothes, bruised but treated deferentially by the Germans, made it obvious that he must have collaborated.

Montag was ecstatic. This was an achievement. The grandeur of it would be recognized in the highest circles. And not for a moment, until the end, had Drach suspected a single thing. The beauty of it. No one would ever suspect his real source, protected because Rostand and he had made a lovely bargain.

The confiscations completed, Montag and three soldiers conducted Drach back to his townhouse overlooking the Seine. As they stepped out of the car, the S.S. major carried a leather case containing a coiled rope. Inside the house, empty now of family and servants, Drach was led into the front parlor.

"So, you see," Montag said, gesturing around the house, "I've brought you home."

Drach said nothing.

Montag shrugged and went to the telephone. He placed a priority call to Reichsmarschall Hermann Göring at Karinhall. As he waited for the connections to be completed, he opened his leather case, removed the rope, and tossed it to one of the guards, nodding toward a crystal chandelier in the room. He stood in the foyer, and held the phone as he watched the struggle.

A guard clamped a powerful hand smelling of onions over Drach's mouth. Then, with some difficulty, the others forced the rope around Drach's neck.

As the trio hoisted Drach into the air, Major Hans Montag was connected with Göring. "Exactly, *mein Kommandant*. Over three thousand . . ." Montag hesitated for a moment, watching Paul Drach's last feeble kicks, then held his breath as Drach's body, sphincter uncontrolled by approaching death, voided itself. "Of course, Reichsmarschall. They'll all be sent on a special train this evening."

Exhilarated by his commander's congratulations, Montag strode across the parlor. He ordered the rope to be fastened to the floor of a bulky armoire. That done, he positioned a Louis XVI armchair beneath the chandelier and called a guard. "Hold it," he said, pointing to the chair.

Using the guard's shoulder, Montag stepped up on the chair and felt through Drach's pockets. In one of them, he found the black fountain pen he had earlier presented. He tucked it in his own pocket and stepped down. *"Auf wiedersehen,* Monsieur Drach," Montag said, overturning the chair.

His work done, Montag thought about the tragedies of war and resolved to celebrate that night with a bottle of vintage champagne at Maxim's.

PART NINE

1979

I

Alex felt Cubitt's finger trace the line of his eyebrow. He opened his eyes and looked across at her. She was smiling playfully. He took her face in both hands and drew her toward him.

"I feel I'm with Robinson Crusoe," she purred. "Let's get away. I know this fabulous place, a little island called Anguilla, in the Caribbean."

Alex narrowed his eyes, stinging from lack of sleep, and caught his lower lip with his teeth, masking a grin. He propped an elbow under his head and with his free hand ran his fingers through her hair.

"This could work," she said. "All we have to do is make that choice."

He continued pushing the hair off her forehead. "It wouldn't be difficult," he said. "It's not as though you and I haven't been through this before."

"Have you really?"

"Once or twice," he said.

"With whom?" she asked, mocking possessiveness.

"All I recall are the suitcases. I always found it more difficult to pack than unpack."

"For me it was just the other way around. I like to pack."

"Maybe we should start by traveling light."

She laughed.

"Think about it," he said, as he slipped out of bed to take a shower.

Ten minutes later, he had finished and went to the basin. He let a trickle of cold water run over his fingers and rubbed his eyes with it, holding his face between his hands. He closed his eyes and relaxed his muscles.

That was his way of withdrawing into himself. Once he understood a situation and had gone through its component parts, he would order them in his mind and, by force of will, determine what had to be done.

He did that now. First he would have to get to Fuller and break him. The way to Rostand was through Fuller. The question of paternity was irrelevant. In a lifetime a man had many fathers and fathered many sons. Sometimes the natural ones were the most hurtful.

Then he would have to resolve his feelings about Cubitt. He liked the way she danced, but he wasn't sure whether they were moving to the same rhythm. It was only intuition, but his feelings usually proved him right.

He rubbed his eyes once more, then returned to the dressing room. On the other hand, she might be the kind of woman he could love. She was alert, lusty, fun to be with and—

—And doubling. . . .

"Jesus Christ," Alex mumbled to himself. He stood frozen, except for his eyes, which moved with Cubitt's reflection in the wardrobe mirror, positioned at an angle to permit him to watch her in the other room. She was going through his desk drawers!

He watched her as she pulled open the middle drawer, picked up the sealed envelope and held it to the light. The envelope was too thick to read through. She set the envelope down, disappeared for a few minutes, then returned with what appeared to be a fountain pen. She unscrewed the top and withdrew a most unusual pair of tweezers.

Microscopically thin, the tongs of the tweezers were four inches long. She picked up the envelope and inserted the tongs into the corner of it. For a brief moment she deftly rotated them round and round.

Drach continued to watch unseen as she finished what he called a French Curl. As she worked with the tongs, Alex was relieved. Not because of what he saw, for it hurt, but because it settled the second question. He should have known. Only he hadn't really admitted it. There was a whiff of betrayal just beyond every embrace. She had chosen sides. Philip's side. Now it came down again to Alex *versus* Philip.

Cubitt withdrew the tongs from the envelope. The report was wrapped tightly around them. She unwound it and flattened it on the desk. Then, from her bag, she took a Swiss-made Tessina 35mm sub-miniature camera, half the size of a cigarette pack, and photographed the two-page report. The Tessina, with a spring-wound motor, automatically cocked its shutter, allowing her to get off eight shots without rewinding. Its internal gears, constructed of nylon, hadn't made a sound.

Finished, she dropped the Tessina back into her purse, then curled the report onto the tweezers and inserted it in the envelope, using the same method by which she had extracted it earlier. She returned the tweezers to their container, replaced the envelope and closed the drawer, just in time to return to the bed before Alex reappeared from the bathroom, his black hair still wet and curly.

"I've been thinking," he said with a smile. "What was the name of that island in the Caribbean?"

II

Philip Rostand was waiting in his father's office when André arrived at a quarter past nine that morning.

"Have you heard the news?" Philip said excitedly. "Bertram Bez has announced his decision to sell his holdings in Art Intrum."

"I'm surprised," André said, half-smiling. "I didn't think it'd be Bez." He went to his desk and flipped absently through his correspondence.

"How did it happen? In one week."

André shrugged, then looked at his son. "Obviously people lack confidence in Marto's methods. I imagine the directors of the A.D.A. are feeling a bit foolish this morning."

Philip sat down. "Marto made a statement to reporters last night following the dinner. He said the collapse of the fund was only a temporary setback, and that confidence would soon be restored."

"I'm certain it will," André said, amusement playing across his face.

"What do you mean by that?"

"I know, because I'm going to do it. This morning I issued instructions to my banker in Zurich to buy up every available share of Art Intrum stock. By four o'clock this afternoon Rostand International will hold the controlling interest."

Philip blew out a puff of air, then dropped back into his chair, a look of incredulity on his face. "You're mad. We'll lose a fortune."

"On the contrary, Philip, we're going to make a fortune. At twelve-fifty a share, and probably less after Bez's statement this morning, Art Intrum is the best buy on the market today."

"But what if the stock drops lower?"

"It won't."

"How do you know?"

"I was the one who undercut it in the first place!"

Philip enjoyed a good laugh. "I don't believe it! How did you do it?"

"Right now I haven't got time to tell you, but I'll explain everything en route to Rome." André paused. "We leave first thing tomorrow morning. I want to clear this thing up with Montag as quickly as possible."

Philip frowned. "Why do we both have to go?"

"I want to see what I'm paying for. I also want you to stay on to see that everything is handled properly after I leave."

"How long will that be?" Philip asked.

"As long as it takes," André replied curtly. "On your way out, find Fuller for me."

"I don't think he's come in yet," Philip said innocently, opening the door to André's outer office.

André looked at him, annoyed. "Check again. It's not like him to be late."

Philip shrugged and left.

André picked up the telephone and called Jane. When she answered, he was unusually solicitous, and in a rare gesture, asked her if she was free for lunch. She agreed to meet him at the Four Seasons, and playfully asked what he was doing for the rest of the afternoon.

He told her he had an important meeting at another gallery. He wondered if she'd like to join him. It was so unusual for André to propose such a thing that for a moment she didn't know what to say.

"Why not?" she said. "Are you buying or selling?"

"Buying," he replied.

"A painting?"

"More than that, Jane. I'm buying an entire gallery."

III

At the New York State Hospital for the Insane, Alex stood beside a white-gowned doctor, looking through a window onto the ward.

He had tried to reach Fuller at his home that morning, but had found his daughter Maggie instead. She was just leaving for the hospital, when she told him about Fuller's stroke.

"It doesn't even look like him," Drach whispered, watching Ray Fuller, propped up in bed, staring into space. Beside the bed, Maggie Fuller, in a wheelchair, sat holding her father's hand. "There's nothing in his face. It's as if . . . as if his cheekbones had crumpled." And then he remembered he'd seen a face like that once before, in London, only three weeks ago.

Embarrassed, the doctor didn't know what to say. To break the silence, he asked, "A relative?"

"No," Alex replied. "A friend."

"His daughter is heartbroken."

"I can see why . . ."

While the doctor talked about the difficulties that older people had coping with the world, Alex remembered Fuller during a happier time. The time he had returned from boarding school with a series of papers to write. Fuller had helped him and the accountant had proudly told half the staff at the gallery that Alex Drach was his young protégé. He used to visit the gallery and Fuller would show him around. Alex referred to him as Rostand's *consigliere.*

Recovering from his reverie, Alex turned to the doctor. "Is there anything you can do for him?"

"Very little. Physically, he's fine, but his mind is completely gone. That's all I can say."

"He's shaking like a leaf, doctor."

"His blood pressure is quite high; not unusual after a stroke."

"He was one of the most lucid men I've ever known. I talked to him yesterday. There was absolutely nothing wrong!"

The doctor shrugged. "It happens." Alex started to interrupt but the doctor added, ". . . Actually there was something . . . I don't know if it's 'unusual,' but . . ." He looked at Drach. "Was Mr. Fuller planning a trip somewhere?"

"I don't think so. He never mentioned it."

"Was he ill before? I mean, before this happened?"

"Not that I know of. Why?"

"I think he must have been. When we examined him, he'd obviously just received an injection. Antibiotics, by the look of it. I could see the needle mark on his hip."

Alex walked through the door separating the doctor's office from the ward floor and approached Fuller's bedside. He looked down at Fuller for a moment and then glanced at Maggie. She sat motionless, her back straight, her hands folded, clenched in her lap.

"Hi," he said.

She looked at him, her eyesockets deep and shadowed with fatigue. She'd always been tiny, but now, sitting there so miserable, she seemed miniature.

"Hello, Alex," she replied numbly.

"Any change?"

She shook her head. "None."

He perched on the edge of the bed. "Do you want to talk about it?"

Maggie shrugged. "What's there to say? Dad called from the office and said he was on his way home. The next thing I heard, the police were telling me he was here."

"Was there anything unusual? I mean the past few days."

"Nothing." She stared at her father. "Once there were four of us. Now I'm the only one left." Tears started down her cheeks. "I can't believe it," she muttered.

"Maggie."

She looked up at him. Her swollen eyes half-closed.

"If there's anything you need, any way I can help, all you have to do is call me."

"Thanks, Alex. I know I can count on you."

Alex bent over to gaze in Fuller's face.

Maggie said, "The other day Dad said something peculiar to me, something about you, I can't remember what. Then he gave me a little manila envelope. He said it contained a key to a safety deposit box. He said that if anything were to happen to him I should give it to you."

Alex stood at the far end of the bed, his heart pumping faster. "Do you have the envelope with you?" he asked, hardly able to breathe.

"It's at home."

"Would it be inconvenient if I stopped by this afternoon and picked it up?"

"Not at all. There's nothing I can do here," she said, reaching out for her father's hand. Fuller continued to stare blankly into space.

IV

It was shortly before half past two that afternoon. Alex approached the corner of Fifth Avenue and Forty-fourth Street. He checked the time of the old-fashioned clock that stood on the corner, his favorite timepiece, the only one like it on the avenue.

The bank was across the street on the southeast corner. He slipped his hand into his outside pocket and felt the tiny envelope. In it was the safe deposit key, together with a tiny slip of paper with the box number inked onto it.

He glanced up and down the street. Nothing appeared to be unusual, but he couldn't be sure. Alex hated appearances; he preferred to deal in sure things. He sensed he was being watched, but ignored the feeling and walked to the corner. He waited for the lights, crossed the street and entered the bank.

The slow-moving escalator took him to the lower level. He walked quickly toward a glass-enclosed area through which he could see an attendant seated at a large mahogany desk. Behind the attendant, through a door, Alex could see rows and rows of steel-encased deposit boxes.

He walked up to the locked gate which separated the boxes from the rest of the bank and nodded, holding up his key.

The attendant left his desk and walked to the locked gate. "I haf not seen you before," he said in strongly accented English.

Alex hesitated. He wasn't quite sure what to say. He had a key, but unless Ray Fuller had left written instructions he wouldn't have access to the box. He wondered if the attendant knew what Ray Fuller looked like. He decided to play it straight.

"I've never been here before," Alex replied. "I'm here on behalf of a Mr. R. J. Fuller."

"Ach, old Meester Fuller," he said, eyeing Drach suspiciously. "And who are you?"

Alex explained that Fuller was quite ill and that he wanted Alex to check something for him. After a delay of several minutes, Alex withdrew several pieces of identification from his wallet and placed them on the turnstile of the teller's window.

The turnstile rotated and carried with it Alex's identification.

Alex watched as the bespectacled attendant examined his papers.

"One moment, please," the old man said. He walked back to a group of filing cabinets. He opened one, thumbed through a series of green cards and selected one. He returned to the teller's window.

"Yes, Meester Drach. We haf you here." He spun the turnstile back to Drach with the green card. "Pleess sign it."

Alex signed the card and returned it.

"Sank you," the attendant said. "Und now you may enter."

Alex waited while the attendant unlocked the gate from the inside, then entered the box area, followed by a guard.

"Vud you like a private room?" the attendant asked.

"Yes, please."

The attendant nodded, took Alex's key and walked through the doorway. He placed the key in one lock, took another key and placed it into a lock just below the first. The keys rotated at the same time, and the attendant pulled out a long narrow box from the steel-encased shelf.

Alex followed the attendant to a small cubicle, where the box was set down on a table. He thanked him. Without saying a word, the old man nodded and left.

Alex sat down before the box. He lifted it. It was lighter than he had thought it would be. He set it back down on the table, hesitated for a moment, then flipped it open.

Inside, held together by thick brown rubber bands, was a packet of old and yellowed papers. Unsettled, Alex picked up the packet, freeing it from the rubber bands.

Beneath the packet a white envelope rested at the bottom of the box. He set the packet aside and reached for the envelope, using his little finger to rip it open at one end.

His heart was pounding. He opened up a folded piece of paper and read a handwritten letter from Ray Fuller. It was dated August 1, 1950.

Dear Alex,

You may never read this, but in the event you do, I won't be around. This will have to suffice as an explanation for what I have done.

Enclosed, you find a half dozen original documents that came into my possession following the war.

At the time I was head of an O.S.S. unit, investigating German War

Crimes, specifically art looting. Among the investigations assigned to my unit was one involving the disappearance of several major art collections confiscated in Paris in June/July 1940. The results of that investigation are here.

The documents themselves are self-explanatory. It is harder to explain my reasons for not disclosing them till now.

Briefly, I want to do that now for you. I owe you that. First, you must understand that my Unit turned up hundreds of cases of collaboration during the war. Furthermore, very few of those cases were ever brought to justice. Rostand's, while one of the most heinous, was certainly not unique.

Secondly, the victims of his collaboration are dead. Nothing can possibly help them now.

Thirdly, the collections, so far as I know, have been destroyed, thus eliminating any reason for pursuing the matter further in that regard.

Therefore, it seemed to me, then and now, that the disclosure of the evidence contained in these documents would serve no purpose other than to punish André Rostand.

On the other hand these papers gave me the one chance I would ever have to assure my family's security. Handled in the right way, they have been worth a fortune to me, not to say the world to André Rostand.

Please understand that at the time I made my decision to withhold this information from the proper authorities, your father had no heirs, as far as I knew.

Your arrival in New York, however, changed everything. When I learned of your existence I was shocked and horrified. Nonetheless, I have kept my silence. I do so because I still believe it is in all our interests, yours, mine and Rostand's, to prevent the dredging up of the past.

My reasons for revealing this to you now are simple. I think you have a right to know the truth about your father. I also believe that these documents have assured my security and represent yours as well. In the event anything happens to me, they may very well be the only way to save your life.

Forgive me. I have always been your friend.

Ray.

For several minutes Alex sat clutching the letter in his hand. Stunned, he was afraid to open up the tattered packet of documents resting before him on the table. Finally, after several minutes, his hands trembling, he opened the first one. He read it.

It was the missing document from Box Number 65 in the Archives, and it proved Rostand was a collaborator. The report was self-explanatory, detailing the arrest of Paul Drach and Montag's role in his arrest. Then, in the fifth paragraph, it documented André Rostand's secret meeting with the S.S. officer in Monte Carlo.

There Alex stopped reading. The meeting had taken place in Monte Carlo. . . . He read it again: "Montag meanwhile was very keen to acquire the hidden collections and took it upon himself to meet the art dealer, André Rostand. He paid a visit to Rostand at Monte Carlo in late June, 1940. . . ."

Then Rostand might have been with Naomi Drach, had to have been with Naomi Drach. They were there at the same time; it would have been inconceivable that they wouldn't have met. There was no other explanation. His father was a collaborator, but not the one the world recognized. André Rostand. It had to be! That would explain so many things. The reason Jocko had sent him to New York. Why Rostand had raised and supported him. Philip's insecurity and hatred for him. It was all rooted there, in Monte Carlo.

For a long time, Alex sat in the quiet alcove, thinking about Rostand. What he must be going through. The duplicity of their relationship all these years. He shook his head as though trying to clear a path through the psychic jungle ahead.

He reread the reports, then put them, together with Fuller's letter, back into the deposit box. Finally, after several more minutes' wait, he buzzed for the attendant. The iron box was locked up again, its contents safe. Then he walked to the large iron gate, where, with a guard, he was permitted to leave.

Instead of taking the escalator, he passed through the lower level of the bank to a set of stairs leading to the Forty-fourth Street exit. He took them two at a time and went out into the sunlight. He checked both sides of the street, crossed it and entered the side entrance of the building on the northeast corner.

He hurried past a bank of elevators, took a short flight of stairs into a coffee shop, walked quickly through it and left the building by its Forty-third Street exit. He turned right toward Madison Avenue, then stopped abruptly in the doorway of a wine shop and glanced back up the street. He waited to see if anyone followed him out of the coffee shop.

No one did. He then continued east to the Pan-Am building and went to his offices on the thirty-first floor. Barely able to contain his anger, he had decided. It was time to act.

As soon as he returned from the bank, Alex walked into Po's

office, greeting his assistant with the words Po always loved to hear:
"We've got a job to do."

Po's eyes lit up. "What's it this time, Number One?"

"A B. & E. . . ."

"When and where?"

"Tomorrow night. Rostand International."

"I think . . ." Po paused. "I think I'm going to sell my shares in
Drach Associates."

"The job can be done," Drach said calmly. "I know the entire
setup."

"Let me in on it."

"Make a list, Po."

There was a momentary pause as Po waited for his employer.
"First, I'll need a complete bypass kit. The induction pickups, a dig-
ital sequencer, you know, standard lineman's stuff. Then, three
power sources: six, twelve and twenty-four volt, and a converter. Get
me a burn bar, a short one, as well."

"Keerist, what the hell are you going to do, rip off the Federal
Reserve?"

"No, just the gallery," Alex said nonchalantly.

"Now he's stealing the stuff. I thought all we did was find it."

Drach turned emphatic. "This is a personal job, Harry. There's no
other way. It's something I have to do."

"OK, no offense. But it sounds like you need a friend. Come on,
give a little. What are you up against?"

"A full house, Po, just about everything: a central station, pro-
prietary console and a lot of new stuff. A Johnson system. One of
those operations that goes on forever. All the intrusion, motion, infrared and god-knows-what-else. They all tie into the environmental
and then report to a very secure console. I can take out the central
station easily enough, but even that has to be slick. I'll need Sam
Kell."

"How much time do you need on the inside?" Po asked.

"A good question. Once I get in I may have to deal with guards.
Movement will be restricted. Maybe half an hour. No more."

"Guards?"

"Four."

"Armed?"

"Yes, but I'm going in sterile," Alex replied. "I don't want anyone getting hurt." He began pacing the floor. "My problem is getting into Fuller's office."

"Why there?"

"I want a look at the stock book."

Po nodded. "Where's your access?"

"Through the place next door. Rostand has owned the whole block for years and now they're renovating that building. If Kell takes out the ADT we can go in through the adjacent townhouse."

"Sounds like you need a lock-and-pick man."

"How did you guess?" Alex said, smiling at Po. "And the Con Ed van for cover."

"It won't be easy," Po said. "The last time I listened to you we ended up spending the whole night in a flooded basement."

Alex laughed. "At least if we get stuck this time, we'll be in plusher surroundings."

V

A very unhappy Leopold Marto sat at the stainless-steel conference table in the boardroom of Art Intrum. He, Duranceau, Kellerman, Feigan and several other board members had gathered to assess their position, made more precarious by the absent Bertram Bez, who, at the opening of that morning's trading, had dumped his five percent of the firm on the London Exchange.

Nando Pirelli, although not a board member, was also present. He and Marto held a brief, whispered conversation, then Pirelli moved to the other side of the room.

Marto, his thoughts murderous, nodded to the secretary, who reached for a gavel. He rapped it on the table.

"Will the board members kindly take their places?" Marto asked.

The room fell silent. The others took seats around the long rectangular table, Pirelli being the only one who did not. He sat in a chair along the wall of the boardroom.

"The Chair calls this special meeting to order," Marto began. "I entertain a motion to suspend the reading of the minutes, copies of which are in front of you."

Ira Kellerman proposed the motion, Duranceau, from the other end of the table, seconded it, and it was carried without objection.

"As the next order of business," Marto continued, "the Chair would like to place Nando Pirelli's name in nomination for the directorship most recently vacated by Mr. Bertram Bez." Marto glanced around the table.

Kellerman again proposed the motion, which was seconded at once by Jules Feigan.

"The Chair calls for a show of hands."

Everyone around the table, with the exception of Charles Duranceau, raised his hand.

Marto, glaring in Duranceau's direction, said, "The motion is carried. In the minutes, it will be duly noted that Mr. Duranceau cast the single opposing vote." Marto turned to Pirelli, motioning him to the table.

The polite applause that came as Pirelli took his place at the end of the table opposite Marto was suddenly interrupted by Duranceau. He rose from his seat, and in a brisk voice said, "I propose . . ."

He was cut off by Marto. "The chairman recognizes Mr. Charles Duranceau."

"Thank you, Mr. Chairman," Duranceau said, nodding in Marto's direction. "I propose a motion that the board appoint a new chairman of the corporation. I further suggest that the present chairman of the board has been grossly negligent in his handling of the firm's business and I ask for his resignation from the board."

Marto was on his feet before Duranceau had finished speaking. Silently the others at the table looked at Duranceau. He paused for a moment, then smiled. "Perhaps I should clarify myself. Actually, I would like to offer the board a nomination for a new chairman, one who should be sitting here with us this afternoon, but who at this moment is waiting nearby for our decision. I offer you the name of André Rostand."

The bluish-red veins of Marto's face stood out like the lines on a map. "The Chair will recognize the motion if it is put in the proper form," he said icily.

"Before a vote is taken on the motion," the Frenchman said, "I suggest the board read this."

Duranceau pulled several sheets of paper from a folder set in front of him. "I have a proposal here which outlines Rostand's conditions for assuming control of the corporation and its assets. I think it is a good proposal, and it has my approval."

Duranceau distributed the papers around the table.

"You will also find a draft letter of resignation to the board. It's from Leopold Marto." Duranceau looked to his right. "Had I known Mr. Pirelli was going to be elected to the board this afternoon, I would have also prepared such a letter for him."

Pirelli was now on his feet. "What's this about?" he shouted. "What right does Rostand have to come in here demanding anything? And since when are you his spokesman?"

Duranceau sighed. "Mr. Rostand has every right. He doesn't want to force us into anything, but he has plans for his share of the company, which, at this moment, amounts to a controlling interest. To put it bluntly, gentlemen, André Rostand owns us."

Silence prevailed for a moment, followed by excited conversations between members of the board. Only Marto remained silent. For a minute or two he stood at the head of the table, then coughed and called for silence. He spoke to Duranceau. "I believe, Charles," he said, "the board deserves some explanation."

"It's quite simple, Mr. Chairman, earlier this afternoon Rostand called me to his office. There he presented me with these proposals and a copy of his 'buy order' for two-point-seven million shares of Art Intrum. I, of course, spent the rest of the afternoon verifying his purchase. The shares are his. I repeat, gentlemen, André Rostand owns a controlling interest in the corporation and requests that the board accept the resignation of the chairman, Dr. Leopold Marto. He also further proposes that the company buy the Marto and Pirelli interests in Art Intrum for seventeen dollars a share. This, I think, is a generous offer considering our present financial position."

Ira Kellerman flipped his copy of the proposal on the table. "It seems obvious to me that Rostand has controlling interest in the firm, but why does he not want all of us to liquidate? Why only Marto and Pirelli?"

"That, gentlemen, I cannot answer. He simply gave me his instructions and asked that they be considered by the board."

Outside the headquarters of Art Intrum, André and Jane Rostand sat in the back seat of their chauffeur-driven limousine. As the motor idled, a grayish-blue vapor rose from its exhaust pipe into the cold February air. André looked up at the windowless concave three-story structure that seemed to him more like a steel vault than an art gallery. The bunker-like building reminded him of a World War II German pillbox. There was no plaque, no brass plate, nothing to indicate the nature of the business inside.

"Ugly, isn't it?" he remarked to Jane.

"Hideous," she replied. "Why in the world are we sitting here?"

André took her hand and gently kissed the back of it. "We have such little time together, Jane."

"Then why spend it like this?"

"Just a moment, you'll see."

Suddenly the car phone rang. Rostand picked it up and listened. "I'm delighted," he said. "I accept." He listened again, replied affirmatively to several questions, then asked, "Is he there?" He nodded as he heard the reply, and hung up. He turned to Jane.

"That was the board of Art Intrum," he said, beaming. "I've just been offered the chairmanship of the firm. Do you think I should have accepted?"

"But isn't that the ring?" she asked, blinking.

"*Was* the ring, darling." He reached for the door handle. "Shall we go in?"

Jane looked at him suspiciously. "Must we?" she asked.

"As the new chairman, I think it's only appropriate they meet you."

They left the limousine and walked up the stairs to the gallery. As they waited for the mammoth steel door to open, André thought about Marto. He had no hard feelings about him. He hoped the old man would take the loss graciously. Pirelli was a different matter.

Without a sound the large steel door swung open. Jane and André found themselves in the large reception area. They heard voices coming from the upper level of the gallery. Art Intrum had no stairs of any kind. The gallery had been designed that way. Marto hated stairs. Instead, ramps circled to the upper levels. The floors were made of textured stainless steel, the curved walls covered with red linen, with chrome moldings and baseboards. The furniture at the landings was also made of stainless steel and covered with black, brown and red embroidered pillows.

As they reached the top level, Duranceau met them. "They're all waiting," he whispered, leading them into the boardroom.

Everyone in the room was standing. "Gentlemen," Duranceau announced, "I'd like to introduce Mr. and Mrs. André Rostand."

There was a polite patter of hands from everyone in the room except Marto and Pirelli.

As André led Jane to the head of the table, a deathly silence enveloped the room. He and Marto momentarily confronted each other. "Forgive the intrusion, Leopold," he said. "The formalities of this affair are as noxious to me as I'm sure they are to you."

Marto grinned. "On the contrary, Rostand. Your presence here is a singular achievement. I'm quite certain you would be as gracious if the shoe, so to speak, were on the other foot."

André looked down the table at Pirelli. Not till then had Jane noticed him. André, following the direction of her gaze, saw Pirelli's eyes drop. Jane looked at André, to find his eyes fixed on hers, her face awash with hurt and shame.

Her mouth tightened and her gaze faltered. But she didn't look away. André, watching the dismay on her face settle, smiled gently at her. There, with a room full of strangers and antagonists, he hoped she would accept it as a gesture, not of vindictiveness, but of love and understanding, the kind of love he had withheld from her all these years, the kind of understanding she had withheld from him.

It worked. He could see she understood. Blinking once, she turned to look at Pirelli, her eyes blazing. Instinctively, without thinking, she clutched at André's elbow. In that instant of recognition of what Pirelli had done, how he had used her, betrayed her, played on her body and deceived her, André reached across and patted her hand lying in the crook of his arm. Then he glanced about the room and, feeling Jane's eyes on him, began to speak.

"I understand the board has kindly proposed that I become the new chairman of Art Intrum. This is an honor, and a responsibility, which I humbly accept. . . ." He looked at Nando Pirelli. ". . . Assuming, of course, that I'll have Mr. Pirelli's letter of resignation from the board, along with his five percent of the company, in the morning."

Pirelli's eyes flared for a brief instant, then with a look of resignation, he nodded, smiled blithely and walked from the room.

In that moment of victory and revenge, André felt like laughing. It couldn't have gone better. Pirelli's humiliation was an unexpected bonus. The sweetest "Amen" would come, however, when he finally dealt with Montag.

VI

The photographs had just been delivered. Cubitt glanced at her watch. It was after four. She would have time to take a bath before calling Alex. On her way to the bathroom the house phone rang. It was Philip.

"Cubitt."

"I wasn't expecting you. Do you want to come up?"

"Try and stop me!"

Cubitt walked into her bedroom, picked up her silver-backed hairbrush from the dressing table and walked into the living room. She brushed her hair and stared south along Madison Avenue. From where she stood she could see the lights sparkling in the shop windows. Dusk was still falling early.

She was annoyed at Philip's intrusion, and wished it were Alex coming to see her instead. Philip was taking her for granted. During the past two weeks she had seen a great deal of him. There had been a score of parties, several nights at the theater, and a weekend in Martinique. It had been fun, but she found his diminishing concern for her, along with a preoccupation with himself, an aggravating combination. He was even too self-absorbed to notice the way she felt.

But she hadn't attached herself to him for either his personality, or his looks. Philip had wealth and power, which he might eventually share with her. She banked on that. In those terms, Alex had nothing to offer.

On the other hand, Alex was a much stronger man than Philip. He appeared to be totally secure within himself, and because of that he was warmer, more considerate and generous, the kind of person who cared about those who cared for him. It was a rare quality, and, though God knows she didn't possess it, she admired it in others.

She thought about the way Alex looked. She'd never been with a man she'd been more physically attracted to. She'd been able to manipulate most men she'd had, but it wasn't that way with Alex. He always seemed to be a step ahead of her. He was new and exciting; maybe that was it.

She thought about the night before. She was certain he liked her.

He was even a little bit in love with her. In that respect, she and Alex were different. She would never fall in love with him until she was sure that he was in love with her. That was only sensible. A man had to love her more than she loved him. Only a foolish woman loved without being loved first.

The doorbell pinged. Cubitt frowned, walked rapidly to the foyer of the suite and opened the front door. Philip stood in the hallway, holding two Great Danes on separate leashes.

"Hi, sweetie," he said as the two dogs bounded through the door. He pecked her on the cheek and passed ahead of her, pulled by the Danes into the living room. He unleashed them and slumped in a chair, ankles crossed. Through his heavy-lidded large eyes, he looked Cubitt up and down. "I called you last night. There was no answer."

"I was with Alex."

"Did you hump him?" As Philip asked the question an odd smile creased his face. Despite the smile and the slump of his massive body in the low-slung chair, Cubitt could tell he was in an aggressive mood.

She ignored the question. "I got what you wanted."

"I'll bet he did, too!"

Cubitt said nothing but went to a tall Chinese desk across the room. She withdrew a manila envelope and the Tessina camera from one of its drawers, and handed them to Philip.

"I just had them developed by a friend of mine," she said. "He's a decorator, very reliable. He doesn't ask questions."

Philip grinned with mock sheepishness, looking half pleased, half resentful. He ripped open the envelope and pulled out two 8" x 10" photographs, along with several negatives. For a few minutes he studied them carefully, his nostrils twitching.

"Did you read these?" he said, looking up at her.

"Of course I did."

"Did you find it interesting?" he asked, slipping the photographs back into the envelope.

She shrugged. "Interesting . . . perhaps. What's it all mean?"

Philip stood and walked toward her. "Fortunately for us, very little."

"Then why all the bother?"

"Was it?" he asked, grinning.

"What?"

"A bother to get them?"

"I had to do it that way. But I'm telling you, I won't do it again."
She turned on her heel and started off for the foyer.

He grabbed her roughly by the arm and spun her round. "I don't
care what you like or what you don't," he said angrily. "You'll do as
I say." He took off his jacket and started unzipping his trousers.
"Take your clothes off," he demanded. The dogs growled, shaken in
their repose by Philip's angry voice.

Cubitt didn't move.

"I said take off your clothes." Suddenly he reached out and, taking
the front of her dress, ripped it from her shoulders. "It's my turn,"
he said.

He undressed quickly and his erection sprang free. The dogs, on
their feet now, watched curiously.

Cubitt looked at Philip for a moment, saying nothing. Then, with a
terrible smile, she slowly began undressing.

VII

Alex entered the Chelsea Bar and immediately spotted Bob Renard.
An old friend, Renard was a New York cop who dressed in form-
fitting shirts, jeans and boots and thought of himself as another Ser-
pico. He had spent twelve years on the force, eight of them as an un-
dercover operative in Narcotics and Organized Crime. Four years
earlier he had been assigned to the Art Identification Unit.

Alex had done him several favors, the kind never mentioned, and
now he needed Renard's help.

Renard stood and took Alex's hand. "You're late, man."

"Sorry. Had a bad day."

Alex sat down, ordered a drink and then reached across the table
and tousled Renard's long hair. "You're out of fashion," he said with
a grin. "Don't you know long hair's out!"

"The commissioner doesn't like it either. I only get away with it
because I work the Art beat. You know, they think we're all weird."

"How's it going?"

"You're looking at it. They busted us up. I've been reassigned to
Property Recovery. Still handle the art thefts, but my unit's gone. No
support up top."

Bewildered, Drach shook his head. "What the hell happened?"

Renard smiled, gesturing with his hands. "It's the same old story. Remember at the beginning how it was fashionable to do something about art thefts? There was all that publicity about how the Mob was getting into the game, setting up the jobs and fencing through the dealers?"

Alex nodded. "It's the best way to launder profits from the drug trade. Set up a dealer, buy paintings, and use them as underground currency."

"Right! So I go out, do some research and find out the trade in stolen art runs close to a billion dollars a year. It's ranked second only to narcotics traffic on the list of the most frequently committed international crimes."

"Big business."

"Big people." Renard leaned across the table, drawing Alex closer to him. "Then what happens! Last month they call me in and tell me they're breaking up the squad. After three years they said I was wasting my time. The truth is nobody wants the strictly legal channels to work anymore. There's too much money involved. I was getting too close."

Alex looked away, feeling Renard's frustration. "So what happened?" he asked.

"So here I am, sitting in my office, under Property Recovery, like the Lone Ranger with no Tonto. I've got no support, no unit. I'm helpless."

Drach shook his head. "It's a lesson we all learned. They're all connected, the people in the trade, the dealers, international rings, politicians, the people who run the legal side, even the police. Business is business."

Alex sipped his Scotch and remembered something that Jocko Corvo had once told him. The Corsican had drawn a pyramid. On one side of the bottom he had pointed to the left, and said, "That's left." At the base of the other side he pointed and said, "That's right." At that level, Jocko told him, there were differences. At the top of the pyramid, however, everyone was the same. There was only one thing. Power. Those at the apex knew it. There, everyone knew everyone else. They protected each other.

Renard leaned back in his chair, shrugged and laughed. "I should have known. The art world is a perfect breeding ground for corruption. What better place to operate from? There's no S.E.C., no checks, no accountability, no pressure from the public." Renard shook his head and drank his beer. "What's your problem?" he said, shifting again toward Drach.

"A big one! Rostand!"

Renard whistled softly. "Transcendent. He's everywhere. What have you got?"

"I think he's dealing merchandise, but I can't be sure. Just a couple of things that came my way." He paused, tightened his lips, then added, "There may be a Nazi connection."

Renard's hands dropped to the table. There was a mixture of wonder and caution in his voice when he said, "Be careful, Alex. If they decide to tap you, they can hurt."

"You don't have to tell me that. I've seen it up close. When I was inside, working for him, I saw what was going on. That's why I left. I figured I'd rather be on my own. The corruption I knew about. The links. The way they operate. But this thing about Rostand is too big. I can't let it go by."

"The only way you can tackle a guy that big is by finding the profit his slide is to someone as big as he is. You can bet no one is going to risk his ass otherwise. They'd be guillotined."

"I need some help from the Nineteenth Precinct."

Renard's eyes narrowed. "Don't ask for too much."

"I need some time, tomorrow night. Say, between nine o'clock and midnight."

Renard looked up at the ceiling pensively. "The Nineteenth . . . Upper East Side . . . between Seventy-second and Ninety-sixth streets . . . the silk stocking district . . . galleries." He looked at Alex and grinned. "A B. and E.?"

Alex nodded.

"Rostand International."

He nodded again.

"And you want me to cover you?"

He nodded a third time.

"I don't want to know anything more about it," Renard said, playing nervously with the gold chain that hung around his neck. "I can get in touch with a couple of friends who handle the patrol assignments in the precincts. You'll have your cover on the streets that night. But let me tell you . . ." Renard hesitated and took a large swig of his beer. ". . . You can be sure the alarms will be connected into the precinct, and if they go off, you've had it."

Alex laughed. "Don't worry. I've got the backup I need."

Renard stood and slapped Alex on the top of his shoulder. "For your sake, I hope so," he said, turned and left.

VIII

Harry Po was in a hurry. It was 8:45. He was cutting it close. Wearing a pair of blue overalls, a light blue nylon jacket and a yellow construction helmet, he walked into Con Edison's Thirty-fifth Street repair station and got into the van parked in the corner of the yard.

Good old Marvin, Po said to himself. Rappaport had left the keys right where they were supposed to be, suspended from a magnet underneath the dashboard. He started the engine, revved it, then drove toward the front gates. As he reached them, a guard appeared from nowhere.

"Fuck me," Po mumbled to himself. "I'm a red banana."

The guard opened the door on the passenger side. "I think you've got a severe attitude problem, fella. You know you can't drive out of here with equipment at night."

"You're an asshole!" Po snorted. "I'm on OT. The junction box in Zone B is fouled up."

"Don't bullshit me," the guard said shining a flashlight in Po's face. "Let me see your job order."

Po turned off the engine and leaped out of the van. "All right, man, I'll level with you. I've got some honey who's just dying for it. But she won't come across unless it's in my van. She gets it off that way."

The guard jeered. "You're kidding?"

"No shit. She goes wild in this thing."

"I'd like to, buddy, but it's against regulations."

Po's eyes pleaded. "Just for an hour. That's all she needs."

"I'm only doing my job."

"Your job? You've got to be kidding! At a time like this."

The guard shrugged. "What can I say?"

"Give me a break, man. I'm com'n' right here."

The guard hesitated for a moment. He looked around the yard, then back at Po. "OK, fella, but just this once." He turned and walked away, shouting over his shoulder, "Be sure and get that van back here tonight. I don't want you running all over town with it."

Po returned to the van and took out a handkerchief, wiping the beads of sweat that covered his face. "Jesus," he said to himself. "He's got to be the dumbest asshole I've ever met."

Po drove the van through the gates onto First Avenue and sped uptown. It was already 9 o'clock.

For Alex it had been a long day. In the morning he had had to see the usual number of clients, held several briefings with Po, and then spent the afternoon drafting a report for an insurance company appraising the value of a collection of stolen paintings.

At a bar across from Grand Central Station, he glanced up and looked at the faces of those seated around him. They were a motley lot, staring absently into nothingness, their anonymous hands gripping tranquilizing drinks and stubbing cigarette butts into small glass ashtrays.

Alex drained the last of his Glenfiddich, then with his right hand reached down and touched the tote bag, unnecessarily reassuring himself that it was still there. Again he itemized its contents, making sure that he had everything. There was a leather pouch the size of an eyeglass case, which contained a set of picks, a collapsible umbrella in a small black case, a pair of rubber gloves, a high-intensity burn bar, a coil of three-inch rope and a small radio transmitter.

He reached into the pocket of his heavy black overalls and paid for the drink. With the tote bag and construction helmet he left the bar and walked to the public pay phone at the back of the room. There, he glanced at his watch. It was ten past nine. Po should be coming through.

Po drove the blue and white Con Ed van north to Forty-second Street and parked. He entered the Daily News Building, went to the first empty telephone booth he saw, sat down in the booth and noted the time—9:12. He was three minutes early.

At 9:15 sharp he consulted a tiny slip of paper and dialed. Through a crackle at the other end of the line he heard Alex respond.

"I've got it, Alex. Where do you want it?"

"The southeast corner of Forty-fourth and Vanderbilt. I'll meet you there."

"OK, trooper. See you there."

Drach hung up and immediately dialed another number. Sam Kell answered after one ring.

"Welcome to New York, Sam," Alex said. "We're on."

"I can't say I'm happy to be back. Where's the marker?"

"Across the street from you. The corner of Forty-fourth and Vanderbilt. A blue and white van in three minutes."

Alex put down the receiver, picked up his tote bag and helmet, and left the bar.

Sam Kell, a paunchy hulk of a man, hung up the phone and stood for a moment in the urine-smelling booth, eyeing distastefully the day's leavings of papers and cigarette butts. He checked his watch, then crossed Grand Central Station to a small alcove off the main rotunda. There he went to a left-luggage locker, opened it and removed a black box about eight inches long. He set the box on the floor and checked the four toggle switches on the front of it, making sure the red and purple wires running from the box were properly mated with an alligator clip. He then closed the box, checked his watch again and quickly walked back across the rotunda toward the escalator leading to the upper level of the Pan Am building. In two minutes he was standing on the southeast corner of Vanderbilt Avenue and Forty-fourth Street. It was cold. He made a wide arc with his arms and flexed his shoulders, partly to keep himself warm, partly to relieve the tightening in the back of his neck. He had never considered himself a reckless man, certainly not a foolish one. He didn't enjoy taking risks. Vietnam, and the thirteen months he'd spent there, had knocked that sort of thing out of him long ago. Admittedly there were times when one had to take a risk, but surely Drach had done his job and knew what he was doing. He depended on that as he had always done, ever since they'd been in Nam together.

He approached the van just as Alex got into the driver's seat. He opened the door on the passenger's side and climbed in.

"Damn cold out there," he said.

"Be thankful," Alex remarked. "There'll be fewer people on the streets tonight." They shook hands, grinning at each other.

"We're still going to freeze our ass out there," Po chimed in from the back.

Kell turned in his seat and smiled. "Howdy, partner."

"You'll be warmer in these, cowboy." Po handed him a pair of overalls.

"You can change in the back," Alex said.

Kell eased himself out of the front seat and climbed into the back of the van, where he put on a pair of overalls, a heavy blue jacket and a yellow hard hat.

At 9:25 the van turned right off Madison Avenue and rolled to a stop in front of a darkened five-story brownstone, next door to Rostand International. Alex left the vehicle, walked around to the back and opened up the paneled doors. Quickly he took out six emergency lanterns and plugged them into the van by cable. He placed the lanterns, lit now, around the perimeter of the van. Then he put four metal stands around a manhole cover and, taking a reel of luminous red plastic tape, strung it from stand to stand.

Kell, holding the black box, joined him with a flashlight, and together they lifted the manhole cover. Then they rigged an electrician's light and ran it down into the manhole, where a series of telephone cables ran underneath the street.

Kell descended into the manhole with the light and carefully examined the underground cables.

"You guys ready for me yet?" Po said, as he emerged from the van beating his arms to warm himself.

"Not yet," Alex replied. "Your act is yet to come."

Po peered down the hole. "Everything OK down there?"

Kell looked up. "Fuck off," he whispered. There was a pause. "I need the box."

Alex handed it down.

"Why don't you just cut the cable and knock out the whole system?" Po asked.

"Clumsy," Alex replied. "He can't cut the cable because all the circuits have supervisors. The moment the cable malfunctions, the alarms at the police station will be set off. Sam has to incorporate a duplicator into the cable. He reads the system with the black box, plugs into it, and then controls it from here."

"What's with the black box?" Po asked.

"Forget it. It's time for you to work."

Alex returned to the van and opened his tote bag. From it, he removed a set of picks and passed them to Po.

"It's a deadbolt type," Alex said. "I checked it out this morning."

"Segalock?" Po asked.

"Yes, but fitted with a Medeco cylinder."

Po frowned. The tumblers of a Medeco cylinder were unevenly serrated. They were the toughest of locks to pick. Po left the van and descended the front steps of the townhouse to the basement level, where he set to work.

Alex returned to the manhole and watched Kell read the system. Alex knew that the first link in any alarm system consisted of sensors at the windows, doors, vaults, transoms and other access points. The sensors were connected to a second link, the electrical circuit, and through them to the alarm control unit.

The alarm control unit regulated the bells and sirens that went off inside the premises, as well as those linked by telephone lines to the Nineteenth Precinct station.

Kell, however, knew his physics. He reached for the little black box, a potentiometer, and then selected the first of eight cables running underground. With a penknife he peeled away the insulation and attached the two alligator clips from the potentiometer to the cable. He checked the meter gauge, looked up in the dim light at Alex and shook his head.

Quickly, he disconnected the clips and reattached them to the second line. Again, not the right one.

He had tried all but the last two lines when he looked up at Alex, this time with a smile on his face.

"I think I've got it," he said. "Number seven. It has to be with a current flow like this."

"You damn well better be right. I don't want to go in there and have all hell breaking loose."

"Don't worry. This is the one."

"How much time do you need?" Alex asked.

"No more than five minutes. I just have to calibrate the right resistance and duplicate it."

Kell attached first the red and then the purple wires of the black box to the exposed cable. He then adjusted the dials on the box and interposed a dummy electrical circuit into the alarm system. This two-step process took three minutes to complete.

Kell stood erect and stretched, almost bumping Alex's alert face reflected in the light from the electrician's lamp.

"OK, Alex, we control the system."

Alex nodded and returned to the van. He picked up his tote bag and then walked the few feet to the basement of the townhouse. Po was still hard at work.

"It's the cold," Po said. "My fingers are numb."

Alex watched anxiously as Po manipulated the picks. He could see it was difficult. The lock also had tapered steel reinforcing rings. It could not be pried or pulled from the door.

Suddenly Alex heard footsteps crunching on the ice. He tapped Po on the shoulder and they edged back into the shadows, hugging the nearest wall. The picks were left dangling in the lock.

Two pedestrians, out for a late night stroll, passed along the street above them. Po waited for a minute before he blew on his fingers and resumed work. Alex remained in the shadows, watching scattered clouds move across the moonscape.

Three minutes later, Po appeared at his shoulder. "It's all yours, maestro," he said. "The door is wide open."

"If anything happens, pack up and leave," Alex said. "I'll make out on my own."

Carrying the tote bag, he pushed the heavy door open and slipped into the dark basement hallway. He bolted the door behind him and waited until he was halfway down the corridor before he slipped on a pair of rubber gloves and switched on the penlight. He found the stairs, turned off the light and, guided by the handrailing, quietly climbed the staircase. One flight up, he switched the light on again, passed the landing and continued upward. Again the light went out and, tentatively, he stepped out onto the roof. By the feeble light of the moon, he made his way to the parapet, looked over the edge and was relieved to find that a gap of only six feet separated him from the gallery's fire escape. He tossed the bag to the other side, then climbed onto the parapet. Balancing there for a moment, he gauged the distance carefully, then jumped, grabbing the railing of the fire escape for support as he landed on the other side.

Moments later, he had climbed onto the roof of Rostand International. There, two electric beams probed the darkness, ready at the slightest intrusion to transmit an alarm to the guards in the central security room. For several heartbeats, Alex stood hesitating. Taking a deep breath, he stepped forward. No alarm sounded. He exhaled slowly, gave a silent thanks to Sam Kell, and went to work.

From the tote bag, he took the burn bar, unwrapped it and, using a piece of paper on which the layout of the top floor had been outlined, located what he calculated to be the gallery's seventh-floor dining room.

He fired the burn bar, and drilled a relatively small hole through the roof, no more than a few inches wide, brushing the plaster detritus out of the way. When the hole was made, he inserted the umbrella through it, opening it when only its handle could be seen. He then began to enlarge the hole around the umbrella, allowing the plaster and cement to fall through. Periodically, he reached down into the growing hole and removed the chippings that had been caught by the umbrella.

Finally, when the hole was large enough for him to pass through, he did so, dropping down onto the conveniently handy dining room table.

He stood motionless for a moment, hearing nothing but the roar of a plane's engines pass overhead. He switched on the penlight, played the beam around the walls of the room and went to the door, alert to the slightest sound of a guard on patrol. With Kell controlling the alarm system, that was all he had left to worry about.

He placed his hand gently on the doorknob and slowly began turning it. He heard it click and stopped. No sound. The door opened a crack. Still nothing. He peeped into the dimly lit hallway. No guard. He stepped from the room, hurried to the door opening onto the stairwell, descended one flight to the sixth floor and entered Fuller's office.

The door shut behind him, he stood for a moment to catch his breath. The room was unbearably stuffy, overheated and quiet except for Fuller's little aquarium of goldfish, which bubbled in the corner of the office. Alex wondered if anyone had fed them since the accountant's departure. He inspected the room briefly and went straight to the desk.

Unless someone had removed it, the stock book would be where Fuller always liked to keep it, at hand, in the center drawer. Alex opened the drawer, probed it with the light and cursed. The stock book was gone. He rifled through the rest of the desk drawers.

He closed the last drawer and stood erect. If the book wasn't in Fuller's office it had to be in Rostand's. Again he moved quietly to the door, listened, then opened it. He was still drawing aces. In black-laced shoes with grooved-rubber soles, he walked noiselessly to the opposite end of the corridor and entered André Rostand's office through the white-and-gold paneled door. He closed it softly behind him, flicked the button on his flashlight and went to Rostand's desk. As always, the desk top was bare. He opened the top drawer and rummaged through a stack of papers, interoffice memos, correspondence and several gray folders tied with blue ribbons. No stock book. He was sliding the drawer back in place when he heard the elevator doors open at the end of the hallway.

He flicked the flashlight off and froze. The squeak of leather-soled shoes started down the corridor toward the office. Alex looked around. There was nowhere to go. He thought a second, then grabbed the tote bag, stuffed it underneath the desk and pressed the hidden button in the paneled wall behind him. The paneling slid open, leaving just enough space for him to stand poised in front of Rostand's bar. He was exposed until he reached around, pressed the button again and stepped back. Just before the panel door closed on him, Alex inserted the tip of his flashlight into the opening, preventing the door from closing all the way. A gap no larger than two fingers remained.

In that instant, there was a long creak as the door of Rostand's office opened. A shaft of light fell across the desk and then, abruptly, the lights went on.

Alex stiffened. He could hear the labored respiration of a guard no more than ten feet from him. He imagined the man's eyes sweeping the room, exploring every recess, sensing his presence. Sweating now, Alex wondered what he would do if he was discovered. Was the bag out of sight? Had he done anything else to give himself away? Would the guard spot the gap in the wall behind the desk? The moments seemed like an eternity until finally the office lights were switched off, the door swished closed and the squeaking shoes receded down the hallway.

Alex waited until the elevator doors opened and closed again, then slipped his fingers down the outer edge of the door jamb to the button. He pressed it and the paneling parted. He stepped out of the narrow space into the office, his body bathed in a tingling sweat.

He considered going back to the street at once, but resisted the impulse. Insead, he turned on the flashlight and went back to the desk. This time he opened the middle drawer and found the stock book.

He sat down in the leather armchair behind the desk, and carefully went through the book page by page. In it was listed the name of every art work the gallery possessed, its point of origin, the date of purchase, its cost and, in the case of those works already sold, the sale price.

Most of the items were valued in six, even seven figures, an incredible inventory. During the past month alone, according to the book, Rostand had turned over thirteen million dollars' worth of canvases.

Alex was almost to the last page when an unusual item caught his attention. An entry, made two and a half weeks ago, entitled "Cityscape of Paris," had Rome as its point of origin. That wouldn't have been unusual except that the painting had been bought for $480. What was Rostand doing with *department store* art? Either it had to be a very good buy—a masterpiece picked up for a song—a wrong entry, or a coverup.

Alex recorded the title of the painting, the date of its purchase, and then continued examining the book until he had exhausted the list. The Watteau was not there.

He closed the book and returned it to the desk drawer, deciding that he had learned all he could from it. Hurriedly, he went through the other drawers. In the bottom one he noticed a small cassette recorder. There was a tape in it, half-played. He rewound it for a few seconds and then listened to the conversation it had recorded.

"What is it, Alex?"

"Just one question, Ray. It's to do with an O.S.S. report. . . ."

Alex smiled sadly to himself and shut off the recorder. Now he knew how Fuller had met his fate. Then, without incident, he made his way out of the gallery, back to the street, the way he had come.

IX

The call reached Special Agent Charles S. Boczka, U.S. Customs Service, at his home in Queens shortly before midnight. He moaned in protest at the incessant ring of the phone beside his bed. He groped for the receiver and murmured, "Boczka."

"Charlie. It's Alex."

Boczka sat up on one elbow and glanced at the bedside clock.

"Jesus, Alex, what a time to call."

Next to him, Boczka's wife turned over, her blinking face framed in a halo of pink and blue plastic curlers.

"Who is it, lovey?" she asked.

Boczka frowned and put her off with the wave of a hand. "Go ahead, Alex."

Boczka hunched over the phone and listened as Alex appealed for his help.

"I wouldn't ask in an official capacity . . . check in the morning for a record of any painting imported from Rome on the sixteenth of January . . . probable valuation less than five hundred dollars. . . . I'm not sure if it's a criminal offense . . . a personal matter . . . looking for a name and an address."

Boczka looked at his sleeping wife and reflected for a moment. "I'm only one of six hundred agents in the country, Alex," he groaned. "Is it important?"

"It's vital."

"OK, I'll do my best," Boczka said yawning. "I'll run it through the computer and be back to you first thing in the morning."

"Thanks, Charlie."

"Good night."

Boczka set the telephone down, reset his alarm for six-thirty instead of seven o'clock, and went back to sleep.

X

"We always seem to do business in the most opulent surroundings, Herr Rostand. It's a pity the demands of my work don't permit me more pleasant evenings like these."

Hans Montag, having shed his cassock, sat with André and Philip Rostand in a suite of rooms in the Roman palazzo of Madame Gérard. The salon in which they talked was furnished with several easy chairs, two couches, antique mirrors, raised fireplace and a magnificently well stocked bar.

Thus far it had been an amicable evening, at least for Hans Montag. He had not stinted himself when it came to the bottle of cognac, now almost empty on the table between the three men.

Philip laughed. "I'm sure, Monsignor, with the funds we've put at your disposal, you'll soon find ample time to enjoy yourself."

Montag stayed Philip's hand as the younger Rostand attempted to refill his glass once again. "I've found, young man, that one's life passes through various stages."

"I presume," Philip said, "there will soon be a change in yours."

Montag's pale eyes lifted inspirationally toward the ceiling.

"I'm afraid at heart I'm really not cut out to be a man of the cloth." He paused and looked at André. "Which reminds me, Herr Rostand. Perhaps we should offer a prayer in memory of the recently deceased Leopold Marto."

Philip gasped and looked at André. "Did you know about this?" he asked.

André shook his head, amazed.

"It was in this morning's paper," Montag said, handing André a clipping from the *International Herald Tribune*.

André looked at the clipping headlined "Leopold Marto, Art Dealer, 79, Killed in Plunge." The article listed Marto's various business interests and then reported that he had fallen to his death the day before from his twenty-fourth floor penthouse apartment. The account stated that Marto had apparently jumped from the apartment and was found shortly after 8 A.M. on the roof of an adjoining building. He left behind a note that mentioned business problems, the police said.

Wide-eyed, Philip accepted the clipping from André. He read it and passed it back to Montag.

"Well, that's good news," Philip said, beaming.

André glared at his son.

"A pity, eh, Herr Rostand?" Montag sighed. "Life must go on, however. As it always has."

André was about to speak when there was a knock at the door. Madame Gérard entered the room and André stood. "Madame! May I present an old acquaintance, Hans Weiller."

Montag smiled, obviously charmed by the woman. Her dark blond hair, long eyelashes and clear pale skin, despite her age, attracted most men she met. Montag was no exception. He appreciated her grace and mature beauty, even though he usually preferred adolescents.

Madame Gérard gazed pensively into Montag's eyes. To the three men her gaze appeared flirtatious, while, in fact, she was wondering where she had seen him before. She smiled. "Have we met before, Mr. Weiller?"

Montag stood erect, bowing slightly at the waist. "I'm sure, had we met, I would have recalled such a charming and beautiful woman."

Madame Gérard looked in André's direction. "Your guests are always so gracious."

André invited her to join them for a glass of cognac. She accepted and Philip raised his glass in a toast. "To a beautiful lady," he said, delighted with himself.

André and Montag lifted their glasses in Madame Gérard's direction.

Madame Gérard nodded appreciatively, and the conversation continued in a light, friendly tone until one of Madame Gérard's young women arrived with a silver tray of canapes. As the girl set the tray on the table in front of him, Montag's eyes lasciviously followed the curve of her buttocks.

Madame Gérard watched him. Montag, alert to her observation, smiled with embarrassment. It was not a smile that came from within. It was a defensive parry, as if requesting her to disregard the lapse. Then, unconsciously, he began to rub the right side of his face with his index finger.

Madame Gérard watched Montag. His gesture was a familiar one to her, but she couldn't place it.

Suddenly, the telephone rang. She picked up the receiver, listened for a moment and handed the phone to Montag.

"It's for you, Mr. Weiller. Please excuse me," she said and left the room.

From the salon Madame Gérard hurried to her office on the floor above. She went directly to her desk. On it sat an elaborate intercom system attached to a reel-to-reel tape recorder. She sat down behind the desk, lifted a switch on the intercom and simultaneously pressed a button on the recorder. This was standard procedure for her—a part of her business which, from time to time, greatly added to her income.

As she sat back in her chair to listen, Montag's voice came through the intercom.

"What was that? I can't hear you. . . . How much time did he have inside? . . . I see. We can probably expect him to show up here. . . . Yes, well, stay with him. . . . No, at the same time, tomorrow morning."

The light of the salon's extension phone went off, but the tape continued to record the Rostands and Weiller as they discussed the call.

Weiller broke the silence. "I'm afraid we have a problem, gentlemen."

"What's wrong?" Philip asked.

"Alex Drach," Weiller replied.

"Drach?" It was André.

"He's just spent half an hour inside Rostand International."
Weiller again.

"At this hour?" Philip exclaimed.

"He had no appointment," Weiller said sarcastically.

"I knew it. . . ." Philip's voice, in anger.

"Who told you this?" André asked.

"We've been watching Drach for weeks," Weiller replied.

"He'll have to be taken care of," Philip said, his voice rising.

"I make the decisions here," André interjected. "I've said it once,
and I'll say it again. I'll handle Alex Drach."

"How?" Philip demanded. "By giving the collection back to him?"

"Perhaps," André said. "Regardless, I'll do it, not you."

"I don't care what you do with the collection," Weiller said. "I
just want the pay-off."

"Don't worry, Herr Weiller," André said sarcastically. "You'll be
content when this is over."

There was a scrape of a chair.

"I have some calls to make," André continued. "I'm at the Excelsior if you need me." A moment later, a door slammed.

For a time there was silence. Then the voice of Weiller said, "He's
getting old, you know. He's not thinking. I'm delighted you've agreed
to take charge here." A chair shifted. "You have a choice . . . just
as your father did once before. Drach or the collection."

"When will the paintings be ready?"

There was a sound of glass being set on a table top.

"They're buried underground, in a catacomb. They're quite safe.
I'll show you and your father within two days. I think you'll find my
repository rather interesting."

"Excellent," Philip said. "If they're in good condition you'll have
your money the same day."

There was a long pause and then Weiller asked, "Drach! Does he
know who I am?"

"I don't know. I don't think so."

"He'll put it together. My God! He's a detective."

"I wouldn't worry. Your friend Baruch can handle him, and if he can't, I have someone who will."

"Really?" Weiller quipped sarcastically. "I didn't think you were the type!"

"Don't underestimate me, Weiller. I'm closer to him than you are."

"Would you be referring to the pretty Miss Keeble?"

Philip laughed. "When the time comes, she'll do what I tell her."

"I'm sure she will," Montag said. There was the sound of a chair sliding back. "You know how to reach me," Weiller said.

A door opened, closed, and there was silence.

Madame Gérard pressed the "Off" switch on the tape recorder and sat back. She closed her eyes. Weiller knows of Cubitt? Without thinking she began to stroke the side of her face with her index finger. Then she remembered. Montag! Weiller was Montag! "Montag," she repeated aloud. "How could I have missed him?"

In a frenzy, she pulled open the top drawer of her desk, pulled out a .38 snubnosed revolver and ran from her office to the salon. She burst into the room too late. They were gone.

Frantically, she picked up the phone. The porter answered and told her Philip and Weiller had just left the Palazzo. She walked to the far end of the room and glanced out the window overlooking the Piazza Navona. It was close to three in the morning, airy and quiet. The Piazza was deserted.

She stared at the fountain of the Four Rivers in the middle of the Piazza and cursed herself. She had waited nearly forty years for this moment and it had slipped by. There would be another chance. She vowed it, just as she had vowed vengeance that night in Lodz forty years ago.

XI

Alex arrived at his office just before nine the next day to find Miss Goodyear looking uncharacteristically bright and alert at her desk. A heifer-like red-haired creature, Miss Goodyear looked like a WAC major with service in the Korean war. She smiled.

At this unusual display of cheeriness, Alex hesitated before her desk. He noticed she had in front of her several sheets of heavy paper which looked like invitations. Then he noticed on top of the filing cabinet there was a vase containing a dozen tulips that emitted a sweet, springlike aroma.

"What's the occasion?" he spluttered. "Is it your birthday?"

Her yellow-brown eyes dropped demurely. "Bertie and I are getting married next week," she replied, thumbing distractedly through a copy of *House and Garden* magazine.

"I'm delighted," Alex said. "Does that mean you're leaving us?"

"Oh! Heavens no," she said, lifting her penciled brown eyebrows. "I'm a liberated woman."

Alex smiled as cheerfully as he could and crossed into his office, where he slumped behind his desk and looked out the big picture window at Manhattan.

The first flecks of a new snowfall mottled the spire of the Empire State Building. Recently at night he had noticed that the tower's top thirty floors were bathed in colored floodlights, a change he abhorred. It used to be that the stately building stood out like an icon, a majestic symbol in itself. Now the City Fathers had turned it into a gigantic toy, in violation of its design. He put Miss Goodyear and the Empire State Building out of his mind and set to work.

An hour later his newly affianced secretary came into the office and, lowering her voice confidentially, said, "There's a Miss Keeble to see you."

Alex wasn't surprised. He nodded, unsmiling, got up and walked into the reception room.

Before he could say a word, Cubitt strode across to him and, looking worried, said, "I want to talk to you."

"Sure," he replied. "Come on into my office."

They walked into his office in silence. He closed the door. "What is it?" he asked apprehensively.

"I had a call this morning from a friend of mine in Rome. Madame Gérard. You remember, I told you about her."

Alex nodded and sat back on the edge of his desk.

"She asked if I knew you, then told me that she had to talk to you."

"Did she say what about?"

"No," Cubitt replied. "Only that it was urgent."

The intercom buzzed.

Alex leaned back and answered it. "A Charles Boczka on the line," Miss Goodyear said.

"I'll take it," Alex replied. He picked up the telephone.

"Alex?"

"Speaking, Charlie."

"I've got your man."

"Go ahead." Alex picked up a pencil.

"We had one hundred fifty thousand entries into the States on the sixteenth of January. I've come up with only one inbound from Rome with a painting valued at less than five hundred dollars. That was Derek Matthiesen. Address: nineteen Via del Giancano, Rome. I checked with Inspector Russell Wilkinson, the agent who cleared him, and he remembered the picture. He said it was a clumsy piece of work. His deputy looked at it too. They both agreed it couldn't have been worth more than a few hundred dollars at most."

"Was it freshly painted?"

Boczka waited before replying. "I didn't ask," he said. "But I can tell you this, this Matthieson . . . or whoever he was . . . is a diabetic."

"How do you know that?"

"He was carrying a bagful of insulin."

Alex penciled the fact. "Got it!" he said, and added, "Thanks for the help, Charlie; I owe you one."

"One more thing, Alex. We checked the street address with the Rome police. No such address exists."

"Figures. Thanks, Charlie."

"Anytime," Boczka replied. "Just call before midnight!"

Alex set down the phone and looked at Cubitt, now standing in front of the large window.

"I know you think I'm paranoid, talking like this, but I think your life is in danger."

He looked at her amusedly. "What makes you think so?"

"After Madame Gérard asked if I knew you, she told me to be careful. She said I didn't know what I was getting myself mixed up in, something about Nazis and stolen art."

Alex remained calm. He wondered if she was setting him up for something. Perhaps she didn't even know what part she was playing. "What are you involved in?" he asked.

A shadow crossed her eyes. "I'm not sure myself, but I'm afraid."

"There's nothing to worry about." He was on the verge of telling her what he knew, then stopped himself. There was no point—either way—of leveling with her.

"This Madame Gérard," he said. "How does she know about me?"

"I asked her that, but she wouldn't tell me. All she said was that she wanted to talk to you. I have her number right here." Cubitt reached inside her purse.

Alex put his hand on her arm. "That's not necessary. I'm going to Rome anyway."

"That's a coincidence. So am I," she said, smiling.

"You are, like hell!" he said.

"Like hell I'm not!"

Alex looked at her sternly. "I thought you were an intelligent woman, Cubitt."

"I'm also a free woman. Free to make the choice."

Alex moved toward her and took her hand, a sharp tingle of suspicion running through him. Her eyes told him nothing. He couldn't tell if she was lying or telling him the truth. He kissed her anyway, and felt her mouth tremble under his. Her arms languidly reached up around his neck.

Suddenly, behind him he heard an abrasive cough. He let go of Cubitt, turned and saw Miss Goodyear standing in the doorway. She had a prim, administrative look about her.

"Excuse me," she said, her voice like a blowtorch. "You've missed one appointment already, Mr. Drach. And the next has just arrived."

"I'm afraid something urgent has come up, Miss Goodyear. Tell them I'm not here."

"But . . ."

"Just do as I say, Miss Goodyear."

"Yes, sir."

"And Miss Goodyear . . ."

"Yes, Mr. Drach?"

"Get me Jocko Corvo, in Paris, on the phone, then book me two seats on the next flight to Rome."

XII

Alex and Cubitt took a cab from Rome's airport to the Bernini Hotel, an ultramodern building on the Via Veneto. After checking in, they went to their room, where Alex placed a phone call to Madame Gérard.

Cubitt, in a chair across the room, leafed through a guide to Rome, while listening to Drach's end of the conversation.

"Yes. . . . Here in Rome. . . . We just arrived. . . . Of course, but I don't think we should talk on the phone. Shall we meet this evening? . . . Seven is fine. . . . Yes, good-bye."

Cubitt waited for him to finish, then excused herself, explaining that she wanted to do some quick shopping on the Via Veneto.

"Okay," Alex said, "but don't be too long. We're due at Madame Gérard's in an hour."

"I won't be long," she said. She walked toward Alex, kissed him and left the room.

As Cubitt entered the elevator down the hall, Baruch came out of a room on the same floor. He walked quietly to Drach's door and from his shoulder bag withdrew a container of hairspray with a one-inch plastic extension attached to the nozzle. He inserted the extension into the lock and sprayed for several seconds.

It didn't always work, he thought. Occasionally, the hairspray was too thin to hold the tumblers of the lock up in their open position. The next time a key was inserted into the lock it would force the tumblers upward. After that, entry was a simple matter. Baruch hoped the hairspray would be effective. He looked forward to his work. The lock sprayed, he retreated back down the corridor to his room, and waited.

Downstairs in the lobby of the hotel, Cubitt went to a telephone booth and dialed.

Philip Rostand answered.

"It's Cubitt."

"Cubitt! What are you doing here?"

"I can't talk long. I'm with Alex."

"Already."

"Were you expecting him?"

He paused, recovered himself and replied, "No, what's he doing?"

"I'm not sure. He has an appointment with Madame Gérard."

"Madame Gérard!" Rostand exclaimed. "What's she got to do with this?"

"She's been in touch with him. She mentioned you and someone else, a man named Montag."

"Montag?"

"Yes."

"How does she know about him?"

"I don't know. All she said was that she knew him during the war and she wanted to get in touch with Alex about him."

There was a pause. Then, "Can we meet?"

"No," she replied. "I've got to get back."

"What's wrong?"

Cubitt spoke rapidly. "I want off this thing, Philip. I don't like what I'm doing. I don't know what's going on, and I think you should get someone else."

There was a pause at the other end. "As you like!" Philip's voice had a hard edge to it. "I think you're making a mistake."

"That's the way I want it," Cubitt said.

"Have it your own way," Philip said, "I never ask anyone to do anything they don't want to do."

"Thanks, Philip. I'm glad you understand. I'm sorry."

"Don't be silly, Cubitt. And don't be sorry. All I ask is that you keep our, uhh, business . . . confidential."

"Of course."

Baruch padded silently down the corridor toward Alex's room. It had been almost an hour since he sprayed the lock, half an hour since Cubitt had opened the door on her way back from the lobby— maybe two minutes since the pair had left the room. Probably going to dinner, he thought. He would need that much time.

He withdrew a blank key from his pocket and inserted it into the lock. He took a deep breath, savoring the uncertainty for a moment, then rolled his hand counterclockwise.

The blank key slid effortlessly through its arc. No resistance. He pushed the door with his knuckles, smiling to himself as it swung open.

The large high-ceilinged room was furnished in eighteenth-century reproductions and had a magnificent view of the Via Veneto. Very romantic, he thought. He removed his clerical jacket and collar and placed them on the bed. He noted Drach's suitcase on the luggage rack. He walked into the bathroom, hung his shoulder bag on the doorknob and pulled a pair of thin surgical gloves from his pocket.

The brass-plated light fixture was ideal, he thought. He slipped the gloves over his huge hands, flexed his fingers as a surgeon might, and went to work.

First, standing on the rim of the bathtub, he unscrewed the light fixture from the ceiling. This accomplished, the bulb dangled down from a clutch of wires that descended from the gaping hole. Gently, without removing them, he loosened the screws that crushed the copper wires to the light's contact terminals.

He was working with his arms above his head, teetering on the bathtub's edge, and this gave him a cramp. He paused, rolled his head and massaged his neck with his left hand. The pain eased. He then put the screwdriver on the vanity and turned his attention to the shower arm.

The plate that joined the shower arm to the tiled wall was a circle of brushed aluminum. Using one hand to hold it in place against the wall, he used his other hand to twist the shower arm around until, eventually, it came away in his hand. Setting it aside, he pulled the plate from the wall and went to his leather shoulder bag. From its recesses he withdrew a Micarta coupling. Made of mica, the coupling would electrically isolate the shower arm from the building's other piping, piping that was sure to be grounded.

He then fitted the coupling onto the pipe and returned the brushed aluminum fixture to its place on the wall. After that, he pushed the shower arm through the hole in the plate, screwing it into the coupling's other end. Now, he was sure the shower arm was no longer grounded.

Next, he took a battery-powered drill from the shoulder bag and twisted a sixteenth-inch bit into its end. Stepping back on the tub, he began to drill a hole into the chrome at the point where the shower arm disappeared into the plate. It was hard work, and the sweat began to pour from him. The drill slipped from side to side, refusing to stay in place. Finally, just as he'd begun to curse aloud, the bit gripped and whined at a slightly different pitch. Leaning his weight into the tool, he felt the metal's resistance and then, moments later, a breakthrough. Brushing the slivers of chrome away, he admired the tiny hole in the shower arm while his hands changed the drill bit for a somewhat larger one.

By now the sweat was rolling down his forehead and the white shirt beneath his vest was darkly stained. Ignoring the pain in his shoulders, he climbed back onto the tub again and applied the larger bit to the ceiling area directly above the shower arm. For a few seconds, flakes of wallboard fell into his eyes, and then the drill pushed through, creating a quarter-inch hole.

He put the drill aside and withdrew a wire coathanger, a small magnet and a roll of electrician's tape. Strapping the magnet to the hanger with the tape, he laid the crude device aside. Then he returned to the shoulder bag and removed a four-foot length of electrical wire and a pair of needle-nosed pliers. Standing before the mirror, he stripped the insulation from both ends of the wire, glancing from time to time at the reflected image of himself.

His clothes were soiled from the task. It bothered him, but a job was a job. His reward would come later.

Returning to the tub's rim, he inserted one of the wire's bare and golden ends in the tiny hole he had drilled through the shower arm. The other end of the wire, and most of its four-foot length, was pushed through the somewhat larger hole he had drilled in the ceiling. Confident now that his job was nearly done, he took the magnetized hanger from the vanity and inserted it into the hole above the dangling lightbulb. He fished with the magnet until he felt it lock with the electrical wire in the ceiling above the shower arm, then gently pulled the hanger back, delighted to find the stripped wire clinging to it.

Taking a penlight from his pocket he clicked it on and placed it between his teeth. The thin beam of light was invisible until Baruch switched off the ceiling light, plunging the bathroom into darkness. Standing on the edge of the tub with the light in his mouth, he attached the stripped wire to the terminals of the fixture dangling above his head. Then, with a screwdriver, he tightened the screws around the wire and stepped down. He switched on the overhead light and stared into its sudden glare. Hot, he thought.

Soaked in sweat, but deeply into the rhythm of his labors, he replaced the light fixture overhead, leaving it virtually as he'd first found it upon entering the bathroom. Then he took a roll of white adhesive tape and bit off a length, with which he covered the small hole. With the hole covered, he bit off a longer strip of the adhesive to tape the electrical wire to the four inches of white wall and white tile leading from the hole to the shower arm.

The job done, he sighed and stepped down from the tub. You could see the tape if you were looking for it. Everything else, however, was quite invisible: the wire, the Micarta coupling, the holes he'd drilled. None of them could be seen. Taking a face towel from the towel rack, he cleaned the tub of its accumulated slivers of chrome. He did the same to the floor beneath the light fixture, wiping up the flakes of wallboard that had fallen from the ceiling. Meticulously, he then removed each piece of insulation which he'd stripped into the sink, tossing the chaff into his case with the soiled towel.

Looking around for the last time, he smiled at his handiwork, stripped off his gloves, put on the black coat and collar, picked up his bag and left the way he'd come. He was terribly pleased with himself. He felt that he was developing a certain style in these matters. Alex Drach would be the second man he'd killed in a bathtub. This time, though, there wouldn't be any blood. Drach would be plugged into the mains. Progress, he thought. But then he frowned. His carnation had wilted and he had no idea where he was going to find a fresh one on the way back to the Society.

XIII

Cubitt, Madame Gérard and Alex had finished their dinner, and now sat together over a bottle of Taittinger 1969 in Madame Gérard's private suite.

She had quieted the table in the course of her discussion of "Herr Weiller," recounting the circumstances under which she'd been raped as a fourteen-year-old, almost forty years ago.

"I was with him for one night, but it was the most horrible night of my life. I've never been able to forget it, though when I think about it, I suspect his reassignment to Berlin saved my life. I heard about the other girls he'd commandeered to serve him. Within a few days he'd tire of them and then have them shot."

"How did you survive?"

Madame Gérard grimaced. *"Survived* is hardly the word for it. I was given to his platoon as a going-away present, compliments of Montag."

"You mean 'Weiller,' " Cubitt said.

"He had a different name in Lodz," Madame Gérard explained. "This 'Weiller' business is a *nom de paix."* She stared at her hands. "He could still be prosecuted for what he did at Lodz, but I'd prefer to . . ."

". . . to do it yourself," Drach finished for her.

Madame Gérard nodded.

"I understand," Alex said. He felt Cubitt's eyes watching him closely as he asked, "This S.S. Captain Montag, he was transferred to Paris, you said?"

Madame Gérard nodded.

"In what year?" Alex asked.

"June, nineteen-forty. I heard he was ecstatic."

Drach sat back, slumping. The table was silent. "What did he do in Paris?" he asked.

Madame Gérard shrugged. "I don't know," she replied bitterly. "I never learned that."

"I know what he did," Alex said. "He was on a special assignment."

One of Madame Gérard's girls entered the room, carrying a tape-recorder. She placed it on the table and left.

"This is what I wanted you to hear," Madame Gérard said. "I have an intercom system between my office and all these rooms. I'm afraid I only got part of the conversation. I left the room when the telephone call came through. It's a custom of mine. No one calls here unless it's important. I like to know what's going on." She pushed the "Play" button, sat back and listened.

"What was that? . . . I can't hear you. . . . How much time did he have inside? . . . I see. We can probably expect him to show up here."

As Montag's side of the conversation played, Cubitt sat listening intently, rigid in her chair. She glanced at Alex and smiled weakly when she heard the telephone replaced in its cradle.

Meanwhile, the tape continued to play as the Rostands and Montag discussed the call.

"I'm afraid we have a problem, gentlemen."

"What's wrong?"

"Alex Drach . . ."

Madame Gérard allowed the tape to play the conversation until the point when Philip said *". . . I wouldn't worry. Your friend Baruch can handle him. And if he can't, I have someone who will. . . ."* Madame Gérard pressed the "Stop" button. She looked at Cubitt, who was now visibly upset.

"Before I play the rest," Madame Gérard said quietly, "I must warn you that what you're about to hear is not pleasant."

Drach arched his eyebrows, puzzled. Cubitt winced, sensing what was to come.

After a pause, Madame Gérard added, "I want you both to know that my loyalties in this case are deeply divided. I considered erasing this part of the tape, for Cubitt's sake, but then I realized the stakes are greater than personal loyalty." She glanced at Cubitt. "Enough said."

She pushed the "Play" button and the tape picked up Philip's voice. *"I wouldn't worry, Baruch can handle him, and if he can't, I have someone who will."*

"Don't underestimate me, Weiller. I'm closer to him than you are."

"Would you be referring to the pretty Miss Keeble?"

Philip's laugh echoed throughout the room. *"When the time comes, she'll do what I tell her. . . ."*

The tape ran on until there was silence.

Cubitt, shaken, covered her face with her hands, and for the first time in many years, she cried.

XIV

Alex and Cubitt returned to their hotel an hour later. The supper at Madame Gérard's had been a brutal strain. Cubitt's clothes were wet with perspiration, and she felt as though she were a completely broken woman.

After the recording was over, Alex showed no surprise. He simply looked at the two women and repeated what Montag had said: *" 'We have a choice. . . . Just as you did once before.' "* That was all. He and Madame Gérard spoke in private for a few minutes and then, with Cubitt, Alex left.

As Alex unlocked the door, Cubitt murmured, "I've got to talk to you, Alex. Let me explain."

"There's really no need," he said. He opened the door and absently took the key from the lock. He began to put it in his pocket, then stopped abruptly. The key was sticky.

He placed his fingers to his lips, pushed Cubitt aside, stepped back, inhaled deeply and kicked the door open wide.

Cubitt stood speechless in the doorway while Alex walked into the room, carefully opened the armoire, then cautiously approached the bathroom door. He opened it, looked around and noticed nothing unusual. Returning to the bedroom, he beckoned Cubitt inside.

"What's wrong?" she asked.

He handed her the key. "Do you notice anything?"

"It's sticky." She rubbed her fingers together, then sniffed the key. "Smells like hairspray."

Alex nodded.

"What happened?"

"I don't know," he replied. "I think the room's been searched or . . ."

He moved quickly to the phone, picked up the receiver, unscrewed the mouthpiece and followed the cord along the wall, looking for a transmitter. Still nothing.

Next, he turned his attention to his suitcase. He opened it cautiously. A tiny wad of paper dropped to the floor. "I must be wrong," he said.

"About what?" Cubitt asked.

He fingered the spitball. "If someone searched the place, he didn't do a very good job. My suitcase hasn't been opened since we left. If they didn't take anything, what did they leave?" he wondered.

Cubitt closed the door and moved toward him. "Maybe we're getting a bit paranoid."

Alex shrugged. "Perhaps. I don't know. . . ." He walked restlessly around the room several times, peering behind the drapes, once looking under the bed. He didn't know what he was looking for, and his efforts at discovering something out of order were futile.

Cubitt looked at him, surprised to see how the tension had turned his face into a menacing dark mask. She had never seen him like this before. There was an almost compelling animal-like force about him that made her want him even more.

"It's all right," she said. "There's no one here. It must be they're oiling locks or something."

"I doubt it," he said, sure that he had missed something. But looking at Cubitt, he shrugged, smiled and then went to her.

In a second he had lifted her off the ground and was carrying her toward the bed.

"Wait, Alex," she said, "I've got to talk to you."

"Later. We'll talk later."

He carried her to the edge of the bed, laid her down and undressed her. Slipping out of his own clothes, he stretched his body against hers and closed his eyes, again marveling at the touch of her soft, fragrant body.

Slowly he ran his fingers up and down her back, ever so lightly, hardly touching her. With his other hand he spanned her dark nipples.

In an instant her legs had moved up around him, crossing behind his back, as she writhed in his embrace. She began muttering in his ear, moaning and rubbing against him, and then gently, very gently, he moved inside her. Cubitt looked up at him and smiled. "Exquisite," she murmured. Slowly she began rocking with an insistent movement of her back and hips. Alex, lost in the lovely ovals of her face, her parted mouth, her lovely green eyes, could focus on nothing but her as she raced ahead in an almost hypnotic trance of her own. She was taking him to a point where he could no longer hold back. She had not been still since the moment he had entered her. Now she reached up to him, pulling him to her more insistently. Rocking still, Cubitt groaned in sympathy, feeling his climax. Then she pressed harder, shoved up under him, again and again, clutching his buttocks with her hands, and finally, quivering, gave way to spasm after spasm that echoed his own.

Afterward, they lay for a long time holding each other. Cubitt, cupped in his arms, started stroking his forehead.

"Can we talk now?" she whispered.

Alex shook his head silently. "Later. Everything will be fine." Alex closed his eyes and smiled, then began drifting off to sleep. A few minutes later, Cubitt slowly lifted herself off the bed and moved toward the bathroom.

Then, as if she had forgotten something, she suddenly turned, walked back to the bed and kissed Alex gently on the lips. "I love you," she whispered. It was the first time in her life she'd ever meant it.

His eyes still closed, Alex smiled. "I'm glad that's settled anyhow," he said. Cubitt walked into the bathroom.

A few seconds later, Alex heard the rushing sound of water as Cubitt turned on the shower. Then, there was a short, strangled, awkward cry.

Alex leapt from the bed and hurtled through the open bathroom door. Cubitt's distorted body lay crumpled in the tub, the water splashing over her. Shouting her name, Alex grabbed her shoulder, but a savage jolt of electricity spun him around and flung him against the wall mirror with such force that the glass shattered. Dazed, he shook his head, recovered a little, began to reach out to touch her again and then hesitated, looking hurriedly around the room. As his gaze traveled across the ceiling, he saw the adhesive tape and the piece of wire running into the showerhead. Frantic, he ran back into the bedroom and returned with his rubber-soled shoe, which he used to slap the taps of the shower into a closed position.

The water off, he stood looking down at the beautiful corpse. He reached down and felt her pulse. Nothing. She was dead. He couldn't believe it. He'd checked the phone. He'd checked the armoire. He'd checked the bedroom. Yet she was dead!

He felt as though he were under water; the sight of Cubitt's tortured face and twisted body rolled in and out of his head like waves. Desperately he tried to break surface.

He leaned over the bathtub and gently pushed a lock of her blond hair back from her forehead. As he did so, he thought that this was the last thing he could ever do for her. He covered Cubitt with one of the hotel's large bathtowels, remembering the sound of her voice saying, "I love you." She had died in his place, for him.

Alex stood and looked around the bathroom. He saw the tape. He stepped onto the rim of the bathtub, stripped away the wire and the tape, balled them up and angrily pitched them into the wastebasket.

Whoever Baruch was—and he supposed it was Baruch, from what he had heard on the tape—he was a professional.

He went into the bedroom and, still dazed, quickly dressed. As he moved about the room, collecting his things and packing his case, the grief and shock slowly dissipated. An overwhelming anger took their place. He went to the window and looked up the Via Veneto, still crowded with late night revelers. He was so immersed in his thoughts that the sound of his bedside telephone startled him.

He walked across the room and picked up the phone.

"Alex?" It was Jocko.

Relieved, Alex replied, "They tried again, Jocko." His knuckles whitened around the telephone.

"Are you all right?" Jocko asked.

"I'm okay, but a friend of mine has been killed."

"Listen to me," Jocko said. "Get out of there! Right now! Where can we meet?"

"Do you know the Piazza Navona?"

"Yes. Go on."

"I'll be at the Palazzo Pambisti in twenty minutes. Ask for Madame Gérard."

Alex put the phone down, picked up his suitcase and then, purposely avoiding the bath, left the room, making certain the door was firmly closed and locked.

He proceeded down the hallway to the elevator, where in his impatience he pressed the "Down" button repeatedly. He would wait to talk to Jocko before phoning an ambulance or the police. In his distress, he did not notice beside him, lying on a bed of sand in an ashtray of brushed chrome, a wilted, blood-red carnation.

XV

Alex, inflamed with anger and hatred, his stomach churning, walked down the Via Veneto, past the Spanish Steps, to the Piazza Navona, watching everyone.

He passed young lovers, their arms locked around each other; tourists chattering; youths with backpacks; an old man selling *granitas;* fountains; beggars; a man with a calliope and crowded bars. As far as he could tell, no one was following him. Finally he entered the Piazza Navona and walked down its length past the Fountain of the Four Rivers.

Finally he came to Madame Gérard's palazzo. He stopped. Two ambulances were pulling away, along with several police cars, their blue roof-lights flashing. He moved on, this time in a rush. A thin-

ning crowd murmured in Italian as he pushed his way through and
walked to the elevator.

"*Che fichi*," the man in the elevator cried. "Incredible!" He was
shaking.

"What's happened?" Alex asked.

"*Terroristi.* Two hours ago." The operator's white-gloved hands
pursed in a gesture of emphasis, then scissored and chopped, panto-
miming what he had seen. On the way to the penthouse, the man explained how three gunmen had invaded the Palazzo, forced their way
into Madame Gérard's, looking for her.

The elevator stopped. The doors opened into the penthouse and
Alex saw a scene of total devastation, broken doors, an overturned
chair and smashed lamp. Shards of glassware crunched under his
feet. Detectives, discussing something quietly, ignored him, as did a
photographer with a Graflex camera. Two stolid-looking women,
taking notes on small pads, also seemed preoccupied.

Alex entered Madame Gérard's office.

He found her seated in the wingchair behind her desk. He took a
chair himself, adjusted its broken leg and placed it in front of the
desk.

She looked at him. A few seconds passed, counted by the ticking
clock on the wall. She mouthed a few words.

"I was out," she said. "Usually, I'm here with my girls. I'm usually here. Last night after Montag . . . I couldn't . . . Three men
came. They wanted to see me. They didn't believe I wasn't . . ."

She looked away, taking in the broken glass, the smashed mirror.
"Every room . . . Three of my girls were beaten up . . . lovely girls.
One of them, from Indonesia, is in a hospital."

"And Cubitt's dead," Alex said bitterly.

Madame Gérard's head snapped back, her face ashen.

"In my hotel," Alex answered.

For a time neither of them spoke. Finally, Alex asked, "Who did
this?"

"I told you. Three men. I wasn't here."

"No. I'm not interested in the men," Alex said. "Who's responsible for it?"

Madame Gérard tensed. "It had to be Montag, of course."

"He must know you can identify him."

"Yes, but how?"

"One way or another. . . . The Rostands."

The pair sat silent again until Alex asked another question: "The *carabinieri*—what have you told them?"

"Nothing yet. I wasn't here. They're questioning the staff who were witnesses. They'll speak to me later. I can tell them a few things about Montag."

Alex shook his head. He stood and walked to the doorway, glanced down the corridor, then returned to Madame Gérard, remaining on his feet.

"Don't," he said, "I don't want you to."

"Why not? After what . . ."

"I want to hurt them myself," he said.

She nodded. "I understand, but let me help."

"Can I count on your silence?"

"Well, yes. Of course. But how will you find him?"

"Through the Rostands," he replied. "When they make contact."

One of the heavy-set women who had been taking notes earlier poked her head through the open doorway. "Are you Alex Drach?" she asked.

Alex nodded. "What is it?"

"There are three people waiting for you outside."

Madame Gérard stood, anxiously looking at Alex. "Were you expecting anyone?"

"Yes," he replied. "They're friends from Paris."

Alex walked back through the penthouse to the front hall. There, standing uneasily under the suspicious gaze of two heavily armed *carabinieri*, were Jocko, his son-in-law, Manetta, and Minta.

Moving surprisingly fast for his size, Jocko was across the hall before Alex said a word.

"Alex!" he shouted. *"Mon Dieu!* Are you all right?" His broad thick arms closed down around Alex's shoulders, and after an awkward crushing hug, Jocko pushed Alex to arm's length for a brief examination.

"I'm fine," Alex replied with a broad grin. He was looking at Minta.

Jocko followed his glance and shrugged with exasperation.

Minta smiled. Her eyes were glistening. "Don't ask!"

"Ask what?" Alex replied.

"Why I'm here."

Jocko shook his head. *"C'est un monde, cette fille.* She insisted. She told me she'd never set foot in my home again if I left her behind." He hooked his thumbs into his vest pockets. "I, of course, refused."

Alex looked at Jocko quizzically.

The Corsican lifted his shoulders, gesturing helplessly with his hands. "What can one do?" he asked. "She's Corsican."

Alex laughed and for the first time in days felt relaxed inside. He turned to Manetta, who, unsmiling, took his hand. Again, as when they first met, he was struck by Manetta's lethal presence.

As they walked toward Madame Gérard's office, Alex quickly explained what had happened since they had spoken on the phone.

"Rostand's here?" Jocko asked.

"Both of them," Alex replied. "And Montag. They're all part of it."

"You're sure?"

"Positive."

They walked into Madame Gérard's office. Alex made the introductions.

"Forgive the disorder," Madame Gérard said, offering them a drink. Alex, Jocko and Manetta accepted. Minta declined, examining Madame Gérard with an appraising eye.

"The first thing I have to do is take care of Cubitt," Alex said. He glanced at Minta, but there was nothing in her face to suggest what she knew or thought.

"We don't want the police. Too many problems," Jocko said. "How did you register?"

"Assumed names," Alex replied.

"Give me the key to the room," Jocko said, holding out his hand. "I have friends in the Union. They'll see that she's properly taken care of."

The thought of Cubitt lying in the bathtub made Alex groan inwardly. He wouldn't permit himself to think further about her. He handed Jocko the key. "The next step is to find Montag. He's moving the paintings with Rostand in the morning. When he does, I want to be there."

"Rome is a big city," Jocko said.

Alex turned to Madame Gérard. "Would a couple of your girls help us?"

"I don't understand."

"The Rostands can lead us to Montag, but they would recognize us. The girls can act as spotters."

"So can I," Jocko said. "Rostand hasn't seen me since the day he left Paris for Monte Carlo during the war. I could get close to him."

Alex shot a sharp glance at Jocko. There it was. Jocko was no fool. He had to have put it together. He'd known all along that Paul Drach wasn't his father. "You're sure?"

"How could he? It's been nearly forty years."

"No," Alex said. "I meant Monte Carlo. Was he there?"

Jocko hesitated, grimacing. He understood the meaning of the question. "Yes," he replied after a pause. "He was there."

Alex nodded and turned to Madame Gérard. "I'd still like your help."

"Well, yes. Of course." Madame Gérard's voice was wary. "My girls . . . I don't know. I don't want them hurt. They don't have the same interest as you and I."

"They won't be in any danger," Alex assured her. "I need them for surveillance only."

"*Surveillance*—it's a French word—" Madame Gérard shrugged. "What exactly do you want them to do?"

"Someone has to alert us to Montag's movements. There's where your girls come in."

"But my girls know nothing of this sort of thing."

"Let me talk to them," Alex said, smiling. "In an hour, I'll have them working as smoothly as lanolin."

Late that night, surrounded by Madame Gérard and two of her beautiful hostesses, together with Minta, Jocko and Manetta, Alex sat at a large table with a map of Rome laid out upon it.

"We'll set up a rotating system of tag-team surveillance," he explained. "Paula," he said to the diminutive Irishwoman with auburn hair sitting next to him, "you start out working the parallel point." Then, to a tall, statuesque Israeli woman, "Allegra, you'll be the first tag. Minta, you're the second."

"What's a parallel point?" Paula asked.

She looked twenty-four, perhaps twenty-five. It was hard to tell. Her shrewd eyes and the way she handled herself suggested she was closer to thirty. But like most small women, she appeared younger than she was.

"It's simple," Alex replied. He drew a circle around the Excelsior Hotel. "This is where the Rostands are staying. We'll deploy around and in the hotel. When they leave, they'll either walk or drive. If they walk, the women will follow. Paula will take up a position parallel with them across the street, walking abreast or just ahead of them wherever they go. Allegra and Minta will follow them on the same side of the street at a safe distance, one behind the other. Allegra, you take the lead; Minta will follow you. Every once in a while, when you can, all of you switch positions so you aren't seen too often in the same place. Remember, though, the one who takes the parallel point must maintain visual contact with the Rostands at all times. She's the eyes for the other two when our two birds turn corners or are momentarily out of sight."

Alex turned to Manetta and Jocko. "If they drive away from the hotel, we'll be in a couple of cars to tail them. Manetta, you and Jocko take up a position south of the hotel in the first car. If they go in that direction, I'll pick up the women and follow on after you. If they go north, I'll be there, waiting for them. You do the pickup and follow me."

Alex looked around the table. "Anything you don't understand?"

There were no questions.

"Good. We'll meet back here, early tomorrow morning."

Madame Gérard stood. "I'd prefer it if you all stayed the night here."

"That's very kind of you, madame," Jocko said. "But we don't want to put you out."

"Not at all. It's safer for all of us this way. And besides, in my line of work, there are plenty of spare beds."

Everyone laughed but Manetta.

While Manetta stationed himself for the night in the front vestibule of the penthouse, Alex, Jocko and Minta went into the drawing room, where Jocko made several phone calls, the last in regard to Cubitt. As he talked, Minta and Alex stood by the windows overlooking the Piazza Navona.

Minta, staring at the airy and serene Piazza below, as though hypnotized by the play of the fountains, asked, "What was she like, Alex?"

"Cubitt?"

"Yes."

Alex thought for a moment. "There were many Cubitts. I knew at least a couple of them. There was the beautiful, selfish courtesan, a woman who never bothered to sort out the good things from the bad.

She never had the time. As a girl she couldn't afford a conscience. Later on, she was too busy climbing to acquire one."

"And the other?"

Alex smiled. "That Cubitt was different. She could be reached. She could care." He paused and glanced at Minta. "Or she wanted to care. The problem was, she didn't care enough about herself."

"Did you love her?"

Inside his jacket pockets, Alex's hands became fists. "Part of her," he replied. "The best part."

Minta was silent, her thoughts turned inward. He waited, letting the silence run its course, until finally she looked up at him. "Someday, I hope you find someone who's good for you," she said.

"Maybe I already know her."

"Think so?"

Alex laughed, then took her face between his hands and kissed her gently on the lips. "Better get some sleep," he said. "Tomorrow's going to be rough."

As Minta went off to bed, Jocko walked across the room to where Alex was standing and handed him a glass of brandy.

"Be careful with her," Jocko said. "She's vulnerable."

Alex looked out the window. There were other things on his mind. "Tell me, Jocko."

"About Rostand and your mother?"

Alex nodded.

"Nothing much to say that you haven't already figured out. Of course I knew something. So did Paul, I think. At least he sensed your mother's feeling for Rostand. I knew it right from the start. I saw it in her eyes the day they met, and when she came back from Monte Carlo, after Paul's death, she had changed. She was pregnant and then she had you." He paused, sipped his drink and then rubbed at the bristle of whiskers under his chin. "Oh, Naomi never told me. But I knew."

"Did Rostand know?"

"I don't know the answer to that. I don't think she ever told him. Like me, though, he must have suspected. Rostand is not stupid."

Alex ground his teeth together and forced himself to push his anger aside. He was tired. An infinity of time seemed to have passed. He hadn't yet confronted the primary question. He didn't want to, but now Jocko asked it.

"What are you going to do to him?"

"Rostand?"

Jocko nodded.

"I don't know. He's left a lot of death behind him. He betrayed Paul and one way or another was responsible for his death. Then, there were so many others. As for me?" Alex shrugged. "I'm part Corsican. You understand *vendetta*. You taught me the word." Alex licked his lips. They were dry. His body was cold and sweating at the same time.

He looked at Jocko. "Why didn't you tell me before?"

"For the same reason I told you to be careful with Minta. I wanted to protect you."

"You shouldn't worry about that. We'll take care of ourselves."

Jocko took out a red cotton handkerchief and wiped the perspiration from his face. "It's hot in here." He turned and started for the door. Halfway across the room he stopped. "You still haven't answered my question, Alex. What are you going to do to him?"

"I'll decide that when the times comes, Jocko. After all, I'm still my father's son."

"The problem is, Alex, which father?"

"No, Jocko. Whose son?"

XVI

The room was stifling. André Rostand awoke with his sinuses inflamed and a cloying bad taste in his mouth. He flung off the covers and slowly slipped out of bed. He glanced at the alarm clock. It was nearly nine in the morning. He took a cold shower, standing under the spray until he felt his heartbeat pick up and the blood pulse to his head. Slowly he began to muster strength. His eyes cleared. He shaved, and then he returned to the dressing room, flinging open the windows of the bedroom en route. The cold air was invigorating.

He dressed, thinking about Montag. The final arrangements had been made. Baruch had given him a complicated set of instructions over the phone the night before. The paintings were ready to be moved. Payment would be in the form of a bank draft issued in the name Hans Weiller, to be handed over on satisfactory receipt of the collection. Rostand had been given a list of the paintings—Monets,

Cézannes, Renoirs, Van Goghs, a stunning, almost unbelievable list—and from that they had settled on a twenty-five-million-dollar buy-out. Nothing had been left to chance.

Still, Rostand was suspicious. He feared something might go wrong. Alex was out there somewhere, hunting Montag. If he discovered them together . . . A shudder went through André at the thought. The poor night's sleep hadn't helped, either.

Downstairs, in the hotel dining room, an impeccably dressed *maître d'* led André to a table by the windows on the Via Veneto. Philip, who had been reading a menu, looked up.

"Good morning, Father."

André nodded and sat down. He caught the eye of a waiter and, without consulting the menu, ordered orange juice, grapefruit, eggs benedict and coffee.

"I don't know how you do it," Philip said. "You eat twice as much as I do but never gain weight."

"High metabolism."

"Mine is the same as yours."

"And hard work."

Philip ignored the remark and reached for the glass of apple juice resting in a bowl of crushed ice.

"Any further news?" André asked.

"Mother called last night. You must have been out."

"I told Reception I wanted no calls put through."

"She's expecting us on the evening flight tomorrow. She also told me that she missed you."

André nodded and reminded himself to pick up a new spring coat for Jane. She liked the Italian designers. "Any word about Drach?"

"Nothing so far," Philip replied. "They've checked the hotels, and a few other likely places. No sign of him."

"And Montag?"

"Not a murmur after Baruch's last call."

"What about the ship?"

"We have space on the next one bound for Buenos Aires. It leaves next week. In the meantime, the collection will be stored in a secure warehouse here." Philip spooned his grapefruit. He ate for a while, then raised the question that had preyed on him for weeks.

"Are you still determined to return the collection?"

"Benevolence has its own reward, Philip."

"That's not an answer."

"Isn't the gallery enough for you? Do you want everything? Even what doesn't belong to you?"

"Why not? We're paying for it."

André shook his head and said nothing, while a sad, almost condescending smile crossed his face.

XVII

"Idiots! You beat up three whores!" Montag screamed. "Fine! But you didn't get the right one, Madame Gérard. Somehow she knows me. Philip Rostand says she can identify me."

Montag, in a murderous rage, paced the length of his office in the top floor of the Society for the Preservation of Religious Monuments and Shrines. Around him, diagrammatic charts and archeological maps of the catacombs hung upon the walls, showing elevation levels, directional indicators, lighting systems, and ventilation ducts.

At the far end of the room, three of his subordinates—Rolf and his two companions—stood subdued and abashed. Between Montag and the trio, Baruch sat leafing through a copy of *Time* magazine. The cover pictured André Rostand. Under his unsmiling face the caption read, "The Art Baron."

"Idiots!" Montag ranted. "I'm served by idiots. Do you think people are interchangeable? Do you think I wouldn't notice the difference?"

Baruch sniggered, hiding his grin behind the magazine.

Montag turned to him, his rage reaching a fervent pitch. He sounded as if he'd swallowed a razor blade.

"And you," Montag screamed at Baruch. "You don't know the difference between one sex and another. You electrocuted a woman, you fool! A woman! My God! She was even working with us."

Baruch snapped to his feet. "Yes, Monsignor. I must be losing my grip," he said laconically. "I didn't think she'd take a shower. She didn't seem like the type who sweated."

Montag, astonished at Baruch's indifference, was silent for a few seconds. Then, in a tone as even as a ribbon, he said, "You know, Brother Baruch, you're a psychopath."

"Yes, Monsignor."

"A psychopath. I have a psychopath working for me," Montag screamed, looking at the three men standing quietly in a corner of the room.

Montag rushed across the room, grabbed the magazine from Baruch's fingertips, and flung it aside.

They stared at each other, Montag trembling. Then once again he began pacing the office. Slowly, he brought himself under control.

"We have a dangerous situation here," he said quietly. "Drach is being difficult, and at this point, brothers, recriminations won't help. Baruch's error was unfortunate, and I'm certain that you men thought you were doing the right thing." Montag's face glared icily in Rolf's direction. "Though, I confess, I cannot imagine what was on your mind. But enough of that! Our problem is to rid ourselves of Drach, take the funds, and get out of Rome."

Montag turned to Baruch. "Have you got the explosives ready?"

"Yes, Monsignor. I've got a half a pound of plastique and the detonators. It's a simple job. I'll be ready when the time comes."

"Excellent. Now, Brother Rolf." Montag addressed the tall, gray-haired man with the silver earring. "Are you ready? I don't want to take the Rostands into the catacombs and have them wait forever while you break through!"

"We're ready to move," Rolf said confidently. "We left the final few feet blocking the entrance to ensure security. It'll take only a few minutes to clear."

"I've got the truck, Monsignor," a jowly heavy-set cleric added. "Between us it should take no more than a few hours to empty the chamber and load them up."

"Good," Montag said. "Rostand has arranged his own storage facilities. You, Brother Damian, will deliver the paintings. The funds will be deposited in a Swiss account as soon as they take possession."

"That leaves Drach," Baruch said.

"Knowing him," Montag said, "we can expect to see him any time now—or even in the catacombs."

"If he does come," Baruch said smiling, "I'll have a nice surprise waiting for him."

Montag, relaxed now, pursed his lips in pleasure. "Yes, a nice surprise," he mumbled to himself. "Just like Hubert Weiller got the day the paintings were buried." At last, the day of his return was at hand.

* * *

It was a hot, sultry day in June, 1944. Fifty feet below ground, however, in the Catacomb of Monte Verde, the air was cool and dry.

Allgemeine S.S. Major Hans Heinrich Montag squinted into the darkness ahead, his washed-out blue eyes carefully registering the twists and turns that led ever deeper into the labyrinth where, for weeks, under cover of night, he and his adjutant, Sergeant Hans Weiller, had hidden a vast fortune in paintings salvaged from the loot the Nazis had stored in Rome. The work completed, it was time to seal the tomb.

With his flashlight, Montag checked the Bruton compass clutched in his hand. "Just two more turns to the north," he said, turning to Weiller, who plodded along behind.

"Yes, Major!"

He'd found a perfect storage facility, Montag assured himself. The soil was volcanic and firm, the chambers dry, and the temperature constant year round. The treasures would be well preserved.

"No one will ever find them down here, eh, Weiller?"

"No, Major!"

"No one," Montag thought. He had spent months mapping the network of passages and crypts that made up the catacomb. There were forty-five ancient catacombs underneath the soil of Rome. He had chosen Monte Verde because it was one of the most complex and least explored of them all. Only a very small number of its three square miles of burial chambers had ever been mapped.

Montag checked the paper on which he had carefully detailed the catacombs' twists and turns. According to his compass readings he was almost there. Without the map and compass he never would have been able to find his way in or out of the labyrinth. In some places the narrow corridors descended a half a mile underground. A yard or so wide and no more than six feet high, they crossed and crisscrossed each other continuously. Some were dead ends and some led off into the blackness beyond.

He located the right chamber and, bending slightly, entered the crypt. Before him the flashlight illuminated hundreds of beautiful canvases, each of them an Impressionist or Post-Impressionist masterpiece. Set in the cubicoli filled with the bones of Christian martyrs, the paintings took on an almost mystical quality. With his fingertips he traced the wine-red birthmark on his right cheek and inspected his private gallery. "Such treasure," he thought. The Reichsmarschall had taken the Old Masters and left him the "Decadents," still worth millions. A pity to entomb them like this. Someday, though, somehow, he'd return for them. Now, he had no choice but to leave them behind.

The Americans had already started to occupy Rome, he and Weiller being among the last of the Germans left in the city. Weiller was all right. He wasn't S.S. But Hans Montag could expect no protection when he was captured and made a prisoner of war. Hardly, considering his rank in the S.S. and events at Lodz. He faced disaster, perhaps even a firing squad.

Montag had a plan, however. If it worked.

He placed a small charge of dynamite before the front portal of the chamber, drew three wires across the domed hall, and made his way back along the passages to the foot of the stone steps leading out of the catacomb. There he placed his detonator.

That accomplished, he withdrew a Luger from his holster and pointed it at Weiller. "I won't harm you," he said. "I just need your uniform. Take it off."

Weiller's face paled. "I don't understand, Major." He edged toward the stairway.

"One more step and I'll kill you," Montag snapped.

Reluctantly, Weiller removed his clothes while Montag took off his own. After the sergeant put on the S.S. uniform, Montag instructed him to recheck the placement of the dynamite.

Weiller started to descend into the darkness, but then shook his head and turned back to Montag. "I'm not going down there."

Montag's lips curved in a thin smile. "I'm sorry, Weiller." He leveled his Luger with both hands and fired two shots into the sergeant's chest. As the echo of the two rounds reverberated throughout the chamber, Weiller's dead eyes stared back in disbelief.

Leaving the body at the mouth of the catacomb, Montag ascended the stairs, connected the wires to the detonator and blew the charge. Next, he quickly removed his gray jacket and shirt, withdrew a cartridge from his weapon, pried open the cylinder head and ignited the powder. As the cartridge flared, he held it to his left armpit where, as all S.S. officers did, he had been tattooed with his blood group. The burn was extremely painful, but efficacious. The scar tissue that formed would, like wave-washed sand, erase the last traces of the past.

Dressed in the uniform of the Wehrmacht, and now as Sergeant

Hans Weiller, Hans Montag walked from Monte Verde, searching for the first unit of American soldiers to whom he could surrender.

XVIII

Alex received Minta's call from the lobby of the Hotel Excelsior just after eleven that morning. He was in a café a block north of her.

"They've just left the front lobby," she said in a low voice. "Both are wearing overcoats, the older Rostand with a cane. This must be it!" A minute's silence. Then: "They've turned right out the door, heading in your direction. Paula and Allegra are moving. I have to go." She hung up.

Alex left the phone booth and walked to the front of the café. He had good sightlines down the tree-lined sweep of the Via Veneto and saw them coming. He had stressed to the women that the success of their surveillance depended on their spontaneity and naturalness. They had to stay loose, act normally and adapt. He had also told them to keep their distance. If they were "burned"—spotted by Montag—they'd never get another chance.

Alex sat at a table inside the café and watched through the window as the two Rostands trekked northward past the crowded café filled with the actors, aristocrats, tourists, models and prostitutes who frequented the luxurious street at all times of the day and night. The three women, dressed as though on an afternoon's shopping expedition, took their positions beside and behind the Rostands. Paula, assimilating herself with the flow of pedestrians, walked on the opposite side of the street, parallel with the two men. Allegra and Minta trailed behind, with an interval of about forty feet between them.

As the Rostands passed by Alex's position, he ducked back, watching for any sign of awareness that they were being followed. There was none.

His adrenalin was going full tilt. The first five minutes were always like that. This was the tense time, the time when everyone was tight, when mistakes were made. He hoped everyone stayed loose. As soon as Paula, Minta and Allegra had passed, Alex glanced up and down the Via Veneto. He was checking for any sign of convoy; a counter-surveillance team that Montag would likely be deploying. The German would certainly be watching Rostand, just as he was.

Alex saw nothing suspicious and left the café. Outside, without pausing, he zigzagged between a group of well-dressed tourists, and darted across the street to a dark green Fiat. He swung into the driver's seat and drove north, constantly checking his rearview mirror. As expected, Jocko and Manetta were there, driving a beige Alfa-Romeo, also rented.

Alex picked up the small two-way radio transmitter that lay in the empty bucket seat beside him. Jocko had been able to obtain the system from a friend in the Union, a low-grade police official in charge of handling unruly football crowds.

"Our subjects have just turned right on the Via Boncompagni," Alex said. "Take the next corner, go east a few blocks and wait for them on the other end."

"Looks like they're not going far," Jocko said.

"Give them time. This is only the beginning."

Alex broke contact and Manetta, driving the Alfa, turned right and drove east.

Alex turned right at the next intersection and parked. Ahead he saw the Rostands cross over to the north side of the Via Boncompagni and continue east.

Paula, who had begun across the street from them, was quick to react. She turned away as they came toward her and entered a tiny shop that sold salt and tobacco. Allegra picked up her pace and hurried up the south side of the street, drawing abreast of the Rostands. Minta, meanwhile, crossed the street, keeping a leisurely pace, and tailed the two art dealers at a distance of forty feet. Paula emerged from the tobacco shop and took up the tail behind Minta.

Alex, still in the Fiat, smiled to himself. The women had learned well; it was a classic execution of the rotation switch. He breathed deeply now and began to relax. The first hurdle was over.

A block farther on, the Rostands stopped in front of a dreary gray stone structure, checked their watches and entered the building through heavy paneled doors. It was a bank.

Thirty seconds later Minta reached the bank and walked in just in time to take a place in the same teller's line the Rostands had chosen. The bank was filled with office workers. She could feel her chest pulse to her heartbeat as she watched the two men waiting patiently ahead of her. In line, between them there was only a young priest and an elderly lady with several shopping bags.

"A pleasant day, isn't it, gentlemen?" the priest observed, smiling at the Rostands.

"Very agreeable," Philip said cordially.

"Are you tourists?"

"On a holiday," André Rostand replied.

"You ought to see the collection at the Borghese Gallery. They have some wonderful pictures there."

"I know it well," André said. "I'm glad that you reminded me. We'll visit the museum before it closes at two." They all smiled at one another, then stood in silence until the Rostands reached the teller's window. André changed several hundred dollars into lire and then, together with Philip, left the bank.

Minta considered leaving her place in line and following them, but she recalled Alex's warning about Montag. He would have his people watching for anyone getting too close to the Rostands. The conversation with the cleric also bothered her. It obviously was contrived. On the off-chance she might be burned, she decided to stay in line and waited until the priest had changed his money and left before leaving the bank herself.

By the time she was outside again the Rostands had disappeared. In an instant the cleric had stepped into a black BMW, and, with two other priests, driven off toward the Via Veneto. Minta, feeling afraid and abandoned, hurried in the same direction. Striding rapidly, her lips pressed in disappointment, her eyes scanning the street ahead, she continued west for two blocks, certain she had lost the tag. She had let Alex down. She reached the Via Veneto and was about to start back to the hotel when she spotted Jocko and Manetta in the Alfa. She looked around, shivered with relief, and ran to the car.

"Where are they?" she asked, getting into the back seat.

"Ahead," Jocko replied. "What happened inside the bank?"

"I'm sure it was a contact." Minta related the substance of the conversation between the priest and the Rostands.

Jocko switched on the transmitter and briefed Alex. "What do you think?" he asked. "Over."

"Minta's probably right. If she is, we've got a chance to set them up. You won't be recognized. Go to the Borghese Gallery. Jocko, you and Minta be inside when they arrive. Manetta can monitor the transmitter. I'll let you know if there's a change of plan."

Alex was parked, the Fiat idling, at the eastern end of the Via Ludovisi. For the past few minutes he had been observing the Rostands walk toward the southern edge of the gardens. Philip, he thought, swaggered with a distinct jauntiness in his step. It would be like his half-brother—it was the first time he'd ever used the term—to savor the intrigue. Paula and Allegra were trailing behind.

Suddenly, near the end of the avenue, André hailed a passing taxi. He and Philip ducked into it and sped north into the Borghese Gardens.

Alex eased away from the curb. He had no time to pick up Paula and Allegra. He wheeled his Fiat in a tight circle and accelerated after the Rostands.

Ignoring the cutoff for the Via Pinciana, he took the left fork of the road and drove through the hilly parklands thick with umbrella pines. The Borghese Museum was directly ahead.

Alex pushed the transmitter button on the two-way radio. "Manetta?"

A crackle, then Manetta answered. "Here," he said.

"They're coming in. Are Jocko and Minta inside?"

"All set."

"Stay put. I'm going to park in the rear of the Villa. Let me know when they leave."

"*D'accord.*"

At that moment, André and Philip were walking through the front entrance of the Borghese Gallery.

On the ground floor, André stopped for a brief moment to gaze at three marble sculptures by Bernini. One was *The Abduction of Persephone.*

"Do you know the legend of Persephone?" he asked.

Philip shook his head, "Who cares?"

André ignored his son's remark. "She's the maiden of spring," he explained. "One day, she was picking flowers, narcissus, as I recall. The earth opened up and Hades, the lord of the underworld, abducted her. She was held captive among the dead until Zeus, worried because her mother Demeter, the goddess of harvests, had refused to let the earth bring forth its fruits, sent Hermes to rescue Persephone. Hades agreed to let her go, but for only part of the year. Each winter she has to return to him as his queen." André paused and looked at Philip. "It's a sad story, don't you think?"

Philip looked away. "I was never much on mythology."

They climbed a staircase to the floor above. There they entered a room full of the masterpieces by Caravaggio for which the gallery was famous.

"It would be nice to have a few of these," Philip quipped.

A heavy-set priest, with a round bald patch at the back of his head, interrupted them. "Have you seen the Raphael in the other room?" he said, taking a piece of gum from a pack and offering some to the Rostands.

André declined the gum, and asked, "Are you a guide?"

"You could say that, at least for the day." He stuffed the piece of gum into his mouth, put the paper into his pocket and started toward the exit. "Let me show you around."

Across the room, Jocko and Minta watched the trio walk to the staircase and descend to the ground floor. They waited a few moments, then followed, catching a quick glimpse of the heavy priest as he passed out the front door of the museum behind the Rostands.

Manetta was through to Alex in the same instant, giving him a description of the black BMW that was then wheeling up to the front of the Borghese Palace to pick up the priest and the two art dealers. Inside the car, Manetta informed Alex of that fact, and then waited until the BMW had disappeared down the avenue before cutting across the graveled parking space, collecting Minta and Jocko and speeding after the departed BMW.

To the left of the long avenue leading from the museum, Alex waited in the Fiat for the black BMW to pass. Now was the most crucial time. The Rostands had made their contact. They weren't operating at the end of a long leash anymore. They were being brought in. There was no telling whether Montag was in the BMW, but Alex thought it unlikely. He wouldn't appear until the last possible moment, probably with the collection.

Moments later, when the black sedan, with two clerics and the Rostands, sped past, Alex pulled away, trailing the BMW through the Villa Borghese to its westernmost point. It looked as though they were headed away from the city. The BMW slowed in the heavy traffic around the Piazza del Popolo, then swung across the Ponte Margherita, and sped to the left along the banks of the Tiber. Alex alerted Jocko on the radio.

"Where are you?" Alex asked.

"We're two minutes behind you," Jocko replied.

The BMW followed the Tiber around the Castel Sant' Angelo, then swerved into the Via della Conciliazione toward Saint Peter's Square. The majestic columns of Saint Peter's lay dead ahead. The sedan cruised across the square until it reached the Via di Porta Angelica and the Gate of Saint Anna, where it turned left and entered Vatican City.

Vatican City, the smallest state in the world, covers an area of 109 acres, a little larger than London's Saint James's Park. With its own printing press, newspaper, railway, television station, mint and postage stamps, Vatican City is bounded by Saint Peter's Square, the Papal Palace and the Vatican walls. Apart from the Basilica of Saint Peter, only two of the Vatican's six entrances are open to the public, the gates on the Viale Vaticano and the Arco delle Compare.

Alex, realizing that he could not follow the BMW sedan further, found a parking space on the Via di Porta Angelica that gave him a direct sightline to the Gate of Santa Anna, and waited. A moment later, Manetta, with Jocko and Minta, pulled up behind him.

Inside the Gate of Santa Anna, Baruch was halted perfunctorily by a Swiss Guardsman, uniformed in puffed sleeves and trousers of yellow, blue and red. Waved on, Baruch drove the BMW straight ahead to the second checkpoint, where a Vatican policeman in a dark blue uniform stopped him and asked him for his pass.

Baruch eyed the slender form of the policeman as he checked the pass.

The policeman nodded twice, handed Baruch the pass and pointed in the direction of the stone archway leading to the Cortile del Belvedere. Baruch drove on past the post office and through the archway, where he was once again stopped by a pair of Swiss Guards, one of whom directed him to a parking place in the center of the huge courtyard.

Baruch parked near the four-streamed fountain in the center of the courtyard, adjusted his clerical garb, then stepped out of the BMW and opened the rear door. André and Philip Rostand emerged from the sedan and followed Baruch to the entrance of the Vatican Library.

"Architecturally impressive," Philip commented as they climbed a long staircase to the top.

There, puffing from the climb, André leaned on his cane with both hands. Looking down, he could just make out the stone terrace three flights below. His strength wasn't what it used to be. His balance was unstable, his breathing labored. He remembered Zurich and the stab of pain in his chest. He blinked his eyes, looked up and found Philip staring at him.

"Are you all right, Father?"

André's head bobbed yes three times. "Fine. Let's go."

At the entrance to the Hall of Maps another Swiss Guard stopped them. Baruch fished three passes from beneath his cassock, and handed them to the guard. "They're valid," he said, in German.

The guardsman stepped back, smiling easily, *"Jawohl, mein Bruder."*

Baruch took the passes and replaced them in his pocket, while the guard opened the door.

The trio made their way down a passageway whose bookshelves, were they put end to end, would extend for six miles. They reached the end of the corridor and entered a gigantic round room whose frescoes, full of bearded men symbolic of learning and philosophy, glared down at them. Off that room was a tiny chamber, and beyond, a stairway leading up to a heavy paneled door.

Baruch knocked once and entered.

Hans Heinrich Montag, dressed in a plain black cassock with a small red line at the base of his clerical collar, greeted them with a satisfied smile. Behind a heavy mahogany desk, he stood, walked around it to André Rostand and extended a pudgy white hand in greeting. "Welcome to the Vatican. After thirty years I've come to feel quite at home here. A pity it's my last day."

André took the hand and pumped it briefly, while looking about the room, which was windowless except for a tiny alcove high in the right wall.

"Your sanctuary, Montag?"

"You'll forgive me, Rostand, if I ask you to call me Monsignor Weiller, at least until we're beyond the walls of the Holy City."

"Certainly, Monsignor."

"You mean the paintings aren't here?" Philip asked.

Montag laughed. "No, of course not. You'll forgive me for putting you through so melodramatic an itinerary, but you'll understand the need for caution. When we arrive I think you'll find it worthwhile." He reached for a black cashmere coat with a velvet collar and led them from the room.

The four men took the stairs and descended to the main level of the court. The stone halls were cool and soundless except for the foot taps, which echoed down the silent corridors. Moments later, they emerged into the sunlight of the Belvedere Court.

As they walked across the court, Montag smiled at a stoop-shouldered bishop walking toward them. It was a polite frosty smile that generated neither warmth nor hostility, with no movement at all at the corners of the mouth.

"Good afternoon, Excellency," he said, a flush of color rising from his collar. "May I present the art dealer, André Rostand, and his son, Philip?"

Bishop Alois Schneider's yellowed teeth flashed momentarily in a drawing-room smile. "Ah, yes. I know the name."

"You flatter us, Excellency," André said.

The bishop grunted and turned to Montag. "Friends of yours, Monsignor?"

Montag grimaced. "On Church business," he replied.

Bishop Schneider inspected André for a moment, sniffed, and without another word tottered off in the direction of the Library.

XIX

At five past one, the black BMW sedan pulled out of the Gate of Saint Anna and turned right, leaving Vatican City. In it were the Rostands and three clerics.

At a respectable distance behind, the tension growing, Alex and Minta maintained pursuit. Further back, in the Alfa, Jocko and Manetta did the same.

In the half-hour they had spent waiting for the Rostands, Alex and the others had regrouped, assessed the possibility of pursuing their quarry into the Vatican, but then, realizing that the paintings could not possibly be stored in the Vatican itself, had delayed their move until it was clear the Rostands and Montag had made connection. Their patience had paid off.

The BMW traveled the open expanse of Saint Peter's Square, headed south along the bank of the Tiber, then turned east toward Trastevere, an ancient, densely peopled section of Rome, where streets twisted and turned in every direction. Pursuit would be difficult here.

In front of Alex and Minta the black sedan continued east, and began to move unpredictably through the complex confluences of Trastevere, crisscrossing streets, turning haphazardly, cutting north, then south, but never losing its pursuers, if that were the driver's intention.

Alex followed the BMW as it turned again. At the next corner, Alex turned right, then right again, then a quick left, and spotted Manetta in the beige Alfa several blocks behind. He slowed, then pulled into the curb. The BMW had stopped for a light.

At the change of the traffic light, the black sedan turned left onto the Via Portuense, swerved adroitly to pass a lumbering truck and sped off. They were now headed southwest, out of Trastevere, on the road to Civitavecchia.

There was a crackle on the two-way radio. Jocko: "They're moving, Alex."

"This could be it," Alex said to Minta, "as long as they don't feel the heat."

Minta glanced at Alex. "I'm frightened," she said. "What if they know you're after them? It could be a trap."

"Maybe it is. Maybe it isn't. If they've looked over their shoulders, they may have seen us, but we can't stop now."

"What are you going to do? There are at least five of them."

"I don't want to think about that. We have to concentrate on not losing them and hope they're leading us to the collection."

After fifteen minutes, the BMW suddenly turned left through a large gateway, flanked by two cut stone pillars. It looked like the entrance to a deserted villa.

Alex slowed and flexed his shoulders. He was stiff, both because he was tense and from fatigue. It had been a long night, and an even longer day. He pulled the Fiat into the side of the road, a hundred and fifty feet beyond the entranceway, and flagged the Alfa down.

Manetta pumped his brakes and slid-stopped into the rough at the side of the road. He and Jocko were out of the car in the same instant.

"Manetta comes with me," Alex said, pulling a Remington .38 from his hip. "Jocko, you stay with Minta. If we're not back within an hour, you'd better call your friends."

"No," said Jocko. "If you're not out in an hour, I'm coming in." Their eyes met. Alex smiled briefly, then nodded.

The day was unseasonably warm and Alex noticed the smell of wood smoke and pine trees as he leaped the low wall bordering the estate. Manetta was over and beside him at the same time. Together they struck out across a small field toward the long line of plane trees that ran parallel to the driveway.

The scene seemed so reminiscent of combat in Vietnam. The fields, hedgerows and trees played before him like a dream, a slow-motion replay of the countryside around Hue. Alex turned toward Manetta. The Coriscan's face, dark and impassive, showed no sign of strain. He was the kind of backup you needed.

Alex floated on, reached the trees, then put out one hand, palm down. Manetta understood. They hugged the trees and listened. There were voices coming from a short way off.

Alex's hands clasped together, a signal for Manetta to hold. Manetta nodded.

Alex silently padded along the line of trees toward what appeared to be an old ruin. A few stone columns and flagstones lying about were all that remained of a Roman villa, once, no doubt, the palatial home of a wealthy patrician family.

From a dreamy, slow-motion pace, everything speeded up. Alex's feet began moving quickly over the damp ground. He broke cover and found a pathway leading down a steep incline to a garden overgrown with weeds, twisted shrubs and tall grass. There, before what looked like the entrance to a cave, Alex saw them. He dropped to his knees and watched. Led by two men in clerical garb, one of them the man Alex remembered from London, with the silver stud in his ear, the Rostands, Montag, and two others began descending a stone stairway into the ground. One more remained behind.

Alex returned to Manetta. "Six in all, not counting the Rostands. What do you think?"

"That makes it almost even," Manetta replied.

Alex smiled, but Manetta's expression remained unchanged. Together, then, they returned to the garden. Manetta looked at Alex, pointed to himself, then to the cleric at the entrance, and made a small circle wih his index finger.

Alex nodded and moved his finger across his throat.

Manetta moved off.

Five minutes later, the cleric had positioned himself on the ledge about the cave entrance. He had a Mauser machine pistol in his hands and was fitting it with a wooden stock, every now and then glancing around the clearing in front of him.

Alex's finger curled around the Remington's trigger. The wait was getting to him. Where was Manetta?

Then he set his teeth. Manetta, with a long stiletto in his hand, suddenly loomed above the guard. Manetta's hand clamped the guard's mouth. In the same instant, the guard's arms shot out, his back arched and he started wriggling upward, trying to free himself from Manetta's grasp. For several seconds, the guard's body twitched violently and shuddered. Then it stopped.

Alex cleared the distance between the garden and the entrance to the catacomb in seconds. A wire guideline led into the darkness below.

He approached the entrance silently, then stopped, listening for any sign of activity on the steps. He heard voices, a murmuring that was indistinct. If he stepped onto the top step, he knew he'd be a perfect target, silhouetted against the skyline.

Manetta, wiping the blade of the stiletto on a handkerchief, joined him. He pointed to the sun and dropped his right hand behind his left, asking if they should wait for nightfall.

Alex shook his head. He didn't want to give them the time. Anything could happen. Others could come. There was also the possibility that there was another exit somewhere else—especially if, the thought suddenly occurred to him, this was a catacomb.

He looked around the entrance, then climbed the little knoll above it and removed the cassock from the dead cleric's body. He hastily slipped it on over his head and started for the entrance. It fitted him perfectly and, with the exception of the small hole wet with blood at his back, it felt fine. He picked up a flashlight lying next to the Mauser.

At the entrance, he clasped his hands, signaling Manetta to stay put, held his breath, and started down.

Nothing. He exhaled and continued his descent.

At the base of the stone staircase, the voices were more distinct. There were two of them, talking some distance away. Alex walked softly for a few more feet and turned a corner. A light glowed softly at the end of the corridor. He walked toward it, still following the wire line. Suddenly, two men stepped out of the shadows.

Startled, Alex froze, his hand tightening around the .38 Remington concealed inside the vent of his cassock. He wouldn't use it unless he had to. The sound of gunfire would surely alert the others.

In the dimly reflected light he saw the thick heavy-set man who had followed him in London. This time Silver Stud wasn't with him. Another man, bigger and more powerful-looking, with a neatly trimmed moustache, stood behind him. The dumpy one spoke. "Easy, Father. Sorry. No tour today. The catacomb is closed for excavation."

Alex heard the snap of his chewing gum. He also noticed that the fat man's hand was hidden behind his back, no doubt holding a weapon. As it was, he would have no trouble with him, but the big man behind him would have time to react. He, too, would have a weapon and . . .

"Mi piace molto vedervi . . ." Alex spoke rapidly in Italian, hoping it preoccupied the guards long enough to position himself between them. He had to submarine them, split them, so that he could then deal with them in turn.

Alex passed the gum-chewer, in spite of a confused protest. "Excuse me, Father."

Alex's flashlight caught the fat man full in the face, dropping him. At the same time, he raised his right knee and snapped his foot back into the shin of the big man behind him. There was a satisfying solid crack. The man let out a scream, and Alex heard a gun clatter to the stone floor. The blow had also spread the big man's legs apart, leaving his groin undefended.

Alex was now operating on instinct, applying the basic techniques of karate he had practiced over and over for many years. He was not a Sensei. He never would be. But he was adequate to the task at hand. It was second nature to him, now, a matter of pure physics and psychology. The physics of it was not complicated, though a very difficult thing to perfect. The energy behind a blow, its power and effect, were determined by its mass multiplied by the square of its velocity. The greater the speed and the more precise the timing, the more damaging the impact. That was the technical part of it. More important was the psychological. It surprised him when he had first begun training to find that it was much more difficult to inflict pain than to accept it. Most people were conditioned to accept pain. Very few, apart from psychopaths, ever learned how to inflict it. It had taken years for him to understand this, but he had no difficulty now.

Alex spun to his left and snapped his foot again, this time higher, into the man's crotch. A strangled, whimpering groan escaped from the back of the big man's throat. He clutched himself and fell forward to his knees, onto the damp travertine flooring. A blow to the man's collarbone stilled him for good.

"For I have sinned," Alex said automatically. He removed his cassock and moved back to the entrance to retrieve Manetta.

When they returned together to where the two guards were laid out in the middle of the passageway, Manetta looked at Alex and, for the first time since he had known him, Alex saw Manetta smile. The two moved on.

With his flashlight Alex led the way, passing quietly through the labyrinth. At the same time, he had to struggle with a feeling of claustrophobia as the beam of the flashlight played over the walls of the passageway, revealing the cubicoli filled with the bones of Christian martyrs stacked, one on top of the other. On one of the arches he passed was an inscription written in Latin:

> *The field wherein was the double cave,*
> *Which he bought to intern his treasure,*
> *In the tabernacle of the Lord.*

Appropriate, Alex mused.

Deeper in the catacomb, Alex tried to calculate the twists and turns of the descent, but he soon gave up. He realized the underground world was too complex. The passages crisscrossed each other, sometimes at short intervals, then dropped to another level and recrossed in other directions. Every now and again there was also a door that led off the passage into a small chamber that he assumed was used by the Christians for family burials and religious ceremonies. In these chambers, he saw chairs and benches hewn out of the rock, the walls pierced with horizontal niches for the dead.

Time became distorted to him, but he calculated that they had followed the wire for a quarter of a mile when suddenly there was a flicker of light ahead. He motioned Manetta to hold, turned off his flashlight and crept on. As he drew closer to the source of light, he could hear voices. Slower now, he crept down the passageway, hardly breathing.

A few feet farther on he could hear the voices distinctly, though he couldn't see their source. The high-pitched voice of Philip Rostand was coming from a small chamber at the end of the passageway.

"You're mad, Montag!" Philip shrieked. "Don't you know anything about paintings? Look what's happened to them!"

There was silence. Then, in a thick German accent, Montag spoke, his voice panicky, "You're telling me that there's nothing that can be done?"

André answered first. "Nothing! Absolutely nothing!"

"What'll I do with them?" Montag asked.

"You can stick them up your ass, as far as I'm concerned," Philip shouted.

"Surely, you can clean them?" Montag said, again pleading.

"I told you," André said. "It's impossible."

"I know you're lying to me. I know it," Montag shrieked.

"There's nothing more to say," André replied. "Now show us the way out."

There was another pause. Montag answered, his voice now menacing. "I'm afraid that's impossible, Herr Rostand. It only stands to reason. If these paintings have no value, you have no value. On the contrary." He laughed. "You're both a liability to me. You know who I am. You can identify me."

"You *are* mad," André said.

"No madder than your own son," Montag shouted. "Am I not right, Philip? You were willing to liquidate Fuller and Drach for these paintings."

"Let us out of here," Philip cried, an edge of hysteria in his voice.

"Again, I repeat, that is impossible. I'm afraid you and the collection will have to remain here on exhibit. You two can enjoy them—for eternity. A rather appropriate tomb, don't you think, Baruch?" Montag's panic had vanished now. He sounded implacable.

"Shall I set the explosives, Monsignor?"

"At once. I'll meet you back at the Society."

Footsteps receded down a distant corridor. A minute's silence passed. Then Philip's voice said, "Baruch. For God's sake what are you doing? We made a deal. I'll give you money. Anything. A fortune in paintings. It's my gallery now, Baruch! Please! Remember?" Suddenly, there was a sound of a scuffle, then the echo of two shots fired.

Alex couldn't wait any longer. He rushed toward the chamber. Halfway down the corridor a bright light to his left transfixed him. It was Silver Stud.

"Baruch?" the voice behind the light bellowed. "It's Drach!"

Alex broke to his right, running aimlessly into a passage that, for all he knew, was a blind tunnel. He heard the thump of running feet behind him. Uncertain which way to go, he decided to keep turning to his right. That way he would remember the way back should the chase prove to be a long one. As he ran, turning through the maze, he noticed that the floor of the passageway had changed. Water trickled in a slow course down the center of the corridor, forming a rivulet a few inches wide, its passage etched in stone for nearly two thousand years.

Stopping to draw breath, Alex listened for his pursuer, but all was quiet. He started to move on, then found that he had entered a cul-de-sac. Switching off his light, he retreated back down the corridor, feeling for a passage that would take him to his right again.

Suddenly, light flooded the corridor. Alex froze, blinded by the harsh glare. Blinking, he tried to focus. Then he saw him, a shadowy figure holding a gun.

It had to be Baruch. In the same instant, a shot thundered, and Alex's left hand exploded in pain. His flashlight crashed onto the floor in shards. Alex threw himself to the floor and at the same time, rolled to his right, firing wildly. Baruch's light, his target, went out, plunging the passageway into darkness.

Hardly conscious of the pain in his hand, Alex recorded the sound of dripping water, the rustle of clothing, scurrying feet—they seemed to be moving away—and again, silence. He waited, crouched low, breathing in shallow gulps. His legs began to ache, but he remained still, not daring to move. Finally, after several minutes, he jammed the .38 into his belt, wrapped his bleeding hand in a handkerchief and chanced the passageway again, slowly inching forward in the darkness. He had gone no more than a hundred yards when suddenly, he felt an arm snake around his neck.

"It won't be painful," Baruch whispered.

The split second it took Baruch to say that was all the time Alex needed. Maybe it was luck, getting that brief moment, before Baruch tried to take him out. It could have been, so easily, all over for him. Right there, in the humid darkness of the kingdom of the dead. He reacted instinctively, grabbed Baruch's wrist and rotated it around and forward directly above his shoulders. It was enough to throw Baruch off balance. The echo of Baruch's shot reverberated throughout the corridor while Alex, driving his shoulder upward under

Baruch's elbow, yanked down on his wrist with every bit of strength he could muster. Baruch's elbow snapped clean at the joint.

Baruch screamed in agony and in desperation tore himself away. Drach fell to the floor, pulled his weapon from his hip and fired in the direction Baruch had run. At once, he rolled to his left, not knowing whether Baruch was still around, but anticipating that Baruch would return fire. Instead, once again, there was silence.

In the darkness, both men remained stationary, each waiting for the other to reveal his position. Baruch, hunched in a corner of the chamber, grasped his arm and grimaced in pain. He'd never lost. Never. He was invincible. Perhaps he had underestimated Drach. He had been arrogant. That was a mistake.

Baruch gripped his gun, now in his left hand. He didn't like guns. They were toys. No style. No delicacy. And in the dark, useless.

Then, suddenly, he felt a strange sensation, a weakness in his legs, heart pumping faster, the mouth dried up. His stomach tightened and he began to perspire.

He sat on the floor, one foot tucked under him, his head hanging down, breathing in short, shallow inhalations. He knew what was happening to him. Nothing out of the ordinary—for any diabetic. It was the preliminary stage of a diabetic coma. All he needed was a quick injection of insulin.

Carefully, Baruch set down the gun and calmly reached under his arm and opened the small leather purse he wore like a shoulder holster. In it was his syringe and the insulin. Quickly he withdrew the syringe, uncapped its needle and reached for a vial of insulin. Then he stopped. Which vial? There were four. Three contained insulin, but the fourth held ten cc's of Triftazine, the sterile solution of pure sulfur that he had used on Fuller. Ordinarily, he could tell the difference. The insulin was clear, the sulfur solution slightly orange in color. But in the dark, he was helpless, unable to tell.

Fingering the vial in his hand, Baruch calculated the risk. To turn on his flashlight, even for a split second, would provide Drach a perfect target. In that instant, at this range, the man wouldn't miss. On the other hand, to choose the wrong vial . . .

The sweat pouring off him now, Baruch appreciated the irony of his situation. Drach or the unseen vial. Either way it was a risk. The percentages, however, were with the vial: four to one. He chose.

Alex, crouched at the opposite end of the chamber, waited anxiously for the slightest sound that would betray Baruch's location.

But his own breathing was the loudest noise he could detect in the chamber. At one point, he thought he heard a muffled grunt, but to fire on that evidence was too risky. He waited, fearing the thumping of his heart would give him away.

His left hand throbbed painfully, but it wasn't seriously damaged. The flashlight had caught the full force of the round Baruch fired.

He wondered how fast Baruch could move. What was he doing? The silence was getting to him. He felt like screaming, but that was stupid, and he found himself smiling to himself.

Five, ten minutes passed. Still no sound from Baruch. He must have moved off again.

Now, with every muscle tensed, Alex hunched forward, hurled himself to his right, then left, then right again and stopped. He went down hard and stayed there, waiting. No sound. He waited another minute, then struck a match. He couldn't believe it. Baruch was there, a hulk slumped in the far corner, his face immobile, his eyes looking out, seeing nothing. Then Alex noticed the syringe dangling from Baruch's right arm.

Drained nearly to the point of exhaustion, Alex walked over to the living-dead man, picked up the flashlight, and started to leave the chamber. He stopped and turned back to look again. Staring into the killer's vacant eyes, Alex thought about Hugh Jenner, and old man Thaw, and Ray Fuller. And Cubitt. He reached down, plucked the carnation from the addled man's lapel, crumpled it in his fist, and threw it aside.

His .38 drawn again, Alex moved back up through the corridors toward the excavated chamber. He didn't know where Silver Stud was, but if he had to bet on it, he would be waiting for him somewhere ahead.

He edged along, feeling the wall for direction. Movement was difficult, the passage meandering in every direction. He was also tired, so tired. He desperately wanted to rest, but there was no time.

"Keep moving," he told himself.

He thought of Montag. It helped. Anger rose in him and the surge of adrenalin it generated kept him going.

The permutations of the catacombs were endless. He was cold and sweating at the same time. He adjusted the thick blue pullover higher onto his neck and wished now he hadn't discarded the cassock. The cassock would . . .

Up ahead of him he heard a muffled cry. He blinked away large drops of sweat that trickled into the corners of his eyes as he cautiously moved ahead.

There was a brief flash of a light up the passage. He stopped, and listened. No sound. Softly he set one foot in front of the other and inched forward. He heard breathing and estimated the man was no more than a few feet from him.

Alex leveled his .38 in the direction of the breathing. No need to think about it. He had no time. He shouted, then dipped and rolled.

"Alex! It's me!"

Alex lodged the .38 under his arm and switched on the flashlight. In its beam he saw Manetta standing over the corpse of Silver Stud. The dead man was bleeding from a slashed throat. The red smile, Alex thought, remembering the day Jocko killed the German soldier.

"Giustizia!" Alex said, walking toward the dark wiry Corsican, who held a bloodied stiletto in his hand.

"Giustizia!" Manetta echoed.

Alex and Manetta went on to the chamber where Alex had first heard voices. They were only a few steps inside when they saw André Rostand kneeling disconsolately beside Philip. He was holding his dead son's hand. Philip's chest had been torn apart. It looked like a .44 Magnum from the size of the gaping wound. Alex's shadow, thrown by the lantern overhead, crossed over the dead man's body. André turned and, wavering on his knees, said, "So you've finally come for them, Alex?"

"You mean the paintings?"

André wagged his head up and down.

"I'm here for more than that. Where's Montag?"

"Gone," André replied, looking at Philip. "I don't know where."

Alex bent over and took Philip's wrist in his fingertips. It was a futile gesture. "What happened?"

"They were going to bury us down here. Philip tried to escape. He struggled with Baruch and Baruch killed him."

For a moment, Alex remained crouched beside André. Then he stood, looked at Manetta and flicked a glance in the direction of the chamber door. Manetta understood and quietly left the room.

"What about the paintings?" Alex asked.

"Ah, your legacy. Your masterpieces. The Drach Collection." André heaved a terrible sigh. "Let me show you."

Rising, André picked up a lantern and began walking through the chamber, the light illuminating hundreds of paintings stacked along the wall. He stepped closer to one of the canvases. As the light fell across it, Alex saw that it was black—pitch black. He looked at the others. They were all perfectly black.

"Monet, perhaps," André said, pointing to the paintings. "Or a Seurat. Look at this one. A Cézanne perhaps, or a Pissarro?" He raised the lamp to cast the black painting in high relief. "Inspiring, don't you think?"

Alex was silent.

"Paintings, young paintings," André explained flatly, "are like plants. They need air and light to survive. Chemically, they're still alive until the oxidation process is completed. It takes about one hundred and fifty years. After that it doesn't matter. They're dead, chemically speaking. But these works were still alive, almost all of them painted after eighteen-fifty. Montag, of course, never understood that." André sighed. "He's destroyed them, because he viewed paintings like dead commodities, things that could be stored in darkness, like the hoard in Fafnir's cave, and then retrieved when the purpose suited him." André smiled sardonically. "Well, as you see, they wilt. Without light and air they wither and die. It's a chemical matter, of course, but I prefer to think that they need to be seen. They need to be gazed upon."

"You blamed it all on Paul Drach, didn't you?"

"Montag did. I acquiesced. I won't say it was all his idea, that I didn't profit, but I was young, Alex. Young and frightened."

"My mother and you were . . . together, in Monte Carlo."

André looked directly into Alex's eyes. "Yes, after the Germans took Paris."

"Did she tell you?"

"No. But I suspected it when Jocko first wrote to me about you. Then, that day you walked into my office—you were fifteen—I knew. I looked at you and I knew at once." André glanced at the paintings, then looked down at Philip. "You know, you resemble my father."

Alex visualized a photograph of Aaron Rostand in its round frame. It had stood on the mantel of André's office, next to a cherry-wood cane. He realized now that he had long since, unconsciously, recognized that face in the mirror. He turned to go.

André clutched at his arm. "Don't leave me," he said.

Alex drew back. "Let go, André."

"Don't!" André pleaded. "You're all that's left. Everything is yours, the art, the gallery, the legacy of Rostand International, every-thing."

Alex shook his head. "I don't want it."

"You don't understand. I always wanted it to be yours. I tried to help you, gave you everything I could. I protected you. I was even going to give these back to you." André's hand swept around the room. "I swear to you!"

"No," Alex said, "you're the one who doesn't understand. It doesn't work that way. You made your choices and you always chose number one. Not once, but twice." Alex shook his head. "That's the sad part. You were given a second chance. You could have nailed Montag then and there in New York. But you didn't. You figured you could have everything your own way. But you weren't the one who paid the price. Everyone around you did. Think about it, André! A lot of people are dead because of you."

"Not me. Montag. Philip."

"You really don't understand, do you? You betrayed your best friend. Your wife. Your son. Both your sons. Don't you realize what that means?"

"Don't you think I know that? Don't you think I've suffered all these years? The guilt, the remorse."

"But you didn't learn the lesson, did you? I guess the philosopher was right. If we don't learn from the mistakes of the past, we're doomed to repeat them. You've lived a lie for forty years, André. You've lied so long, you even lie to yourself."

Alex started for the chamber door.

André went after him. "What are you going to do?" he shouted.

"Find Montag!"

XX

Montag waited. There was no need to rush. They wouldn't discover his escape for hours. Idiots! Did they really think they would trap him? He hadn't survived the war and the aftermath to be caught in his lair. Like a fox, he had found several ways in and out of the Cata-comb of Monte Verde. While Baruch took care of Drach, he would settle with the whore. First he would find out how she knew who he was. After that, he'd finish her off.

He glanced around the Piazza Navona looking for any sign of danger. His practiced eye saw children playing jump rope; women, on their way to or from the market; old men playing dominoes in a café; and in the very center of the Piazza, a group of girls and boys jostling flirtatiously with each other around the fountain.

Montag felt for the gun, made certain its butt did not protrude from the pocket of the long black coat he wore over his cassock, and started for the entrance of the Palazzo Pambisti. He walked quickly. The faster the job was done, the sooner he could leave Rome.

He scurried through the gate of the Palazzo and crossed the interior courtyard to the elevator. Everything was quiet. No one in sight. Perfect. Maybe he'd have some fun with her. She still had tits, after all.

When the elevator came he entered it, nodding to the operator with a pleasant smile.

"Good day, my son," he said.

The operator's eyebrow raised slightly when Montag asked for Madame Gérard's penthouse.

Montag disregarded the man's curious gaze and got out at the foyer of the apartment. He started down the corridor toward the office, his right hand fondling the butt of the weapon. He felt himself growing more and more excited. The throbbing spread from his fingertips through his trembling body. Yes, he thought, he'd have a good time before killing her.

He released his grip on the weapon and reached to rub the side of his cheek. It was a fatal mistake. Had he had his hand in his pocket he might have been able to turn, withdraw his gun and fire the moment Madame Gérard appeared in the doorway to his left.

As it was she had him helpless at point-blank range.

"Stop where you are," she said calmly. She held a snubnosed revolver in her right hand.

Montag froze.

"Now," she said, "keep your right hand on your cheek." She stepped forward, patted his coat from behind and pulled out the gun. "Walk toward my office," she ordered.

Montag hesitated, side-glanced and smiled. Then he moved down the corridor toward her office.

Madame Gérard stayed behind him. "Faster," she said. They walked past the salon, and entered her office.

"Stand against the wall," she said. She sidestepped past him and stood in front of her desk. It was dead quiet. "You don't remember me, do you, Montag?"

"Weiller, Madame. Monsignor Hubert Weiller. You mistake me for someone else."

"Lodz, Montag. Think. May, nineteen-forty. The death pits. A tall blond girl. Fourteen."

Montag shook his head. "I'm afraid, Madame . . ."

"No, Montag. You're not afraid. And it makes no difference whether you remember or not. I do!"

"I must talk to you," Montag said. "I came to see you, Madame, because we have so much in common." He took a step toward her.

"Get back!" she shouted.

Montag backed against the wall. "I'm rich, Madame. I have millions. We could share them."

Madame Gérard lowered the gun a few inches, aiming it squarely at Montag's groin.

"*Mein Gott,*" Montag shouted. "One chance, that's all I ask, one chance!"

"What chance did you give them?"

"Lodz was necessary. We were fighting a war."

Madame Gérard aimed the pistol.

Montag dropped to his knees, holding his arms out, pleading, "I beg you. Please, I'll give you anything." His face twisted in fear. "*Please!*"

"I want nothing from you," Madame Gérard said quietly. "Nothing but to see you dead."

"Wait!" he cried. "Listen to me."

She didn't listen. She wasn't interested. She was also surprised. She thought she'd enjoy this moment more. She didn't. Perhaps it was the distance from Lodz and all that happened there. Whatever, there was no passion in her revenge. The impulse to see Montag in agony had been watered down by time. For years she had thought about how she would make him suffer, but strangely, nothing was left except the conviction that he should no longer exist.

She looked at him babbling incoherently. In truth, she was meting out punishment to a stranger who bore Montag's name. The man

who had raped her and murdered her family had been replaced by a
sick, aging stand-in.

She hesitated an instant, lowered the gun a few more inches and
squeezed the trigger. The gun exploded into Montag's crotch.

Montag spun sideways, as if hooked, then lay on his side, his legs
twitching, looking up at her and screaming in pain.

"They're thick walls, Montag; you can scream all you like." She
leaned back against the desk and pointed the snubnosed revolver at
Montag's stomach. She began to speak quietly.

"Once I was happy and alive. I was a beautiful girl. I had my
whole life ahead of me. You killed that girl and everything she cared
about. In her place you created your executioner. That, Montag, was
a mistake. You should have shot me."

Montag was whimpering now, writhing on the floor, his hands
stanching the flow of blood oozing from between his legs. *Mein
Gott, Mein Gott,* have pity on me."

Madame Gérard smiled. She was surprised he could still speak.
Apparently, he wasn't suffering enough. She moved closer and leveled the gun at his lower stomach. That's when he moved, charging
at her like a bull, clutching for the gun.

The weapon never wavered, nor the hand behind it. Madame
Gérard's index finger squeezed off another round. The blast ripped
Montag's stomach open.

He catapulted back against the wall, sinking onto his haunches,
staring up at her. Saliva and, soon, blood dribbled from the side of
his open mouth.

"You're not man enough to stop me," she said softly. She sighed.
"It's not over yet, is it?"

Montag's pale eyes narrowed. He snarled and in one last desperate
attempt sprang forward, lunging at her. "You fucking whore," he
screamed, through a spray of blood.

Madame Gérard waited until he was almost upon her, until the
last possible instant, until he thought he had her, and then she fired
twice.

Montag grunted in agony as he was thrown back for the third and
final time. The two rounds had found their mark where she had
wanted them: the first in the center of his throat, the other through
his right eye.

"How does it feel, Montag?" she asked quickly, knowing that he
had only a little time remaining. "Can you talk to me?" she said.

He stared up at her blankly.

"I should be thankful to you, Montag. You've played your part perfectly. How many of us ever really have our dreams come true, even though they're nightmares?"

He had maybe one or two seconds left, enough time for her to say, "Go to hell, Montag."

Montag slumped forward, dead.

XXI

Outside Palazzo Pambisti, Madame Gérard walked into late winter sunlight. The Piazza Navona was like a huge terracotta park crowded with clusters of tourists with cameras, afternoon couples sitting over coffee, children laughing and playing. A tall, lithe monk, leaving the church of Santa Agnese, deftly kicked a scuffed soccer ball a group of boys had let fly in his direction. The coffee drinkers, the children, the browsers at the newsstand—Madame Gérard took them all in with a feeling of rejuvenation and new life. Surprisingly relaxed, she continued past the Fountain of the Four Rivers to the far end of the Piazza and sat at the rim of another fountain where, above her head, Neptune struggled with a dolphin. She had been there for a long time, watching the parade of people pass leisurely through the Piazza, when she saw Alex and Minta coming toward her.

Across the expanse of cobblestones, they recognized her. Their pace slowed as they approached, relief on both their faces. They sat down on either side of her.

There, by the fountain, they said nothing, listening to the cries of the balloon sellers, the rush and gurgle of the fountain, watching the play of life go on.

Alex was the one who broke the silence. "That was Montag, back there?" he asked, thinking of the horribly contorted, one-eyed corpse he and Minta had just seen in Madame Gérard's office. It had struck him then that dried blood and pigment had the same texture.

Madame Gérard nodded, looking straight ahead. "It's finished." Then she looked at Minta. "You're the kind of girl I would have been if . . ." She stopped, and they could see the pain of her past shoot through her. Her eyes roamed restlessly, regretfully, around the walls of the Piazza, changing color in the sunlight, and settled on a second floor window in the curve of the north end. The gold lettering in the window read "Galleria Navona."

Alex followed the direction of her gaze. Inside the gallery, he could see people moving back and forth in the artificial light, staring at the paintings as though entranced.

Early the following morning, the body of "Monsignor" Hans Weiller was interred in an unmarked grave near Civitacastellana, a tiny village fifty miles north of Rome. Five other "clerics" were buried with him. Their death certificates, signed by the village physician, attributed their end to a car crash on the *autostrada* outside of Rome. In attendance were half a dozen gravediggers, together with a heavy-set, dark-haired man wearing a gold medallion.

After the last of the wooden boxes had been lowered into the ground and earth covered them, he turned and walked to a waiting Alfa-Romeo. Then he and another man, wiry and dark, drove to Leonardo da Vinci Airport where they took the next flight to Paris.

As Jocko's Paris-bound jet traveled toward the Alps, the sun rose high in the sky, brilliant and cold over the peaceful English cemetery in Rome. Alex Drach, his eyes glistening from the wind, his hands clenched in an effort to stop from shivering, stood over Cubitt's grave. He had brought a dozen roses with him and left them scattered over the mound of earth at the head of the grave. He felt hollow inside, watching his breath vaporize in the freezing air.

He looked at the rich color of the red roses against the clay-brown soil and thought about how many ways there were to die. Cubitt snatched away just as she was beginning to live. Ray Fuller, whose life spurted on in a mindless vacuum that was a living death. Philip, annihilated by his own hired assassin. But perhaps the cruelest death of all would be that of André Rostand, a psychic death, when he carried the body of his son back to New York, broken and alone.

Standing in the cemetery for foreigners, Alex couldn't help thinking about his own life, how lucky he was to be alive. He remembered Jocko's last question at Madame Gérard's. Whose son was he, after all?

Inside him, there was an utter stillness. The answer was harsh, with one sparse mercy. The truth was that he'd never had a father. But then, after all, it didn't really matter anymore.

After a few more minutes, he left the graveyard and climbed into the taxi that had brought him there. He told the driver to take him to the airport, where Minta was waiting for him. Then he settled back and closed his eyes. They had time enough to make the flight to Corsica. There was a carnival there. Appropriate, he mused. It was time for Carnival.

Appendix

The Reichsmarschall of
the Greater German Reich

Headquarters, 31 May 1940.

The battle against Jews, Freemasons and other
affiliated forces of opposite "Weltanschauung" is
a foremost task of National Socialism during the
war.

I therefore appoint Major Hans Montag to form
Staffs in occupied territories for the purpose
of safeguarding all research material and cultural goods of the above-mentioned groups, and
transporting them to Germany.

All Party, State and Wehrmacht Services are,
therefore, requested to give all possible support
and assistance to him, in the discharge of his
duties. The above-mentioned is requested to report to me on his work, particularly on any
difficulties that might arise.

/s/ Göring

T O P   S E C R E T
Confidential
Postal Censorship

OFFICE OF CENSORSHIP   RECORD NO. SJ FIN 12583
UNITED STATES OF AMERICA

FROM: TO:
Rostand International   Hans Montag
New York   Bank Leu & Co. Ltd.
                               7, Rue de Lion d'Or,
                               Lausanne, Switzerland.

---

1. Date of Communication: 4 Sept. 1940

2. Date of Despatch: 5 Sept. 1940

3. Type of Communication: Cable

4. Register No: 477

5. Serial No: 5005

6. Language: French

7. Previously censored by: Switzerland 512

8. Station distributor: Nov. 1940
                                DR
                                BER
                                D10-10 ND
                                FIN-CPC   TRI

9. Disposal of original   H
   communication: R
                                C
                                RS

10. To be photographed: Yes

11. Reviewer: R.J.F.

12. Examination date: 2 Nov. 1940

DR use only.   <u>COMMENTS</u>

1. Sender, a French citizen taking refuge in
    New York, transfers Sw.Frs. 1,500,000 to
    recipient.

2. Sender states the funds are payment for
    the following paintings:
    Portrait of a Bishop   Sw. Frs. 5,000.-
    Meister von Delft,
        Tryptichon   Sw. Frs. 27,000.-
    Pietro Longhi, two Vene-
        tian family scenes   Sw. Frs. 27,000.-

3. Sender has been offered Sw. Frs. 25,000.- for
    a Cézanne. He states that H. Montag, Locarno,
    has a party in Zurich who is interested, and
    that it is possible that the Sw. Frs. 1900.-
    deposited on a Gauguin could be freed with
    Montag's help.

Oberkommando der   BERLIN W 35, 30 October 1940
Wehrmacht   Tirpitzufer 72-76

Az. 2 f 28 J (1a)   Tel: Local Service 21 81 91
No. 1838/40 g   Long Distance 21 80 91

TO: Army Commander in the Netherlands.

As supplement to the Führer's Order No. 2850/40
(Secret) dated 5 July 1940, addressed to Reichsmarschall Göring through the Adjutant of the Chief
of the Army High Command, to the effect that
lodges, libraries and archives in occupied territories of the WEST will be searched for material
valuable to Germany, and in order to safeguard
this material through the Gestapo, the Führer has
decided:

The ownership status before the war shall be the
criterion; in France, the status prior to the
declaration of war on 1 September 1939. Trans-
fers of ownership to the French State, etc.,
completed after this date, are irrelevant and
legally invalid, except in special cases authorized by Reichsmarschall Göring. Reservations
regarding search, seizure and transportation to
Germany on the basis of the above reasons will
not be recognised.

Reichsmarschall Göring, and/or his deputy
Reichshauptstellenleiter Montag, has received
clear instructions from the Führer personally,
governing the right of seizure; he is entitled
to transport to Germany cultural goods which appear valuable to him and to safeguard them there.
The Führer has reserved for himself the decision
as to their use.

It is requested that the services in question
be informed correspondingly.

> The Chief of Army High Command
> By Order:
> Signed /t/ REINECKE

R E S T R I C T E D

The Reichsmarschall of the Greater German Reich
> ROMITTEN, 21 November 1940.

Dear Party Comrade Montag,

Hearty thanks for your letter and most of all
for the wonderful paintings you have secured
for me.

I should like to inform you briefly as follows,
relative to the cultural goods seized in France.
I have especially welcomed you, after much vacil-
lation, as authority for the collection of the
articles was finally decided upon although I must
point out that other authorities also claim to
possess power from the Führer: first of all the
Reich Foreign Minister, who several months ago
sent a circular to all authorities, claiming,
among other things, power for occupied territory,
and stating that the safeguarding of art treasures
was his responsibility.

Moreover, the Reich Propaganda Minister is still
also delegated, I believe, to determine the data
relative to those cultural goods, which once were
stolen from Germany and which should now be returned. This, however, pertains mainly to the
articles that are found in the possession of
enemy museums.

I have promised to support energetically the work of your staff and to place at its disposal that which it could not hitherto obtain, namely, means of transportation and guard personnel, and the Luftwaffe is hereby assigned to give the utmost assistance.

In addition, I should like to call to your attention that I have been able to obtain especially valuable cultural goods from Jewish owners. I obtained them from hiding places that were very difficult to find; I discovered these a long time ago, by means of bribery and the employment of French detectives and criminal agents. This activity continues, as does the activity of my foreign exchange investigation authorities in scrutinizing bank vaults. In both cases the results will be communicated to your staff, which will then be required to seize the articles and transport them. I consider the cooperation between your staff and my office in PARIS as excellent and answering its purpose to the highest degree.

In order that no incorrect ideas arise regarding the articles that I want to claim for myself, and those I already have obtained through purchase and others which I should like to obtain, I wish to communicate the following:

1) I already possess today through purchase and barter perhaps the most important private collection in Germany, if not in Europe. These are works of art that I include in the category of early Nordic masters: that is, consequently, the early German, the early Dutch and Flemish, the works of the French Gothic; that is, paintings as well as sculpture.

2) A very extensive and highly valuable collection of 17th century Dutch.

3) A relatively small but very, good collection
of 18th century French, and finally a collection
of Italian masters.

This whole collection will be housed appropriately in KARINHALL and will come later into
the possession of the State as my legacy, with the
provision that the gallery remain in KARINHALL.

The Führer has welcomed my plan, as well as
supported it.

Thanking you again for the paintings, I am
with

                    Heil HITLER !
                    Yours,
                        /s/ Göring

The Reichsmarschall of the Greater German Reich
BERLIN W 8, 30 May 1942.
Leipzigerstr. 3.

Dear Party Comrade Rosenberg,

Your staff for the seizing of cultural goods in
Paris has, I believe, been brought into a false
reputation in your opinion, as if it fostered
artistic trade itself. I know the work of the
staff very well and must state that there is no
service for which I can express such absolute
praise for continued work and willingness as for
this service and all its co-workers. It was
probably I who caused this reputation of
fostering the artistic trade, since I asked some
gentlemen, who were special experts, if they heard
anywhere during their stay in Paris or France that
paintings or other art objects were being sold by
art dealers or private citizens, to look at these
things and report them to me, if there were anything of interest to me. Since the latter was
frequently the case, I again asked the men to
oblige me by obtaining the things for me, for
which purpose I provided a depot for them. If,
therefore, several gentlemen were industriously
engaged in maintaining connections with art
dealers, this was done for me exclusively as a
personal favor, for the benefit of the enlarge-
ment of my collection. Since very many intended
purchasers for art objects search in the occupied
territory, I can imagine that these people may be
in ignorance of the situation; perhaps also out
of jealousy the gentlemen of your staff have been
suspected in a wrong direction.

I feel compelled to give you this explanation
and to request that this procedure be maintained.

On the other hand, I personally support the work
of your staff wherever I can, and the seizure
of a great part of cultural goods became possible
through the fact that I was able to assist your
staff through members of my staff.

With best greetings and Heil Hitler!

Yours,
/s/ HERMANN GÖRING

C O P Y

SUPREME HEADQUARTERS
ALLIED EXPEDITIONARY FORCE
Mission (France)

AG 000.4-1

APO 757
18 February 1946

SUBJECT: Report on the French dealer, André
Rostand.

TO: Supreme Commander Allied Expeditionary
         Force (Main), APO 757 U.S. Army (Attn:
         G-5, MFA&A, Major R. J. Fuller)

Enclosed is information supplied by the
D.G.E.R. relating to the French dealer and his
activities during the occupation.

For the Head of Mission:
/s/ F. W. Jones, Jr.,
/t/ F. W. Jones, Jr.,
Major, AGD
Adjutant General

S E C R E T

17 February, 1946

SUBJECT: Watch List.

TO: Major Ray J. Fuller
             G-2 Censorship — SHAEF
             Main Headquarters
             APO 757

1. Returned herewith is the list containing the
names of art dealers whose correspondence should
continue to be the subject of a special watch.

NAME	KEY WLM NO. DATE		LETTER, CABLE, PHONE	
BRANDT New York City	P&D WLM/2082 8/2/45	(Q)	Yes	Copies
GALERIE TISCHLER Lucerne	P&D WLM/2082 27/11/45	(Q)	Yes	Copies
KELLER New York City	P&D WLM/2082 8/2/45	(Q)	Yes	Copies
WENDELANDT, Doctor Geneva	P&D WLM/2082 27/11/44	(Q)	Yes	Copies
ROSTAND, André	P&D WLM/2082 8/2/45	(Q)	Yes	Copies

COPY
8123 11 13
D.I.R.A.
R.J.F.

24 February 1946

Special Report
on
the firm of
Rostand International

Paris art dealers

———————

Note: The information on which the following report is based has been obtained
partly from original documents and partly
by interrogation of some of the persons
most closely concerned. The interro-
gations were carried out at the Special
Art Interrogation Center in August 1945.

———————

1. The mystery which has hitherto surrounded
the activities of the Jewish firm of art dealers
Rostand et Cie. in Paris during the years of
the German occupation is now beginning to clear
as a result of newly discovered documents and
the interrogation of Reichsmarschall Hermann
Göring. The following would now seem to be the
story.

2. This report supersedes the memorandum sub-
mitted 8 January 1946 by Wng. Cmdr. Hugh Jenner
to this office. Field inquiries subsequent to
Jenner's investigations are as follows.

3. A representative of Reichsmarschall Göring, Major Hans Montag, visited Paris after the defeat of France in June 1940. At that time he was in charge of confiscating Jewish art collections on behalf of the Reichsmarschall.

4. One of those arrested by Montag was Paul Drach. Drach was arrested because he had information as to the whereabouts of numerous hidden art collections. It is not clear what happened to Drach while in detention, but Göring claims that he refused to cooperate with the German authorities.

5. Montag meanwhile was very keen to acquire the hidden collections and took it upon himself to meet with the art dealer, André Rostand. He paid a visit to Rostand at Monte Carlo in late June, 1940.

6. Göring stated under interrogation that it was at that time that he was told that the most important part of the Rostand collection had been loaded on a boat sailing for USA, that the boat had been intercepted by a German submarine and forced back into an Italian port, where its cargo was unloaded and the collection seized by the Italian authorities.

7. These facts, however, should not be lost sight of when considering the subsequent developments. Göring states that the following is a summary of his representative's conversations with M. André Rostand.

(a) Montag proposed that in exchange for information about Jewish art collections he would release Rostand's collection held by the Italian authorities.

46

(b) Rostand was very eager to do business. He also proposed to acquire from the Germans those works of art they did not want. It was agreed that Rostand was to have first option on these paintings.

(c) To do this Montag and Rostand discussed the possibilities of aryanizing Rostand's art gallery in Paris. Rostand accordingly asked Montag to make the necessary arrangements.

8. Both parties were apparently greatly satisfied with the results of this meeting, and directly after his return to Paris, Montag arranged the release of the Rostand Collection. Details of what happened during the next few months are not quite clear but it appears to have been the joint idea of Montag and Rostand that Rostand's gallery should be aryanized. The role of Montag in the affair seems to have been that of using his semiofficial position and his papers from the Reichsmarschall to negotiate with the German authorities in Paris, e.g., Dr. STENGER, the Commissioner for Jewish Affairs, etc.

9. The Rostand Gallery is one of the best known and most reliable galleries in the world. Since Rostand has had dealings with a study group investigating art looting in occupied Europe, this report is extremely sensitive. For this reason a classification of Top Secret has been requested.

/s/ R. J. Fuller
Major